TANGER GOLD

A Dak Donahue Novel

STEVE DWIGHT NICHOLS

This book is a work of fiction and the product of the author's imagination. Names, characters, places, events, incidents, business entities, religious entities, and organizations are used fictitiously. Any resemblance to actual places, organizations, business entities, religious entities, incidents, or persons is entirely coincidental.

Books

1. Murder and the Preacher's Wife

2. The Sinner's Reckoning

3. The Good Samaritans

4. The Last Revelation: The Beginning of the End

5. The Inception War

6. Tanger Gold

7. To Kill a Blueblood

8. An Angel Never Prays

Prologue

General Cuez motioned for the three guards to hold off on his prior order. General Cuez walked closer and looked at the young soldier's face and hand, "What damn message?"

"The leader told me to tell you exactly word for word, 'When he finds you and you crawl out from under the rock you've been hiding under, he is going to cut your head off."

Chapter 1

Dak stood and peered at each of his friends, "I need to know where you five stand. You are my brothers and sister. I do not wish to be the tribe leader, but we must have leadership. Our government is a monarchy, and we must have a king or queen." He then glanced first at Veronica knowing she was the outspoken one of the group and if she agreed the others might follow suit. No one said a word at first and he then peered at the other three friends. Four of the five stared back at him. "We all know the tribes' counsel will not take me seriously unless they see you have pledged to fight with me. You know we have no choice. I know each of you love our tribe, the same as I love our tribe. Our plan must work, or our tribe will die."

Hulk glared straight in front of him as he stood in The Dive looking out the window at the white caps of the ocean in the eastern horizon. Dak knew where his best friend, Hulk, stood. He had been instrumental in conveying now is the time to attack the Normand navy. Hulk had also listened to his father, Billy Ray, speak over the past six months of the need to stifle the malcontents located at Meadow Bottoms. Dak needed to hear from the others.

During the hesitation, Dak reflected back over time how he and his friends built the log house where they now stood. He wondered if they all would agree with him and Hulk as he glanced at the structure. The group had always been friends. Dak remembered the good times as he and his friends built the shack when he, Robin Hood, Veronica, and Hulk were ten years old. Trey and Tommy Boy were nine and eight. They named the shack The Dive. It started out with one room and was a hangout for the group. Over the next four years the group added additional rooms and then when they turned fourteen the guys moved into The Dive.

Hulk kept his gaze on the ocean and his voice was stern, "This is the only way we know. This is all we know. We have heard the elders speak of a different way where people are elected to lead by a democracy by winning the most votes. We have also heard where the government owns everything, and the leaders at the top live like gods. What we know is for close to seventeen years your mother, Dak, has been our queen, and she has led our tribe in good times and bad times. She has made certain everyone has a roof over their head and food on their table. Everyone is required to work and follow her rules. My parents have mentioned no one could have done a better job and most of the people respect her as the queen."

Dak glanced at his five friends and then held his gaze at Zenith. "We know what we must do, but first I will have to address the tribal council and then address the problem in our tribe located in Meadow Bottoms in which Hulk speaks. I need each of you standing with me."

Trey looked at his friends and then back at Dak, "I am with you. I will go south with you, and we will defend the innocent people and our tribe. We will bring the war to those damn Normands."

6

Robin Hood motioned his head in agreement, "I am with you. Staying here and waiting is not the answer. We all know war is coming. We all know we cannot survive, and our tribe cannot survive unless we act. If we wait for the Normand Army to crash through the defense we have set up along the jetty, we are doomed."

Tommy Boy also shook his head in agreement, "Me and my sword are with you. I am ready to die for you, my friends, and our tribe."

Veronica cleared her throat and then at looked at Zenith. She knew Dak was always special and was not surprised with Zenith falling in love with him. He had matured quicker than Hulk and Robin Hood. He always been more independent than the others and more driven. He had always been a great hunter and pushed himself to be a great warrior. He would train for hours and push the rest of the group to train. She turned her gaze to Dak and noticed his stern jaw line as he stood waiting for her to speak. "Dak, I will fight for you to the end. I believe your mother will pull through, but we have no certainties dealing with the poison injected into her system." She noticed everyone was now looking at her, as she turned back to make eye contact with Dak. "Dak, you are our leader. This is your destiny to be the King of Cliff Tops."

Hulk turned from the window and looked at Dak and nodded his head in agreement. "Your friends are all in. We have discussed the plan for close to eight hours, and this is what your mother would have done if she had been able. We will leave at first sunrise."

7

Dak smiled at Zenith. He owed her his life and now he knew he loved her. He also knew she had run away from her home, her father, and her Blueblood community because of him. She did not know her mother who had died in labor from complications giving birth to a second child and now she was estranged from her father and stepmother. She had never had to want for anything with her father working for the Blueblood Senate which was established in a coup years ago in Merlin. "Your people were produced in a laboratory and genetically enhanced at least a decade before the Transition Period. We know biologically your ageing process was accelerated, and you are genetically enhanced Blueblood. Now Zenith, we are your people. Zenith, I have fallen in love with you, and now we must hide from the Blueblood Senate. You know they will track us and try to kill us after you broke me out of their dungeon. I owe you my life for assisting me in escaping." He did not take his eyes off Zenith, "This is not your war. We cannot expect you to fight alongside of us. You can remain here with our tribe."

Wrinkles suddenly appeared on Zenith's forehead as she looked surprised and responded without hesitating. "I go where you go. I will not stay here with the tribe while you six march off to fight this gorilla war of yours. I choose to love you. It was my decision. I believe in you Dak Donahue, and I made my decision what I would do when you were in the dungeon. I am not going to change now."

He smiled at Zenith. "I did not want to speak for you or ask you to fight with us. This is going to be a deadly mission with tribulations. We will not be able to protect all the innocent people. We will not be able to stop the Normand Army moving north. At best, we hope we can disrupt their supply lines and maybe build an oppositional force to help us fight in the future. Our main mission is to open the Continental Trail for the passage of food and supplies. Otherwise, we will not be able to survive when the Normand Army in full strength attacks. There are just too many of them and not enough of us. Our tribe needs food and supplies to fight and hold out against an extended siege." He was stern in his voice, "We have no choice if we are going to survive, we must undertake this mission. The prisoner Hershel will come with us. We must trust someone, and I trust you six with my life. I also somewhat trust Hershel to guide us. We will not arm him, and we will need to restrain him every night. We cannot afford for him to escape. For us to be successful, we must be in stealth."

Chapter 2

Doc Johnson stared from his seat at the kitchen table at Delores, Wayne, Mia and then Samuel as they lingered. The doctor looked tired. "It really has been a miracle. The silk clothing must have protected her from the arrows being able to transfer the lethal dose of snake poison. Who knows," he raised his hands, "Some of the poison may have evaporated over time from the tip of the arrows before they were shot. She may have received just a small trace into her blood system. Normally with poison in the human body, we in the medical industry introduce parenteral fluids which we have done with the use of the blood infusion and the water infusion." He looked at Samuel. "I believe the quickness of us providing the Blueblood's blood must have help purify her blood and fought off the effects of the poison." Doc Johnson looked at Samuel understanding she was still in danger. "All four of these things along with our Lord and the tribe's many prayers may have saved our leader. I know she is not out of the woods yet, and she is young, healthy, and a true fighter. Sometimes a doctor must deal with uncertainties while treating a patient. There are grey areas." He shook his head and rubbed his left hand over the thinning hair on the crown of his head with a perplexed expression on his face.

Delores was the first to speak. She was relieved with the report. "Will she have a full recovery?"

"I do not see why not. The two wounds are healing without infections. I gave her the Herbal tea that will help her sleep. Her body needs rest and nourishment. We want to keep her in bed as long as possible. The poison might be dormant and any additional moving or exercising could activate it. In time it will dissipate through her system."

Samuel interrupted. "My blood is designed to fight off infections. I will provide her another pint of my blood. There has been enough time since the first transfusion. You need to make this happen now," he commanded.

***

Dak walked across the compound in front of the fourplex. Others were out doing their chores. It was a cold afternoon with snow on the ground and overcast clouds. He bellowed in a challenging voice, "You Blueblood, how do we know it is not you, the master assassin?" Delores heard the loud command and came out of the fourplex with Mia and Casey. They stood on the front porch watching the two men facing each other. They also noticed Zenith and Dak's five friends all standing behind him. Billy Ray walked out of the blacksmith shop covered in both sweat and soot carrying his sword. Little Jimmy and Eric of Newport approached from the sawmill area both carrying their weapons. Wayne rode in on his black horse with two other men. They all watched in silence

11

with a concerned expression watching the two men facing each other in the middle of the street.

Samuel never had someone question him or challenge him unless they were a Blueblood Senator or a commander in the Merlin Army. Immediately after the Transitional Period, he had risen to the status of General in charge of the Blueblood Army, and he had been commissioned to travel through the Midlander's territory with Aquarius to the city of Cliff Tops and report back to the Merlin Senate the possible threat coming from the Normand Army. He was stationed in Merlin, and his reputation was that of a killer. He looked surprised at the accusation. He stopped walking and turned and faced Dak and his friends. He knew how he felt about Dak's mother, Vicky, lying on her death bed. He knew he loved her, and the news about her recovery had been the best news he had heard. He could not wait to kiss and hold her. He also knew their romantic feeling for each other had to be kept quiet. He thought about her every day. Now, her son stood before him accusing him of trying to kill her, why this unfounded accusation? "Young Dak, I am not the master assassin. I have apologized for allowing the two assassins to shoot Queen Vicky at the gorge. I do feel responsible for not stopping the assassination attempt and for that I failed."

Dak loudly interrupted him, "We find it coincidental you showed up and then two days later my mother was shot with two poison arrows while you were sitting next to her. You led her directly into a trap at the bridge of the gorge on the day of the

Battle of New York. The two assassins were waiting for her at the gorge. Before we could interrogate the two assassins, you killed both. This is what we know. You devised this will conceived plan." Dak unsnapped both of his straps holding his Sai swords secure in the sleeves hanging from his belt on both his sides. Samuel did not dare tell anyone how he felt about Queen Vicky. He knew he could not fight this young man being in love with his mother.

"I would have stopped those arrows if I could."

Dak responded, "But you chose not to. You, sir, are a liar. You are an experienced Blueblood warrior. You would have been aware of the danger and if one, let alone two assassins, were plotting to kill someone, you would have been aware of their presence. The only reason you did not stop the arrows was the assassins worked for you. You planned the trap with the deceptions of being friendly to the queen and our tribe. You know the Blueblood Senate has requested you to kill me, Zenith, and our Queen. You led her right in front of your men. That is why we have not been able to locate the third assassin until now." He stared at Samuel.

Several people in the tribe stepped forward toward the two men facing each other. The spectators were surprised at the scene with one mother gathering her small three children and forcing them indoors. Hulk, Trey, and Tommy Boy unsnapped the straps holding their swords in place. Robin Hood and Veronica fanned out to each side with their arrows loaded and the strings on their bows pulled halfway in position. Zenith stepped next to Dak with her right hand resting on the grip of her sword.

Wayne jumped off his horse and yelled, "Hold it right there!"

Dak turned to Wayne and proclaimed, "You are not in charge. I am your leader until my mother recovers, and if she does not recover, I will assume the role as the King of Cliff Tops. At that point in time, I will execute this man for murder." He looked at Samuel. Wayne hesitated with Dak commanding he was in charge. He noticed the rage in Dak's eyes and face. He tried to fathom if the accusation could be true. Could Samuel be the third assassin?

Vicky's closest friends now looked at each other with perplexed expressions. They had not considered who would lead the tribe if Vicky had died, and they also had not considered Samuel being the master assassin. Everyone knew Wayne was the queen's most trusted friend, advisor, and he was placed in charge of the work groups and the running of the tribe's affairs. He worked with the farmers, fishermen, loggers, and hunters. He would negotiate with Captain J.J. regarding the trading for the goods. He tried to make certain everyone was treated fairly and compensated for the work performed in the community.

Aquarius also dismounted his horse. He had been on the ride with Wayne to assist with advising the New York tribe leadership and make certain the gates leading into the tunnel and at the end of the Continental Trail were secured and well-guarded. Wayne respected Aquarius's ability both as a senate advisor in Merlin and as a soldier. He had been trained by the military men in Merlin to be a general before he opted out to work in the Blueblood Senate. Aquarius knew from experience in Merlin he did not want to be involved with the political issues of Cliff Tops. His experience had taught him individuals in politics could have strong feelings for certain issues and hatred of other people and these feelings were hidden deep inside the politicians' psyche. He also was aware no one alive had ever threatened Samuel and lived. He was surprised to hear Samuel talk to Dak in such a humble and polite tone. The only person he took orders from was the Blueblood commander of the Army and the Blueblood Senate. Samuel would kill this young man, his friends, and then Zenith would no doubt fight Samuel to the death. This entire situation was about to escalate. He causally announced, "I am a Blueblood like Samuel and my daughter Zenith." Everyone turned to Aquarius and watched him step forward. "We cannot protect everyone. We are all sorry your mother, the Queen of Cliff Tops, was shot by two assassins. I however can assure you Samuel is not the master assassin." He lifted his hands in a pleading gesture. "Our guards in Merlin have killed several assassins, and they are very deadly. Dak, your mother is still in grave danger. Samuel is the best qualified person to protect her, which he has been doing since she was shot."

Dak replied, "He watched her get shot. That is my point. You were made aware of his orders that came from Senator Dale. The first thing he mentioned when we met him on the trail heading west from Old Thomas' Outpost was the fact, he was going to arrest Zenith and myself. He was ordered to bring us both back to

Merlin dead or alive. We know for certain that was one of his orders. Why are you taking up for this man? I understand you dislike him."

Aquarius raised his hands again in a gesture of compromise, "Being a leader, you will learn to take advice from your trusted allies and advisors." He looked at his daughter Zenith and Dak's five friends standing behind him in support of his claim as the leader. He considered the accusation against Samuel. "Samuel is an honorable man, and how I personally feel about him does not mitigate his integrity as a person. I can assure you; he is no master assassin from the Asian continent. What you say about his orders from Senator Dale is true. I do not know his hidden agenda or if he has a hidden agenda. I was told to seek your tribe out and report back to Senator Blackmon about your ability to wage war and the validity of the threat of the Normand empire."

Samuel stood in a relaxed posture. He knew he could not fight Dak. He only had one choice to diffuse the encounter. He reached to his buckle and released the belt holding his sword in place, allowing the sword and knife to fall to the ground. He stared at Dak.

Aquarius was surprised by Samuel's gesture. The Blueblood army was taught to fight to the death, or otherwise they could be held prisoners and drained of their blood. Sometimes, they were imprisoned for weeks, and the process repeated over and over for months or years. The blood from a Blueblood made the normal person immune to all viruses.

Dak commanded, "Take him to the jail and lock him in a cell by himself." Trey and Tommy Boy pulled their swords and walked over to Samuel and motioned for him to walk toward the jail. The three men walked off with them entering the jail door and closing it behind them. No one said a word. Wayne looked at Dak. "What are you proposing we do?"

"Everyone on the council needs to meet me in conference to discuss that issue in five minutes. The rest of you people need to return to your jobs. I am going to check on my mother first and then I will be in the meeting." Dak walked past Delores, Mia and Casey standing on the front porch into the fourplex without looking at the women. The women stared at their kids unsure of what to do as the rest of the town folks returned to their jobs.

***

Little Jimmy leaned against the wall. Everyone knew he loved his queen, and he would do whatever she asked. He was a huge man and had been her trusting bodyguard in the old world fighting against the slave industry and terrorists. He waited for his son, Trey, and his daughter, Veronica, as they would also be attending the meeting in the church/banquet hall.

Billy Ray did not look happy as he leaned against the other wall. Billy Ray was just as loyal to Vicky. He had been her most trusting warrior in the fight against the slave traders. He had respected her decisions and her leadership. If someone needed to be killed, she

17

would pull the trigger. She would lead the mission and place herself in the front lines of the operations and not hide like most leaders. She embodied more courage than anyone he had ever fought beside. He also knew she loved her friends and her God.

The two large men, Billy Ray and Little Jimmy, were both on the Cliff Tops Council and looked intimidating as they position themselves along the two sides walls in the auditorium and were prepared to watch the meeting without taking a seat at the table. The church had been used by the tribe over the years for the community meetings and indoor meals. Delores sat down at the table between Eric of Newport and Wayne, and no one said a word. Mia walked in and stood next to her husband, Little Jimmy. Aquarius opened the double doors and walked into the meeting and took a seat at the table. Zenith and Robin Hood walked through the double doors and sat next to each other on the last row of seats in the church. Next Hulk, Veronica, Trey, and Tommy Boy walked in and found seats on the opposite isle from Robin Hood and Zenith. The double doors opened, and Casey walked in and looked at her husband, Eric of Newport, who was sitting at the table and announced, "I know I am not on the council, but I would like to be part of this meeting. I want to know what is going on." Eric of Newport motioned for her to take the seat next to him. Silence filled the room. Dak's friends avoided eye contact with their parents and the other adults.

After Casey sat down, she looked at her husband and then at her son Robin Hood. She gritted her teeth, "What is the meaning of this?"

Robin Hood glanced at his mother. "We have a plan."

Casey snapped, "You have a plan. You are not in charge. What do you mean you have a plan?"

Hulk raised his head and glanced at his father who was staring at him. He looked back at the floor.

Aquarius voice boomed across the room. "I am not certain I should be here. I am not certain why I was asked to be in this meeting."

Zenith stood and spoke softly in response. "You were asked to be here Father for your insight and advice. Dak will be here in a few minutes. He will make a statement and answer your questions."

A minute later the doors opened and in walked Dak. He proceeded to the head of the table where his mother normally sat. He scrutinized the group. "I am glad everyone on the council could make it, and the rest of you are welcome. I just talked with Doc Johnson. My mother is your ruler, and we pray she is on the road to recovery. The doctor and I prayed at her bedside for her recovery." His face hardened as he spoke with authority, "That is the good news. However, she could still slip into a coma, and there are no certainties. In her absence, I am the lawful heir to the leadership of this tribe, and I will lead." His focus narrowed to those seated at the council table and then rested on Wayne, "If

19

there is anyone in this room that disputes me being the rightful heir, you need to speak now. If you do not agree with me leading, you can leave the tribe." His expression was one of a harsh tone. He leveled eye contact with the adults.

Delores focused on the tabletop, and tried to sound calm, "Your mother will recover. I just know she will."

Dak lessoned his tone, "We all pray she does. I know each of you have been praying for her and helping to care for her. I thank you for both your prayers and care. However, she is still in danger from the third assassin. We have been assured by both Samuel and Aquarius, the Asian assassins work in groups of three with one master and two apprentice. She also is not out of the woods from being poisoned. The doctor is concerned with the traces of the poison still in her system. He is suggesting she lie still and is concerned if she becomes active, the poison, which is dormant, could be transferred faster through her blood system and kill her. I know how each of you love my mother, and she loves each of you. I never thought about being the leader of this tribe until now." He looked at Wayne and then Delores. "But someone has to be the leader."

Eric of Newport looked at Dak. "You know we all love you, Dak. We all prayed for your safe return from your trip to Merlin. You are a loved member of this tribe."

Wayne said, "I have watched you grow up. I have watched all you kids grow up. I have been loyal to your mother ever since I started working with her years ago. I held her as she buried her husband. I held you when you were first born. There is a time and a place to discuss the leadership of this tribe. This is not the time."

Dak looked at Wayne. "I love you like an uncle. However, my mother cannot make decisions that need to be made. We are at war. I disagree with you. This is the time and the place. Your responsibility as a member of the council in the past was to advise your queen and then carry out the order the queen rendered. Can you provide me the same loyalty as your acting king? Can all of you provide me the same loyalty as you did my mother?" Dak knew if Wayne agreed the others might agree. Wayne had always been the second-in-command, and the people in the tribe went to him for help and advice. He would step in and resolve most conflicts which arose between people of the tribe. He was also her most trusted friend and advisor. Dak watched Wayne's body language trying to anticipate his response.

Wayne sat still and appeared to be thinking. He knew Doc Johnson felt Vicky would recover with time and rest, but the timing was the question which might be hours or days? The possibility of her entering a coma was slight. Her vital signs had been steadily improving, and she had received two pints of the Samuel's blood. The blood would fight off all viruses and should heal any infections hidden inside her body. There however was no known cure for the Hook-Nosed' Sea snake poison that was thought to be on tip the assassin's arrows. Wayne also knew of multiple times when Vicky had saved his life. He remembered her shooting the Highway Patrolman in Butler, Tennessee through the

21

mouth as he was being tortured. He also knew Vicky was the reason they all had lived through the Transition Period. He felt he owed Vicky and if being loyal to her son was what he had to do, he would agree. He motioned his head and proclaimed, "I will support you the same as I have always supported your mother. I will provide you with advice as you request."

Dak immediately turned his attention to Little Jimmy. "Little Jimmy, I need your support. What will it be?"

Little Jimmy was thinking about Wayne's response. He too was loyal to Vicky. She trusted and respected Dak, but she would want her advisors to offer guidance to him as they had to her. He nodded his head. "I will support you."

Dak turned to Billy Ray. Billy Ray thought back to the first time he had met Vicky on the Navy ship. They had flown into South America, and they were taking on gun fire from all sides. Little Jimmy had driven their vehicle over a small retaining wall and broke the axel causing the vehicle to breakdown in the middle of the compound. Billy Ray had rolled out of the front passenger door and looked up as a guard hired by the perpetrator was about to shoot him. He had no way to hide in the large circular driveway. He was out in the open with the guard having the high ground. He could not raise his gun fast enough to fire a shot. Vicky had tracked the man running across the roof line and exited the rear door shooting the man and saving his life. She then ordered him to take the safer assignment of watching the exterior of the large home while she and Little Jimmy busted through the door knowing there was an ambush waiting. They captured the man who had purchased the twin boys and saved the two kids from being raped and killed. Billy Ray, at the time, was the hired gun from the United States Military Special Forces. He respected a leader who accepted the danger and did not force others into something they would not do. He knew where he stood with Vicky. He motioned his head in agreement.

Eric of Newport had always been loyal to Little Jimmy and Vicky. They had pulled some strings and got him released from prison for working in an auto theft ring. He had hated being in prison and wasting his young adult life behind bars. He owed Vicky. He said, "Your mother would expect nothing less. I will support you as the leader of this tribe until which time your mother says otherwise."

Dak looked at the last person on the council. Delores had a look of concern. "Delores, what is your answer?" The room was silent as Delores hesitated.

She looked at the table and avoided eye contact. She finally announced, "Your mother is going to recover. I vote we wait."

Hulk looked at his mother, "Mom, you need to agree with Dak. All of us have, and we need to move forward. The tribe needs to move forward. We have a plan, and we need everyone's support. Now is the time to make the decision of leadership."

"What is your plan?"

Tommy Boy, Delores's youngest son, spoke, "Mom, you know we love you. We have pledged our allegiance to Dak until which time Queen Vicky recovers. You need to do the same. The tribe needs to move forward, and we need to attack while Captain J.J. can assist us."

She looked at her two sons, "I want to hear the plan. We on the council should hear the plan."

Dak noticed the stalemate with Delores and stepped to the side of the table. "We will leave on Captain J. J's boat in the morning. I will lead a group down the coastline to Harpers Ferry Harbor. Our goal has three objectives. We have talked to Captain J.J. He has provided us with intel on the Normand navy. We will destroy the four Normand ships anchored in port. The four vessels are classified as Bargue ships. They are the largest sea vessels-capable of transporting a five hundred soldiers per ship. We believe these four ships will be used by the Normand navy to attack us by sea. We must sink those ships."

He held up two fingers. "We will open the Continental Trail for a short period of time to transport needed supplies while at the same time disrupting the supply lines of the Normand army. You know we need to stockpile food and weapons."

Dak held up three fingers. "We will also try to verify if there are resistance warriors in that region. You know we must take the battle to the Normand army. We cannot stay here and hope someone is coming to help us. There is no help coming. The Blueblood army and the rest of the soldiers in Merlin are not going to assist us in the upcoming war. I have listened to you advisors talk of this for months. We will go south and be the sword of

24

justice." He hesitated and in a command voice, "The group will consist of us six plus Zenith and our prisoner Hershel. We have talked with Zorro. He is healing from his wounds and is ready to return to the New York tribe. He will make certain the guards have the password for us when we return through the tunnel and the Continental Trail. You all know this is what we must do. We must have reliable intel on how strong the Normand army is and if there are resistance fighters in that area."

He looked at Billy Ray and Wayne, "We have listened to you talk ever since the first Normand sailors showed up seven years ago outside out jetty and announced our tribe had trespassed on King Solman's land, and they were going to collect rent and taxes. Sitting here and doing nothing is not going to work. They are not going to just go away."

Wayne raised his eyebrows in surprise at the plan and the fact the group had decided such a risky, but well thought out strategy. Wayne also knew they needed to have someone take the fight to the enemy and sinking those troop-carrying ship was a necessity. He and Vicky had debated the situation prior to the Battle of New York. She understood they needed to attack, but they did not have enough warriors. Wayne also was aware Vicky was not willing to take a chance on loosing Little Jimmy or Billy Ray in a battle in the south. She needed the two men next to her to control the people migrating north from the New York tribe. The group in Meadow Bottoms was not cooperating with them or her command. Neither

Wayne nor Vicky had considered sending the young warriors on such a dangerous mission.

Delores turned to her husband, Billy Ray, looking for support to try to talk her two sons out of going. "We need to wait for Vicky to recover. This is a decision she needs to make. She would want to have input into the plan and make the final decision. I know our queen, and she would not devise a plan for her teenage son to lead his friends and proceeding south to wage war."

Dak looked at Delores, "We do not have time. Captain J.J. can transport us now. He will not wait. I am in charge, and I have spoken. I am the leader."

Aquarius looked at the faces of the council members sitting at the table and then looked at Dak standing. "I am not certain I should speak."

Dak motioned his head to proceed to Aquarius, "That is why you have been summoned here. You are both an experienced diplomat and soldier. Your independent suggestions are appreciated."

Aquarius hesitated and tried to get his thoughts in line. He slowly stood. "Allow me to speak openly."

Dak motioned his head yes.

He looked at Dak, "The plan is a good plan. You might be able to establish General Cuez's weaknesses and his troop's fortitude to fight. In addition, there might be several soldiers like Hershel who would like to switch sides. You will need to locate resistance fighters south of the New York tribe and create a network. This war could last for years. I doubt it will be over in a short period.

"Being a member of the Blueblood Senate, we discovered conquering of people is one thing but forcing them to be loyal and not sabotage is another issue. Killing the opposing soldiers on the battlefield and trying to secure the land can be costly but not nearly as costly as holding the territories from the hidden warriors in plain sight in the villages. The kids and women in the villages can be lethal. We in Merlin discovered we lost more soldiers after we conquered the tribe of people. They sometimes would attack our troops who were working in the capacity as police officers. They would attack our soldiers while they were asleep in their barracks. We tried to set the tribe up to govern themselves, and they would turn on us and kill our troops. This is one problem General Cuez will face."

He glanced at the others. "Also, feeding his army will be difficult. He will want a fast victory. If you can make it difficult for them to supply the front lines of his armies, this will slow them down. Soldiers sometime reach burn-out if the conditions are miserable. They might start defecting.

"War is coming and sitting here doing nothing as all of you know will not work. You cannot defend your tribe without help. You will need additional food and supplies to hold out under a possible siege. I agree the City of Cliff Tops is a natural fortress located high on top the cliffs on the peninsula in the northeast most part of the continent which can be defended. But the realm of your territory is vast, and there are ways for a large army to penetrate your defenses, and once the defenses are compromised, your soldiers will fall like dominos. You have the radiation fields to the west, but as you now know soldiers can travel from Merlin to Cliff Tops. I am proof of that. You have the frozen north barren land, but a squad of well-trained soldiers could attack you from the north simultaneously as they attack from the east from ships or land army from the west. The cold turbulent ocean helps to keep large battleships at bay, but Captain J.J. sails into your jetty and so can the Normand navy. The deep gorge and bridge to the south separate you from the New York tribe, but if the New York tribe falls from an attack, you will also fall. I would agree with Dak's plan to make life hell for General Cuez and the Normand army."

He looked at Dak and raised his hands in a gesture of compromise. "You asked me to advise you. I do not mean to oppose you on this issue. Matter of fact, I agree with your plan. I will volunteer to go with you on this mission." He looked at Zenith knowing he wanted to protect her. He then hesitated and was somewhat cautious.

Zenith finally said. "What is on your mind, Father? Speak now. Dak will listen."

He continued watching his daughter. They had hardly spoken. She had avoided him, and he knew she was mad he had not helped her when she repeatedly requested his help in Merlin. He now was here, surrounded by strangers in a foreign land on other side of the continent. His daughter had a large reward leveled on her-dead or alive. She could never return to Merlin as a trusted citizen. He turned to address his comments to Dak, "If I may. I do believe you made a mistake arresting Samuel. I do not believe he is an assassin trying to kill your mother. I believe he is trying to make amends for not stopping the assassins prior to them shooting her and now he feels he must protect her. He knows of the danger the assassins represent. The assassins know how to go undetected and sometimes the only time you know they were in your village is when you locate a corpse. You need to understand the assassins are a very formidable opponent. They work as a team, and once they are successful with the mission, they disappear into thin air."

Dak looked at Wayne. "Wayne will be in charge while my mother is recovering and while I am gone. If my mother dies and I die, Wayne will be your leader. Once we leave on the voyage, and Aquarius, you leave for your trip back to Merlin, Wayne you may release Samuel from lock up."

Aquarius turned to face his daughter, Zenith, and then turned back to Dak. "I am going back to Merlin alone?"

Zenith stood. "Father, you need to choose sides. If you choose to fight the corruption against the Merlin Senate, you need to stand with me. I cannot side with the Senate. I know the people of Merlin are good, decent people, but they have changed little by little over the years, and now the Bluebloods live with a privileged style of life which they do not deserve. No one deserves to live like a god where everyone else is a slave." She stared at him the entire time. "If you do not want to fight alongside me, then Dak has indicated he will allow you to return to Merlin a free man. However, if you elect to side with us, you need to report both me and Dak were killed in the journey by Midlander's, and you escaped when Samuel was killed. We need you to be our eyes and ears in the Blueblood Senate. The Senate is corrupt, and at some point, the armies of Merlin will join the war on the side of King Solman. Senator Dale will have to be dealt with if we are to survive."

Delores looked surprised and turned her head looking at Dak. "So, you do not believe Samuel is the master assassin, and you had him arrested anyway?"

Dak replied, "I have ordered additional guards to guard my mother. Hulk and I had a rather forcible conversation with Captain J.J. He finally admitted he dropped the three men off at Lower Cove south of the New York tribe. They must have scaled the cliff and entered our territory after they across the gorge. He indicated he vetted them before he allowed them on his ship. He did not know they were assassins and headed for Cliff Tops. There is an assassin out there somewhere."

Dak looked at Wayne, "The assassins work in a group of three with two apprentices and one master assassin. We do not know if Samuel killed the master assassin or two apprentices." He looked at Delores, "I did not wish to give Samuel a chance to intervene in this mission. I do not trust him. Once we leave port and Aquarius has left for Merlin, he can be released. We need to keep Samuel here if possible. He is the best warrior on the planet. We need him as a trusted member of our tribe. He might not return if Aquarius returns prior. He knows if he returns to Merlin and is reported dead by Aquarius, the guards will then kill Aquarius for treason. Samuel and Aquarius are genetically induced brothers. We hope Samuel will cooperate." He turned to Wayne knowing Wayne would have to deal with Samuel.

Wayne nodded his head he understood.

Dak then turned toward Aquarius, "Thank you for offering to go south with us, but Aquarius, you will need to leave for Merlin at first light. You will need to locate the underground resistance led by Iven Chezon and assist them in the fight for the freedoms for which those people deserve. You will also need to keep the map of the route to yourself and send us a warning if the armies from Merlin march toward us. We will need updated intel on Merlin armies and their intent. I am asking you to be a spy." Aquarius looked surprised but was impressed with the clever strategy.

Dak then added, "What do we really know about our advisory in the south? We know King Solman is not a Christian or studied the Holy Bible. He has elected his name for other reasons. The correct spelling of the King of Israel as noted in the Holy Bible is Solomon. We also were concerned with how fast, strong, and well equipped his armies have become in such a short period. According to Captain J.J. the further one goes south the less vegetation and natural resources. Most of the old forests that survived the Transitional Period are located in the middle and north part of the continent. The cost to construct and maintain an army that size would cost more than the southern continent posed. I listened growing up as you adults talked about the expense levied on certain countries before the Transition Period to provide a large army, and how the cost was a sacrifice by certain countries which were willing to spend all those resources to maintain the defense of their country. The question I have is how is King Solman paying to maintain his expensive army? We need to find out and cut off his funding.

"Zenith mentioned the chess plates in Merlin were made of a bronze metal. Hershel has confirmed the Normand army received their bronze chest plates by merchant ships. The only country that has the wealth to finance and equip King Solman's army is the Blueblood's of Merlin.

"I have traveled to the west coast and back. Merlin is situated at the narrow part of the continent. I counted four nuclear waste pits as I cross the continent. I believe most of the nuclear bombs in the old-world war did not make it by the North America missile defense system. The nuclear bombs did not damage this continent near as bad as we once thought. There are vast forest and animals not damaged by the nuclear war in the middle part of the continent. In addition, Hershel has confirmed there is no nuclear wastes pits in the tip of the southern hemisphere. The earth, with the continent's reshaping changed our world more than the nuclear bombs. You parents and leaders taught us the world was a wasteland caused by nuclear holocaust which is not the case. I believe you tried to scare us from traveling. This was the second war where nuclear bombs were utilized. In 1945 two bombs were dropped on a county called Japan and twenty years later the damage caused by the two bombs were not noticeable. The damage caused by the nuclear war was not near as bad as we were taught."

Wayne stared at the floor. He knew what Dak had mentioned was correct. The adults had taught the kids to fear the outside world. He was also aware the missile defense system called the Patriot Program was able to shoot down over ninety-five percent of the rockets launched from the adversary countries. He also did not want to answer for the parents.

Aquarius stood still as he now realized the truth about Senator Dale and the bank of Merlin. He knew he would need to expose the treachery by those in charge in the Merlin Senate to finance the Normand army. He now realized he must return to Merlin.

Delores glanced at Wayne with a perplexed expression. She had never given the young adults enough credit for being intelligent and understanding the landscape to fight a war.

Dak looked at Delores and then Wayne. "Before we leave on our mission south, I am going to ride to Meadow Bottoms and carry out lethal punishment for the man they call Sie. They were called to arms, and Sie talked the people in that community out of fighting with us in the Battle of New York. He is pushing for us to sign an agreement with General Cuez. You know there are more people living in that community than with us in Cliff Tops. He would like to have an election where he is the one elected to be in charge. My mother has allowed this to go on far too long. I am going to stop the insurrection before I leave in the morning." Dak looked at Little Jimmy, Wayne, Eric of Newport, and Billy Ray. "I need you four to accompany me."

Delores understood what Dak was suggesting. "Do you not think you need to provide your mother the opportunity to recover and let her decide what to do with Sie and the people of Meadows Bottoms?"

"This has gone on far too long. We cannot afford to allow this treason to poison our way of life and expand to other areas in our realm. I have spoken." Dak walked out the front of the church with his friends following him.

Delores turned to her husband, "You are not going to be part of this. The Queen, I am certain was going to deal with this issue."

Billy Ray interrupted Delores, "And now Dak will deal with the issue. I will ride with Dak. These insurrectional acts should have been dealt with years ago. Those people need to be made aware who the leader is and obey the law or leave. It is that simple." He turned and walked out followed by the other men in the meeting.

Chapter 3

As the sun was setting, the twenty men, Veronica, and Zenith rode into the Meadow Bottoms. The community of Meadow Bottoms was located close to five miles southwest of Cliff Tops. The community was in a valley with large fields which allowed for gardens and ranching. Several of the people living in the area had migrated from the New York tribe. A few had once been sailors or immigrants from further south and had opted to live in Cliff Tops and had been transported north by Captain J.J.

The people of Meadow Bottoms lived in homes with mostly along the main dirt road. The community had a store, school, and church. Dak slowed his horse from a trot to a walk and then stopped in front of Sie's home. Over fifty people walked out and lined the street watching the riders and some were armed with swords. Dak stared at Sie as he walked out his front door followed by his wife. Sie seemed cautious as he noticed the several riders and commanded, "What is the meaning of all this?"

Dak did not take his eyes off Sie. He was an overweight man with a beard, full head of hair and was close to six feet five. Dak figured him for a bully. Dak commanded, "I am your king until which time my mother recovers."

Sie interrupted Dak and announced loudly so all could hear, "We the people of Meadow Bottoms do not see it that way. We have voted, and the community has elected me to be the leader.

There are more people living here than in Cliff Tops. I am the elected leader of Cliff Tops. The democracy has spoken. You will take my orders. There will be changes. You will lay down your weapons. I will negotiate a treaty with the Normand command. We do not agree with your war." He smiled at Dak and then the others facing him on horseback. He seemed to be very confident.

His wife walked further out of the front door of the home and stood next to him. She was a plump lady that did not smile. She held several pieces of paper up and waved them. "This is the record of the votes. Since the majority has voted for Sie, the election is complete. We are in the process of setting up a court and a sheriff department. My husband will be making all the decisions dealing with the foreign policy." She then added, "He will set himself up with an elected committee to manage the realm."

Dak knew he needed to be punctual and complete the sentence before the community could resist. He very much wanted to limit the carnage. He also knew they were trying to intimate him because of his age. He tried to hold his rage in check as he dismounted his horse and walked over to Sie. Dak was surprised to hear of the election, and Sie may have been in touch with the Normand command. "It is rude to interrupt your King." Dak hit him in the face with his gloved fist and then kicked him in the sternum knocking him backward into his front porch railing. Sie fell to the ground, coughing and trying to get his breath. Sie tried to get up, but Dak walked to the side of him and kicked him in the ribs before he could stand. Dak motioned for Trey and Tommy Boy to pull him over to the wood pile. Dak then turned to the people of Meadow Bottoms. He noticed some men had walked forward with swords in their hands. Dak spoke loudly, "We are at war with the Normand army and King Solman. There are no compromises or treaty we can sign with the Normand empire that they will not break. They cannot be trusted to keep a treaty. We either fight or die. They are wanting our land and our freedoms. Your Queen called the people of Meadow Bottoms to battle and none of you showed at the Battle of New York. This man has committed treason, and he deserted his Queen's army. I, Dak Donahue, appointed King of Cliff Tops, sentence this man named Sie to die for his acts of treason and leading this insurrection. The rest of you will need to decide if you will stay in my realm. If you elect to stay, you will follow the laws. If you are caught committing treason, you will be punished. This is the only warning you will receive."

The men from Cliff Tops dismounted and either pulled their bows with loaded arrows or their swords ready to fight. The man walked forward. Dak recognized him as the preacher. He held out his hands in a gesture of good will. He then looked at Sie and Sie's wife who was trying to help him up. The preacher said, "You have no right," as he looked at Wayne for help.

Wayne held his sword in the ready position and said, "Your King has spoken. This man is guilty as charged. The paper with everyone's name on it is proof of treason."

Little Jimmy and Billy Ray walked in front of five men with their swords pulled and were watching them. They were ready for a fight. The men seemed to back down when they saw Little Jimmy's steel rod with the hammer on one end and the sharp spear on the other.

Dak pointed for Trey and Tommy Boy to place Sie over the wood pile with his head hanging over the wood. Hulk handed his four-foot-long sword to Dak and then walked over and held the wife and pushed her toward her home. Sie tried to fight back but the two men were too strong. Dak loudly commanded, "Let me make myself transparent. Our form of government is a monarchy. We do not have elected officials unless I elect them. I am acting King until which time Queen Vicky recovers. If you live under my realm, you will do as I say. The penalty for treason and desertion is death." Dak paused and walked toward the wood pile. "Any last words or request of our Lord?"

Sie yelled, "Everyone stop them. You elected me to be your president. This an illegal coup." He tried to stand, but Trey placed his body weight on the back of Sie's legs forcing him to lie still while Tommy Boy held his shoulders in place.

Tommy Boy looked at Dak and motioned his head as he pulled his hands down toward the lower torso holding Sie's hands forcibly behind his back. Before anyone could say another word Dak turned with the sword held high in his right hand and swung hard, decapitating Sie.

There was a sudden gasp from the town folks as they watched in disbelief. His head rolled on the ground, and the blood spilled out from the neck cavity. Dak turned to the people and declared, "You men will report to basic training at Cliff Tops in the morning. All men." He looked at the preacher. "If anyone here would like to leave, I will grant you safe passage to the area past our borders. Most of you people came here from the New York tribe. You may return. But if you elect to stay, you will fight, and you will follow the laws set by your King or Queen. Is there anyone here that disagrees with me?"

The preacher was in shock. He tried to talk and was speechless. He looked around at his flock. The only sound was the widow on her knees crying. The people looked at the preacher as a leader. "These people are God-fearing people. What gives you the right to command them?"

"Did Jesus not say give to Caesar what is Caesar's?"

"Yes. He did say those words."

Dak interrupted him, "We must have a ruler. My mother, your Queen, settled this land along with her friends. She has been recognized as your Queen. In her absence, I am acting King, and I will kill any man who says otherwise. We must have a government and this government is a monarchy. Do I make myself clear?" Dak walked in front of the preacher looking him in the eyes. He whispered quietly so only the preacher could hear him. "The other preachers in realm follow the rules and laws set out by Queen Vicky. You have elected to side with this man named Sie. You now have two choices. You need to either take your place at the wood pile or tell these God-fearing people to obey their king."

The preacher looked at the people and then at Wayne, Little Jimmy, Eric of Newport, and Billy Ray with his hands extended out by his side with his palms up. His attention turned to the crying wife of Sie sitting on the porch. He realized Dak was going to kill him if he did not comply. Dak whispered a second time, "What will it be? You need to decide right now. These people need a preacher, and I can appoint another preacher if you want to walk to the woodpile. It is up to you." The preacher looked at Dak and noticed the blood on the sword. He could see the determined expression on his face and in his eye.

The preacher faced the towns people, "You people of Meadow Bottoms." He hesitated. "You people of Meadow Bottoms. Your king has spoken. He has provided you two choices. You need to decide. I will obey King, Dak. We were wrong in allowing Sie to distract us from the leadership of our community. If you do not side with your king, you will need to leave and seek a home elsewhere."

A thin man stepped forward. "I do not agree. I will not kill another man." His wife came to his side and tried to pull him backward. "No Ethan." The man looked at his four small kids and his wife. "What type of man would I be if I denied my God?"

Dak noticed Zenith had walked next to him. She had pulled her hood back revealing she was a Blueblood. The people of Meadow

Bottoms had never seen a Blueblood. Zenith whispered, "He may serve another way. Not everyone is cut out to be a soldier."

Dak was surprised by the man's boldness. His wife had tears in her eyes and the small girls were crying. "I know some of you people. I have hunted and fished with some of you. I have worked next to you. You know Wayne, Little Jimmy, Billy Ray, and Eric of Newport. All of us are fair, reasonable men. You know the rules. You know what I require. You know Queen Vicky to be fair and honest. She provided you a place to live and allowed you to have refuge on her property and eat her food. You know why you are here. You know the other territories are not a place you would like to live. She provides you protection from the Midlander gangs and the soldiers in the New York Tribe, and in return, from now on when requested your presence on the battlefield you will fight."

He looked at the man. He was standing rigid. Wayne looked over at Billy Ray and Little Jimmy with a grim expression. Dak asked, "Ethan, are you disputing me as your King, or are you unwilling to fight for your family, friends, and your King? Do you want me to have my men place you on the wood pile where I will remove your head in front of your family?"

The man said, "I am no killer. I love my Lord with all my heart. I do not dispute you as being the leader. I do not believe in killing another man. My time here on earth is short. My time in heaven servicing our Lord will be long. I did not sign that paper voting for Sie as the president. It is a sin for me to kill another man. If you must, go ahead and carry out your sentence."

41

The preacher looked at Dak, "He comes from a family which has a strict belief against taking a human life. He does not come to my service. He is a good man in the community. He speaks the truth." The preacher hesitated, "He and his family members did not sign the petition for Sie. I beg you to show mercy."

Dak hesitated. He knew he did not want to kill anyone else. "Are you a brave man?"

"Yes, I am a brave man. I stand before you and this community ready to die for my Lord."

"You sir will report to Doc Johnson in the morning. He will teach you how to be a medic in our army. You will be trained as a medic and then assigned to the medic division to assist our troops. In order to be a good medic, you must be brave, and I believe you to be the bravest man in Meadow Bottoms."

He looked relieved. "Yes, King Dak, I am a brave man."

"Then, do you agree to your assignment in our army?"

The man looked at Dak, "Yes, my King. I agree. Thank you for being a fair and reasonable King."

Everyone turned as three teenagers ran from an old barn toward the group of people. They started crying and yelling with one of them demanding, "What happened to my father?"

Sie's wife stopped crying and ran into the street and tried to pull her sons out of the street. Dak looked at the three teenagers, "Your father committed treason, and I passed judgment on him. You three can bury your father tomorrow. Then two days from now, you will report to Cliff Tops for basic training in our army."

The oldest yelled, "You bastard. He grabbed the ax next to the wood pile and came toward Dak. Trey grabbed him and threw him to the ground. He stood over him holding the ax and then pulled the ax out of his hands. Dak could tell the young man was no warrior.

Sie's wife started crying and begged, "Please do not kill my boys."

Dak looked at the teenager lying on the ground with a violent expression looking up at him and the mother in tears. "If you ever yell at me again, I will cut your tongue out. If you ever pull a weapon on me again, I will kill you. Now, you and your two brothers need to decide if you wish to live under my rule or leave. Otherwise, you better be in basic training in two days to learn how to be a soldier in my army." Dak and the others walked to the horses and mounted them and rode back to their homes.

Chapter 4

Hulk looked over the side of the ship's rail at nothing but the cold sea as the ship sailed through the turbulent water rocking constantly up and down. "As far as I see, there is nothing but waves and ocean."

Dak looked over at his friend and smiled. "We will be on land soon enough. Hold your lunch. I am not certain what to expect, but you better be ready to fight. The Normand army has provided no mercy for these people, and we will provide no mercy to them."

Hulk smiled, "The guys are all nauseated with the motion sickness. I am not certain how well we could fight right now if we were attacked. I guess we could puke on the enemy." Dak smiled. He knew Tommy Boy and Trey both were seasick and lying down inside the cabin of the boat. He had not seen Robin Hood since a few minutes after they left port. The waves were between ten to twenty-feet high forcing constant motion for the passengers. The three men had upchucked several times.

Veronica walked carefully with the constant motion on the deck and leaned against the rail next to Hulk. "Have you two become use to the boat ride? Trey and Tommy Boy turned green from the motion sickness." Hulk and Dak smiled.

Hulk replied, "So far, I am holding my lunch in place. This is the fastest way for us to go south, and we hope we can avoid Normand entanglements. I also hope Captain J.J. can be trusted to drop us off in an isolated area where we can sneak ashore, or this is going to be a short boat ride and a short mission."

"If he is setting us up in a trap, I will make certain he is the first to die. The first sign of another ship flying the Normand flag, I will gut him. I am not certain we should not kill him anyway. He tried to lie about dropping the three assassins off prior to docking at our jetty. He said he thought the three Asian men were silk traders. Give me a break." She looked at both Dak and Hulk, "He is not someone to be trusted," Veronica announced.

Dak looked at his two friends. "We must trust someone. He did not know of this mission until we all gathered and got on his boat."

Dak then grimaced and asked, "Did I do the right thing in Meadow Bottoms?"

Veronica replied, "Sie was nothing but trouble. My mother had urged your mother to take steps two years ago. He would stand up in church and talk about how he would do things different if he was in charge. He used the church to promote his platform to reorganize the government. He was selling land owned by your mother to other people. She is the Queen. He was making money off the herds of cows your mother provided the community which she traded for with the New York tribe."

"I agree with Veronica. Hell, if you had not cut his head off, I would have. There is no signing a treaty with King Solman," announced Hulk.

Zenith walked out of the lower cabin in her warm coat. "I just cannot get used to this cold weather. I have on four layers of very

45

warm clothing, and I am still cold. How do you guys stay warm in this cold wind?"

Hulk smiled and noticed Dak's was also smiling. "I was about to take off my coat. I am burning up." Zenith rolled her eyes at Hulk.

Zenith then offered, "My father used to take me sailing when I was little, and I am accustomed to the motion at sea. I am not feeling seasick." She grinned and pointed toward the cabin, "Those friends of yours are not acclimated to traveling by ship at sea. The smell inside the cabin area where those guys have puked is unmerciful." She waved her hand in front of her nose. "I told Robin Hood he was going to be dehydrated if he puked one more time. He then asked me to kill him." She laughed.

Hulk declared, "Four-day old dead cats in a small room does not smell as bad as their puke. Maybe I should go offer them a chicken to eat." Dak laughed along with the others.

Zenith smiled, "Hulk, that is terrible. I am certain the thought of eating a chicken would force them to upchuck." They all laughed.

Dak smiled, "Come here, and I will hold you." He opened his bear-skin coat, and she walked into his waiting arms as he wrapped the coat around her and held her tight against his chest. "You are a west-coast girl not accustomed to this cold environment." He kissed the top of her head.

Dak said, "I just asked Hulk and Veronica if I made a mistake in Meadows Bottoms. Should I have done something different?"

Zenith turned while being held by Dak and looked at both Hulk and Veronica, "I do not think you made a mistake. You made a

46

difficult decision, and you made the correct one. That family will always hate you. His wife, I bet, was the driving force behind him wanting to be president. In Merlin, all the male politicians have a wife advising them and pushing them into public office. I would not turn your back on any of them. Samuel would have convicted the entire family and killed the family, so he would never have to worry about being stabbed in the back or poisoned by one of those sons. You showed wisdom by sparing Ethan's life."

Veronica announced, "I respect Ethan for standing in front of us and being brave and not wavering with his commitment to our Lord. He will make a great medic."

Hulk said, "I know that is correct. I looked at Sie's wife when her husband was lying on the ground dead. She looked evil. There is no way you will be her king. If you had asked her if she was going to accept you as her king, you would have had to kill her."

Veronica added, "She would have lied to save her three sons."

"That is why I did not ask, and I sincerely hope her sons show for basic training. I told Wayne to escort them over the bridge and force them to live in the New York tribe if they do not comply. Zorro owes us a favor or two," replied Dak.

Veronica announced, "I see land." She pointed west toward the horizon and could barely make out land in the far horizon. The group turned. The lookout located on the front of the boat yelled, "Land to the west."

"Thank God. Maybe we can depart this misery," announced Hulk.

Chapter 5

Wayne and Little Jimmy walked toward the jail house. Little Jimmy asked, "Are you comfortable providing him his sword?"

Wayne did not slow his pace, "She said for us to give him his weapons and release him immediately. I tried to convey to her without his sword and other weapons, we might have a chance against him. She told me this was an order and not a request."

Little Jimmy asked about the status of the captured Normand soldiers.

Wayne felt his pulse increase, "We have interrogated the soldiers captured in the Battle of New York. Most of the soldiers seemed to say what they think would keep them alive without being tortured until the Normand army marches north and liberates them. They also are aware the captured soldiers in the New York prison had been beaten and killed during the interrogations. All the information is about the same. These soldiers do not know when the Normand army will attack or with how many men. Now I am stuck with eight soldiers being held as prisoners, and I do not want to keep them. Billy Ray suggested I should return them to the New York tribe and allow the New York tribe to handle them the way they desired. He pointed out the soldiers had attacked the New York tribe, not us here at Cliff Tops. It takes too many resources to keep the men in prison. I must make certain there is always at least one guard on duty, and no one wants to be in the jail watching the enemy soldiers. Our Queen has ordered prisoners not to be tortured, and I understood without torture, the men will not confess any meaningful intel. We have no leverage over the prisoners."

The two men approached the jail, "Do you have any suggestions?"

Little Jimmy raised an eyebrow as he stepped on the porch of the jail, "I have nothing." He could sense Wayne's frustration and smiled at Wayne.

"I had hoped the prisoners would be like Hershel and provide us with insightful intel. I now realize these prisoners are either lying or do not have helpful information." He spit on the ground in aggravation. "This is the life of a city manager."

The front door of the jail was propped open to allow fresh air in the jail house. They glanced at the guard who was leaning back in the chair with his cap pulled down over his closed eyes. The guard awoke as they walked past him into the larger room housing two jail cells. The guard immediately sat up in his chair and straighten his hat. Wayne and Little jimmy glanced at the captive Normand soldiers in the one crowded cell.

They walked in front of the door to Samuel's cell. Samuel looked up from his bed with a blank expression on his face. Wayne at first had not noticed the Normand soldier lying on the floor of the other cell with blood running across his face. He had a large head wound where his scalp had been peeled back exposing skull tissue.

Little Jimmy asked in his deep voice, "What happened to him?"

49

The Normand soldier in the far corner angrily voiced his concern, "I will tell you what happened to my comrade. That crazy bastard did that to him." He motioned toward Samuel.

"I am over here in this cell. I did not touch him. I believe he slipped and fell." Samuel smiled as he laid in his bed on his back with his hands and fingers interlaced behind his head.

Wayne looked at the group and then back at Samuel. He tried to visualize how the soldier must have gotten too close to the bars between the two cells. He could see blood and part of the man's scalp stuck to the common bar wall of the two cells. "Our queen has woken and wants to talk with you. She told us to give you back your weapons and release you." Wayne glanced at the Normand soldiers as Samuel stood up. The soldiers all had fear in their eyes as they watched Samuel stand and walked toward the door of the jail cell.

Wayne unlocked the gate, and the hinges made a screeching noise as the door to the cell opened. Samuel stood and walked out the door of the jail cell. Little Jimmy handed him his sword and two knives. He hooked his belt holding his sword around his waist as he stood with his back to both Little Jimmy and Wayne. He stared into the cell of the eight Normand soldiers with the one lying on the floor. He placed his knife in the top of his boot and the other knife on the holder fastened to his side. He then asked, "So the Queen wants to see me?" He then mouthed the words to the Normand prisoners, "I will be back." The Normand soldiers all looked concerned.

The three men walked toward the interior jail doorway. Wayne turned to the guard sitting in the outer room of the jail, "You need to summon Doc Johnson to look at the injured prisoner lying on the floor. He might be dead. And for God's sake Walter try not to sleep the entire shift."

Walter looked surprised at the news of needing to summon the doctor.

The three men walked in the front door of the fourplex. Wayne pointed to the stairs, "She is still not fully recovered. She wants to talk to you." Samuel smiled at Wayne and Little Jimmy and walked up the stairs.

When he arrived at the door, he hesitated to think about what he would say. He opened the door quietly to the apartment. He walked to the bedroom door and saw Vicky lying in the bed. Her hair had been washed, and her sheets had been cleaned. She had the cover pulled over her as she was using two pillows to position her head looking forward. He noticed her smile, and he smiled at her.

"I am so sorry you were placed in the jail. Please forgive me. I will talk with my son about his actions." She hesitated, "After I ring his neck when he returns." She smiled, "I am truly sorry. I know you are not trying to kill me. I told my men to return your weapons."

He rushed over to her and kissed her hand as he knelt by her bed. "Please do not apologize to me for anything. It was my failure. I should have been on alert at the bridge and spotted the

51

two assassins and acted before they shot you. I was concerned about the Normand soldiers attacking from the other side of the gorge, and I never considered the possible assassins. I am so sorry. I was so scared we lost you. My actions could have cost you your life. You know I love you." He bowed his head as he held her hand.

"My son should not have arrested you. I am truly sorry." She reached over and took his hand. "The doctor says I should recover. I need you to help me train. I need to be prepared for the war to come. But I understand if you must return to Merlin."

He reached over and kissed her on the forehead. "You will love me as I love you. Give me a chance. Based on your need for me here, I will stay with you. I will retire from the Merlin army."

Vicky looked at the man on his knee next to her looking her in the eyes. She thought, "Could he love me as much as he says. He seems so sincere." She knew he wanted to make love to her nonstop for hours. She had truly enjoyed his company. The romance part of her life had been missing for the past seventeen years. She thought back to her college days, and the men she had been with while her boyfriend watched. He would coach her on how to be great in bed and please a man. Her boyfriend would be turned on and made the entire scene so fulfilling. That sinful lifestyle had been very difficult to forget. Now, she had become cynical as she aged and looked at Samuel with her doubts. "Samuel, Aquarius has returned to Merlin and will report you, Dak, and Zenith were all killed on the trip by Midlanders. If you return to Merlin, Aquarius will be killed for lying and treason. That would not go well with Zenith if you caused her father to be executed."

She looked at him with concern. She had been surprised with the plan Dak and his friends had implemented. Samuel looked a little surprised. "In addition, Samuel, my son, Zenith, his five friends along with Hershel, the captured Normand soldier, have gone south to wage a raiding war against an army led by General Cuez."

He stood and looked at her, "I should have been a member of the raiding party. I will fight for my Queen. They would need my help."

She smiled, "Samuel that is why you were in jail. So, you could not stop Aquarius from returning to Merlin. Dak knew you were not the master assassin." She did not want to tell Samuel about Dak's plan with Aquarius being a spy. She still did not know how much she could trust Samuel. She smiled and pulled the cover back showing her legs and her short white nightgown and playfully extended her left foot off the bed into his belly. He rubbed her foot and knelt by her bedside and kissed her foot. She pulled her foot back and under the covers with a devilish smile. "I will be better soon."

"You tease me. I have fallen in love with you. I was scared for you. I think about you every moment of every day. I was by your side at the gorge to protect you, and I failed."

"Even the right reasons have the wrong consequences sometimes in life. I do not blame you. Matter of fact, I owe you for providing me two pints of your blood. I will be better soon. The doctor felt I must have received a small trace of the poison. Your blood may have saved me."

Chapter 6

They rowed the small wooden rowboat into the cove. Tommy Boy jumped out and held the tow rope tight holding the boat in place. Hulk jump out and ran approximately twenty yards bent over to the tree line looking for signs of soldiers. He knelt on one knee with his bow loaded with an arrow and then motioned for Veronica and Trey. Zenith and Dak were the last two off the boat. Dak helped Tommy Boy pull the rowboat into the bushes as the others spread out and watched for a Normand beach patrol. The two wiped the sand on the beach area with pine tree limbs to conceal the footprints. When they were finished, Dak looked back toward the sea as Captain J.J.'s ship could barely be seen on the horizon sailing southeast. He then walked next to Hulk, "Lead the way."

They walked in a column close to ten feet apart across the ground which was covered in thick hedges and weeds until they cross the meadow. They then proceeded into the pine tree forest as they ascended the small mountain. Hulk led the raiding party up the steep mountain approaching the ridge top. From this advantage point, they could look down into the town and the harbor. Hulk held his hand up for everyone to halt as he approached the ridge line. He watched through his binoculars and then motioned for the others to join him. He whispered, "There are seven ships, not four. Three ships have been fitted with a large catapult on the front and rear decks. The other four appear to be troop carriers with tarpons attached to the platform on the stern and another on the bow decks." He handed the binoculars to Dak.

Veronica pulled her binoculars down and said, "They have over a thousand soldiers in the field outside the town. They will have search parties and scouts on the perimeter."

Dak lowered the binoculars down, "They have moved three additional boats with men into the harbor. We will need to strike fast and move out. I suspect they are looking to fortify the Midnight Hole region. We will wait for darkness. Four of us will swim out tonight before the moon rises and place the explosives on the bottom of the three vessels caring the catapults. Trey, you will place your explosive on the large troop-carrying boat near the dock. We must take out those catapults. Those are designed to take out our tribe at the top of the cliff. We will need to place our explosives, swim back to the beach, and then we will head inland."

***

Zenith had been watching. She pulled down the binoculars and looked at the others, "What is missing are kids and women. I do not see a single child or a female. Just soldiers." She turned and looked at Hershel, "What would they have done with the kids and women?"

Hershel looked saddened. He thought back to when he was separated from his family. That was the last time he saw them

56

when the Normand soldiers carried them away in a wagon and forced him and other men to walk into a prison camp. He hated the thought of the camp. In order to survive, they had to fight other men. The winner was made to be part of the Normand army. He had killed a farmer from another province as the Normand men exchanged gold as they bet from the ring side. The loser was buried in a mass grave. He would never forget the hot branding iron when it was stuck to his back marking him as a soldier. He remembered the guard holding the iron smiling at him and then left the hot iron for an extended second as his back burned in pain. He still had nightmares about killing the farmer and the look on his face when he rammed the sword through his belly. He looked at Zenith, "I am sorry, but the families have been split up and the men will either fight or be killed. The families will not ever see each other again."

Dak could see the pain in his eyes and immediately ordered, "Robin Hood, you and Veronica stay hidden but follow the ridge and complete a recon on what is west of us. We will need to head west as soon as we sink the ships." He hesitated. "See if you see any town people. It is imperative you are not seen. Our primary mission is to blow these ships and then head northwest. Be back before dark." The two headed along the ridge at a trot.

The group laid down and rested as Zenith watched the town. As the evening started to shift to darkness, Veronica and Robin Hood returned. Robin Hood whispered, "We located the towns people. They are in a large prisoner camp." Hulk and Trey looked over at

Robin Hood. "They have killed several hundred people. The dead are lying on the ground for everyone to see."

Hershel said, "They are trying to break everyone. If you are a parent and a male, the men will end up fighting for them to protect their kids. All the old and handicapped have already been killed. They have no use for them."

Dak looked at the three and said, "Get your gear on. We need to check our devices. These four bombs must work. I wished we had three additional explosives for the other three vessels. Make certain they attach securely with the force aimed inward toward the bottom of the ship. We must breach a hole big enough to force the ship to sink. You will not be able to see in the darkness underwater. If the explosive is not tight and held in place or aimed in the correct direction, it will not work." Dak thought about how the explosives were made. They had tried one as an experiment. They only had enough material for the four explosives they carried, and the one used in the experiment. The nitroglycerin was made by the engineer in the tribe with a small amount of nitric and sulphuric acid. The engineer, Val, had been able to salvage a small amount of sulfur, and Doc Johnson had a small quantity of nitric acid from the heart medication he had preserved from the old world. "We need to make certain these explosives work. This is all the nitric acid our tribe was able to locate. We will take out the four ships, meet back here, and then head northwest. We will need to stay hidden for the second part of the mission to work."

Veronica asked, "What about those prisoners? They will all be killed in retaliation for the ships sinking. The Normand command will assume the sabotage was carried out by hidden people from this community."

"We need to stay in stealth and move further inland. We need to reach the Midnight Hole before the Normand army fortifies that position. We need to open the Continental Trail and push supplies north. Now, the four of us are heading for a swim."

Zenith looked at Veronica understanding how she felt. Dak had intentionally not mentioned the prisoners. She like Veronica wanted to help the imprisoned people. They had talked on the boat ride. There was just no way everyone could be saved.

Dak looked at Hulk, "Provide me a hundred-yard head start. My target is the furthest away. Tommy Boy, you need to provide Hulk a hundred-yard head start. Trey you will need to wait for Hulk to clear his boat before you start your swim. And, make certain Tommy Boy is one hundred yards out to sea. Let's set these explosives for fifteen minutes and blow these ships. Have your gear packed. We will then head Northwest on a run."

Dak entered the water and started swimming. The ocean had three-feet high waves at the small cliff at the entry point. The tide was up and covered the beach. Hulk waited until Dak was one-hundred yards out and then he entered the cold ocean and started swimming. Tommy Boy waited and did the same. Trey was the last to enter the ocean.

Dak could only hope Tommy Boy and Trey had waited. He did not want to be near the ship when the first explosion took place. He swam to the darkest side of the ship. As he treaded water with the boat rising and lowering in the waves, he shivered and almost dropped his bomb. He was so cold his hands were shaking as he pulled his screwdriver and attached the band around the bomb to secure it to the bottom of the wooden boat while going under water and holding his breath in the total darkness of the sea. He felt for the timer and flipped the switch on. He returned to the surface and started swimming back to shore close to five hundred yards away. He was trying to stay in the ship's shadow as long as he could. He had not noticed any guards on the deck when he had approached, but they had seen multiple guards on board each ship while planning the mission. He knew he needed to be close to shore when the first bomb detonated, or he could be spotted. If spotted, he would be killed. He could not out swim a rowboat with several men rowing toward him.

The seal skin clothing helped keep him warm, but he knew he needed to hurry. Freezing to death was not the way he wanted to die. He did not have time to look for Hulk or Trey. He would assume they had set their explosives and returned to shore. He kept pushing through the cold waves trying to get closer to land. His muscles were starting to cramp. He could feel his arms and legs starting to give way to fatigue. He dared not turn over on his back and float and rest for fear of freezing to death. His point of entry near the small cliff suddenly came into view through the ambient light of the rising full moon. He kept straining with every movement of his arms and legs. He refused to give in to the fatigue and excruciating pain. There was a rip tide making his swim more difficult. The strain to push forward was miserable. He was about one hundred yards from shore when he heard the first explosion from Hulk's bomb. He looked at shore as he pushed his muscles harder. He heard the second explosion, which would have been his bomb. He kept swimming. He looked up and saw Zenith waving for him to hurry. The third bomb detonated. He pushed harder, and finally, the fourth bomb detonated. He floated into the small embankment and could hardly stand in the shallow water. Hulk jump down and helped him to the shore with Trey reaching down and pulling him up over the embankment. Hulk jumped back over the embankment, "You need to start running. Are you okay?"

Trey had been watching the boats. He returned to Dak, "The first boat appears to be going down. The other three are starting to sink faster. We did it."

They all looked at Dak and could tell he was ill. Zenith urged him to run. He instead laid on his back breathing. He could hardly stand when they tried to lift him. His muscles were cold and aching. He was exhausted with fatigue. He tried to force them into action. Trey whispered, "He has been in the cold water to long. He was in the water longer than all three of us added together." He pulled a fur hood over his head and placed a fur coat around him. Dak started running up the small embankment toward the ridge line. The group met at the ridge line and Zenith told Dak to change clothes. He was shivering as he stood still. Once he started removing his clothing, he seemed to look better. She looked at him with concern, "Are you going to be okay?"

Dak motioned his head yes.

Hulk ordered, "Robin Hood, you know the way. We will follow. Now let's get going." He then looked at Dak with concern. "You need to get moving. Your body needs to generate heat, so you do not suffer from hypothermia."

Dak motioned his head he understood as he stood with a concern look on his face. He could not stop shivering.

Chapter 7

The next morning, Vicky walked down her interior steps and by the kitchen doorway and noticed no one saw her. She could hear the two cooks talking as she passed the kitchen doorway. She eased the exterior door opened and proceed down the three steps. She felt a sharp pain in her leg as she descended the last exterior step. She smiled and hid her pain as she said hi to several people as she first stood at the bottom of the porch steps and then walked further into the road. The cold morning air felt nice with the clear sky and the warm sun. After eating breakfast in bed, she was bored of staying inside. The last couple of days had been uneventful as she had laid in her bed waiting for the doctor to provide her clearance to walk and exercise. She walked through the snow on the path toward the cliff-top area. She wanted to peer out over the ocean at magnificent view. She knew she was still not healed enough to ride horseback. Her leg still hurt with the sutures still in place. She tried not to limp, but the pain was constant. She waved to Little Jimmy and Billy Ray working side-by-side in the blacksmith shop. She proceeded to the top of the cliff and the view was uplifting, but she also realized her injuries were not healed enough for this stringent walk. As she walked, she worried about her young warriors. She thought how wonderful the view would be if she was able to see Captain J.J. and his ship sailing back into the ocean side of the jetty with Dak and his friends safely on board.

She then turned and looked at the small cottage her son and his friends had built and made their home. She smiled at the thought of the name of the home, The Dive. Dak would not tell her why they picked the name The Dive, but Robin Hood had told his father the name came from the two-hundred-foot headfirst jump to the jetty below. She found out Dak and his friends would take a running start and jump from the cliff, and she had Wayne install a sign at the top of the cliff, "No Diving."

She had first thought she would walk the additional one-hundred-yards to The Dive with the intent to walk through the structure. She smiled as she thought of the guys and their lack of housekeeping. However, she now realized this had been a mistake. She felt the blood oozing out of her upper leg with the piercing pain. Doc Johnson had told her the sutures were installed loosely to allow the wound to drain. She turned and started walking back toward the apartment.

Wayne and Samuel walked out of the barn and were headed her way. As Wayne approach, he stated, "You are not supposed to be out of bed. The poison in your system we hope is dormant. Unnecessary activity could activate it." She looked down and saw the blood on the outside of her boot. She turned away from Wayne, as to position her left boot so the two men could not see the blood.

She changed the topic, "What are the plans?" she asked.

"Eric of Newport and I are going to ride and meet with Zorro. We need to know where they stand with supply of food for the winter. Some of our men are going seal hunting. They will hang the meat up on the racks out of the reach of the bears. We might have to kill a cow or two. The people in Meadow Bottoms are wanting to sell us two of your cows." He hesitated for Vicky to understand they were acting like the livestock belonged to them. Vicky did not show any emotion. Wayne continued, "We will also see if Zorro has enough grain and hay for the winter."

"Go at once and buy the two cattle from the rancher in Meadow Bottoms. They have complied with reporting to basic training. We need to work with them to establish a monetary system. This is not easy for them to accept me as their queen." Wayne started to say something about the people in Meadow Bottoms, but this was not the time or place. He turned to leave and headed toward the barn.

Vicky looked at Samuel as Wayne was close to twenty-feet away. "I am nauseated and about to pass out. I do not want anyone to know. Can you help me and let's walk back to my apartment?"

Samuel immediately approached closer and noticed the stain-soaked blood through her pants on her upper thigh with the blood spreading to her butt. He could see her boot with the fresh drops of blood. He stepped to her side, and he held her up as they walked toward the front door. Once they cleared the door threshold, Samuel closed the door, and he picked her up in his arms and ran up the stairs. He closed the door. "What were you thinking? You must have busted the sutures in your leg." He carried her to her bed and removed her boots, coat, and shirts. He then removed her pants and her silk lined undergarment and the bandage. "Yes, the sutures are ripped." He walked over to the table and grabbed two towels and wet both. He immediately pushed one rag against her thigh and held it in place with pressure. "We need to stop the bleeding. The suture has pulled loose. Doc Johnson placed two layers of sutures. I believe the bottom layer might also be pulled loose. The arrowhead lodged into your femur cracking the bone, and he had to cut the tissue more than normal to remove the arrow. What were you thinking? It will take time to heal."

He glanced at Vicky lying on her back looking at the ceiling. She glanced at him, "I was going crazy in here by myself. I thought a short walk would help. I wanted some fresh air and to look at the view over the ocean." He reached over and started cleaning her leg and wiping up the blood while holding the other rag in place. He noticed the only clothing she had on were her socks. "The doctor told me not to get out of bed for a few more days. I do not want the doctor back in here telling me he told me so. I do not want to hear him complaining about having to sew me up a second time. He has too many other patients."

"I need to get the doctor, and he needs to add a few sutures to hold the puncture wound together. You got blood on your sock."

"I do not want a doctor. You can pour alcohol over the wound and then place a butterfly bandage over it. You know how to tear the towel into rags and tie the strips around my leg to hold the bandage in place." She looked at Samuel and then rolled over on her side away from him. She then reached over and pulled her two socks off.

He smiled to himself. He loved she was so independent and disobedient all wrapped in a five-foot-four-inch perfect body. He placed a bandage over the sutures. He noticed the bleeding had stopped. He picked up the towel and cut the towel in two long narrow strips to hold the bandage in place. He lifted her cover and pushed it to the side as he placed the one strip between her upper thigh and pulled the strip tight and tied it over the bandage. He repeated this with the second strip as he glanced over her nude body as she lay on her side facing the exterior wall. He smiled to himself, "I have no choice. I need to go and tell Doc Johnson about his disobedient patient."

She turned over very fast on to her back, "You will do no such thing. I will have you arrested, beheaded, quartered and your remains thrown over the cliff."

He ran his hand over her lower leg and looked at her foot. "I believe I got all the blood off your leg and foot." He pulled the cover up over her and tucked the top blanket in around her. If you would like, I can stop and check on you later tonight."

"Any word on our missing assassin?"

Samuel stood, "Wayne ordered a search two miles out in all directions with bloodhounds. He had men also search the cliffs. He made certain all the small rowboats were in storage. So far, there is no sign of the third assassin." He looked perplexed. "They found nothing. I do not understand where he could be hidden. I know in the past, they always attacked in groups of three with a master and two apprentices. Wayne has mentioned removing the additional guards from your door and outside. I feel he believes the third assassin must have left the area." She did not answer, and she watched him stand and walk out the door.

Chapter 8

They were all breathing hard after the seventeen-mile run. Tommy Boy declared, "I need to rest." He laid down behind the rock located at the edge of the field. The area was covered in large granite rocks and weeds. The forest had turned from a small thick pine forest to an older hardwood forest.

Hulk pulled out his radiation device and turned it on. He held it over so the moon light would assist. He announced, "We are clear."

Dak knew something was wrong. "I need to get out of these wet socks and shoes. We should be clear of the Normand army. We need to rest." Dak sat still and started shivering. The sweat created from the run chilled him. He was exhausted as he sat been over with his back to the tree.

Veronica looked at Dak knowing he was not feeling good. "This is good ground. We will camp here. I will get the firewood. We need to warm you up. Tommy Boy, you make a round about two-hundred-yards to make certain this area is clear. Robin Hood, you see if you can find us some fresh food. Zenith you need to see if you can warm Dak's body temperature." Zenith looked at Dak understanding Veronica's concern.

Dak's teeth chattered, "I will be alright. I just need to get some warm clothes on."

"Take off your clothes. You and I are going to lie together in this bed roll next to the fire."

Hulk started picking up limbs for firewood. He asked Trey to stand guard as he watched Tommy Boy walking up the small mountain to the ridge line.

Within in an hour, the fire was hot, and the raccoon Robin Hood had shot was cooked. The group sat and started eating. Dak held Zenith tight under the bed roll and listened to Tommy Boy report about the small village with horses located over the ridge line close to half mile west of their camp. He heard Robin Hood say the wind was blowing the smoke away from the village. "They should not be alerted to our presence. We will need their horses."

Tommy Boy added, "The village is dark with a little light coming from a couple of fires. The people are poor, and the horses are not much. The main road going north goes through the village. There is a Normand flag flying outside the village."

Hershel said, "The Normand army has already taken all the good livestock and the men for warriors."

Dak finally stuck his head out from under the cape. "We need to bypass this village. Based on the map, we need to go close to ninety miles north before we reach the Continental Trail. Part of our mission was to stop the Normand navy. That was easy. Now we've got to open those gates and send supplies north."

Veronica looked at Zenith who had pulled the cape down from over her head lying in front of Dak. "I am concerned about the prisoners. They will be killed in retaliation."

Trey looked up after taking the bite of his food. "We did not kill those people, little sister. We are not going to be able to save everyone. I talked to Wayne in private before we left. He said something I never thought he would say."

Dak and Zenith both got dressed and then got out of the bedroll and sat next to the fire. Hulk handed them each some of the cooked meat. Dak looked at Trey, "What did Wayne say?"

"This war is going to change all of us. We are going to do things we would never think we would do. No one ever comes out of a war the same." He hesitated. "He said in every war there are more innocent people that die than warriors, and our army will kill some innocent people. Then, we will have to learn to live with ourselves and our guilt."

Hulk looked over as he pulled a joint out of his pocket. "We need to be successful with our mission while we are on this side of the divide. Once we go back home, we will sit and wait for the war. While we are here on this side of the Continental Trail, we need to make things right."

Robin Hood smile, "You are going to share that with us, right?"

"I was going to give this to Zenith and Dak. They need a smoke after what they been doing under the bedroll."

"We have been doing nothing but trying to get warm." Zenith then added, "That might help Dak warm up."

Hulk walked over and smiled as he handed the joint to Dak.

Dak took a smoke, "Pass this around. We need to bring General Cuez out in the open, so we can kill him. Hershel, did you march this road when you were with the Normand Army?"

Hershel watched the group eat and converse. He was a quiet man and never spoke unless someone asked him a question. He wanted revenge. He also wanted to see if his kids were still alive. He missed his wife and family further south. "I do not think you realize what you are up against. Now they realize someone is roaming the area, they will send search parties out in every direction. They have bounty hunters they use, and they will kill whoever they have to locate those responsible for blowing up those ships. We are not safe here."

Hulk was concerned about how they were going to travel, "If the Normand army has all the good horses, that is where we need to go first. We need horses. We need to find one of their outposts and steal their horses."

Zenith said, "If what Hershel is saying is correct, they will send soldiers north from the large camp at the harbor. They will talk with the people of that village and try to find out information. They will be on horseback."

Hulk shook his head in agreement, "We need to be waiting. If they travel in a column of fifty or less, I say we attack them in an ambush. If more than fifty, we travel by foot."

Dak still shivered. He knew he needed to warm up. "Hershel, we will send you into the village tomorrow morning and scout it out. Now, everyone needs to sleep. The sun will be coming up in a couple of hours. Tie Hershel's legs and hands. We should be okay without a lookout tonight. They will start looking for us tomorrow."

Hulk looked at Hershel. "Do you need to relieve yourself first?"

***

Robin Hood had been the first to wake. He had been surprised that Dak had not wanted a lookout during the night as he looked around the area to make certain it was clear. He put his boots on and drank some water. He loved the morning hours when nothing was moving, and the sun was just rising in the eastern sky. He looked at his friends all under their capes and bedrolls, still sleeping. He walked up the hill to the ridge line. He looked across the meadow. The villagers had not awakened, and the sun had just risen and not melted the dew from the roof tops of the huts and buildings. He saw one elderly man gather some wood and return indoors. The fog was starting to dissipate in the valley. He was alarmed when he looked south toward the horizon over a mile away and saw the riders approaching on the road at a fast pace on horseback. He ran down the hill to the camp. "They're here. Two columns of Normand soldiers. There is close to fifty of them. They are riding in from the south."

Dak and the others jumped up and strapped their swords and bows on. "Trey, cover the ashes and try to hide the fact we were ever camped in this spot. The rest, come with me." The group ran up the incline to the crest of the ridge.

Hulk was watching through his binoculars, "They have made everyone come out of the village standing in two lines."

The group was surprised by the massacre, and how fast the villagers were killed. The villagers were cut down with swords and shot with arrows. Veronica, stood and said, "We must help."

Dak grabbed her and pulled her down. "You will stay down." He looked at his friends in a commanding voice with clenched jaws, "Everyone remain here. We must stay hidden."

"You cannot mean we are not going to do something about the families being slaughtered right in front of us," Tommy Boy whispered.

"No one is attacking. Everyone stand down and stay hidden."

Hulk was mad and looked at Dak, "You mean we are going to hide and do nothing about this? They killed the people who had no way to protect themselves. They lined them up in two rows and executed them." He pointed toward the field, "A small boy was killed while he was trying to escape."

"I am not going to repeat myself. We are staying hidden. We are not the ones killing the innocent people. We will not engage them. Now is not the time."

Zenith had seen the young child running away on the road as the Normand soldier shot him with an arrow. She ducked her head in dismay, "This has been a massacre. The Normand soldiers knew they were going to kill these people before they arrived this morning."

Hershel could tell the group did not agree with Dak, but he knew Dak was correct. He looked at the team. "They killed them because they did not pay the taxes and provide them with more cattle and sheep. Notice the grain silo is empty. The soldiers think the villagers are hiding their livestock and storing their grain somewhere else. The Normand soldiers will ride north to the next village. They are on patrol looking for food. We need to pray that the next village has the tax, grain, and livestock to provide them."

Dak asked, "So, they will return heading south along this same path?"

Hershel nodded his head yes. "I believe they will. They are stationed at Harpers Ferry Harbor. Notice the uniforms. Those are not the normal soldiers stationed at the outpost. Those men are part of the Normand Front Guard team. They work directly under King Solman but are assigned to General Cuez as his loyal security team."

Dak looked at his friends as they all watched the Normand soldiers ride north in the two columns. "We must be smart. If we had attacked, the villagers would have been just as dead. We would not have been able to save them. We would have been in the open and with them on horses, we would have also been killed. We cannot fight trained Normand soldiers on horseback in the open when they out number us five to one. We must remember our mission. We must hurry and cover over nine hundred miles north and open the lower gate temporarily to send livestock through the gate to our tribe. We also need to establish how strong their army is and if there is anyone left to fight in this region. Stories of this type of massacre will spread, and the opposition will grow, and I must believe more and more people will fight with us. We also will need to stay hidden from the villagers when we can as we travel north. There are several thousand small communities north of us and some will be loyal to the Normand army."

Veronica turned and looked harshly at Dak. "I do not care if they are Front Guard Soldiers. We should have helped those people."

Dak held his hand up as to say, I am not finished. "We will go north now and look for our spot, and when they return, we will hit them. With their armor, we will have to fire high velocity arrows in close to bring them down. If you noticed, they wore the metal breast plates and steel helmets. Our steel-tipped arrows need to hit them in the perfect unprotected area or be fired in close. We only have few of the high velocity arrows. Most of our arrows will not cut through the metal armor. Also, they are watching outward away from their column when they ride. We must use their training against them. We will need to get inside their protected zone, which is inside their column, and take them down with our swords, That is not going to be easy against horse soldiers."

Hershel was surprised and asked, "You are not considering attacking a squad of fifty Front Guard Soldiers, are you?"

Hulk looked at Hershel, "Yes. They all need to die. We need to set things right and let the people know there is hope. They will start taking up arms against the Normand army if they have hope."

Hershel was surprised and fearful. He thought these young people and himself were going to die. He suggested, "You do not need to attack them in the open. You need to wait and get in close. For example, if you had on their uniforms, you might be able to fool them." Hershel doubted these young people's ability to wage war against a well-trained Normand combat unit. He looked concerned, "Dak is correct. They would have killed your team out in the open field." Hulk and the others looked at Dak and then Hershel understanding the two men were correct.

"Now let's head north. The next village most likely will be ten to twenty miles north. We will set our ambush, and we will take out these soldiers." Dak took off jogging along the ridge line and then down the hillside heading toward the road leading north. He wanted to cover as much distance as possible. As he ran, he thought about how his team acted while watching the massacre. It was his responsibility not to be spontaneous, or they would not survive. They had to stay hidden. He tried to place the thought of losing one of his friends out of his mind as he kept pushing himself as he ran. Hershel had assured them; the Normand army would not rest until they located the people who sank the ships. He explained the guards on those ships will be blamed and at least a couple will be executed in front of the watching army. General Cuez forces other guards to remove their heads with the ax and the dead are left impaled in the open for others to see. There is no mercy provided by the Normand commanders. Several of the imprisoned people of Harpers Ferry Harbor will be killed in front of the other imprisoned people in an attempt to force someone to talk. Dak then considered the brutality of this conflict, and what he and his friends must do to win. He kept running and thinking about the war.

After close to fifteen miles, Hulk caught up with Dak. "This is the spot," proclaimed Hulk, "This is the best spot for an ambush. You said we need to be close. We can hide in the rows of Rhododendron under all this tree foliage. We can hide on both sides of the road a few feet back and be totally hidden." Dak looked at his friend. He knew the group was tired and hungry. He did not want to spend too much time stationary, but he wanted to kill those Normand soldiers who massacred that village. He was disgusted as they were.

Dak looked around. While resting, the more he absorbed the surroundings, the better he was able to visualize the ambush. The group had been spread out on the fifteen-mile run with some having a faster pace and in better physical shape than others. He and Hulk were the first two to arrive. Some of the group paired off and talked as they ran.

Dak saw Trey, Tommy Boy, and Hershel walk into the area and sit down. Then, Veronica and Zenith walked over and sat down along the trail and drank their water. They looked down the trail and spotted Robin Hood approaching. He made certain no one surprised them from the rear. Robin Hood walked into the narrow

78

area in the road and noticed the thick Rhododendron forest which was located under the large tree canopy. "This is a perfect spot for an ambush. The Rhododendron trees are an evergreen, thick with leaves, and low to the ground. We could literally hide four feet off the trail and fire arrows at point blank range. If the Normand soldiers are coming this way, this is the best spot to set things right."

Dak smiled, "Robin Hood you echo Hulk's suggestion. I agree with both of you."

"We could also penetrate between their columns of riders and take them off the horses with our swords," proclaimed Zenith.

The group talked about what they were going to do. They also discussed the worst-case scenarios with the Normand soldiers being spread out in one column instead of tight together in two columns. Dak finally announced the plan. "Remember they may have on steel helmets and chest plates. You need to make your arrows count." Dak explained his final part of his plan. The group acknowledged they understood.

***

The Normand commander was angered by the simple lives of the country people. The anger turned to hatred. He hated the way they dressed, and the way they talked. He thrived on his revulsion he felt for them, and he enjoyed having his men kill the people in the villages and take their land and their belongings. His men also

79

enjoyed killing the villagers. The soldiers kept track who killed the most villagers. It was a matter of pride between the elite soldiers under his command.

Dak and his friends listened to Hershel explained how the Normand command dealt with the villagers. The villagers had been naive and believed the Normand commanders who had sold them on the great opportunity for selling the Normand army the food and their livestock. After the communities were stripped of their land and livestock, the young men were taken as slaves, and there was no mercy provided for the villagers.

On this trip, the commander had hoped for more grain, more horses and wagons to transport the materials back to Harpers Ferry Harbor. The two wagons full of grain, chickens, stored corn, and other farm grown items, was not enough for the Normand army all winter.

The captain had led his platoon from Harpers Ferry Harbor the morning after the ships were sunk. He wanted to be the commander assigned to locate the responsible men. He wanted to show General Cuez he knew how to capture those soldiers and then skin them alive. He felt the job of gathering food from the poor villagers was beneath him. He led twenty of his best men at a faster pace. He wanted to return to Harpers Ferry Harbor and be permitted to find the responsible saboteurs. His ambition was to be a general in the Normand Army. He wanted to be noticed by General Cuez. He figured the people in the Harpers Ferry Harbor community would know who sunk the ships, and he decided he would start with torturing them.

His mistake was, he had not anticipated the people behind the sabotage of the four ships moving north so far and so fast on foot. He had figured they would be in the outskirts of the harbor town. The region located off the main road was a rough terrain and hard to travel fast yet Dak and his group and been able to run along the ridges of the mountains and slope down the hills and through the valleys. Once they had gotten on the road north of the massacred people, they had moved at close to eight miles an hour on foot.

The captain ordered the rest of his troops to head to Harpers Ferry Harbor with the slower wagons and livestock. He was impatient to return and receive the better assignment. He had seen General Cuez from a distance yelling at the captain in charge of the security of the ships and camp. He had thought this was his opportunity to move ahead in the ranks by first capturing the people responsible and then presenting their heads to the general.

He turned the curve in the dirt road and fast approached the thick hardwood forest on the narrow section of the road. The woods turned from a young pine thicket to an older hardwood forest and then as they started to ascend the mountain, the captain noticed the thick underbrush. He and his men relaxed, and he had not ordered a scout to proceed the troops. The villagers were thought to be the only people in the general area and were weak and complied. If they disagreed with his commands, he would have them killed. They had ridden through the area earlier the same day

81

and did not anticipate an ambush. As he was riding following his four front riders, he noticed the sudden quietness. There were no birds flying or squirrels running in the trees as before. His men were all watching outward as they were trained. As he entered the area, he looked closer at the surroundings. He stared at the shape of a person hidden in the underbrush. The small trees were so thick, he could hardly see past a few feet off the road. He heard a bird sing which sounded like a whip-poor-will with the sound coming from behind him. His mind did not register the threat until the arrow pierced his throat. Several of his men had taken off the metal breast plates which provided the needed protection from arrows and swords for the upper front and rear torso region. The breast plates were not comfortable on long rides with the extra weight. The arrows pierced through the heavy wool coats into their chests and backs.

Dak saw the man in the blue helmet stare at him. He let the arrow fly hitting the man in the throat as he heard the bird sound produced by Trey. He reloaded his second arrow and shot the man next to him in the ribs. He fired his third arrow and hit the soldier on his side of the trail in the back. Dak saw the two front riders' bend over their horse's mane and the other another fell from his horse with arrows fired by Hulk. Dak pulled his two swords and jumped from his hidden spot. He stood in the middle of the small trail and cut the rider across his thigh and then stabbed him through his side below the ribs.

Hulk was responsible for killing the front riders. He fired his three arrows from the opposite side of the road hitting the front three soldiers. The plan was for both Dak and Zenith to fire three arrows each and then attack the column from the center of the trail. They wanted to stop anyone from riding away and warning the other soldiers. The group trapped the soldiers between Hulk at one end and Trey and Tommy Boy at the other end.

Robin Hood was hidden in the middle area where he could fire arrow after arrow. Zenith was positioned down the trail a few feet from Dak and had hit three soldiers with her three arrows and then pulled her sword. She killed three wounded men riding toward her with her cutting them as they tried to ride past.

Trey and Tommy Boy were hidden on opposites sides of the trail and watched as eighteen riders passed. As soon as the last two riders were even with them, Trey whistled the sound like a whip-poor-will. With Trey and Tommy Boy stationed at the area at the end of the trap, they had been able to shoot the soldiers next to them on the trail and then each shot four additional men in the back as they rode further up the trial.

Hershel was concerned when he thought about the training the Front Guard Soldiers had completed. They were all killers. He knew he would be killed by the Normand commander when he was captured. These men would all want to have the honor to kill him. He knew he would not be able to convince them he was a prisoner. He had asked Dak for a sword. He had offered to fight with them. Dak had indicated they did not need his assistance with this confrontation. Hershel did not understand how these young people could survive an attack on a fully armored experienced Normand squad of Front Guard Soldiers. Prior to the ambush, he walked the path with Dak and agreed his friends were all well-hidden next to the trail. He then ascended the hill close to twenty feet and hid behind a large Tulip tree sitting behind the thick Rhododendron bushes. He was amazed as he watched from behind the large tree as Tommy Boy and Trey fired three fast arrows in less than three seconds hitting the Normand soldiers in the backs and heads who were at the end of the column. He watched as every one of the soldiers took on several arrows from both sides of the road. He saw Hulk, Zenith and Dak jump out of the thick underbrush with their swords and kill the injured Normand soldiers on horseback and the soldiers lying on the ground. Only one soldier seemed to survive, and he rode south with two arrows sticking out of his body. One in his shoulder and another in the back. As the horse started to pick up speed, he saw the rope being pulled tight from across the road catching the rider in the neck, knocking him backward to the ground as the horse kept running south. The man landed on his back and started gasping for air. Veronica rushed him from behind the trees and walked over him and plunged her sword through his chest. She looked at Dak, "The next time we ambush these killers." She hesitated and wiped the blood from her sword on his cape. "You can work the rope, and I will be in the middle of the ambush. This is the only asshole I killed." The group laughed.

Dak smiled, "Hurry, we need to be prepared. The rest of the soldiers will be coming soon."

Hershel walked from his hidden spot from the thick Rhododendron underbrush. He stared at the dead Normand soldiers lying in the narrow dirt road. He slowly walked over and stood over the one with the blue helmet. Zenith observed Hershel, "Do you recognize him?"

Hershel slowly looked at Zenith and then at Tommy Boy, Trey and then Robin Hood. Dak had not taken his eyes off Hershel as he had walked from the tree line. Dak wanted to trust him, but trust had to be earned. Dak said, "She asked you if you knew these men."

Hershel turned to Dak, "I do not know these men. These men are an elite group of warriors. Notice the blue helmet on the captain and the blue bands on the right arms of the dead soldiers. They are called the Captain's Guard. They should have a tattoo on their left bicep of a creature with horns. They also have tattoos of teardrops. Each tear drop represents a man, woman, or kid they have killed." He looked concerned. "King Solman has hand-picked these bastards. How did you kill so many Normand soldiers so quickly? Not a single arrow missed the target. You killed these twenty men in less than forty seconds."

Dak was still watching Hershel, and the two men made eye contact, "We have trained for war since we were three-years old. We were taught how to wage war, and you noted we were all hidden within ten feet of the trail."

Tommy Boy held up a coat. "None of these uniforms will fit me." He smiled looking at Hershel, "This was like shooting fish in a small barrel."

Trey said, "I found the biggest coat on the soldier over by the front of the line. I am going to make this uniform fit. I will try to cover up the hole made by Robin Hood. The arrow hit in the center of the uniform located in the middle of his chest. Damn good shooting Robin Hood."

Robin Hood was pulling an arrow from a dead soldier, "I fired off seven arrows and all hit the targets. I need some more arrows."

Dak smiled, "I am going to wear the blue helmet and the captain's uniform. He is no longer in need of it. Now let us get the dead off the trail. Zenith you and Veronica can help me locate eight horses. We need to hurry."

Hulk walked by Hershel dragging a dead soldier. Hershel noticed he had his uniform removed. Hulk said, "Hershel, you need to get you a uniform and start dragging these soldiers into the thick underbrush. See if you can remove the arrows from the dead. We will need all the good arrows we can find. Check them for weapons and gold. Maybe the next battle, we will allow you to swing a sword."

Tommy Boy looked up from pulling an arrow out of a man's back, "Are we not going to bury these men?"

Hulk shook his head. "The bears, buzzards, and coyotes need to eat the same as the worms. These bastards do not deserve a proper burial. Besides we need to hurry. The rest of the fifty-man platoon

86

will be coming down that road, and they will not like us killing their friends."

Chapter 9

The assassin had left the jailhouse and circled back around after he watched Samuel leave the jailhouse and return to the main building. He crawled through the bushes along the top of the cliff and was careful to stay hidden. He had noticed the young people who had stayed in the shack overlooking the ocean had all left by ship. He crawled in the small crawl space the first night and waited until dawn. The temperature was so cold he knew he could not survive another night in the crawl space. When no one entered the shack the next day, he crawled out of the crawl space and hid inside the home. He found the home a perfect place to hide where he watched the area. He knew when his master had been killed so quickly by the blond-headed man, and the other apprentice had been knocked out, he needed to hide and wait. When he realized the key to free the other apprentice from the jail cell and unlock the lock was not with the guard, he knew he had to kill both the guard and his countryman. The other apprentice could not be left to talk or be tortured. He remembered how close he had been to being caught after he sliced his countryman's neck. The man was chained to a pole in the jail. He raised his neck and accepted the blade. He then had run into the woods as the blond headed man was approaching the jail. The jailor had confessed when his third finger had been cut off, the man who killed his master was a Blueblood from Merlin.

He was surprised. The Sect Leader had not reported that a Blueblood would be involved. He had indicated the female target was not guarded but could be a difficult target. The Sect Leader had emphasized not to underestimate her. Kill her at the first opportunity and, "Do not allow her to see you coming." He wanted proof of her death. He now also knew if given the opportunity he would kill the Blueblood after he killed this woman. He owed his master. He thought about the Christian teaching he was forced to endure. The cult leaders wanted the assassins to fit in and understanding the different religions were required. He said to himself, "Leviticus 24:19-21, an eye for an eye."

As he watched out the window of the home, he wished he had known why they were summoned by the Sect Leader and the High Priest to travel so far to kill this woman. He wondered who she was, and how the High Priest and Sect Leader had known of her. He missed the hot dry climate on his continent and his young wife. He however knew this mission was an honor. The task had come from the High Priest, his council, and the leadership of his Sect.

He was confused how she lived after being hit with two poison-tipped arrows. He had assumed she would have died within two-to-three hours. He also knew these people would bury her after a funeral. His Sect had forced them to study their religion and customs to be able to go unnoticed. He had watched from the home for four days. From the bedroom on the north side of the home, he could see the graveyard located behind the church. The home had been a perfect place to hide, but he knew time was running out. At some point someone would enter the home and if he was discovered he would have to kill that person. He made certain there was no funeral for her just the men that died in the battle on the other side of the gorge. He waited and watched for the news of her death.

He was surprised after four nights when he looked out the kitchen window in mid-morning and saw her walk down the front stairs. He was confused how the poison from the sea snakes had not worked. One arrow should have killed her. His master had showed him how to milk the Hook-Nosed Sea snakes and retrieve the poison. He had guaranteed them the poison always worked and just a few drops could kill multiple people. They had killed other men with the poison. The person would stop breathing after losing the ability to walk. They would salivate from their nose, their mouth, and upchuck uncontrollably. The poison would attack the body's nervus system, and the person would then go into shock and die.

Her apartment was well guarded with people coming and going through the front door all day long. He hoped she would keep walking toward him. He noticed she had a limp caused no doubt by the other apprentice's arrow. His master had been the first to shoot, and the arrow should have killed her. It had hit her in the upper torso. His partner in training, the other apprentice, had not aimed high enough and hit her in the upper leg. With the tips of both arrows coated with the poison, she should have died. He wanted to make certain this time as he felt his knife strapped to his side in the holder attached to his waist. He saw her gaze out over the ocean and then look directly at him as he was watching from the rear window. He then noticed the men walking from the barn and talking with her about halfway up the path. They separated and the Blueblood walked her back to the apartment. He kept watching and knew he might be discovered soon. He needed to strike in the night and then leave as planned through the New York territory and south along the Continental Trail. They had planned to obtain a seat on a trade ship in Harpers Ferry Harbor and sail back to Asia. He hated this cold weather. He looked forward to receiving the glory from his God once the Master Priest and the Sect Leader had appraised him after he had completed his mission and killed this infidel female.

***

As the sun had slowly disappeared in the western sky, the assassin was watching and comparing the body language of the two guards as they made their rounds to the prior nights. The first night after the Battle of New York, the guards appeared to be more attentive and peering in the shadows created by the moon as they worked as a team making their rounds. He noticed they now appeared to be more relaxed and, in a hurry, to return to the indoors. The cold wind was relentless. The assassin hated the cold frozen ground covered in snow. He took a deep breath and looked all around him. The area was clear of people and dogs. He hated a barking dog that could alert guards to his location. He ran to the large rock at the top of the cliff area. He cautiously looked around the area and noted the street was still clear. He ran down the path to the corner of her building. He looked around to make certain the guards were nowhere near. He listened and did not hear any sounds from the Queen's upstairs room. He could hear someone talking on the lower level of the end apartment. He jumped and grabbed hold of the deck and pulled himself to the railing and climbed over the rail to the balcony. He stood on the balcony with his back against the wall out of the moon light in the shadow of the roof soffit. He heard someone closing a door somewhere in the distance at another home, and he dropped to the floor of the balcony. He waited.

Vicky had hated being bored all day. She knew Doc Johnson coming by her apartment to check on her was no coincidence. He had worked endless hours with the help of others mending the injured after the Battle of New York. Doc Johnson had successfully removed Zorro's kidney and mended over fifty injured men in addition to delivering a baby for a lady living on the outskirts of Cliff Tops. The men and women mostly received cuts from swords or punctures from arrows during the battle and had to be checked and re-checked for infection and any symptoms of the deadly B12 virus. The B12 virus blanked the earth and killed more people than the following war. Even seventeen years later the B12 virus was still killing people.

In the battle, some had lost a limb or in Zorro's case his kidney. The doctor was too tired to socially visit. She knew Samuel must have told him to come and see her.

Doc Johnson provided her with Herbal tea containing a sedative to help her sleep. "This tea has twice the sedative. It will force you to sleep." He had smiled as he inspected the cut-up towel used to hold a rag and then a butterfly bandage over the leg wound. "I see you have been a bad girl." He smiled, and she never answered. He applied a couple of sutures and a bandage. She thanked the doctor as he was leaving and assured him, she would drink the tea and rest. She laid in bed for over an hour worrying about Dak and his friends. She knew the doctor had told her friends not to visit her. She held the cup of tea and thought about drinking the contents but decided to wait until later in the night, so she could sleep all night. She thought she heard a sound outside on her balcony, but she always heard noises in the apartment. The wind was always blowing on the mountain top creating noises with tree limbs rubbing against each other in the woody area near their home. The small animals would come out at night and run through the bushes. Occasionally a racoon would scratch against the log siding as it climbed to the roof. She heard a hot amber pop from the large hickory log in the wood burning stove located in her great room. Her apartment was on the second floor and was situated in the middle of the three lower apartments. Her apartment was bigger than the other three apartments on the first floor. She could hear Wayne every night closing doors downstairs and walking on his wood floors in his boots. Eric of Newport and his family living below her were always loud. Sometimes, she could hear Billy Ray and Delores late of a night. Those two seem to really enjoy making love to each other. She took a sip of tea and started dozing off.

He looked through the edge of the window. He noticed there was no one in the main room. He eased his knife between the door jamb and lifted the tumbler upward, and the latch clicked as the door was opened. He eased the door further open and stepped across the door threshold. The assassin slowly and silently walked into the room as he intentionally left the door ajar. This was his escape route, and this mission would be over in a few seconds. He knew she was injured and by herself. He licked his lips and cautiously walked to the bedroom door and peered into the bedroom. He could see the covers pulled over someone lying with their back to him and noticed the sound of someone lightly breathing. His heartbeat accelerated with the anticipation of killing her and then fleeing. He thought of his master, the revenge and his glory with his God.

***

Samuel never complained about the cold wind or the cold nights. He liked the open territory and the people in this village. They all helped one another. He liked talking with the young children. They were happy, talkative, and loving. He also knew there was a third assassin in the area hiding somewhere. Wayne

94

and his men looked all around the town of Cliff Tops for any signs, and they had not been able to locate a single footprint in the snow or a sign someone was hiding in the caves, mines, or along the cliffs. They used dogs in the search, but without the exact scent, the dogs had not been able to locate anyone. He wondered if there were only two assassins. Maybe Wayne was correct. Maybe one had died once he came ashore. Wayne provided guards for the first three days and nights but had removed the guards when there were no signs of the third assassin in the area.

Samuel knew the two city guards were not up to the task of stopping the assassin. He was aware of how deadly the killers were. The assassins had killed a few Bluebloods over the years in the city of Merlin. His men killed several of the assassins at different locations on the west coast. At first, ten to fourteen years ago, the assassins could easily be spotted. They could not speak English, and their clothing was different. The thin cloaks were designed for the deserts and hot climate of Asia. Over time they had been taught English and learned to blend in with the poor families in and around Merlin. They were taught the customs and forced to read the Holy Bible just so they could fit in with the poor people. By quoting Bible verses, they were able to be accepted and fit into the poor communities. The security force in Merlin had not spotted an assassin in two years. The assassins had just stopped coming.

The assassins were sneaky in the methods of killing their prey either in an ambush or after an extended stakeout. Stabbing an innocent person in the back was collateral damage and acceptable. They learned to be patient and wait for the perfect opportunity. The assassins Samuel and his men had captured had never demonstrated remorse for killing anyone. They had been trained to kill and welcomed death with honor. When they had been tortured, they had never been broken. They chanted to their God for mercy, guidance, and strength. They were finally killed when they would not provide the needed information.

The assassins were skilled killers with multiple types of weapons. They preferred the blade of a knife or sword, but they could kill with their hands, and were very accurate with a bow and used venom from the Hook-Nosed Sea snakes rubbed on the tips of the arrows.

He walked down the street looking in all directions. He knew the two guards walking the perimeter would try to stay inside in the warm jail house as much as possible. He walked in front of the fourplex and noticed the footprints in the snow leading to the front corner of the fourplex. He looked up to the door located on the balcony and noticed the door was ajar.

***

The assassin smirked to himself as he moved slowly across the floor. He wanted to look into the eyes of the infidel as she took her last breath. He wanted to tell the High Priest how he stared into her eyes as she died and in stole her last breath. This killing needed to be glorious after the master and the other apprentice had been killed. He approached the foot of the bed as he noticed his heartbeat had slowed down. He felt calmness within himself as his confidence was certain.

The bed was positioned on the opposite wall from the door with the headboard positioned against the exterior log wall. The bedroom had one window which was covered with a large drape. The moon light coming from the balcony door he had just entered provided a small amount of ambient light along with the hot embers from the cracked opened door of the wood burning stove. He slowly pulled his knife. He started to walk to the side of the bed when, suddenly, the person rolled over, and he saw the motion of their hand. He immediately knew something was not right. His body felt strange but could not register what had happened. He felt some type of liquid on his hand as he rubbed his stomach. He glanced down and saw the end of the object sticking from his belly. It looked like a large needle used for sewing leather. His mind was trying to comprehend what had happened. He reached down and pulled the sharp steel object from his belly and realized he had been hit by a well-balanced throwing spike which was close to eight inches long. The woman had pulled the spike from her hair and in one fast motion threw the spike with the sharp end penetrating seven inches into his belly.

After a second passed, he realized his stomach had been punctured. He now knew he would die. The acid in his belly was toxic to the rest of his internal organs. He knew he only had a few minutes before death. He also knew he was going to complete this mission and gain his personal glory with his God. He gritted his teeth. As he lunged on top of her mattress, she anticipated his move and headed toward the bedroom door. He jumped off the bed and chased after her.

Vicky knew her best chance was her sword. With her injured leg, she limped toward the open door. He caught her from behind, tackling her to the floor. She immediately turned as she was falling and before he could restrain her, she landed her right fist on the bridge on his nose. His head absorbed the blow, but his nose bone broke, causing him a second of delay. Vicky used the time to reach with her left hand and grab the blade of the knife and holding the knife away from her. At first, she appeared to be stronger with the knife cutting into the palm of her hand. She hit him a second time in the nose with her right fist. She knew it was a matter of time before he killed her. He was on top and had the leverage, and she could not hold the knife's blade much longer. She could feel the knife cutting into her left hand and the oozing of blood running down her fingers. He tried to pull the knife backward away from her at first. Then, he tried to hit her with the handle as she clung to the blade.

She heard the door from behind her abruptly open with the door casing flying into the room and landing near her. She noticed the eyes of the assassin register the fact someone else had entered the room. The assassin looked down at Vicky, released his hold on the knife, and then rolled backward. He stood in one motion and ran out the balcony door, jumping headfirst over the rail.

Samuel chased him to the balcony and looked down at the man lying in the snow-covered street with the blood near his body. Samuel hollered for the guards. Vicky heard Eric of Newport running out the front door into the street. She heard Wayne and Delores rushing up the stairs. Samuel ran back to her side and held her. He immediately asked Delores for a wet rag to stop the bleeding. "The assassin is in the street. We need him alive if possible."

Wayne looked at Vicky and noticed all the blood on her midsection. He had assumed she had been stabbed. Samuel looked for the knife wound, and he also assumed she had been stabbed. Vicky whispered, "That blood is not mine." She held up her hand showing her palm and the deep cut. She was a little confused, "He jumped headfirst over the balcony. Who would do that?"

Samuel looked at Wayne, "Her only injury is to her left hand."

Delores held the wet rag against the bleeding hand wound as she glanced at the open balcony door. Wayne turned and ran down the stairs. He met Billy Ray and Eric of Newport in the street. The two guards were approaching on foot. Little Jimmy opened his front door and approached from his small cottage. Other towns people also showed up.

Eric looked up. "He is dead. There is a puncture wound in his stomach region. He landed on his head. I believe his neck is broken." The men turned and looked up at the balcony.

Wayne said, "She will be alright. She has a deep cut on her left hand."

Chapter 10

As she placed a rope around the white gelding standing in the woods, Zenith said, "These are all magnificent horses. They are trained for combat. They do not scare easily."

Dak was riding on a horse and had three tied off to the saddle horn. Veronica took two other horses tied off to the horse she rode back to the team. He watched Zenith rub the neck of the horse and let it smell her. She pulled an apple out of her pocket and allowed the horse to eat the red apple off the palm of her hand. He looked around making certain no one was nearby. "The horse I believe likes you." He smiled at her. "You certainly are a beautiful woman, and this is a romantically quiet place in the woods."

She smiled and kept rubbing the horse, "I see that you are over being cold from your swim last night." She looked at him and smiled, "We need to be going. We will not have much time. Those other soldiers will not be far behind." She jumped on her horse and rode past Dak heading back to the ambush spot. He followed her to the road and the others.

Hulk announced, "We have done what we need to here. These dead men deserved no mercy. What do you want to do? Do we wait or head north?"

Dak noticed the other guys were all watching and listening. Dak glanced south along the dirt road. "I do not want to be caught between a large force coming up from the south and these soldiers heading south. We will head north. We need to keep moving north. We need to make our way to the Midnight Hole before the area is reinforced with additional soldiers. When word reaches the Normand command at the Midnight Hole about the four ships being sunk, they will double the guard detail."

***

"Here they come. They are pulling two wagons full of grain, several chickens in cages and other livestock. This area is open. There is no way we can approach without them seeing us." Hulk looked over at Dak lying next to him in the weeds at the top of the knoll. The others were standing behind the embankment holding their horses directly behind them listening to them talk.

"With our diversion and these borrowed uniforms, we will fit right in. All we need to do is get close without them being alarmed. The diversion should work." Hulk glanced at Dak with a smirk and then glanced back a Veronica.

Veronica looked at Dak, "Why don't you run across the field naked?"

Robin Hood smiled, "Well, Veronica, two reasons. First, we assume the soldiers to be heterosexual." He over emphasized the word "heterosexual" and used both arms and hands making the imaginary description of a curvy female. "Meaning, they like females, and we are betting the soldiers have not seen a pretty-looking female in days. The second reason, Veronica, is you have a body like a Venus, and they will notice you even from a great distance." The guys all smiled, and Zenith laughed with Robin Hood's over describing the situation.

"I know what heterosexual means," snapped Veronica. She handed her bow to her brother, Trey, and pulled her coat and top wool sweater off. She pulled her boots off and then her pants. She removed her two top shirts, bra, and then her socks, "I am not removing my panties for you guys to see me. This is all I am willing to do." She stood still looking at the group with a smile on her face.

Zenith smiled, "You will have done your part. If any of those soldiers get close to you, I will kill them for you."

Dak looked concerned, "This might not be as easy as the prior ambush. We need to be sharp. Let's make this look good. There are thirty soldiers we need to take down."

Veronica waited. Robin Hood was lying on the ground at the top of the knoll hidden behind the weeds watching through the binoculars at the approaching soldiers and the two wagons. He announced, "I believe we are good." He descended the knoll and jumped on his horse Trey was holding.

Veronica looked back at her friends as she dropped her big coat on the ground for Trey to pick up. "The things we do in war." She turned and ran over the hill and down the dirt road heading toward the oncoming soldiers. She glanced back as she approached the Normand team of soldiers to give the appearance, she was running from someone. When she was close to one hundred yards from the

103

front two soldiers on horseback, she acted like she was surprised to see them, and she turned to run perpendicular into the field away from the road and the oncoming soldiers.

Dak commanded, "Let's go."

Dak, Hershel, Hulk, Robin Hood, and Trey headed for the column of soldiers with swords pulled. Dak still did not trust Hershel one hundred percent, but he knew he needed him to talk to the soldiers. Dak's accent could not be disguised, and they needed every second to position themselves for the ambush.

They ran the horses toward the column of soldiers as the dust from the dirt road rose and then settled back to the ground behind them. The leader was staring at Dak with his blue helmet as they approached. Dak and the others kept the face mask pulled down over their face and the uniform tight against their bodies. Hershel announced as the sergeant of the Normand soldiers approached. "We ran into some villagers." He pointed at Veronica as she was running across the open field. "She is young, frisky, fast, but worth the chase. We have already killed her friends. We removed her clothing, and she then escaped. We are going to enjoy her this afternoon."

The soldiers watching her run smiled.

Hulk and Robin Hood had ridden past the front of the row of troops and out flanked them on both sides. The soldiers in the rear of the column had ridden to a stop next to the soldiers in the front of the column. With all the soldiers observing Veronica as she slowed to a trot. The anticipation of taking turns with her was peaking. Three of the soldiers rode toward her with an understanding they would have her in the field first. Dak rode next to the sergeant with his right hand on his sword. The sergeant looked at the man in the blue helmet and study him. He noticed the brown leather-seal skin boats, he started to yell, but one quick stroke by Dak's sword took his head off. He pulled his second sword and stabbed two soldiers through the gut as he rode between them. The fourth soldier turned to see what had caused the other soldiers to fall when Dak cut him across his face with the sword in his right hand. Hulk used his one sword and swung the blade with force, killing the fifth soldier and then a sixth soldier. Both Robin Hood and Trey made their first swings count as the soldiers were not prepared to be stabbed and slashed from behind. They all swung the swords, hitting the unprepared soldiers and then proceeding to the next ones.

Tommy Boy and Zenith headed over the ridge in the direction of Veronica. The three Normand soldiers were further away from Veronica and were surprised with the attack. Zenith had not wavered. She took out a soldier on the right and one on her left as she passed between them. The third soldier tried to turn his horse to face her, but she blocked his swing with her sword and then rotated her sword downward cutting deep into his exposed thigh. Two of the men died immediately and the third laid over his saddle holding onto the horse's mane. Tommy Boy rode behind Zenith and turned to the injured soldier and with one hard swing, cut the wounded soldier's head off.

By the time the soldiers realized they were being killed by men dressed in Normand uniforms, half of them were either dead or severely wounded.

Trey jumped from his horse into the wagon and attacked the man riding in the back of the wagon with a downward swing. The first swing had been with great force and the recoil caused the soldier to fall backward. The second swing cut him across his face and deep into his unprotected belly as the soldier riding in the back of the wagon was now dead. Trey turned as the driver realized his guard had been mortally wounded. The driver panicked and jumped from the wagon. Trey jumped to the driver's seat and stopped the wagon and then placed the brake on. He jumped from the wagon with the sword in his hand killing other soldiers. Robin Hood pulled his bow and shot the man on the ground and also shot three other soldiers, two of which were in a second wagon. Dak killed three additional men who were all at the front of the column and were slow to understand he was not the commander. The hesitation cost them their lives. Hulk proceeded like Dak, killing the men, and then moving to the next man.

Hershel fought a soldier on horseback with both men blocking the swings of the other. Hershel finally grabbed the soldier with both falling to the ground. They wrestled and rolled over on the ground trying to be the one on top. They each hit the other with their fists as they rolled over a second time and then a third time. Dak and Hulk noticed all the other Normand soldiers had been killed. They jumped off the horses and watched the ongoing wrestling match between Hershel and the Normand soldier. Robin Hood rode up and watched with a loaded arrow. Tommy Boy had ridden into the battle scene after the three soldiers had been killed in the field. Zenith and Veronica rode into the area with Veronica jumping off the back of Zenith's horse.

Hershel rolled over on the Normand soldier struggling to win the fight. The soldier pulled Hershel over and now was on top. The soldier pulled a knife from his boot. Dak anticipated the soldier's move and grabbed the man's wrist when he was about to plunge the knife into Hershel's unprotected side. Dak announced, "The fighting is over," as he pulled the knife from the man's hand. Hershel hit the soldier in the mouth as he stood, knocking the man back down to the ground. Hershel looked over into the field and saw the three dead soldiers that had gone after Veronica and the dead bodies of all the other soldiers lying on the road. He then glanced at the one still alive lying on the ground with his lip bleeding. He looked at Dak, "It is a good thing you stopped the fighting; I was about to kill him. I left him alive, so you could interrogate him."

The group laughed as Dak played along, "Yes, I believe you would have pulled his knife out of your rib cage and killed him with his blade. Hershel, I do believe you are our bravest soldier and our best warrior." The group continued to laugh.

Dak noticed Veronica still had not covered her body. She stood in just her panty and then walked with her shoulders and back straight with confidence as all watched her. She picked up a sword from one of the dead men. She approached the soldier on the ground, "So, you want to rape me?"

Hulk stepped in her path and held her arm as she approached the soldier lying on the ground.

Dak said while looking at the soldier, "She is going to kill you if you do not talk. Where is General Cuez?"

The soldier noticed the naked female had pulled her arm free from the grasp of her friend. He then glanced around him at his dead comrades and then realized the other soldiers who rode ahead had all been killed, and these men were wearing their uniforms. There would be no help coming. There were no other Normand soldiers on patrol in the area. "He is in the Harpers Ferry Harbor with two thousand of the best soldiers on the planet. They will kill scum like you." He spat on the ground in protest.

Dak held his hand up motioning for Veronica to halt, "I hope they are better than you and your friends because I did not even break a sweat providing justice to these murderous ass holes. How many men are at the gate on the Continental Trail leading to the New York Tribe?"

They watched the man look at the ground. The soldier knew these were the soldiers who had blown up the four ships in the harbor and killed his commander and friends. Trey walked up carrying a metal rod he had pulled from the wagon. The rod had a braided handle on one end and a brand on the other end.

Trey looked at the soldier and asked, "What is this brand used for?"

The soldier glanced at the brand. He had watched hundreds of men, women, and kids all scream when the hot brand was stuck to their skin. He did not answer but looked away.

Hulk walked past Veronica and kicked the soldier in the side. Hulk clenched his jaws, "What did you do with this cow brand?"

The soldier did not answer.

Zenith dismounted, "That is enough." She pulled the clothing from her saddle bag. She walked over to Veronica and handed her the clothing. Veronica took her time placing her long socks on first and then her tight-fitting silk under pants and then her other pants. She sat down and placed her boots on. She stood facing the men as she took her time as she placed her bra and two shirts on while all watched.

As Dak removed his blue helmet, he staired at the soldier. "I am going to ask you one more time. How many soldiers do the Normand army have stationed at the cave leading to the New York tribe? We call the area the Midnight Hole."

The soldier looked up. "You know I cannot reveal this information to you. I am a Normand soldier, and we do not sell out our comrades. Go ahead and kill me."

Dak looked at Trey, "Start a fire. We can eat a couple of those chickens." Dak then turned back to the soldier. "We are not going to kill you." He then looked at Hulk, "Tie him up."

***

Zenith walked up next to Dak and in a soft voice, "What kind of parents will we be if we start doing things like this. Actions like this affect people. The memories will always be with us. Is there not a better way?"

Dak was caught off guard by the statement. He hesitated and looked around to see if anyone could hear them talk. He looked into her big, beautiful eyes, "I love you. I want you to be the mother of my children, but if we do not stop the slaughter by the Normand army, we will not have an opportunity to be parents."

"That is not what I asked. I am afraid we will be mean parents with no patience, full of hatred, and full of revenge. Is that what we will become? Doing things like this affects us all. You can talk to anyone of age, and they will tell you they live with some type of guilt."

Dak finished placing the gold from the dead soldiers into the saddle bag. "What I know is we are at war and if we do nothing we will not survive. I already live with guilt. I cut a man's head off in front of his wife and friends, and I might be forced to kill his three boys once they try to kill me." He turned and walked toward the fire and picked up the brand. The Normand soldier saw him walking toward him, and he tried to embrace what was about to happen. "Hulk, you and Trey hold him still."

"Please don't. Dear God. Please." He did not take his eyes off the glowing orange part of the brand.

"Is that what the men, women, and children said to you before you branded them?" asked Tommy Boy.

Hulk held his face firm and Trey held his body still. Dak stood over the soldier and position himself looking down with the brand in his right hand. The man was gritting his teeth in anticipation of the pain. Dak stuck the hot brand to his forehead and held the brand in place for a second pushing inward. The man screamed and cried as the smoke rose from his face and the smell of burnt flesh filled the air. Dak commanded, "Untie him." He handed the brand to Robin Hood. "Are you right-handed or left-handed?"

The soldier laid on the ground crying in pain. Hulk kicked him. "He asked, are you right-handed or left-handed?"

The soldier looked up with a questionable expression, "I am left-handed."

"You are a liar. Your pouch for your arrows on your back is facing your right side. You are right-handed. Hold your right hand up."

"What for?"

"I said hold your right hand up, or I will cut your arm off."

The soldier was quivering with pain and anticipation as he held his right hand up. Dak quickly pulled his sword and stuck his sword blade between the middle finger and the ring finger and jerked his sword with the blade cutting off the two fingers next to the thumb. The man recoiled in pain, looking at his two fingers on the ground.

"Your days as an archer are over. You will no longer be shooting any more men, women, or children with your bow. Now get up. I need you to go deliver a message to General Cuez for me." The soldier at first had trouble standing with a grimaced expression. He looked at Dak with his hand bent into his belly and his other hand holding his burning face. "Tell him I am coming for him and when he crawls out from under the rock where he hides, I am going to cut his head off. You make certain you tell him this. I am coming for him." The soldier looked at his hand holding it tight trying to stop the bleeding then at Dak. "What is the message?"

The soldier replied, "You are going to cut his head off." The soldier started walking south and then started running. He finally cleared the knoll. Dak turned, "We need to drive these animals and grain back to the people in the village ahead of us." He looked at Zenith not knowing if she accepted his decision as he walked to the fire.

Tommy Boy cleaned and cooked four chickens. He figured it was his turn to cook. Plus, he did not want to be involved with the one soldier being branded, he announced, as the soldier cleared the hill, "The chickens are done."

Chapter 11

Aquarius examined the map Dak provided. He noticed his route since he had left Old Thomas's Ranch. Once he left Old Thomas place, his first marker was the nuclear waste pit to the south. He headed north into the cold wilderness. He was thankful for the extra food, small tent, and the extra pack horse. He hoped Dak was correct. Dak suggested the Midlanders might have migrated south for the winter. They had not seen any permanent type structures during their trip. The Midlanders camps were portable, and they seemed to move from location to location. He hoped he could avoid them. He gently folded the map and placed it in the waterproof leather satchel.

On the fifth day, he cleared the first river. He knew there were a total of three rivers. He also was aware, if he had to, he could go further north and follow the second map which Zenith and Dak made as they crossed the continent. No one knew the exact miles from the east coast to the west coast, but the best guess was between nine-hundred to one thousand-four-hundred miles from Old Thomas Ranch to the west coast. The west coast of old earth in the North American continent had changed with several hundred miles inland sliding into the Pacific Ocean during the Transitional Period and the low-lying land being covered in ocean waters. The event caused rising ocean waters that permanently flooded the land mass to cover the old state of Missouri up through the Dakotas.

Merlin was located on the west coast where the continent turned inward along the coastline creating a huge ocean gulf. Dak had explained the nuclear bombs had missed most of this area with the large open plains and mountains and tree forest leading into the old country of Canada.

Aquarius glanced behind him to verify he was not being followed and the items on the pack horse had not shifted and fallen off as he rode through the wooded area. He then thought about what Dak had suggested, "Could the Blueblood government in Merlin be secretly financing the war in the south." He thought about the Blueblood people in the government who had mystically died inside the walls of the Blueblood sanctuary area. No one linked the random deaths. He and a few of his friends had guessed the Merlin Senate and Merlin army may have orchestrated the assassination of the one senator, the city mayor, and the guard posted outside the senator's home. He kept thinking as he rode several additional miles. He recalled the man in charge of the Merlin bank. He, like the prior mayor, was not a Blueblood but was appointed by the senate to manage the bank. His name was Bob, and some called him "Bob the Banker." Bob had been found dead four years ago. At first, the guards reported death caused by the B12 virus, but the doctor from the Blueblood University, Dr. Vandergriff, had suggested the cause of death to be murder and was due to a high level of B12 virus being injected in his blood system. Doc Vandergriff was Aquarius' friend and told him secretly Bob had been murdered, and the killer went to a lot of trouble and risk to make the death to randomly appear to be caused by the B12 virus. The level of the virus in the body was four times the level of a normal person who died by the naturally observing the virus into the nervous system. Now, a second-generation Blueblood had been appointed by the senate after the strong recommendation of Senator Dale to manage the Merlin Bank. Aquarius thought as soon as he could, he would need to infiltrate the bank's security and establish if the money was being moved to assist the war in the south. He also wondered, "Why would Senator Dale and others transfer money to King Solman. There is no relationship or is there?"

As he rode west, he was conflicted as considered who he could trust in Merlin. He also made a mental list of who he could not trust. As days turned to weeks and the trip had been harsh, Aquarius become bitter as he thought about Zenith and her choice. He was dejected as he approached the third river and realized he may never again see his daughter. He also knew he should be in Merlin in a few days and start his dangerous work to uncover the plot.

Chapter 12

Vicky inspected her hand wrapped in the bandage as she contemplated her near death experience. The three assassins had been sent by someone. As the group was quiet and finished breakfast, Wayne finally declared, "I agree with Samuel. I do not believe the assassins were sent by King Solman or General Cuez. The Normand army has us out numbered. They do not need to send assassins to kill you. They will send their entire army to kill all of us at some point. Killing you does not provide them a tactical advantage. Based on what we understand about the religious Sect located in the Asia continent, they would never work for King Solman. They believe all of us are infidels. The sooner they kill all of us the better. They hate us all. Captain J.J. has indicated the Asia religious sect would like to purify the entire world with all our blood. The Asia continent is in total conflict and wars are constant between the clans."

Delores looked up from eating the last of her eggs, "Who then would be sending the assassins? I never heard of assassins that would martyr themselves on an assignment. Who would be their employer?"

Wayne looked at Vicky and hesitated to say what was on his mind. Vicky finally looked at Wayne, "You think it is Zanbar?"

Delores looked confused. "Who is Zanbar?" Little Jimmy ducked his head and blew out air. Eric of Newport placed his toast on his plate and looked worriedly at Vicky but appeared to understand and agree with Wayne.

No one answered for a few seconds. Mia finally said, "If Zanbar or any of his family members are still out there, they would send assassins. They declared they would have their revenge."

Delores and Samuel waited for someone to explain. Samuel finally asked, "Who is this man named Zanbar? I need to know."

Billy Ray looked at Samuel. "We had a mission over nineteen years ago. The mission got a little ugly."

Delores blurted out, "You think this has to do with a mission nineteen years ago during the old world before the Transition Period? Tell me this is not so. Who would still be alive to orchestrate such a vengeful mission after everything the world has been through?"

"Zanbar or his family would," said Wayne.

Samuel looked concerned, "Who is this Zanbar person?"

Wayne answered, "He was a Saudi National, and his oldest son was caught purchasing a young child in the human slavery business from Columbia, South America. The son was very wealthy. The entire family was extremely wealthy like so many Saudi men who received stipends from the oil money from their government. The family diversified into the world banking business and shipping business and made billions. They owned yachts, homes, huge buildings located all over the world, with jets to transport them. Whatever someone could buy with billions of dollars, Zanbar did."

He looked at Delores and then Samuel, "Zanbar's son purchased a young girl from one of the gangs in South America. The girl was thirteen. He paid two thousand dollars for her. His plan was to rape the virgin girl and then throw her dead body into the ocean when he was finished with her. We stopped the rape and the murder. It did not end well for Zanbar's son. He was killed on his yacht, and what was left of him and most of the crew was discovered by the Saudi Government when the yacht sailed into the port of Jeddah on the Red Sea a few days later."

Vicky looked up, "I do not believe Zanbar would have survived during the Transition Period. We can dismiss that thought."

Mia looked at Vicky. "If Zanbar or his family survived all these years, they would not hesitate to send assassins after you. The news around the world is spread by the merchant ships and traders. Some of the traders go to the other continent and deal with the people of Asia. Not all the Asia people are part of the religious sect. That is where the silk comes from that Captain J.J. brings us that we use in our uniforms to protect us from the arrows. I would not discard the possibility too quickly. Rumors and stories like the Battle of Cliff Tops and the Battle of New York spread like wildfire. You know how we are so eager to receive updated news when Captain J.J. sails into our dock. Others around the globe will be just as eager. The Normand army lost all those men. Those stories travel fast, and you are the leader of the oppositional army. Your name has been broadcasted worldwide."

Chapter 13

The villagers all cautiously observed the face covered riders with contempt and fear as the group rode into their small community on the Normand owned white horses. The mothers tried to gather the children back inside the huts and small homes as the elderly stood frozen in their standing positions. Dak and his group rode slowly to the corral and forced the cows and horses inside the fenced area. Trey jumped down from one wagon, and Tommy Boy jumped down from the other wagon. Both men led the extra white horses tied off to the rear of the wagons to the corral. They left their horses and wagons tied to the corral fence. The villagers noticed some were dressed in Normand uniforms and the others appeared to be warriors holstering multiple weapons. Dak noticed this town was about three times the size of the small village where the massacre occurred. The group dismounted and went into the small saloon. They all ordered and then ate the meals and drank the ale. Dak asked the waitress to send for the mayor. He laid three gold coins out on the table and paid for the meals. The restaurant owner came over and looked at the gold. He was an elderly man and looked apprehensive, knowing there could be a trick. Dak announced, "We pay for our meals. We also will pay for those Normand solder's meals and their rudeness in the way they treated you and your community. We know they stole your livestock and food." Dak flipped him a fourth gold coin in the air.

The man reached for the gold coins and immediately went into the kitchen.

Hulk looked at Dak, "Are you going to give away all the gold we got from those dead soldiers?"

"We need to buy good will. These people are scared. You can see fear in their eyes."

After the meal, the eight walked outside. They noticed several men arrived from the farms and others were on their way into town, approaching from the road north and south. Dak knew the towns people had a security network set up between the families to help each other. He knew they had not had time to hear about the smaller village south where the Normand soldiers butchered the villagers. He also was aware the people had reservations about the Normand army. The stories from the south had spread over the past few years. A tall, bald man walked over. He announced he was the mayor. He cautiously looked around and seemed nervous.

Dak ordered, "Spread out and be on alert. Some of the people might be beholden to the Normand empire. The danger is not knowing who to trust." Dak noticed the farmers were all carrying tools such as axes and hoes. Dak walked into the city street removing his Normand helmet and jacket revealing to the people his group were not part of the Normand empire. He turned and faced the mayor and the gathering people. "You people might not like what I have to say, but I am going to say it anyway. We have brought your animals back to you and your grain. We have also brought you some additional horses. They are your property, and you may do what you wish with them. If you want to give them to the Normand army when they return that is your decision." He looked around at the families, and the men who had gathered. "Of the fifty Normand soldiers that arrived here forty-nine of them are dead. My friends and I killed them."

The mayor looked scared and stuttered as he replied. "Well, how did they die?" The people looked confused.

"We ambushed the soldiers and killed all but one. We let one go in hopes he would tell General Cuez his forty-nine comrades were not killed by you. We do not want them to seek revenge on the innocent people in your community. You will find out soon enough those same soldiers at daybreak rode into the small village south of here and massacred everyone. They killed every man, woman, and child in that village. We tracked them to set things right."

The man standing near the corral with his three grown sons did not appear to be timid. He stood holding an ax and demanded, "Who are you?"

"We are not from around here. We have elected to fight the Normand army. Someone needs to stop the massacres." He pointed at Hershel. "He once was like you and then he was forced to fight in the Normand army. They will not stop until all of your men folk are part of their army, they own all your land, and own all your freedoms. You, Mr. Mayor, will be the first to die as the town watches. I am not here to advise you. I am not here to fight for you. We will be gone in the morning. I am telling you; you will not

121

survive unless your tribe unites and every one of you agree to fight. You will also need the other tribes to unite. All the villages around this region will need to create a militia to fight. We left their swords and bows lying in the field for you. There are additional horses which are wandering around where we killed the soldiers. There are additional soldiers lying in a pile at the pass where the Rhododendron forest creates a narrow passage ascending the mountain. There you will find additional weapons. You will need to run or fight. But if you stay here in the open, you will die. Ride south and see the village and the massacre of your neighbors. They have imprisoned or killed the people in Harpers Ferry Harbor. You will have two choices to hide or fight if you want to live as free men. If you stay here, they will take you as slaves and force the men to fight in their army. Please allow Hershel to tell his story."

One of the young men holding a pitchfork yelled, "Can we come with you? Some of us will fight."

Dak shook his head no. "You cannot come with us. I am sorry, but we must leave in the morning. You people will be on your own. I am not going to lie to you. If you stay here, most if not all of you will die. I am sorry to bring you this news." Dak walked over to his horse and led the animal toward the stable. The others followed.

Veronica was the first to say something inside the barn. The horses all were eating grain and drinking water. They could hear Hershel telling the people of the village about his past, and what he had witnessed. "They are going to kill every one of these people." She looked at Dak.

"Veronica, they were going to kill these people whether or not we came through this area. Once the supply of food runs dry, The Normand army will not need them. The Normand army is going to send bounty hunters after us with a large sum of money demanding our heads. Zenith and I already have a wagon load of gold offered for our heads in Merlin. The planet is getting smaller for us. The only way this is going to work in the short run is if we kill General Cuez. We need to force General Cuez into the open and kill him. That is what I am trying to do. These people will now need to decide if they want to be slaves, run, or fight."

Hulk then added, "Or they need to decide how they choose to die."

When they opened the barn door and walked outside, they were surprised with the men standing and waiting. Trey and Hulk pulled their swords. Dak looked at the men. The group had grown to over thirty men. The one in front spoke loudly, "We want to fight alongside you. We all want to fight. We just do not know how. We are not scared. We are farmers. We will come with you."

Dak looked at the men. "We do not have time to train you. You will need to find another. We are on a mission. I would suggest you travel north and seek out other brave men from other villages and build a militia to fight and protect your families. We will be back at some point to help you. I am sorry friends, but you cannot come with us. The Normand army has two-thousand men in their camp in the Harpers Ferry Harbor with another ten-thousand men further south. They will be coming through here at some point and they will need your food. Once your food runs out, they will no longer need you. They will be sending patrols, mercenaries, and bounty hunters this way to clear the path for their armies. They need your livestock. They will need some of you to be slaves. Most of you will be killed. That is their way."

***

Dak whispered, "We need to leave before sunrise."

Zenith rolled over and kissed him. "You are a smart man. You are a natural leader. Now I see why you allowed the one prisoner to report back to General Cuez. You provided these people a chance."

"I hope they take their chance. I would rather be an average person and not be forced to decide who lives and who dies. But now that you mentioned I am the leader, we need to do it one more time? After all morning sex is better than no sex."

She smiled. "Twice last night was enough. We must save our strength and get going." She kissed him on the cheek and then smiled looking him in the eyes.

Zenith and the others were waiting at the stable. Hershel walked over. He had been talking with the young men during the course of the night. The winter cold air was refreshing to Dak and his friends. They were accustomed to rising earlier in Cliff Tops when the temperatures were fifty degrees cooler.

Dak looked at Hershel. Dak could tell he wanted to ask something. "Please thank the people of the village for providing us extra food for our traveling." He noticed Hershel looked concerned, "What is on your mind?" The other six stood with their horses ready to ride north. Two other young men walked out and stood next to Hershel.

"Am I your prisoner?"

Dak looked at Hershel, "Do you want to remain here?"

Hershel raised his hands in a gesture of friendship. "You have said several times, we need to do what is right. I understand you have a mission ahead of you to help your tribe and those people north of the Midnight Hole. These people are going to need a lot of help. I want to stay and fight with them. It is the right thing to do."

Dak smiled, "You are free to do as you please. Thank you for your help."

Hulk smiled, "So we are not going to be tying him up any more at night?" The group laughed.

Trey and then Tommy Boy walked over and hugged Hershel. The two had ridden next to him for most of the journey talking with him as they traveled. Robin Hood hugged Hershel, "Keep your head down. One of those Normand soldiers might scalp you." Both men smiled at each other.

Hulk walked over and hugged him, "Good fortune, my friend."

Veronica smiled and hugged him. He looked at her, "If you ever need a husband, please send for me. No matter the distance, I will make the journey." She smiled at him.

Zenith walked over and hugged him. He smiled at her, "Keep him safe."

"I will."

Dak walked over and hugged Hershel. He held the hug and looked at Hershel, "When we return, we expect to see you leading one of the best armies this continent has ever seen." They smiled at each other. Dak became serious, "Be smart and pick your battles carefully. Do not allow them to draw you out into the open or trap you and your men in an ambush. They are bigger and stronger. Remember this, my friend."

"I will do my best. I have learned a lot watching you and your friends. Good fortune to all of you. Please do come back. We will need you fighting with us in the battles to come."

***

The group rode north at a fast pace for close to ten hours in nonstop rain. Dak motioned for Hulk to stop. "This is a good place to camp. The rain has finally stopped. We will be in the village of New Foundland in a couple of days." The group all stopped and started setting up camp. They knew what to do without being asked.

Once the fire was going and the food was being cooked, the group sat around the fire waiting for the three rabbits to cook. Tommy Boy looked over at Dak with Zenith leaning against him. "I hope the information Hershel told you is correct, and the road from the village of New Foundland to the Midnight Hole is a safer route."

Dak had been considering this very question. "What those villagers told us, and Hershel repeated sounds correct. The Normand army is stationed along the Continental Trail at different locations. We should be able to bypass their squads and camps. So far, we have not seen any signs of the Normand patrols in the small communities we have rode through today. This route is longer by about fifty miles. Hopefully, the Normand army will not anticipate us taking this route."

Veronica looked at the guys and then added, "Next time someone else can run across the field in the nude. I stepped on a briar with my barefoot, and it still hurts."

Robin Hood smiled, "Like I said before, the Normand soldiers are not gay, and you have a body like a Venus."

"Don't say that again." The guys could tell Veronica was mad.

Dak looked at Veronica. "All I know is you are a very pretty young lady and an exceptional warrior and friend." Veronica looked at Dak and then at Zenith who was leaning into his lap watching the fire burn. "The plan worked perfectly. I was able to cut the head off the sergeant of that squad and before his head hit the ground, I struck two other men with my two swords. Hulk was able to do the same. Once the commander fell, the platoon hesitated, and that gave us the precious time we needed. These Normand soldiers are drilled to take orders and then act. They have trouble thinking on their own and with the leader dead, they hesitated. They are very well trained how to fight with swords, spears, shields, and bows but once we can get in close one on one, we have the advantage."

"Why not order Zenith to run through the field naked? She is prettier than I am."

Dak smiled at Hulk. Dak also knew his friends had tried to talk and be friends with his wife. Zenith had been reluctant to share herself, her history, and her feeling with anyone except him.

Zenith looked at Veronica. "You are very pretty. You have loving parents and a loving brother. You are very fortunate." The group did not say anything for a few seconds.

Veronica looked at Zenith wondering if she was being nice or was she envious of not having a family, "What is the significant reason of classifying you Blueblood warriors as first, second or third-generation Bluebloods? Your father and Samuel are first-generation, and you are third."

Zenith looked at Veronica wondering why she was quizzing her. "The difference between second and third-generation is age and not how pure our blood is. The first-generation Bluebloods were all hatched in a lab using what the scientists felt were the perfect DNA material inserted into the chromosomes. The process as you know enhanced our reflexes, our strength, our intelligence and among other things we mature at an accelerated rate. The first-generation are all thirty-five to thirty-seven years old, and they all have one name. The first-generation were paired, and then several were found to be sterile and could not reproduce. They lived in a closed community and hidden from the governments of the world. The Blueblood leaders lived by a code and law they passed mandating no divorces and no affairs. The Blueblood government would not allow the pairs to be split. Then, the Transitional Period occurred and approximately ten years later, they realized my people were dying out in wars and fighting for the people in Merlin. Several hundred died during the Transitional Period. The ruling body of the Blueblood people rushed and forced the pairs to break the bonds of marriage and forced them to reproduce. Most of the offspring, which were second-generation Bluebloods were paired with a first-generation Blueblood. They needed warriors, and without the academy training one cannot learn how to anticipate an opponent, or how to fight with a sword like I can.

"The offspring were identified also as second-generation Bluebloods. I was labeled the third generation because I was young. Most of the second-generation has at least one parent that was from the first-generation offspring. I am a young third-generation Blueblood. My parents waited until after the Transitional Period to mate. When I entered the academy to become a Blueblood warrior at six, I was the only third-generation Blueblood in the class with parents who were both first-generation. Most of the second-generation Bluebloods are not as pure genetically as me and very few third-generation Bluebloods are. The original Blueblood ruling council tried to keep the blood line secure by controlling the mating."

Hulk looked at Zenith, "So, the Blueblood council tried to control the breeding and it backfired. The genetic code has not been protected, and the Bluebloods are now being born with certain problems either physical or mental?"

Zenith at first was offended by the question, then she realized the truth hurt. "Yes. It is just like the normal families passing the genetic code into their offspring. Some turn out to be great and some turn out to be failures, but most are in between."

Dak remembered early in the relationship telling Zenith how he was raised. He was with his friends everyday with school, working, hunting, fishing, and playing. Dak spoke, "The parents of my friends all assisted with the activities of the group. We enjoyed sleep overs. My mother made a point to tell me every day she loved me. I never knew my father. My mother used a doner, and the doctor had used the old technology of scrubbing both the sperm and egg which enhanced me genetically. My friend's parents had used the same doctor and the same process, and their abilities have likewise been enhanced similar to you Bluebloods." Everyone sat still looking into the fire thinking about what Dak had mentioned.

Dak sat and remembered when Zenith spoke briefly about how she was raised with the normal female maid being paid to feed her and prepare her for the day's activities which consisted of training to be a Blueblood warrior since she turned six-years old. She did not have friends, and her mother died while she was young. Her father worked extended hours, and the maid would rush home to spend time with her kids as soon as her father arrived home. He knew Zenith was envious of his childhood, which was filled with love and friendship.

Robin Hood smiled, "Yea, us guys like women with pointed ears and without pointed ears."

Zenith smiled at Robin Hood knowing he was joking. The rest of the guys laughed.

Dak was grateful for Robin Hood's comment, because it broke the nostalgia mood. He finally said, "Veronica, I am not going to order our best sword fighter to lay down her sword. We need Zenith with a sword on horseback. Besides, we won that battle. We made those men pay for killing the innocent kids and people of that first village. I feel vindicated. You are not our weak link. We are all well trained and excel in fighting. You know I love you like a sister and the rest of you guys like brothers."

Tommy Boy looked at Veronica, "Zenith killed those two soldiers riding out to rape you quicker than any two of us could have. No one is questioning your ability to wage war, but Zenith is better than all of us."

Hulk smiled at Robin Hood. "Were you successful at commandeering some more weed from those farm boys?"

"Yes. I talked them out of one joint. They said once we make it to the Midnight Hole, I need to talk to a man by the name of The Weed Eater. Evidently, The Weed Eater is on the next level at

131

growing pot. I will roll us a joint, and then I am out. Veronica you can have the first smoke since your foot was wounded in the combat with the Normand soldiers." The group laughed.

"I pulled the thorn out." She looked at Zenith. "Thank you for killing those soldiers in the field." Zenith smiled at her. "You know until I watched you in the battle of New York, I did not believe someone could block incoming arrows with the broad side of a sword blade."

Zenith moved her head up from Dak's shoulder. "We are taught how to do this in the academy. You really must have trust in yourself, because if you miss the arrow, you die."

Trey announced the food was ready. The group started eating and continued talking until they all fell asleep.

Chapter 14

The Queen leaned back and relaxed as she soaked in her tub with the warm saltwater to help her heal. She stared at the scars from the two arrows as she rubbed them. She always had been vain about her appearance, and the scars bothered her. She then rubbed ointment on her scars hoping they would dissipate. She had considered her needs as a woman as she sat in the tub. She knew she needed to fight her forbidden desires. She stepped out of the tub of hot water and placed the silk robe around her. She noticed in the moon light the snow falling by her window and was glad to be indoors from the cold weather. She loved the luxury of hot baths with the hot water generated from the hot springs and the wood burning stove to warm the room. The twelve-inch-thick log walls provided extra insulation and kept her apartment toasty. Plus, the heat from the three apartments located below her kept her warm. She walked over to the window in the glass door and looked out over the compound below. She saw movement and then recognized Samuel walking from the cliff area toward her building. He always wore the brown leather coat with the fur around the neck. She thought about him, his looks, and his abilities. She also knew he had a crush on her. She remembered her prior boyfriend would always tell her how powerful a woman could be that knew how to use sex as an instrument to win over a man. Her boyfriend would watch her on the floor of the small condo in an intimate entanglement with another man patiently waiting his turn. The intensive sex after the other man had left was tremendous.

She thought back to living in California. The first time she attended Sunday School at her boyfriend's church, the lesson had been about Samson and Delilah. The adult class had joked about how Delilah had used sex to conquer Samson. Without further thought her hand reached for the door handle, and she opened the door to her balcony. She walked out the door and stood on the snow-covered balcony barefoot looking over the rail of her balcony down at Samuel in the courtyard below.

Samuel saw her door open and watched as she walked out. He slowly approached as he felt his throat go dry. When he stopped and looked up at her, he could not help but notice she was staring at him. She wore a thin silk robe. The Queen slowly removed the robe from around her and allowed it to fall to the deck. He walked over to the wall, jumped up, and pulled himself to the top of the balcony. He stepped over the rail. He reached her and pulled her into his arms. He hugged her and moved his lips toward her lips providing her an opportunity to kiss him. After the kiss, he opened the door and pulled her inside, closing the door behind him. He walked over in front of the wood burning stove and felt the heat. He placed the large bear fur blanket on the floor in front of the stove. They kissed while he removed his clothes, and she motioned for him to lie down on his back. She sat on him arching her back and rotated her hips. They made love all night in front of the wood burning stove on the bearskin rug.

Chapter 15

Delores knew her husband was tired. He worked while standing all day making weapons in the blacksmith shop. Some of the men were going on fishing trips and others going on hunting trips. The tribe was trying to store enough food for the winter and also store extra food to sell to the New York tribe. The tribe was concerned with the threat of a possible siege, and the tribe looked forward to meeting Captain J.J. when he sailed into their harbor with an update on the wars in the south. The best guess was the attack from the Normand army would occur in the first part of the spring of the next year. Everyone in the tribe was tired. The women turned the seal furs into warm needed clothing, the silk was made for the bottom layer of protection in the uniforms, and the cow hides and other animal furs for the additional warm clothing.

Delores was tired of worrying about her two sons. She was disappointed her husband had not stood with her when Dak announced he was the heir to the leadership of the tribe. She was happy the Queen had recovered enough to take over her role as the leader. No one had ever discussed how someone was going to be appointed king or queen in her absence. No one had elected Vicky to be queen. She had just assumed the role. She was in charge of the CIA unit in the old world, and the leadership role carried over.

Delores looked at her husband washing off. She knew he did not want to talk with her about the politics of the tribe. She also knew he supported Vicky and if any person in the tribe ever questioned her authority, the person would have to answer to him. "Do you think Vicky will agree with Dak that he is the heir to be the king of Cliff Tops?"

Billy Ray straightened and looked in the mirror, "I do believe she will discuss the leadership role with us at some point. But for now, she is the leader." He smiled knowing Delores loved Vicky. He then added, "And saying otherwise is treason."

Delores walked into the bathroom and rubbed her husband's back, "I was surprised Dak sent Aquarius to Merlin and left Samuel here with us. Have you talked to Samuel?"

Billy Ray smiled and looked at Delores in the mirror. "He came into the blacksmith shop and asked me to make him two curved sharp eighteen-inch hatchets. Each hatchet was designed very precisely with a four-inch spike on the backside of the curved handle. He had drawings of the hatchets with his specification listed. He does not talk much. He always has a mean look on his face." He finished drying his face, "I asked him about the spike on the back of the hatchet. His reply was the spike needs to be designed to penetrate the steel helmets of the Normand soldiers and also have the lateral strength to stop a sword with a one-hundred-fifteen mile per hour velocity."

"That is all he wants is two hatchets?"

"I do not know what he wants. That question, my dear, is above my pay grade." He laid his rag down.

"Where does he sleep at night?"

136

"I believe he walks around the city watching out for assassins."

Delores smiled at her husband as he turned toward her. Billy Ray picked her up and carried her toward the bed. "It is late and both of us are tired. Have you now switched your concern to Samuel instead of the leadership of the tribe. At first, you were concern about our sons, second it was who should be the leader of the tribe, then it was Aquarius and now Samuel."

She smiled as he laid her on the mattress. "Does it not seem strange to you there is a Blueblood walking around Cliff Tops, and no one watches him? I mean what does Vicky say about him? Where does he sleep?"

Billy Ray looked at his wife knowing she must know something. She had asked twice where he sleeps. "I understand in talking with Aquarius, it is the mission and completing the task that drives Samuel. He does not care about the journey. He is concerned with completing the assignment. He felt responsible for Vicky being ambushed and almost killed. So, he watches our village. I will make him the two hatches to help build a rapport with him. I have no clue where he sleeps. I know Dak had him sleeping in the jail cell for a couple of nights and Little Jimmy told me the Normand soldiers in the next jail cell pissed on themselves with fear after he reached one of them through the bars and slammed the man's head into the steel bars killing him.

"Wayne mentioned he is a strange man that keeps to himself." He started kissing Delores, and she started to relax. "I have this seal oil I can rub over your perfect body."

Delores loved her husband because he had compassion toward people, lived with grace, and a great father. She knew he loved his sons. "Please help yourself to everything I have. You know I love you. Please taste me." She leaned back on the bed and spread her legs.

Chapter 16

The group slowly approached the small village. They rode under a sign hanging from two poles, 'New Foundland'. The people of the community looked but did not smile. Dak felt an ominous gut feeling with the greeting on the out skirts of the town area. He pulled the reins back on the horse and stopped as he peered up the dirt street into the main section of the town. He then announced, "We need to split up. Hulk, Robin Hood, and I will enter the tavern. We should be able to learn more about these people in the bar area of the tavern than any other place. Trey, you, and Tommy Boy loop around the town and then head to the stables and keep your eyes open and be careful. Veronica, you and Zenith check in the lodge a few minutes after we enter the tavern. You can pay for two rooms. Something does not feel right. We need to be careful."

Tommy Boy asked, "What has you so concerned? They are not flying a Normand flag, and so far, we have seen no Normand soldiers."

"I want to make certain there are no traps. It is what we don't see that has me uneasy. I do not see any men. Where would the men be? This might be a trap. Remember these people are not our enemy."

"We hope they are not our enemy," Hulk replied.

The three pulled up to the rail for the horses at the tavern. Dak noticed a couple of older men watching from across the street

139

whispering among themselves. The three dismounted and walked through the doors. They spread out with Hulk going to the bar, and Dak and Robin Hood took a table. A few seconds later, the waitress took their orders, and the bartender took Hulk's order. Dak and Robin Hood sat quietly and started eating their food. They were trying to listen to the conversations around them and act normal. The place had been loud when they first entered, but now the customers seemed to be quiet. The waitress was very pretty and friendly. She placed her hand on Hulk's shoulder when talking with him, and Robin Hood raised his eyebrow as he noticed and suspected she was flirting with Hulk. She walked behind the bar and then leaned over in front of Hulk revealing a woman with very noticeable amount of cleavage as she poured Hulk another drink and provided him his food.

Robin Hood glanced to see if Dak had noticed the lady seemed overly friendly as she flirted with Hulk. Robin Hood whispered, "She is taking him to one of the back rooms."

Dak glanced over, and Hulk smiled at Dak and Robin Hood as he left the bar heading for the rooms in the back of the establishment. Dak whispered, "How old do you think she is?"

Robin Hood looked at Dak. "I guess she is in her twenties. What difference does it make?"

"She is as old as your mother."

Robin Hood was surprised, "My mother?"

Dak glanced around and then looked very serious at Robin Hood, "When this goes down, you need to be ready. Dumbass just walked into the trap in the back room."

The door opened and in walked seven men all carrying swords. The oldest man saw Dak and Robin Hood and walked over and rudely sat down across from Dak. He looked at Dak with a stern look, "We don't care for strangers. Who are you, and what do you want?"

Dak peered at the man, "Friend, we are passing through. We stopped at the village south of here, and they suggested we come here to New Foundland on our way to The Midnight Hole."

"They did not suggest any such thing. You are riding horses owned by the Normand army. You are scouts working for the Normand army."

"Friend, we are not soldiers fighting for the Normand army. We killed the soldiers and took their horses."

The man looked like he did not believe that to be possible.

"I believe you to be a liar. You two could not kill Normand soldiers. They roam this area in squads of twenty or more. They would hunt you two down and kill you."

Robin Hood said, "That is why we came to New Foundland and did not stay on the Continental Trail on our way to the Midnight Hole. They are looking for us." As Robin Hood talked, he used his hands to emphasize the trip and the reason they came to the tavern.

Dak felt uneasy about the conversation. The man was too serious and had not smiled at Robin Hood's attempt to be funny with his statement of them hiding from the Normand soldiers. Dak reached under the table and unsnapped his swords and watched the men carefully.

Two of the men had walked over and stood next to the bar where Hulk had eaten. They both turned and were watching Dak and Robin Hood. The other people in the restaurant all watched. An old man in the corner stood and loudly asked, "What is it you three desire? We know that the other fellow is with you. And you better not be lying."

Dak slowly turned his head to the elderly man and answered, "We seek safe passage. We are heading to the Midnight Hole."

The man sitting down across from Dak jumped up causing his chair to fly across the floor as he pulled his sword. "Why would you go to the Midnight Hole unless you want to meet up with your comrades? There is one maybe two battalions of Normand soldiers stationed there."

Dak was trying to figure out which side these men were on. He did not want to have to kill them. "We are going to the Midnight Hole to kill the Normand soldiers stationed there and then proceed down the Continental Trail. We hoped to hook up with some resistance fighters we left at the small village. The Normand army is amassing at Harpers Ferry Harbor. They will wait until spring to proceed north. So, friend, I need to know what side you are on. Ours or theirs."

Dak then stood up. He pulled one of his swords and twisted it around his fingers for a few seconds like a baton and then stuck it back into the sleeve. All the people watched the twirling exhibition. The older man at the other end of the bar announced, "I hope Vulture knows what he is doing. That was damn fast."

The rest of the men pulled their swords. Dak motioned for Robin Hood to lead the way out the front door. Dak wanted to fight in the open, and he also was now concerned about the others.

Dak and Robin Hood backed out of the tavern and turned to see over fifty well-armed men waiting. The two were now surrounded.

Hulk walked around from the rear of the building without a shirt and his hands tied behind his back. His face was red, and he looked like he had been hit in the face. His hair was messed up, and he looked frustrated.

The man from the restaurant walked out the door and commanded, "You two need to drop your swords." The two men pushed Hulk forward so Dak and Robin Hood could see him.

Dak announced, "If you are Normand sympathizers, then we are ready to fight you and your men to the death. We will not lay down our weapons."

Another man approached the area. He yelled, "Now, everyone please hold it right where you are. I am the mayor of New Foundland, and I am telling you two to drop your swords."

Veronica stepped out of the shadow of the building and walked up behind the mayor and placed her knife against the mayor's throat as she held his head still with her left arm wrapped around his neck. She whispered through her gritted teeth, "You need to tell your men to back away. My knife is an eightieth of an inch from your Carotid Artery. You flinch, you die. Let me make myself very clear, you will be the first to die on this street."

The men standing around Dak and Robin Hood turned and saw Veronica's threat to the mayor, but they could not hear what she had whispered. The mayor said in a pleading voice, "Friends, we all need to consider the delicate situation. Vulture, you need to ask your men to step back, lower their weapons and leave."

The man named Vulture appeared relaxed, "She is bluffing."

In a pleading voice, "No, she is not bluffing. I will be the first to die."

"We can elect another mayor. Besides, we have their friend."

The female waitress walked out of the tavern and announced, "I believe him. If he had been with the Normand army, there would have been more of them. Have you ever seen three soldiers off by themselves. Besides, they do not have female soldiers," as she pointed at Veronica. "The young man over here is circumcised. I have never seen a young Normand soldier that was circumcised."

Everyone hesitated. The mayor announced as he felt Veronica's knife digging deeper into his neck, "Thank you, Becky, for your input. Vulture, you need to tell the men to back away. This one is not bluffing."

Tommy Boy and Trey each had gone unnoticed and had walked in behind the men holding Hulk. Zenith walked into the circle and faced the man named Vulture. She pulled her hood back exposing her pointed ears and blond hair. Everyone appeared surprised as they recognized her as a Blueblood warrior. "My friend will cut

144

your mayor's head off, and then I am going to cut you down. You will be the second one to die on this street, and there's not a thing you can do to prevent it."

Vulture looked at the first Blueblood he had ever met. He then turned and declared, "We are not friends with the Normand empire. We must be careful. Come on in, and I will buy you a drink." He looked at Dak and then Zenith. The men seemed to agree, and everyone relaxed.

Tommy Boy walked up behind the two men holding Hulk. The men seemed surprised to see Trey and Tommy Boy with their swords pulled standing a few feet behind them. Tommy Boy looked at Hulk, "How did that lady know you have been circumcised?" The one guard reached over and cut the rope free, so Hulk pulled his hands in front of him. The other guard threw him his two shirts.

The guard then smiled, "That is no lady. Becky is known to be a whore and a good one."

Tommy Boy and Trey watched as Hulk smiled and proclaimed, "I need a drink." Hulk followed Dak and Zenith into the bar, and the three started drinking.

The waitress seemed to still like Hulk, and her flirting did not slip by Zenith. Before long, Robin Hood was asking the waitress if she had a friend or a sister. Dak watched, laughed, and drank until the door opened and in rushed Veronica.

Veronica tried to go unnoticed. She quickly walked up to the table, "There is a squad of twenty Normand soldiers headed this way in a hurry. They are about to reach the bridge. We need to leave now." Dak dropped a gold coin on the table and the group jumped up and headed for the door.

Robin Hood announced, "I guess we will know soon enough what side these people are on. We need to get on our horses and be ready to fight or run."

Dak looked in the direction of the approaching squad, "We do not have time to run. We have walked right into this trap."

Hulk knew they were in trouble, "We are in the open, and they will see our horses. They will know we killed the Normand soldiers."

Hulk pulled his sword. Dak pulled his swords and Robin Hood set his bow and turned a complete circle looking for combatants. The city street was empty. The people of New Foundland had disappeared.

The Normand riders all stopped their horses, and the captain commanded, "You need to drop your weapons. In the name of King Solman, you are to be arrested."

Dak looked at the captain, "I do not think so. You and your men need to drop your weapons and get down off those horses."

The Normand soldiers all laughed.

"I don't believe you understand. There are twenty of us on horses. We have you surrounded. This village is our village. These people have pledged their allegiance to King Solman. You ride horses that belong to King Solman. You are horse thieves."

The men from the tavern stepped out from the sides of the buildings blocking the escape routes. Vulture stepped out further from the tavern and stood in front of Dak facing the Normand soldiers. He looked at the commander of the Normand squad and announced, "We had a town meeting in your absence. We reconsidered our alliance." The Normand soldiers appeared to be a little nervous as they started looking around the small town.

The commander yelled, "This is treason, and you will be killed if you do not do as I say. Now arrest these horse thieves."

"We decided against being slaves of the Normand empire. You need to drop your weapons." Vulture raised his arm and then dropped his arm and several arrows hit the Normand soldiers. The men from the village had been waiting, and the ambush had worked. The villager's attacked from all sides with some men were position on top of the tavern, the motel, and barn with all firing arrows. Other men rushed out from the hidden places taking the soldiers off their horses and killing them. Robin Hood aimed his bow and shot three fast arrows, hitting three Normand soldiers in the face, neck, and head. Dak and the other five watched as the Normand soldiers were killed by the villagers.

Vulture walked over and looked at Robin Hood, "You are very skilled with that bow. I noticed you shot three arrows killing three soldiers in less than three seconds. We could use you to be part of our revolution."

Robin Hood looked at Vulture, "Dak is better with a bow, Hulk and I are about the same, and Veronica maybe a close second.

Those two large guys are also very skilled with bows. The blond lady with the pointed ears is a Blueblood warrior. She is better than we are."

Vulture studied the group, "We could use all of you."

Dak watched as the Normand soldiers were being stripped of their uniforms and searched for gold and other valuables. "We have a mission we must complete. I would suggest you talk with a man named Hershel located south of here in the small village. They have decided to fight the Normand invaders. The Normand army will send troops north from Harpers Ferry Harbor. You can ambush them in the Rhododendron forest. They will most likely send scouts so be on the lookout. You will need to choose your battles carefully. We will be leaving at first light, and I hope to see you in the future. May your God smile down on you and your men."

Dak arched his eyebrow, "I do have one question. How did you know the Normand soldiers would be coming here tonight?"

Vulture smiled, "We can go back inside and finish our drinks." They started walking toward the tavern. "Because they told us they would. We had agreed to their terms, and then we heard rumors from traders that they had lied to us. Last night, we had a coming to Jesus type of a meeting, and we decided to fight. When you showed up, we were very suspicious of you." He looked at Dak with a questioning smile. "I have one question for you. What is your mission?"

Dak looked at Vulture and two other men who had walked over to their table. He thought about the twenty dead Normand soldiers. They had all been butchered to death with no consideration for taking prisoners. He knew these men were ready to fight an extended war. They would be very difficult to root out of these mountains with a fast-flowing river next to the village which created a natural barrier. "You will find out soon enough. Now that these soldiers are dead, can we assume we should not run into any additional Normand patrols tomorrow as we approach the town, The Midnight Hole?"

"We have scouts watching. There should be no patrols on the road. There are close to one thousand soldiers in the area. They are recruiting the local people to fight with them. If they refuse, then they kill them. The Normand patrols took herds of livestock from the people to feed their army."

Dak decided to confide in him, "We sunk four ships in the Harpers Ferry Harbor a few days ago. The next morning at dawn close to fifteen miles north, we watched the people in the small village get massacred by the fifty-man patrol. We set two ambushes, killing all but one soldier. We enforced the revenge for the people who were massacred."

The two men talked while the rest of the people got loud and drunk. Vulture, from time to time, would glance at Zenith. She was talking with Veronica, Robin Hood, and Tommy Boy. He motioned toward Zenith, "What is her story?"

Dak knew the reward on their heads would be tempting for any man. Plus, they would want Zenith's blood to protect them from B2 virus and other viruses. Dak's eyes narrowed as he turned toward Vulture, "She is with me."

He watched Vulture for a reaction. Vulture was in his forties and noticed the younger women. He watched Veronica and Zenith as they laughed and talked at the end of the table.

"Good for you. She is very pretty."

Dak noticed the awkward void in the conversation as Vulture stared at Zenith. Dak said, "We will head out at first light. I would suggest you contact Hershel at the other village at the bottom of the mountain. He is a good man. He will fight with you." Dak stood and walked behind Zenith and motioned for the rest to follow him.

Chapter 17

Hulk looked at his monitor, "The radiation level is low on the ridge. I believe the higher we go on this mountain the higher the reading. I am picking up a small trace in the air. We should be okay for a short period of time." He was sitting bent over and wrapped his detector up in the small leather satchel. He glanced at Dak who was peering with his binoculars into Midnight Hole located below in the bottom of the valley.

Dak heard the report on the radiation and did not move. He kept his view on the target, "They appear to be saddling their horses in two separate columns. I believe they will send some of the men south along the Continental Trail to the village where Hershel is located and some toward New Foundland. They would have heard by now their men have been killed. We will need to strike once they leave."

Dak felt a gut reaction of concern knowing there were still close to five-hundred soldiers stationed below. He also recognized the need for urgency in attacking.

Hulk lifted his binoculars and scanned the area below, "I believe by now the soldier you spared might have found a stray horse and made it back to Harpers Ferry Harbor. General Cuez might send additional men." He adjusted the binoculars. "To the west are the cattle and sheep herds. I wonder." He hesitated and dismissed his thought as he kept watching the Normand soldiers and the large herd of cattle.

Dak looked at Hulk. "It has been twenty-four days since we landed at Harpers Ferry Harbor, we need a plan. What were you thinking?"

"It is too crazy, but I thought about creating a stampede and pushing the animals through their camp and then the tunnel to the New York tribe. All we would need to do is take out a couple of units of guards stationed on the outskirts. We would need to have the New York tribe open the gates at their end."

Dak quickly placed his binoculars in his pouch, "Let's go. We must hurry and get in position. The soldiers will be pulling out soon."

"In position for what?" Hulk was confused.

"We are going to do exactly what you just said. We are going to stampede those cattle through their camp and run them through the tunnel to the New York tribe."

Dak stood and ran quickly down the path. The walk up the two-mile-long hill had been difficult forging through the brush and scaling rocks on the steep incline. Going down was easier.

Dak hurried to meet with the group. Hulk caught up with Dak, and he sat down out of breath. Dak announced, "We must hurry. They appear to be splitting their troops into three separate groups. As soon as the two columns of Normand soldiers head south along the Continental Trail and toward New Foundland, we are going to position ourselves for a surprise for those soldiers left behind. The

152

numbers will be depleted, and they will not be expecting us. We will strike tonight."

Zenith asked, "What will happen to Hershel and those men in that small tribe? What will happen to the men in New Foundland? Both these groups will be attacked from both sides. You know General Cuez will also be sending soldiers north from Harper's Ferry Harbor."

"I told Hershel they cannot count on us. They will have to pick their fights and not get caught in the open. I also told Vulture he and his men cannot attack the Normand army in the open ground. They would be slaughtered. We must get the cattle pushed through those gates. We will surprise the Normand guards left behind to watch the Continental Trail. I can only hope they send the majority of their troops south. Hulk and I confirmed what Vulture told us, 'They have over one thousand men stationed here at The Midnight Hole.' They have two columns of troops preparing to pull out. We must strike tonight."

Veronica looked at the faces of her friends, "This is going to be very risky, at best."

Dak interrupted her. "Veronica, I need for you to be the one to move north to the interior gate and proceed to the other end of the tunnel and repeat the password 'Rumpelstiltskin' to the New York tribe guards. If that gate does not open, this plan will not work."

"You know if your plan does not work, you will not be able to go home, and I will not be able to return through the gate with their army stationed here. I do not want to leave you guys." She looked sad. "Dak, you treat me like I am the weak link in our group, and I am not. I can fight as good as any of you."

The others ducked their heads as Veronica looked at each of them for support. She did not want to be the one left out and forced to return home.

Trey said, "One of us must make certain the gate is open at the other end. Veronica, if you do not do it, then which one of us will?"

Dak was tired of having to make concessions with his plans. He interrupted, "This is my decision, and I have spoken. Now everyone get your gear, and we must be in position before the moon comes up."

***

Zenith could tell Dak was apprehensive with the plan. She walked over to him. "You are right to be nervous about our attack. They have us greatly outnumbered. In order to be successful, we must kill the guards in the outpost positions then stampede the cows right through the camp." She smiled, "I believe this is the craziest thing we have ever done. I know nothing about driving cattle. I hope you and your friends are cowboys."

Dak smiled, "The Normand soldiers are heading south. They have divided into two columns of three hundred men with one column heading up the mountain road to New Foundland and one heading south on the Continental Trail. If we are going to attack them, this is the time. The rest of the soldiers will be in the tents too far out to respond to our stampede. We should have to deal with a few guards who will not be expecting our attack." He smiled, "I drove five cows for two miles years ago. I guess that makes me a cowboy."

His eyes narrowed and his smile grew. "This is nuts, but this is the best we have."

***

Zenith looked over at Dak as he was watching the Normand guards through the binoculars, "You know you were rude to Veronica in telling her she must leave and head north. You know she loves you guys and wants to be part of the group. She feels you do not trust her and her abilities to fight."

"I might have just saved her life. Trey will assist her getting through the entrance on this side and then all she must do is head north and provide the New York guards the password to get through the gate. Zorro and I agreed on the password, and I hope his guards recognize us. This is going to be risky. We are outnumbered by several hundred men. I started to send you through the gate to protect you."

Zenith snarled, "I would have ordered you through the gate." She noticed the smile on Dak's face. "She is the only female with all you guys. I believe she tries harder than any of you guys to fit in with your group."

Dak pulled the binoculars away from his face and looked at Zenith. "You know I love you, but I am the leader of this group."

"Yes, I know you love me, but I do not agree that you are my leader. You lead your friends. I am a Blueblood warrior. I do not take orders from anyone."

Dak looked at her thinking he was glad his friends did not hear Zenith.

"Listen Dak, I am here because I love you. You know I fell in love with you. That does not mean you are my leader. Look, the soldiers are starting to leave."

Dak looked through the binoculars and thought about trying to order Zenith in the future. He quickly changed his thoughts. He knew she was not going to take his orders. "There is close to six-hundred of them leaving on horseback. They are traveling light with no long-term food supplies. They all are dressed in full armor. They are going to war."

"I really hope Hershel and Vulture's men are prepared. I pray those men are smart enough to realize they need to fight and then retreat. Those soldiers will track them and try to root them out of their hiding places."

Dak said, "Yes, I hope so too. They are going to be greatly outnumbered. I also hope our team can hit the three different stationed guard posts at the same time. There is a myriad of things that could go wrong with this plan." Dak looked at Zenith knowing the likelihood of the men fighting with Hershel and Vulture surviving was not good. He also knew he had to keep his mission in check, and sending this herd of cattle through the gate to his home was the priority. "We must wait until the sun goes down."

***

They all waited in their hidden spots. Hulk noted the time and when the sun dropped below the horizon, he could see the silhouettes of the four guards near the open fire. He rode his horse into the camp. Four guards were watching the western perimeter of the camp and relaxing around the warm fire. One man on horseback did not surprise or alert them. One soldier hollered at Hulk as he approached, "What is the news?" The guard was squinting into the darkness, attempting to identify the approaching horse and rider.

Hulk did not waver. He kept his horse at a trot. When he got within forty feet of the first standing soldier, he extended his reach and aimed the bow. The arrow passed all the way through the man's torso. The other three were still sitting around a campfire as their comrade fell to the ground with an arrow sticking through his heart as he suddenly laid dead. As one guard jumped up, Hulk fired the second arrow and hit him in the middle chest. He loaded a third arrow and hit the third guard ten feet away in the face. Hulk jumped off his horse and faced the fourth guard, who had pulled his shield and his sword. The guard was blinking quickly as he was jittery trying to prepare himself for battle as Hulk approached.

157

Hulk did not hesitate. He swung his sword hard, knowing the guard would block the sword with his shield. He also knew the guard would recoil from the hard swing and try to counter with his sword. Hulk stepped toward the guard before he had time to swing his sword. Hulk used his body weight as leverage to push the Normand soldier backward, forcing him off balance. He also held his arm, which prohibited the man from swinging his sword. Hulk then stepped between the shield in the left hand and the sword in the right hand and head-butted the soldier. The soldier fell backward, and before he could defend himself, Hulk rammed his sword deep into the man's gut. The soldier laid limp on the ground, and Hulk finished him with a second stab into the man's heart.

Tommy Boy and Robin Hood approached the four guards on the south area who were also sitting around a campfire. The guards had not expected anyone since the town people had been conquered and the other soldiers had been ordered south. They were happy to be on guard duty. They felt lucky not to have been ordered to travel south and fight a battle. Two guards, sitting near the fire with their backs to Robin Hood and Tommy Boy, took the first two arrows in the center back. The other two guards located on the other side of the fire had not warned their comrades the approaching two men pulled their bows. Robin Hood shot the third guard before he could pick up his shield. The fourth guard picked up his shield in time to block the arrow fired by Tommy Boy. Tommy Boy jumped from his saddle and dropped his bow as he charged the soldier. The soldier tried to block Tommy Boy with his

shield, and he had planned to stab Tommy Boy. The force of
Tommy Boy running into the shield with a bull rush forced the
man to fall off balance to the ground. With one quick surge,
Tommy Boy first cut his right arm off at the wrist and then cut him
deeply across his neck.

Robin Hood said, "These men are all dead," as he wiped the
blood from his knife. "We need to hurry."

Trey and Veronica walked in the shadows. They made their way
along the bottom of the cliff and stayed hidden in the bushes and
small trees. Veronica looked at her younger brother. "Trey, I got
this. They will not be expecting a woman. You stay hidden."

As he started to disagree, Veronica looked at him, "I said Little
Brother, I got this."

She dropped her warm coat on the ground and walked out of the
bushes. The first guard saw her and smiled. The second guard
approached Veronica, "Where did you come from?"

"General Cuez asked me to come over here and entertain his
best guards." She kept walking.

The first guard was young, naive, and he looked confused.
"General Cuez asked you to do what?"

Veronica pulled her knife at three feet away and rammed the
blade into the older guard's gut. She then turned and threw the
knife hitting the young guard in the chest. Both men collapsed.
Trey raced to her side. Veronica stood over the first guard and
rammed her sword through his neck. The other guard was trying to
crawl off. He was in shock with the hilt of the knife sticking out of

his chest. Veronica and Trey walked over to him. The guard looked up, "Help me. Why did General Cuez order you to kill me? Oh my God, I am going to die."

Trey swung down, stabbing the man in the center chest. "We need to hurry. You need to enter the tunnel. There might be additional soldiers in the tunnel. I will guard this entrance and ignite several torches in the entrance. Veronica, please stick to the plan."

Dak and Zenith rode swiftly into the center camp with the ten guards sitting around the fire. The area was open, and there was no way to sneak up on these guards. The guards could hear the riders approaching. They all watched anticipating additional guards from the main camp. One guard stood and was looking into the dark night when Dak's arrow went straight through his chest. The other guards saw their friend fall over dead. The second arrow hit the guard in the front of the fire. Zenith reached over with her sword and hit the soldier nearest the fire, cutting him down. She then pulled her horse to the left and ran over another man. Dak hit the fourth man in the stomach with an arrow who was watching Zenith. Dak jumped off his horse and pulled both his swords. The three soldiers looked at each other and then attacked Dak.

Zenith turned her horse and cut the man through his ribs that had fallen and was trying to stand. She saw the man release the arrow standing near the fire. She held her sword up and blocked the arrow. The man stood and watched in disbelief. She cut him across the shoulder as she ran past him. He stumbled and fell into the fire.

She turned her horse and ran after the other two soldiers. The one on her left tried to swing at her from his standing position. At the last instance, she turned the horse, and the horse bumped the man causing him to fall. Zenith did not slow. She held the saddle horn and leaned over and sliced the man across his face with a downward swing of her sword. The other man shot an arrow, and she blocked the arrow with her sword. Zenith turned the horse toward him and charged. The soldiers dove to the ground to avoid the charging horse. Zenith held to the saddle horn and reach down as she swung her sword cutting the soldier across his back. She immediately turned to look for Dak.

Dak caught the first swing of the guard on the right between his small blade and the large blade on his Sai sword. He twisted the sword so hard the man lost his grip on his sword. Dak stuck his other sword through the man's chest. He did not hesitate. He blocked the next man's swing who had been in the middle position. Dak dropped to one knee as he blocked the swing, and then with the other sword, cut the man across his thigh deep into his femur. The blade stuck in the bone and the man fell. The last man backed up as Dak approached. He looked scared. He swung at Dak. Dak stepped into the swing and blocked the blade, and he kept his sword moving forward slicing the man's right arm off. He then kicked him in the chest, and the man fell backward. Dak walked over him and shoved his blade through the man's midsection, killing him.

Dak ran over to the man and pulled his sword out of the man's left leg. The man was covered in blood. "Help me." Dak disliked killing an injured man, but he knew they could not take a wounded prisoner. He stabbed the man in the chest.

Dak looked at Zenith, "I never like taking another man's life, and I hope that does not ever change. Life is precious and should not be taken for granted."

Zenith could tell killing the injured man did not sit well with Dak, "We need to hurry. These men have made their choice to be soldiers and have done far worse."

Dak and Zenith rode in behind the herd of cows. "We need to locate the lead bull. He will be the one with the large cow bell tied around his neck. We need to force him in the direction toward the tunnel. The cows will follow their bull."

Robin Hood, Tommy Boy, and Hulk rode over. They looked at each other and with the nod of the head by Dak, they started yelling and waving their hoods, running the herd east toward the gate.

The soldiers inside the guarded area were off duty. They all had relaxed and enjoyed their time relaxing and feeling blessed not to have been in the units going south. Most were happy they had not been ordered to ride out earlier to track down and butcher the men who killed their comrades. The rider from Harpers Ferry Harbor reported four ships had been sunk in the harbor and the patrol of the fifty-men squad riding north had been ambushed with forty-nine of the squad killed. The commanders knew there were some resistance fighters in the out-skirt villages. This was part of being a soldier and having to deal with small tribes. They were ordered to kill the men in the small villages along the way. The women, children, and old people were not an immediate concern. The plan had been to trick the larger villages into submission and kill people in the smaller villages. It took less time to kill the people than to conquer them and beat them into submission. The Normand commanders knew there was no retaliation from a dead man.

First, one soldier stood and looked to the western fields with a perplexed expression and asked, "What is that noise? Listen. Everyone be quiet."

A couple of the other men stood. They too were confused. A few men walked out of the tents and were looking into the direction of the noise. The first man squinted, trying to see into the darkness. He finally turned and yelled, "Stampede," as he ran for the tree line. The other soldiers did likewise. A couple of the soldiers stood behind the wagons and watched as the herd of cows ran through their camp site. The other men ran into the woods and tried to stay clear of the stampede. Through the darkness of the night and the dust created by the herd, the men could make out a couple of horseback riders directing the stampede toward the tunnel, but they could not tell who they were in the darkness.

Trey stood to the side, with the corral fence behind him directing the herd into the large tunnel entrance and then kept waving a large blanket directing them north into the tunnel.

One soldier stepped out from the tree and yelled at Robin Hood, asking what was the meaning of stampede? Robin Hood shot him through the chest with an arrow. As the last cows passed their positions, the commander yelled for the soldiers to get their weapons. Hulk saw the commander in the field yelling for his men, trying to rally them. Hulk turned his horse and ran it toward the commander. The commander turned as Hulk's arrow went through his stomach. Hulk rotated and shot another soldier. In the mass confusion, the Normand soldiers had not grabbed their weapons and now the tents were all trampled and at least one wagon was turned over.

Veronica approached the guards sitting at the camp inside the tunnel. She could smell the smoke from their campfire as the smoke was carried out the top of the tunnel by the draft coming from the north entrance. She glanced above her at the dark ceiling close to twenty feet above her and then peered toward the campfire. These men were on guard duty and watching for anyone entering the tunnel from the north entrance where the tunnel ended at the New York tribe. She looked down at part of the old steel railroad track left behind from the old world with the large size gravel under the track. The path located next to the track in the tunnel was packed down dirt and rock. She knew she needed to stay hidden in the shadows as she planned her attack. She could see the burning fire and the silhouettes of three men. She slowly approached as the men were talking. Two of the men were facing north with their back to her. The other one was placing wood on the fire and was the one talking. She walked up behind the two men and went unnoticed. She slowly held her sword out to her side and swung the blade hard. The sword stuck through the one man in the back and came out his belly. He fell forward into the small fire. The other two men looked puzzled at the sight of their comrade falling forward from his sitting position. She stepped across the dead man and rammed the other man in the chest as he watched his comrade fall forward. The third man rolled backward and then tried to see who had attacked his comrades. He panicked and stumbled, trying to stand. Veronica stepped back into the shadow placing her sword in the sleeve, and once he stood, he struggled to see through the light of the campfire to discern who killed the other two guards. He hesitated as he realized the attack was coming from the Normand control side of the tunnel. As he rushed off bent over toward the New York tribe, Veronica quickly pulled her bow and in one motion loaded her arrow. She carefully fired her arrow into the darkness hitting the man square in the back with the arrow sticking out his chest. She picked up a burning log and lit several torches as she proceeded further north in the tunnel.

As she walked around a curve in the large tunnel, she could see the light at the exit and the large bar gates with the two guards from the New York Tribe peering into the tunnel. She yelled, 'Rumpelstiltskin.' She waited. She heard the gate open, and a soldier approached her. She walked toward the guard, "You need to clear a path and set torches in the tunnel. There will be a stampeded cows headed this way in a few minutes."

The guard looked surprised and turned and ran toward the gate and the barricade. Veronica walked out of the gate as the last of the barricade was being removed. She noticed the four large campfires and the large number of burning torches. The captain of the guard looked at her cautiously. "We have sent for Zorro and his guards. He will be here soon."

Veronica noticed the heavily armed men watching the gate. The New York tribe had built several platforms and barriers to fortify their position behind the gate. "Tell Zorro these cattle need to be moved to Cliff Tops. I am going back to my friends."

***

Dak looked at his friends while resting on one knee behind the embankment, "We will retreat through the tunnel. We will need to regroup and bring more soldiers."

Hulk was both surprised and excited with Dak's order, "The people will all be killed, including the tribe where Hershel is staying and the people of New Foundland. They need our help."

Dak looked at Hulk, "If we stay, we will be killed. There is close to three-hundred and fifty Normand soldiers regrouping as we talk. We have been successful with the herd of cattle and some of the sheep have been funneled through the tunnel. That was our goal. There are another six-hundred Normand soldiers that left this camp earlier today. We will need to meet with the council and return with more men. Our mission was not to go south and die. We have done what we set out to do. Now, we need another plan with more soldiers. We have no backup plan, and no one to support us if we try to defend this ground." He pointed south into the darkness and the flat area out from the tunnel entrance, "Here comes Robin Hood."

Robin Hood was the lookout stationed near the turned-over wagon. His horse was on a dead run. He pulled the reins back and stopped the horse in front of Dak and the others, "Here they come. We need to get the hell out of here."

***

Veronica looked south along the dark tunnel. She heard the horses galloping toward her. The tunnel in certain areas was pitch dark with now burning torches located at the north end and south end. In the middle section, which is close to a quarter mile in length, the tunnel has a couple small curves, and the view to the end of the tunnel was restricted. One could hide in the shadows created by the direction of the light from the torches. Trey had lit several torches to create light for the cows at the south entrances and now the New York soldier had entered the north end of the tunnel and done the same. Veronica was in the middle of the tunnel hidden in the shadow area on a small ledge. She waited. She could not tell the number, but she knew she had to stay hidden as the riders got closer and approached the curve in the tunnel. She gripped her sword and looked down at as the first rider rode by with a mask. The tunnel was too dark to identify the other riders. The riders were spaced close to twenty feet apart. She saw the second and then the third rider. She saw the fourth and fifth rider. She waited and heard another rider approaching.

Veronica considered her being trapped in the tunnel. If these five soldiers were just the beginning of several hundred Normand soldiers approaching the north through the tunnel, the New York soldier would be forced to close the gate and defend their territory. She realized she only had one choice which was to fight her way through the five Normand soldiers that had just rode past her. She positioned herself to the edge of the ledge and jumped out at the side of the sixth rider. She took him off his horse, and he landed hard. She heard his voice when he grunted from the impact of the hard landing on the bottom of the tunnel floor. She quickly held her sword up facing the man on the ground, "Dammit Robin Hood. I almost killed you. I thought you guys went south to rendezvous with Hershel."

"I think you broke my shoulder. We need to hurry. The Normand army is on our tails. Dak changed the plan."

"Get up. Can you run?"

Robin Hood tried to move, and he squinted in pain. He could not place any weight on his hand. "Yes, I can run." He looked like he was about to pass out. Veronica reached his other arm and helped him stand. She glanced south down the tunnel and could see a light along the wall of the cave as the Normand soldiers were moving their way. "We need to get moving."

Hulk was the first through the gate. He noticed the large number of New York soldiers well-armed and ready for combat. Tommy Boy then Trey came through. Then, Zenith and Dak rode side by side.

Zorro stepped out in his warrior uniform with his pearl handle sword on his side to greet them. "Hi young Dak. It is good to see you. I hope your mission was very successful."

Dak looked at Zorro, "You need to come with me to meet with my tribe. We need to take the battle to them now before they fortify the Midnight Hole. I've got one more coming through and then you need to close that gate."

"What about the other female? I believe her name is Veronica. She went back into the tunnel and said she wanted to be with her friends."

Dak was irate and turned and saw Robin Hood's horse gallop out of the tunnel, "Give me a torch. Hurry. Come on Zenith. We need to find Robin Hood and Veronica. The rest of you stay here. If we do not come back, close the gate, and prepare for battle." The two rode down the incline through the gate. They made it to the first turn to find Veronica holding Robin Hood up as he was limping. They could hear soldiers coming. Dak jumped off his horse.

Veronica said, "I believe his lung has collapsed. His shoulder might be broken. He cannot lift his arm. He is about to pass out from the pain."

"Come on and get on my horse. Robin Hood, you need to ride out of here." Dak lifted him on his horse.

Zenith said, "Give me the bridle." She pulled the horse behind her horse and rode toward the gate with Robin Hood leaning over the mane of the horse holding on the saddle horn with one hand."

Veronica and Dak followed running hard. They came around the last turn and saw Hulk and the others waiting on them. Hulk commanded, "Hold up. Here they come." As they rushed through the gate, the guards closed the large iron gate and pulled the locks down into position.

Chapter 18

General Cuez looked at the soldier from his chair in the middle of the doorway. The large door close behind him as he walked into the room. The soldier felt alone and knew General Cuez would not hesitate to remove his head. Failure was not acceptable in the Normand army. The soldier walked into the open area and stood. General Cuez's captains were all in attendance lined up in a row watching. "Captain O'Dell, please come forward." The captain walked out of the line of captains trying not to show fear. "I have read the reports. Your blunder has cost me my opportunity for a fast and easy war." He yelled, "You lost the battle to an ill-prepared New York tribe when you had the surprise and numbers. You did not wait until all the soldiers were ready. Now they have secured the gate at the end of the tunnel." He was red in the face. He looked evil at the captain.

"Sir, my men thought they could win, and they attacked prior to me giving the order."

"Who is at fault? You as the leader or your brave men?" He stared at the captain. "As a captain, you are to make certain your men follow your orders and if they do not, you will punish them. That is what a Normand commander does in his leadership role. That is what I must do as the acting General of the Normand Army."

"Sir. If you give me another opportunity, I will prove myself to you. Through my leadership, my men and I have conquered the territory north of Harpers Ferry Harbor. I have been the spear of the northern assault."

Cuez yelled. "You know what the punishment is." He stood and looked with a fake expression of sympathy. "If I allow you to have another chance, then everyone of these other captains will demand another chance. I must have captains that are true leaders of men." He motioned for his guards. The four guards ran into the middle of the floor and apprehended Captain O'Dell. One stood behind him and stepped into the back of his legs at his knees forcing him down on the floor. The other two held him down on the floor and the fourth stood with the sword. The guard held his sword up. The captain did not plea for help or mercy. He knew what was coming. General Cuez motioned his head. The guard swung and Captain O'Dell's head rolled over on the floor. The other fifteen captains stared at the head, the body, and the blood.

General Cuez said in a calm voice, "Now that we dealt with his failed command, we need to move forward." He looked at the soldier standing. "I do not like cowards. Matter of fact, I hate cowards. There is no room in my army for a coward. Do you know what I do with cowards?"

The soldier shook his head no, "Sir. I am not a coward. I have the tattoos to prove I am a great soldier."

"I feed the cowards to my dogs. You say you are not a coward, but here you stand. The other forty-nine men in your squad died bravely. Did they not?"

"Yes sir, they all died brave men."

He looked at his row of captains, "Does this man look brave to you?"

They all loudly responded in unison, "No sir."

"See son. All these commanders disagree with you. They all believe you are a coward. Are you telling me, my commanders do not know the difference between a brave soldier and a coward? Are you telling me they are lying to me?"

"Sir, I am no coward. I was the last one alive in the squad. I was told to bring you a message."

The general interrupted, "How many of their men did you kill? How many men did King Solman's forty-nine elite Guard Troops kill before those brave soldiers died on the battlefield?"

"None, Sir."

"What did you just say?"

"None, Sir."

The General walked forward from his chair and looked at the soldier, and he then glanced at his captains. He stared with madness and demanded, "Step forward, soldier." The soldier walked forward further into the light and stood behind the dead body of Captain O'Dell.

"Those were elite Guard Soldiers and all forty-nine died without killing a sod buster. Do not lie to me." His voice increased louder as he spoke with his face turning red in anger.

"Sir, the six men and two women killed the forty-nine soldiers and left me alive. They indicated they ambushed Lieutenant Ranken with his nineteen men and then ambushed us while wearing their uniforms. Sir."

"Why was the guard unit separated?"

"Sir. Lieutenant Ranken was not patient. He was returning to receive better orders. We had taken all the grain and the remaining livestock from the second village. We killed all the villagers in the first village earlier that morning. They had not complied with our tax mandate and our request for grain and livestock. We were on the road heading south when we were ambushed." He made eye contact with the General. "Sir. After I was released, I walked south and discovered Lieutenant Ranken and the first squad of soldiers naked lying dead in a pile in the woods being eaten by wild animals. I then located one of their horses and rode here to report to you." He looked at General Cuez without blinking, "The eight soldiers killed all twenty-nine of the remainder of your unit except for me in less than one minute. Sir, they were no sodbusters or ranchers. They were all very schooled in the art of combat with a sword and bows like nothing I have ever seen. They did not break a sweat killing us."

"You mean to walk in here and tell me forty-nine of my elite soldiers were killed by six males and two females?" He pointed his

174

index finger and looked at the soldier. He laughed and then said, "You are a liar and a coward. Guards remove his head." The guards started toward the soldier.

The soldier pulled his hood back and the bandage off his head. "They butchered my face with the hot branding iron, Sir. They held me down and branded me with one of our brands. I did not do this to myself. They did this to me." He turned so the captains could see his face with the deep red brand in the middle of his forehead. The captains stared at his face. "Their commander cut off my two right fingers, so I could no longer shoot a bow." He held his hand up with a thumb and two stumps then his ring finger and his little finger. "Then, he told me to deliver a message to you, Sir."

General Cuez motioned for the four guards to hold off on his prior order. General Cuez walked closer and looked at the young soldier's face and hand, "What damn message?"

"The leader told me to tell you exactly word for word, 'When he finds you and you crawl out from under the rock you've been hiding under, he is going to cut your head off."

Chapter 19

Vicky and the council listened to Dak's report and his suggestions. They had caught the Normand command unprepared and accomplished more than Wayne had anticipated. She looked at Wayne and then Billy Ray, "What do you think we should do?"

Wayne stepped forward. "If we can help the freedom fighters survive and teach them how to fight, we need to take advantage of this opportunity. We need all the men we can gather. We need to save the people in the south. This is a rare break, but we need to mobilize quickly and attack."

Vicky looked at Billy Ray. Billy Ray spoke, "I agree. We need to send our army south through the tunnel and fight them before they fortify that area and kill all the resistance fighters. We need to take with us no fewer than six-hundred men."

Delores looked at Vicky and then her husband, "We need to attempt diplomacy. We need to try and set up a conference with their leaders. Besides, where are we going to get that number of fighting men?"

Dak was upset at Delores with her mentioning diplomacy. He had seen first-hand the Normand army, and how they butchered the poor farmers and ranchers. "We have them on the run. We must strike now. We can try diplomacy once our position is strengthened. The New York tribe has more men than us. They will send four-hundred, and we will send two-hundred. We can take one hundred men from Meadow Bottoms. It is time they fought with us. Time is running out. We need to leave tonight at midnight before they regroup with their entire army. When we left them, the Normand army was in disarray, but they will quickly regroup. We need to push them south and out of that region."

Vicky looked at Dak with scorn. She tried to hold her temper in check. "Dak you and your friends did better than we could have done."

"Yes mom. We worked together. I would like to lead this assault."

"What you did at Meadow Bottoms is not acceptable. Billy Ray and Little Jimmy will lead the assault. You will go with them. Then you will need to answer for your actions."

Dak was surprised with his mother's attitude. Her demeanor had changed. "I have answered for what I did, and what I did was I cut the head off a man who had committed treason and disobeyed your orders to fight and protect our tribe." As he spoke his voice got louder with each word and his face turned red with anger. The rest of the audience did not dare say a word. Dak then added, "I would do it again. You should have addressed the festering problem years ago, and for the record we need to send more men. We could send four hundred men from Cliff Tops. We need to ensure we will win the battle."

She turned red in the face with anger and wrinkles appeared on her forehead, "I am the Queen, and how dare you raise your voice to me. I will not leave our home unprotected. I will send one-hundred men from Cliff Tops and one-hundred from Meadow Bottoms. How dare you administer capital punishment without my authority. You do not have the authority to kill one of my citizens. Our tribe needs to grow. Once word gets out, we kill our own people, others will not come here to live. The diversity in our people will make us stronger. We need more workers and soldiers."

Dak started to say something, but he knew he should not. He stood still. He glanced at Samuel standing to the side of the room. He was in full armor. Dak had hardly noticed him. He had stayed in the background and had not participated in the planning of the attack.

Dak looked at Samuel, "You Blueblood. What would you have done if someone had not obeyed you and would not defend your tribe and tried to instigate a coup?"

Vicky answered prior to Samuel. "It does not matter what he would have done. I am the Queen, and you do not have the authority to kill someone without my approval. What makes us any different than the Normand army killing our own people?" Dak was surprised. His mother now was the Queen and not his mother. She leaned over the table placing her hands on the tabletop for support and was staring at him. He knew her question was a rhetorical question.

"You were not in a position to rule, Mother. Four of your five tribal leaders voted me into office and four of the five accompanied me to Meadow Bottoms to administer the

178

punishment. I did what had to be done. I have answered for my actions. I was acting in the role as the King of Cliff Tops."

Vicky noticed Dak was still looking at Samuel. She ordered, "Clear the room. Now. Except you Dak.

Wayne closed the door behind him as he was the last person to leave. Vicky turned to Dak, "You do not understand."

Dak was mad. He could not hold his temper in check. He had not slept, and the fatigue was setting in on him. "I do not believe you understand. This is war. The opportunity to attack is now. If we are lucky, we can push them eight hundred miles south all the way out of Harpers Ferry Harbor and maybe all the way to the deserts of Southern City. I have seen the war firsthand. We need to assist the people of the south to set up resistance fighters. Those people need our help, and we need their help."

Vicky noticed how upset Dak was, "Dak. I've killed a lot of men. I never killed one person that did not deserve to die. I felt I was helping the poor and the people who could not protect themselves. I thank our Lord for giving me the fortitude to kill those monsters. However, killing people can make you a monster. I do not wish my son to become a monster. A parent's prayers are answered if their kids are loving kids and grow into loving adults. That is what concerns me."

Dak looked at his mother and felt bad for his outburst. "We are at war. Some of these warriors I have killed might not have been bad men, but they were forced to fight us by our adversary. I did not have the luxury to determine who I was killing in these battles.

I just know we must stop them. If I am lucky and live through this war, I will need to be like all the other soldiers and deal with the consequences of my actions."

"You do not understand. Decapitating a man will haunt your memories and those of the people who bear witness."

"Listen Mom. Robin Hood has contacts inside Meadow Bottoms. They were alerted to the battle raging in the New York Territory prior to us receiving the notice. They are closer and could have responded. Your friend Sie did not tell the others and held the battle in confidence. Some of those men would have fought if they had known. We almost lost the battle. There were dead bodies all over the ground stacked up like firewood. If we had not responded like I ordered, we would have lost." He raised his voice, "The Normand army would not have made the same mistake. They would have gathered in mass in the New York Territory, rested their soldiers, then came across our lines and across the gorge and killed all of us. You need to remove Delores from your council. She does not understand what we are up against. Staying neutral is not going to work. There is no possible reason for King Solman to grant us a treaty that he would stand behind. The only thing he understands is power, and his armies are three times the size of ours. They are better trained. They are better supported, and they have better leadership."

She was mad at his response, "You need to rest and eat. I will direct Zorro to have four-hundred men ready to leave at four A.M. Billy Ray will advise them on the mission. I will not remove

Delores from my council. She provides me a political balance in my decisions. If everyone on the council always agreed, what would be the point of having a council." Vicky turned and walked out the church doors. Dak sat down on the church pew and prayed.

Wayne walked into the church along with the others. They spread the map out on the table in the front auditorium of the church. Dak sat on the front bench thinking and could hear the men talking about the plan and logistical problems to move the soldiers into position. He listened to Hulk describe the location of the freedom fighters and last known position of the Normand soldiers. Dak stood and walked to the rear of the church. He glanced at the people standing around the table and noticed Samuel was not in the church. He wondered what his advice would have been. He quickly dismissed his thoughts about Samuel to focus on questions from the other men looking at the map. Billy Ray ended the meeting by saying, "We must be in position at dawn. We need to catch them while they are still asleep. Everyone needs to get some rest, and we will leave at midnight and hook up with the New York tribe soldiers before dawn."

Everyone walked out leaving Dak and Wayne. Wayne looked at Dak, "I was with you in Meadow Bottoms. I supported you then, and I will support you now, but please do not make me choose between you and your mother. I will talk further with her when the time is right." He turned and walked out. Dak turned and looked at the altar and thought of his actions. He then turned and walked out.

***

Wayne sent a messenger to Meadow Bottoms to send one hundred men, and they needed to be prepared to leave for battle at midnight. He wanted them saddled and ready for inspection thirty-minutes before departure. He told Billy Ray to inspect the soldiers and provide them an explanation and stress the importance of the battle prior to them leaving. He secretly hoped the men of Meadow Bottoms showed up. He did not want to have to administer capital punishment to the deserters. He knew Vicky, and he knew she would not tolerate deserters. He was also surprised at her decision to challenge young Dak in front of the tribe's council and other men.

He liked the attack plan. He had accepted there was no alternative to war. The Normand army was going to kill them. He just worried about the unknown within the upcoming battle. They could not afford to lose. They needed every soldier. Wayne worked with the women on providing food packages for the troops for the remainder of the night. He made certain stable employees had the horses fed and saddled.

Chapter 20

Dak awoke with Zenith lying across his chest. He looked at her. "We can stay in the warm bed if you desire." He was tired. He had not slept more than a few hours. He was frustrated with his mother and as he tried to sleep, his thought kept him awake. She had never used that tone with him. He was confused about what she expected. This was war and not a mission to take out a single target like she had done in her past life. He had never seen her so angry as when she walked out of the council meeting.

Zenith got out of bed and dressed. In a gentle tone, "You need to hurry if you are coming with me, Billy Ray and the guys."

Dak smiled, "I finally fell asleep a few minutes ago." He knew he would like at least an additional three hours of sleep, but he also knew he needed to be leaving with the army.

"Zenith hold on and wait on me. The plan is simple. I am going to lead Trey, Hulk, Tommy Boy, and you along with twenty of the New York tribe men on foot down the tunnel. We suspect the tunnel will be guarded and maybe booby traps set along the way. We also know visibility will be an issue. The use of a torch would draw attention. We need to make it through the tunnel before anyone knows we are attacking. The morning temperature is below zero, which is a blessing. The Normand army is mostly southern men. They will be cold and staying in their tents."

Dak got out of bed and noticed Zenith had already put on her silk underclothes and her leather pants and top. She was lacing her boots. "We need to secure the path, and Billy Ray will then lead the army on horses through the tunnel. We will hook up with the freedom fighters and push the Normand army out to sea and out of Harpers Ferry Harbor. Hopefully, this will be a one-month journey."

Zenith looked at Dak, "Dak, I like your optimism, but they have the numbers and better experienced army. Some of our soldiers have never fought a single battle. We cannot push the Normand army out of Harpers Ferry Harbor in one month. Harpers Ferry Harbor is over eight-hundred miles south." Dak smiled at Zenith as she placed her hair in a ponytail.

"Maybe forty days," he grinned.

Chapter 21

Dak knelt on one knee from behind the rocks on the ledge. He scanned the area with the help of the ambient light from the moon. He did not see any soldiers. He did not see any campfires or camps. He glanced over to his right, "The place looks deserted."

Hulk eased up next to him and looked over the embankment. "How can this be? There should be close to three-hundred Normand soldiers waiting on us. Tell me they did not just pull out and leave."

Dak turned to the captain of the New York tribe and motioned him forwarded. The captain crawled up next to Hulk and Dak. "The Midnight Hole appears to have been abandoned. This could be a trap. Send one of your men back to notify General Claiborne we are through with no resistance. We will need to send out two-man scout teams in all three directions." He paused while he kept looking from his hidden advantage point behind the rock embankment. "They might be hiding and waiting. I do not want to walk into an ambush."

"Roger that." The captain turned and motioned for a squad of men to move forward. He told one to proceed north through the tunnel to the waiting comrades. He pointed for two men squads to go in the three directions. Dak and Hulk watched the two-men on the left proceed to the tree line while looking at the surroundings as they ran. Then, two more men ran straight for the wagon laying on

185

its side two-hundred yards straight out from their position. The last two-man squad ran right to a large tree close to one-hundred yards out. They all motioned the area was clear. Dak turned and motioned for the rest to advance. He then stood and walked into the open with Zenith and Hulk following. He glanced at the two men to the right and the two men to the left as they were still signaling no movement. Dak walked to the wagon and looked toward the village close to two-hundred yards south of his location. The full moon had shifted to the western sky and provided the needed ambient light to see the silhouettes of the huts, buildings and other structures. There was no sign of anyone. He watched as a dog crossed the street in the village. He thought what a good place for an ambush. The buildings and homes could conceal over one-hundred Normand soldiers. He looked at the New York Captain, "We need to send scouts into the village and out further into the forest and fields. They need to report back to us in one hour. We need to know what we are up against. Make certain they report back in one hour."

***

Billy Ray rode out of the tunnel entrance followed by a column of the soldiers. He dropped his torch and proceeded to the wagon. Hulk turned to his father, "They have abandoned the village. Dak has sent scouts further out on foot. They were instructed to report back in one hour. They appear to have left their dead without burying them. I guess you saw the dead soldiers lying in the tunnel."

Billy Ray commanded, "They must have figured their supply lines are too long, and they were ordered back to Harpers Ferry Harbor. That is where they will make their stand and fortify their position. They can be re-supplied by the sea." He looked in all directions. "They fled in a hurry. They left their men where they laid. No army would do that unless they were in a hurry."

Dak kept his gaze into the village and the Continental Trail leading south. He had not turned around and looked at Billy Ray or the column of horse soldiers. The sun was about to rise over the eastern horizon. "General, I would suggest we wait for the scouts to report to us. If the Normand army has retreated south, I would suggest we split our troops and send fifty men north to assist the men of the New Foundland tribe. Then, General Claiborne, I would suggest once we reach the small village approximately one-hundred-twenty miles south on the Continental Trail, we send another fifty men north on that road toward New Foundland. We watched yesterday as the Normand soldiers rode toward New Foundland. We could trap those soldiers. In addition, we need to reinforce that tribe. They are good men who want to fight with us."

Billy Ray smiled at Dak as he spoke, "I am no general."

Dak turned and looked at him. "Yes, you are. Our Queen has placed you in charge. You are to oversee this army." Billy Ray thought back to the meeting two weeks prior where Dak announced he was the acting king of the tribe in his mother's absence.

Tommy Boy smiled, "Holy heck, Dad, you are a general. Congratulations on the promotion." The men laughed.

Billy Ray said, "Okay, I am a general. I agree we wait for the scouts to report. Then, I will make my decision on how we will proceed." He thought about his men and this army. Four-hundred of them were men from the New York tribe, and he had just met them. He knew how well Trey, Tommy Boy, Dak, Hulk and Veronica could fight. He had trained them. He was impressed with Zenith and her courage and abilities. The one-hundred men of his tribe would fight, but he was concerned about the one-hundred men from Meadow Bottoms. He thought most of these men were ranchers, farmers, and carpenters. They had been training for a week. He knew no one could turn into a soldier in a week. They all needed more training and experience. He knew some of these men would piss on themselves before battle when confronted with a stronger, more confident squad of soldiers.

The first two scouts approached, "There is no one in the village alive. There are several headless villagers." The scout looked away and then back at Billy Ray, "Some are children and a couple of babies. There was no mercy. They were all left in the open for us to find."

The quietness was deafening as no one said a word for a few seconds. "Damn them. Send some men to bury the dead. We wait for the other scouts to report," declared Billy Ray.

Thirty minutes later the two other teams of scouts reported. The one that had gone east reported they located a herd of sheep and goats. "The ranchers at first were reluctant to come out of hiding. They saw the Normand soldiers riding toward them yesterday, and they fled into the mountains and hid. The soldiers left during the night heading south. They randomly killed several hundred sheep for no reason."

One of the scouts from the west reported there were close to three-hundred horses heading north toward New Foundland. "We found no soldiers hiding in the woods. We combed the area about five-hundred yards north of this location. We tracked the horses for half a mile on the road headed for New Foundland."

Billy Ray looked at the first scout. "Ride back to the ranchers and tell them they will be provided safe passage through the tunnel. They can take their herds either to the New York territory or Cliff Tops. Tell them it is inevitable the Normand armies will return at some point and the animals will be taken from them." He turned to his son, Hulk, "Take fifty men and go north. We will send an additional one hundred troops from the small village twenty miles south of here. We will surround the Normand squad and kill them. You will need to let us get the other one hundred soldiers in position before you attack them from the rear."

Hulk looked at his men from Cliff Tops. "Fifty of you follow me. It is payback time."

Billy Ray then added, "Do not take any risks. If we are attacked by the main army, I will send a messenger. You will need to

189

immediately retreat to the New York tribe and secure the gate. Otherwise, you and your men will be cut off. We cannot afford to lose fifty men."

"Yes sir."

Billy Ray knew he needed to be ready to fight and then retreat in case of over whelming numbers of Normand soldiers charged them from the south. He feared his son and those men would be cut off from retreat and surrounded.

***

Dak and Zenith rode for five hours and came to the field on a knoll and Observed the small village south of them was void of people. He could see smoke coming from the fire damaged hut and large building. They waited to advance before the horse army led by Billy Ray approached from the north.

Dak looked at Billy Ray as he rode up to the top of the knoll. Billy Ray motioned for the column of soldiers to halt. Dak announced, "The village is void of life. We have not seen any movement."

"Send a ten-man scout team," ordered Billy Ray.

Dak motioned for Tommy Boy and Zenith along with seven New York tribe men. They rode into the village with three men proceeding around the left and three going around the right. Dak, Zenith, Tommy Boy and one other soldier advanced up the middle. They met at the far end. One of the New York scouts from the left reported, "The entire village has been burned. I did not see any bodies."

The other scout team from the right side announced, "No bodies. No one is here. There are wagon tracks leading into the mountains and also tracks leading to the New Foundland village. They might be a couple of days old." Dak looked further south along the Continental Trail. The view was clear for close to a mile until the trail turned and went into a pine forest. He did not see any signs of anyone. He wondered whether the Normand army could be hidden in the pine tree forest covering the small mountain.

Dak commanded, "Report back to General Billy Ray Claiborne. He needs to send soldiers west. Zenith and I will go south and scout the road. We will need to be flanked on both sides about one-hundred yards. Tell General Claiborne we need to anticipate an ambush."

Chapter 22

The dirt road ascended the mountain, and Hulk recognized the area from his prior trip. He held up his hand to halt. He turned to the men, "New Foundland is about a quarter mile ahead." He looked at the men of his village. "We can advance a little further then we must proceed on foot. I want us to sneak up on the Normand soldiers."

***

Hulk could view the length of the dirt road to the village from the ditch line and his hidden spot behind the large tree. He glanced behind him, and his men were spaced out close to ten feet on both sides of the dirt road all trying to stay hidden as they proceeded toward the village. He knew this was the first time in battle for most of them. He could see the fear in their eyes. The Normand soldiers were on one side of the bridge and river. New Foundland towns people had built a log wall across the bridge. He could see where the wall had been set on fire and burned at the bottom of the wall. The fire must have burned out. The wall was still standing. He continually scanned the area. The Normand soldiers were resting, and no one was attacking. He could see a couple of dead Normand soldiers hanging from a tree on the far side of the river. He remembered the river and rapids and the riverbed with large granite rocks when they had crossed the bridge and the river a few days prior. There was only one way for a horse to cross the river and that was the wooden bridge. He did not believe the people of the village could hold out much longer. The bridge had been the key. The Normand soldiers could jump from rock to rock and then walk across the three feet deep river, but the horses could not cross. He turned to the men and walked back down the road and gathered the platoon leaders. "We will attack. We need to have two platoons attack the middle and two attack the right flank and two attack the left flank."

"You don't want to wait for the reinforcements?" Asked one of the platoon leaders.

Another leader said, "Your father told you to wait until the one-hundred men from our army approach from the village south of here, so we would have them surrounded."

Hulk knew these men were not warriors. They had trained for battle, but they were mostly loggers, ranchers, fishermen and two were blacksmiths. They all had families. He knew they had reservations about killing another man. He could see the fear in their eyes. "We have them surrounded. If we do not attack now, those people in New Foundland will all be dead by tomorrow. General Claiborne was counting on their support in fighting the Normand division. Now, you men know this is what war is about. You are going to kill those Normand soldiers, or you will be killed. You saw what those bastards did to the villagers. You and your families are next. Now pass the word back through the men and follow me." Hulk knew the men questioned him being in charge at his age. He knew he had to earn their trust. He could also tell the platoon leaders were looking for encouragement from one another. They were scared.

Hulk quietly proceeded toward the bridge. He glanced behind him and noticed his men were following orders. The Normand soldiers were spread out along the riverbank both east and west of the bridge. They were hidden behind the large granite rocks and large tress that lined the river. Their attention was focused across the river at Vulture and his men who were also lined along the opposite side of the river. The Normand captain and squad of men were stationed behind the trees and large boulders near the bridge. He knew that was his point of his attack. The Normand soldiers were trying to open the bridge, so they could ride across the river on horseback. Hulk glanced across the river and smiled to himself. Vulture and his men were killers. He could see three Normand soldiers hanging by a rope from tree limbs. He knew the battle had been brutal, and he was surprised the Normand soldiers had no one watching their rear flank.

He and his men approached slowly and walked up the shoulder of the road as the dirt road ascended the hill. Hulk and his first twenty men were ten feet from the battle line when the first Normand soldier realized they were about to be attacked from the rear. Hulk knew he wanted to first take out the captain and two lieutenants stationed behind the large boulder and hope the chaos would cause the Normand soldiers to panic.

Hulk killed the first two soldiers who turned and sounded the alarm. He rammed his sword straight through the first man's face mask and blocked the swing of the other Normand soldier. He then ran into the man knocking him to the ground where he crushed his helmet with his sword killing the man with blunt force trauma to the head. His men did not hesitate. They fought as they had been trained. The men looped around both the east and west area of the battle lines at the river and attacked the Normand soldiers lined up and down the riverbank.

The announcement went out from inside the small village the Normand soldiers were under an attack. Vulture ordered the gate opened, and his men rushed across the bridge to fight. The battle scene turned bloody as every man fought for his life. Hulk had gone from one soldier to the next cutting them down. He killed the first lieutenant by first blocking his swing of the sword with his left hand and then ramming his knife into the man's neck under the facemask.

Hulk had no time to hesitate. He quickly charged the captain. The captain was a large man in full armor. Hulk knew he was a superior warrior compared to the other soldiers fighting with a sword. He also knew the armor prevented the captain from being quick and agile. He swung his sword with his left hand and dropped low, knowing the captain would block the swing. Hulk slid down on one knee and reached behind the captain cutting his hamstring with his knife.

The captain was preparing to counter with a swing of his sword when he grimaced behind his mask from the acute pain in his left leg. He started falling and Hulk finished him by ramming his sword under the protected breast plate through the captain's lower belly.

His men pushed forward through the Normand flanks. They were first trying to eliminate the archers and then take out the infantry men in the hand-to-hand combat.

The Normand soldiers fled east along the river with four being captured. Hulk and his men attacked the tired soldiers and surprised them. Without the commanders, the infantry men along the east area overreacted and fled on horseback. They had assumed they were being attacked by several hundred troops and panicked when the two lieutenants and one captain were killed at the beginning of the battle.

Vulture walked over to Hulk and noticed he was covered in blood, sweat, and dirt after the battle. "Thanks. I have never been so happy to see someone in my life. I don't know how much more we could take. We lost a quarter of our men trying to keep them on their side of the river. Their archers are damn good."

Hershel walked up and smiled. "Their archers are all dead thanks to our friend named Hulk and his friends. We knew we could not defend the small village in the valley. It sits wide open in the huge field. We came here to fight and teamed up with these people."

Hulk smiled at Hershel, "It is good to see an old friend. You made a good decision. The counter-offensive has begun. Stories of battles like this will spread and others will join the cause." He looked at the men standing in front of him. "The Midnight Hole has been abandoned. We planned to take it but then found out the Normand soldiers marched south." He hesitated with a grim expression. "They killed everyone, even the kids. We saw the remains of a pregnant woman. Her belly had been pierced by a sword. We buried the villagers."

Vulture spit on the ground and looked at the four prisoners. "We need to kill those bastards."

Hulk looked at the men of New Foundland, "Send them to the prison camp in the New York territory. Keep them separated from one another. They will need to be properly interrogated. We will need all the information about the Normand army we can gather. We now will ride south to hook up with our army. We believe the Normand army is preparing for the winter and will make their stand at Harpers Ferry Harbor. They need that harbor to land their ships. We could use the help with our assault pushing the Normand army south."

Hershel looked around. "Where is Dak, Robin Hood, Trey, and Tommy Boy? Where are those two pretty women, Zenith and Veronica? Please don't tell me they have been killed."

Hulk smiled, "None of them have been killed. Robin Hood unfortunately had to have surgery on his shoulder. He is healing. Dak and Zenith are scouting out the road south on the Continental

Trail headed for Harpers Ferry Harbor. Trey and Tommy Boy will be leading a column of soldiers up from the village down in the valley. The plan was for us to trap the Normand soldiers between us. I will be honest-we figured you had either been killed or ran. When I saw your tribe trying to fight, I knew we needed to help you. The other column would not have arrived until tomorrow at the earliest."

Vulture looked at his men. They had been without sleep and were tired and injured. "My men need rest. We have fought for over twenty-four hours straight without sleep and little food."

"I understand. We will be leaving, heading south." Hulk looked around, "Where are the females and the children?"

"We knew we were going to be attacked. We built the wall on the bridge in two days with green trees. The Normand army needed the bridge to cross the river on horseback. They tried to burn the wall, but wet green wood will not burn like dry wood. They wanted the bridge intact. We used the river as a barrier, but this time of year the river is shallow. They were going to be able to cross at some point. We could not have held out much longer. We sent the females and children further north in a hidden area near a radiation dump. We decided to fight to the end."

One of the men who had tied Hulk up when he had first met Vulture laughed, "Vulture, he is looking for Becky." All the men, even the Cliff Tops men laughed. Robin Hood and Trey had told the entire Cliff Tops community about how Becky had discovered Hulk was not a Normand soldier because he had been circumcised.

After the laughter died down, one of the blacksmiths from the Cliff Tops announced, "You may laugh, but I noticed he killed two dozen Normand soldiers including their command team. He certainly can swing that sword." The group looked over behind the boulder at the dead captain and the two dead lieutenants.

Hulk said, "The soldiers in all that armor are the easiest to kill." He pointed at a dead Normand soldier with his leg cut and the metal helmet dented in near the right earhole. "They cannot move fast, and they are vulnerable from the back of the legs. They have no protection on the back of the legs. All you must do is cut through the hamstring and then watch them fall. If they had metal protection on the back of the legs, they could not bend over. The other option would be to hit them in the head real hard. With the metal helmets, they cannot see peripherally. Walk up beside them and hit them and watch them fall. Once on the ground, ram a small blade in their ear hole, cutting into the brain." He held up his knife and wiped the blood off the blade. Vulture and the men watched Hulk clean his knife.

Chapter 23

"We have received word." Vicky glanced at Wayne as he walked into the kitchen. "They still have not met any resistance from the main army. I am concerned with our troops going so far south. We will not be able to reinforce them, or they will not be able to protect us if we are attacked."

Wayne replied, "Our army is proceeding as planned. They are making certain they are not marching into a trap. It has been two weeks, and the only resistance was around the village of New Foundland. The freedom fighters were trenched and holding their own against a formidable number of Normand soldiers. Hulk led a platoon of fifty men and attacked them from the rear. General Claiborne sent another unit of men from the route north of the village the next day. The Normand squad was annihilated. The New York tribe has the four prisoners in lockup. Billy Ray, I mean General Claiborne, believes the Normand army retreated to Harbor Ferry Harbor. They burned the villages as they retreated, killing many villagers."

Vicky smiled at the fact everyone started calling Bill Ray, "General." Wayne then added to his report, "The pigeons cannot fly direct from that far south with the reports for fear they will fly through the radiation fields. We are basically using a pony express type of mail system."

Vicky asked, "Do you think there is any chance we will be attacked by sea. They will know we have sent most our warriors south. We are vulnerable to a sea attack."

Wayne hesitated and looked worried. "If we are attacked, we will all fight. That is all we can do."

"Any other news?"

"The herds of animals we received are eating the grass they can find under the snow. We do not have enough grain or hay for all the cattle and sheep this winter. The goats will eat anything. They eat the vines and bushes. The ranchers say the fields south have more to offer. They can hand cut the hay and haul it north."

"Send them south to their old fields. Send soldiers with them to guard and protect them. Send women and kids to help cut the hay. Everyone must work."

Wayne stood looking at Vicky. He remembered the first time he met her close to twenty-two-years ago. He thought then she was the prettiest woman he had ever met. She had not aged like most women. She had no wrinkles or grey hair. She looked mature, intelligent, and very attractive. She was always put together with her attire in a very attractive manner. He noticed she seemed to have a glow about her the past few weeks. She smiled more. She seemed to be happy.

She was gathering breakfast on a tray and looked over at Wayne, "Is there something else?"

Mia, Delores, and Casey walked into the kitchen. "No, I have nothing else to report."

"I noticed you have been sleeping in the shack. Why is that?"

Wayne glanced at Delores, "There is a view of the ocean from the porch, and I watch the ocean for possible ships of a night. Plus, I help Robin Hood with his shoulder healing from his surgery."

Casey looked at Wayne, "Thanks for watching out for him. It would be okay for me and his sister to sleep up there with him."

Vicky set her coffee down. She picked up the large tray of food. She carried the food out the door and up the stairs.

Delores looked at Wayne, "You are such a liar."

Casey smiled, "I was not the one lying. Me and Jessie will be glad to sleep in The Dive." The three women all laughed.

Delores looked at Mia and then Casey, "It has been nonstop every night for two weeks straight. I hope Samuel can hold out and based on the tray of food she was carrying; he should have plenty of protein."

Casey smiled, "I never knew a bed could make so much damn noise. Mia and I went in the apartment when she and Samuel went for one of their horse ride and tried to tighten and oil the bolts holding the bed together."

Delores smiled, "Some of the moans are coming from Samuel and not our Queen."

Wayne smiled, "Our queen had close to seventeen years of not dating after her husband died, and she had a lot of stress built up in her body. I sleep a lot better in The Dive where it is quiet." He sat his coffee cup down, smiled, and walked out.

Delores smiled at Mia and Casey once Wayne cleared the exterior door, "He better enjoy his sleep. According to Tommy Boy and what he told his father, Dak, and Zenith make just as much noise."

Mia stopped laughing and asked, "Do you think anyone has told Dak about his mother and Samuel dating?"

Casey laughed and said, "I mentioned to Robin Hood something about Samuel and that he was standing guard for the tribe of a night. I did not want to be the one who spilled the beans. He did not mention he knew about the two dating, and he did not seem to make the connection."

"He is a guy. They would not notice a woman in love," announced Mia.

Cassy said, "Mia, I told Robin Hood he needed to forgive Veronica for jumping him and injuring his shoulder. The surgery for his torn rotator cuff went well. We all know it was an accident."

Mia said, "She cried that night. Dak and Hulk won't talk to her. They avoid her. She was ordered to leave the area, and she went back into the tunnel and Robin Hood was injured. Robin Hood told her to stay away from him. He never wanted to talk to her again. He said she was the weak link and would not listen or take orders."

Casey looked up, "He is upset. He is lying in the bed recovering from his shoulder operation and his friends are marching south. Our kids are like us, they have been best friends for life. They will come around."

Chapter 24

"We have been camped here for two-days, and our men are well rested. We must have a fast victory. We have spied on the Normand army from the same ridge. This is the same spot when we landed from the boat close to two months and half ago. When are we going to attack and take back Harpers Ferry Harbor?" asked Hulk.

Dak looked over at Hulk, "We will attack when General Claiborne gives us the order and not before. They have the access roads blocked. We will have trouble breaching the gates. They have a lot more soldiers than us. They want us to attack. We would be in the open with their archers to pick us off. This is not going to be easy."

"We provided them with additional time to reinforce their trenches and fortify the gates on the bridge. Would you not have already attacked?"

Dak looked at his friend Hulk. "It does not matter what I would do. I am not in charge. We have a meeting in forty minutes. We might find out the plan. Now, come on and follow me." The two men walked over to their horses and rode down the ridge and descended the bluff of the mountain heading for their camp.

***

Dak walked under the canopy with Trey, Zenith, Hulk and Tommy Boy. Dak looked at Little Jimmy and said, "hi". He then nodded at Eric of Newport and the captain of the New York men along with three other men from the New York tribe. He noticed Veronica but did not acknowledge her. Billy Ray looked up from the table. He had been studying the map. "I know some of you thought we should have attacked immediately when we arrived two days ago." Hulk bowed his head and looked at the floor. "I elected to be patient and gather information. We cannot rush into this battle." He hesitated and smiled, "You can make one woman pregnant and the process of making a baby takes nine months. You cannot make a baby faster by making nine women pregnant. It still takes nine months. I have been patient for a reason and now I have decided, we will attack at sunrise." He looked at several of the captains in attendance and then continued, "They have plenty of stored food, and we have none. We cannot wait them out. We are not prepared for the winter, and we will have no supplies coming from the north."

Billy Ray looked at Dak and then his two sons. "This is what we know. You have confirmed General Cuez is in the building here." He pointed to the spot on the map. "He is well guarded with six personal heavily armed guards which are always with him when he walks outside. They go where he goes. We will assume they are elite guards and very well trained. There is no way we can reach him without significant loss of life." He pointed to the road leading into the town and the lay out of the battlefield. "They have well enforced trenches which will be very difficult to breach with a frontal assault. The three roads leading in are cut off with gates on the bridges. They have a large number of their troops stationed along the trenches backed up with archers from the hill area. All total over thirteen-hundred infantry men and two-hundred sailors. The three gates are flanked with towers and additional archers." Everyone was quiet. The men who were going to be leading the assault looked grim.

Bill Ray looked at the New York captain. "You will attack at this point with two-hundred men. Little Jimmy, you will lead two hundred men from the New York tribe and attack at this point in the middle. Eric you will attack on the left flank with the rest of the men from Cliff Tops. Every man will need a shield to protect himself from the archers. As we attack, we will be in the open. We have approximately six-hundred soldiers." Billy Ray watched Dak as he stepped back and let the plan sink in along with the other men.

The New York captain was the first to speak. He was cautious as he spoke and knew he had to do as he was told. Everyone had heard about the man named Sie from Meadow Bottoms who had been decapitated in front of his wife for treason and was classified as a deserter. "What about the trenches?" He looked at Billy Ray with concern. Billy Ray watched the others. "They have us out numbered two-to-one with infantry men and have the high ground with archers supporting those positions."

No one said a word. Billy Ray could see the concern on the faces of everyone.

Dak looked at Billy Ray, "Why have they not attacked us? They have the experienced soldiers. They have the numbers, and we are in the open. At best we could retreat eight-hundred miles to the Midnight Hole and fight them as we retreat."

Finally, Billy Ray stood. "That is what we had hoped. We were waiting for them to attack us and stretch their supply lines. We could pick them off as we retreated. That is why I have constantly sent ten men units north of us to make certain, we have an exit route. I was fearful we could be cut off by Normand soldiers hidden in all those villages we passed, or the villagers decided to fight against us. Very few joined our ranks. I will tell you why they have not attacked us. They can sit where they are and watch us suffer from the towers and heated buildings this winter. They can be resupplied with food from ships coming into the harbor. They know we must attack. If we attack, they win. This plan is doomed."

Hulk and Dak both said at the same time, "What are you planning?"

"This is a decoy. The way to cut the head off the snake is to kill General Cuez. The problem is we think he is a Blueblood hidden under all those surgeries." He looked at Dak and noticed the confusion.

Hulk said, "Blueblood?"

"The four Normand soldiers captured in the Battle of New Foundland were taken to the New York tribe and were interrogated by Wayne. That report was received a few hours ago. We understand from Wayne's report, General Cuez backs up what he says with his sword. His men all fear him. He trained his six personal guards. Only a Blueblood could be that good with a sword. No one under his command will challenge him, and there are no other Bluebloods reported to be located inside the city of Harpers Ferry Harbor."

Zenith looked at Billy Ray, "If he is a Blueblood trained with a sword, your men will not be able to kill him. It would take a trained group of Bluebloods to kill him. I know this because in my training in Merlin, we were told stories of rogue Bluebloods. At first the stories sounded like a myth and none of us students believe the stories. Then, the trainers set us all down and told us the truth. There was a secret Sect of Bluebloods from the German region of the old world. They are not part of my clan. They were very violent and very deadly. We outnumbered them and hunted them down with squads of Bluebloods from Merlin. This all occurred in the earlier years after the Transition Period before I was a Blueblood warrior. We were told they all were psychopathic killers, very smart, very hard to spot, and very difficult to kill. They figured out the need to have their ears altered surgically to hide."

Billy Ray looked at the audience, "Samuel has confirmed this to our Queen, and she told our council. I am certain General Cuez is a Blueblood from the German region. He must have undergone surgery on his ears to look normal. That is why I held back the attack. He wants us to attack, so he can kill all of us with one quick swipe of his sword. He ordered a retreat from the north and the Midnight Hole, so we would be alone with no supplies and no way to reinforce our front lines." He looked at everyone, and he noticed the men from the New York tribe were apprehensive about the situation. "I propose to send three soldiers in from the ocean side west of us. They must go unnoticed. They will enter the ocean tonight on a small raft and exit here." He pointed at the map. "They then will proceed under the cover of darkness to this building where the General is staying. A small raft with three soldiers should go unnoticed in the darkness. They will need to stay close to four-hundred yards from the closest anchored ship. They have several guards on the ships. Now, their navy is better prepared for an attack on the ships after you guys sunk four of them." He paused. "The three soldiers would need to stay away from the two watch towers in the harbor." He pointed at the towers. "They have placed guards on the ships and towers which rotate every twelve hours." He pointed at the building near the beach. "The three will hide until the rest of the army attacks. The mission is for the three-team unit to kill the guards and assassinate General Cuez. All the while our six-hundred troops are acting like they are attacking. The attack must look legitimate enough to fool the Normand commanders. We want to pull the captains and other soldiers to the battlefield away from General Cuez." He looked at the New York Captain, Little Jimmy, and then Eric of Newport. "This is going to be a high-risk mission. If he is a Blueblood, it will take you Dak and Zenith working together to kill him. He will be better with a sword than anything you have seen. This is a volunteer mission only. I understand if you decline."

"So, the attack is going to be a decoy?" asked Dak as he looked over the map.

Eric of Newport said, "Little Jimmy and I volunteered along with Billy Ray, but we are apprehensive with us three being able to kill an experienced Blueblood warrior and six guards. You are better with a sword than we are. If you do not want to go, we will."

Zenith spoke up, "The raft will be our escape route. There needs to be four of us. I want Veronica to ride in with us and protect our exit route."

"Zenith this is going to be extremely dangerous."

"Dak, I am going. Either I am going with you, Hulk and Veronica, or I am going with Little Jimmy, Eric of Newport, Billy Ray, and Veronica. You two need to decide if you are going." She looked at Dak and then Hulk.

"Zenith, this is going to be too dangerous for you. I do not want you to go." Dak stared into her eyes.

"I do not want you to go. I am going. This is the only chance we will have to kill that bastard. I saw his troops kill those kids at the small village. I have seen the remains of pregnant women slaughtered by his troops. Someone must be willing to stand up to him. I will take this chance. I like this plan. We would lose half our army in less than three hours if we attack them in the open with them hiding behind those trenches and gates." She looked at Dak.

Dak announced, "General Claiborne, we will leave tonight."

***

Little Jimmy stood in knee deep ocean water and held the raft. Dak noticed the peaceful dark night. The water was cold, and the wind was chilly blowing from the northwest at less than eight miles per hour. The four approached the raft one at a time. Each stepped over the side of the raft and started paddling. Little Jimmy whispered to Dak, "Good hunting."

They paddled for thirty minutes out to sea without talking. Zenith knew Dak was upset. She was not certain if he was upset with her going on this mission because of the danger or the fact she insisted on Veronica being part of the team. "Veronica, there is no way your father, Billy Ray, and Eric of Newport could fit on this raft. We are constantly taking on water from these waves." Dak smiled knowing Zenith was trying to break the ice.

Hulk snarled, "Robin Hood could have been with us if he had not had a rotator cuff tear."

Veronica said, "I told him I was sorry and besides you did not follow orders as you attacked the Normand soldiers at New Foundland. You were told to wait on Trey and Tommy Boy along with the other one-hundred men."

"I was not going to watch those men be butchered. The Normand soldiers were better trained and covered their attempted assaults against the New Foundland men with superior archers.

211

Once we killed the archers, the battle turned in our favor. You are right Veronica; I did not follow the orders. I also did not injury Robin Hood's rotator cuff."

Zenith looked at her two friends and her husband, "Dak, your mother took time to explain to me. You three have all been genetically gifted which was a gift by your parents with the process of cleansing the sperm and the egg during the start of the pregnancy. The process has made you, Hulk, Tommy Boy, Dak, Veronica, Robin Hood, and Trey all superior warriors. The technology was lost during the Transition Period along with volumes of other technologies developed during the old world. The Queen wished me to know this about each of you for a reason. I do not believe Billy Ray, Little Jimmy, and Eric of Newport would have been successful with this mission we are facing."

No one said another word for ten minutes. The three seemed to agree with what Zenith had mentioned.

Dak whispered, "We need to head for that point. Remember we need to be quiet, and let the wind take us further east out to sea before we cut into shore. The sun will be coming up over the horizon in about two hours. We need to hurry."

When they paddled in three feet of water near the beach, Hulk jumped out and pulled them into the shore. Veronica pulled the raft under the small pine tree thicket, near the sand dune and laid the paddles on top of the raft. Dak looked at her, "We will be back if all goes well in thirty minutes after the horn sounds for the battle to start. If we do not return, pull the raft out and head further east back down the coast. You will leave us, and you will live to fight another day. Cover up the sand and our footprints in case they send out a beach patrol and stay hidden." He made certain he established eye contact with Veronica as he provided her orders.

Hulk led the way across the sand embankment and the rough thorn-covered beach area. They had to run bent over zigzagging through the thorn-covered bushes. The area had grown thick with all types of thorny bushes and small cactuses.

Hulk motioned for them to stop. He watched and listened. He turned to Dak and Zenith and signaled with his hands to approach his position. "They have two guards walking the rear elevation and they lope around the two side elevations of the building. We will wait for the guards to walk around the corner of the building on the east elevation. When they clear the rear corner and head to the front be ready to run to the large dune. We need to hide behind the dune before they circle back to the rear of the building," he pointed to the sand dune. "Also, watch out for large number of thorns. I am bleeding. The thorns went through my gloves."

Dak looked at Hulk as Hulk watched the rear elevation of the building. He smiled at his friend, "You literally have thorns sticking to every inch of your pant legs. You are doing a good job of clearing us a path. This thorn covered beach was not part of our known challenges. I will have to tell General Claiborne he did a very poor job of considering our route."

Hulk kept his gaze on the building, "Good luck with that complainant. It will be fled in the folder with the other items under the label, do not give a shit." Now. Follow me." As soon as the soldiers turned the corner, the three ran for the cover of the small sand dune fifty-yards ahead located at the rear of the building. They laid with their backs on the ground hidden behind the dune. Hulk turned and peered over the edge of the top of the dune. He then waited for the guards to walk back across the rear area and turn the corner along the west elevation. The three then crawled to the rear retaining wall of the beach front and placed their backs against the wall as the two guards made another lap. Dak motioned for Hulk and Zenith to be ready. As soon as the guards cleared the corner, Dak knelt on a knee for Hulk to step on his shoulders and scale the ten-foot-high wall. Hulk stood on Dak's shoulders and reached for the top of the wall. He pulled himself over the wall. Hulk reached downward for the weapons as Zenith then stood on Dak's shoulders. Hulk placed the weapons on the floor of the large porch and then reached downward to pull Zenith over the top of the wall. Dak took several steps back in order to use his momentum to scale the wall. He ran toward the wall and lunged upward as he ran up the wall and then he grabbed the top of the wall as Hulk reached and pull him by his coat over the top of the wall. They heard the footsteps approaching the corner as the guards approached for another round. They scrambled and hid under a table positioned on the rear patio in the nick of time as the guards approached making another lap. Dak peered from under the table and noticed the sand on the sidewalk where they had crawled across the deck and hid under the table. He also could see blood from Hulk's hand on the top of the wall. He thought the guards will see the clumps of sand and blood on the deck and wall. He pulled his sword and waited. He motioned at the sand and blood and noticed the recognition in the eyes of Hulk and Zenith. The guards turned the corner and walked by them as their attention was focused looking for ships at sea. They had not considered three people hiding under a table on the rear patio. As soon as the guards cleared the corner and disappeared, Dak and Zenith crawled from under the table and used their hands to brush the sand off the sidewalk and spread it out on the walkway. Dak wiped the blood from the wall, and they then crawled back under the table.

They waited for close to thirty minutes and were in position as the sun started to rise over the eastern Atlantic Ocean horizon. The horn then sounded, and they crawled out from under the table. "The war has begun," whispered Hulk.

Dak could feel his adrenaline increase. He looked at Hulk who looked worried. He noticed Zenith appeared to be ready with a determined expression. Dak tried to hide his anxious feeling and took a couple of deep breaths. He thought about the scope of the mission and how he or Zenith would have to kill one of the most dangerous men on earth. He thought to himself, "A rogue Blueblood with his enhanced reflexes, strength, and elevated intelligence is designed to be a psychotic killing machine. Trying to kill him will be precarious." He looked down at the walkway and prayed for Zenith and Hulk. Dak just realized the chances of all of them living through this mission was slim.

From the front porch of the building housing General Cuez, the battle could be watched. General Cuez liked the view and commandeered the community hospital for his office. The building was a two story with the back overlooking the harbor and ocean with the front of the building facing north into the town. The three knew they had to wait for the battle to be on going for fifteen minutes before they approached. They could hear men yelling orders and horses with riders riding away from the building to the battlefield. The plan seemed to be working as the captains of the Normand army were leaving the building into the battle lines along with the squads of soldiers. Hulk listened while standing at the east rear corner and then turned and motioned two guards were heading their way. Zenith stepped behind the large stone pillar holding up the second-floor porch. Dak and Hulk forced their backs against the wall. They could hear the boots smacking against the concrete sidewalk as the two guards approached. Once the guards turned the corner, Hulk pulled the inside guard toward him and shoved his knife up through the soldier's upper neck and the blade stuck out the top of the skull.

The second soldier tried to pull his sword and yell. Zenith stepped from behind the pillar and shoved her sword through the man's spine and out his belly. Dak pulled jackets off both men and then dropped the men over the retaining wall to the side of the porch and let them fall next to the sand dune and the ten-foot-high wall. They fell against the wall out of sight. Dak said, "They will not be making any more rounds. We need to move forward with the plan. The other guards will wonder what happened to them. Follow me." He and Hulk placed the two jackets on. Dak led the two around the rear and then the west elevation of the building.

Dak paused once they came to the front corner. He pulled the shaving mirror out of his inside shirt pocket and used the mirror to inspect the front elevation. He looked at the mirror and adjusted the angle up and then down. He held up two fingers for Zenith and Hulk. They heard someone run down the stairs inside the building and then out the front door as Dak pulled back the mirror. The soldier was a messenger for the captains in the field.

Hulk glanced through the first-floor window on the side of the building and motioned with his hand that General Cuez was on the second floor watching the battle. The messenger had run down the interior stairs. There were two guards watching the interior stairway.

Dak counted down from three to one.

Dak stepped out from behind the wall and walked behind the first guard. The two guards were fixated on the battle as they were standing near the steps leading to the sidewalk and the yard. He cut the first guard across the back of the left leg cutting the hamstring, and Hulk followed and shoved his knife in the injured guard's ear hole, killing the guard quickly. Dak tried to be quiet. The second guard was closer to the other side of the porch. His peripheral view was restricted with the helmet. Dak cut his throat from behind as he forced his knife under the metal throat protector and forced him down. Zenith had not hesitated. The guard was going to yell as she rammed her sword through the thin metal in front of the mouth.

Dak turned and picked up a shield from the dead guard and ran across the porch and opened the two doors. Once inside the building, the two guards stationed in the back near the stairway aimed their cross bows. Dak blocked the arrow with the wooden shield as the arrow stuck into the front of the shield. He blocked the second arrow with the shield as he ran toward the guards. He kicked the bow upward and then forced his sword through the man's chest. Zenith followed him and killed the second guard as he was trying to reload the cross bow. She was the first up the stairs.

Hulk closed the double doors and rammed the bolt into the floor, securing the doors shut. Hulk removed his Normand coat and watched Dak run up the stairs behind Zenith.

Zenith opened the double doors for Dak and stood to the side. He walked through the double doors with Zenith right behind him. To his surprise, General Cuez was in the back corner of the large room and not at the balcony watching the battle. The room had an extra high vaulted ceiling and was close to twenty feet by thirty feet in size. They were mid-way across the room when they realized their mistake. The guards were all gathered watching the battle from the balcony. General Cuez was not scared or surprised. He ordered, "Guards kill the intruders."

The six guards were all watching the ongoing battle from the view off the balcony. The six men turned toward Dak and Zenith. Dak noticed these men did not wear the extra heavy shields and bulky armor. He knew they would be quicker and deadlier than the other Normand soldiers. Dak quickly removed the Normand guard's coat and immediately absorbed the swing from the first overconfident guard catching the blade with his Sai sword between his small blade and the large two-foot-six-inch blade with his left hand. Dak caught the swing and rammed his second Sai sword through the man's chest. He pushed the dying man in the path of the next oncoming guard.

Zenith blocked the swing and stepped backward as the guard came forward. The guards were very aggressive with the attacks against both Dak and Zenith. She was trying to keep engaged with one guard at a time and out of reach of the other guard. She however knew time was not on her side. She anticipated Dak would need help. She also knew she did not want to turn her back on the deadest man in the room, General Cuez. The other guard was trying to out flank her as she kept trying to slide to the side and face the area where the General was watching. She stepped forward in an aggressive move between the two guards, killing the one on the left with a cut to his carotid artery. She swung her sword backward without looking and caught the second guard in the face. She then turned and swung her sword full force, decapitating the second man.

Dak jumped backward at the swing. The second guard swung from his side. Dak caught the second guard's swing with the Sai sword in his left hand and slid under him and planted his foot with a Karate kick to the man's knee cap. He then turned and blocked the other man's swing with his blade sliding down the length of the longer blade and stopping at the handle with the small blade on his Sai sword in his right hand. Catching the blade between his sword blades, Dak twisted the sword with force. The man was not expecting his wrist to be twisted as he tried to hold the handle of his sword. He dropped his sword. Dak was too fast on his feet and rammed his other Sai sword through the man's belly. He turned, and the man had fallen from the Karata kick, and he could not defend himself. Dak cut him deep in the other leg and then stuck his other sword through the man's chest. Dak was watching General Cuez as the guard died.

Zenith had been in a sword fight with the last of the six guards. She was able to back him up against the double doors leading out on the balcony and then cut his arm. The man dropped his sword, and Zenith ended his life. They both turned their attention to the only other person in the room.

General Cuez clapped his hands, "Great display of fighting. Is there any chance you two would come and work for me? I will pay you three times what the other side is paying you. I will make you a deal worth a lot of land. You may have your own region of this territory. All you must do is pledge your allegiance to me as a soldier in King Solman's army and of course kill a lot of the soldiers in the field facing us." He grinned and seemed confident in his suggestions.

Dak walked toward the rear double doors to cut off his possible retreat, "There is no way in hell I would work for you," snapped Dak.

"That is a shame. The alternative is I kill both of you. I could use you two handling the pockets of resistance in the region. I could make both of you captains. You will want to be on the winning side when all this is over." He pulled his hatchet. "I really like your two Sai swords. I have never seen someone fight with Sai swords. My men saw the shorter swords with the two shorter blades coming from the handles and misjudged your abilities. You handle them very effectively. After I kill you, I will take them and train with them. I might switch my longer sword and hatchet for them. You don't mind, do you?" He smiled. "I hate to put pressure on you, but I will kill both of you with easy. You are no match for my skills with a sword."

Dak adjusted his position as he moved closer with his right foot out front, "The pressure you speak of is a privilege, and it is a privilege to kill one that has orchestrated mass murder all over the southern part of our continent."

"So, you think you and this female can kill me? I assure you; I will kill both of you without breaking a sweat. You have no clue about my power."

Zenith stepped closer, "You have ordered the killing of thousands, and now I am going to kill you." She pulled back her mask and hood revealing her blond hair and pointed ears.

General Cuez was caught off guard by the revelation these two people who had just killed his six guards were Blueblood warriors. He quickly recovered from underestimating the situation. He pulled his four-foot-long sword with his right hand and held his hatchet with his left hand and smiled. "So, you two are Bluebloods. I now assume you were trained in Merlin. The Merlin Bluebloods are all inferior to me. I will kill both of you. Then my soldiers in the field will kill your scum friends." He glanced at Zenith, "I can now sense your fear." He glanced at Dak, "Why can I not sense your presence?"

"Because I do not fear you."

He studied Dak with a perplexed expression, "No. That is not the reason."

We will deal with you the same as we dealt with the three assassins you sent from Asia to Cliff Tops," Dak announced.

"You are wrong on both accounts." He stepped forward looking at both Zenith and Dak. He appeared to be lining them up and determining which one to kill first. "I know nothing about assassins from Asia, and I will kill both of you. I will kill you first, so she can watch you die and then I will rape her. I will then make her available to all my soldiers before I kill her. You two are no match for me." Dak knew he was trying to anger him to attack without Zenith's support.

Dak snapped, "We know you are a Blueblood. You, King Solman, and Senator Dale are Bluebloods from a genetic pool from the old German country. Your genetics were tampered with by some sick scientist."

He looked at Dak with a surprised expression. How do you know about the sect of Bluebloods from Germany?"

"So, you admit you three are Bluebloods."

"I admit nothing except I am getting bored with you. After I kill you and your army, I will attack your homeland and take that hidden coal from your tribe."

Dak looked at General Cuez with a perplexed expression.

General Cuez smiled, "I am the only one who knows your secret."

Dak looked at Zenith, "You need to take my lead. He is very deadly, but he can be killed."

General Cuez looked relaxed and confident, "You are not the first pair of Bluebloods I have killed, and you won't be the last. I cannot believe your army with less soldiers thought they could defeat my army. You came right into my trap."

Zenith moved closer, "What about your superior guards lying on the floor bleeding and dying? Was this part of your plan? I don't think so. You have fallen into our web. We have got you isolated and trapped. There is no one coming to help you."

Dak quickly approached and swung his sword with his right-hand. The General was prepared and blocked the swing and then immediately swung at Dak with his hatchet before Dak could pull his sword away. He had been lucky to block the hatchet with his blade with the second sword in his left hand. The General's

223

reflexes were a lot more attuned for battle than his guards had been. The quick response forced Dak to jump backward. Zenith had not hesitated and swung her sword four quick times with the General blocking all four swings twice with the hatchet and twice with his sword. The General moved away from Dak, so Dak could not attack him at the same time he was engaged with Zenith. He aggressively went after Zenith pushing her backward with both his sword and his hatchet swings while blocking her swings. Dak approached fast and swung his sword in his left hand, and again, the General turned and blocked the swing, and doing so, he stepped away from Zenith's reach. He spun and kicked Dak in the chest knocking him down on his back. Dak immediately rolled over and stood and ran back toward the General. Dak was scared he would kill Zenith if he did not press the attack. The two kept pushing the General toward the wall with each taking turns swinging and then recoiling, waiting for the other to swing. They knew he could only move backward so far.

They finally had him pushed against the wall with Dak on the left and Zenith on the right. He stood straight and peered at both, "I am going to kill both of you. Matter of fact, you two will be the ninth and tenth Blueblood soldiers I have executed. You are not near good enough, and now I will show both of you."

The confidence in his voice spooked Dak. Neither one had been able to infiltrate his defenses with both trying to attack at the same time. The General had been able to move from side to side so quickly, he was always fighting one at a time and out of the reach of the other. Dak knew Zenith was no match for someone who had killed so many men in battle. He was not certain he could take him. The general seemed to know what he and Zenith were going to do before they did it. Dak now realized the General had trained for hours fighting multiple men at one time. He was very well prepared. He had easily blocked every swing. Dak noticed the confident look in the General's eyes. Dak sensed he was going to draw Zenith in closer and then kill her first. Dak yelled and threw his sword from above his head in his right hand toward the General. The General blocked the sword with his sword making a loud clanging noise when the sword bounced off the wall behind the General and then fell to the floor.

Zenith had seen out of her peripheral vision as Dak pulled the sword in his right hand behind his head to throw it overhanded with force. She knew with Dak only having one sword she had to make a daring unpredictable charge. She slid under the hatchet and went low without trying to block the swing. The hatchet swing had missed her by a fraction of an inch as she bent her torso backward while staying on her feet. She then dropped to her knee and swung her sword upward cutting the General in his left upper arm forcing him to drop his hatchet. She immediately placed her sword above her head with her left hand holding the blade with her right hand on the handle and blocked his powerful downward swing which would have split her head. The swords made a loud sound with the two metal blades colliding. She immediately tumbled backward and stood.

The General grunted as the blood started oozing from the left humerus bone area. Dak stood back and watched. He asked, "How long? Two minutes."

He tried to lunge forward toward Dak. Dak stepped further backwards. "We can wait two minutes for you to bleed out. You will need to lay your sword down to clamp off the artery in your arm to stop the bleeding and when you lay your sword down to install a tourniquet, apply pressure, and the clamp, I will cut your Blueblood head off. I will then show your head to your soldiers, so they will know they are the ones on the losing side."

The General looked at both Dak and Zenith with hatred. He now was afraid, and fear showed in his eyes. He was desperate to have a fast win. Dak stood facing General Cuez constantly switching his one sword from his right hand to his left hand and not allowing the General the advantage of knowing which side to attack. General Cuez ran toward Dak with his sword held high above his head. When he swung downward, Dak blocked the sword with the sword in his left hand and planted his right forearm in the chest of the General and drove the General backward slamming him hard against the wall. Dak was angry with General Cuez coming so close to killing Zenith. He grabbed the sword from his left hand and held the General's right hand out to the side with his sword pressed against the wall. He repositioned his right forearm in his neck while now holding his sword in his right hand. He used his body weight as leverage to force him against the wall with his forearm pressing against his throat.

226

Dak gritted his teeth. "You psychotic asshole. I want you to know the man that killed you is not a Blueblood, just a simple rancher, part time hunter and fisherman." He held the General in position, and the two men stared at each other. The General started to lift his left arm with it hanging limply by his side bleeding. The arm would not respond and could hardly be moved. The excessive amount of blood was running out of the humerus area of the arm unto the floor.

Zenith hesitated, not wanting to take a chance hitting Dak. She knew the General still had a lot of fight left in him. She swung her sword down cutting deep into the General's left ankle as it was positioned against the wall a few inches from the back of Dak's right leg. He started to fall, and Dak removed his forearm hold against his neck and in one quick motion he pulled his sword blade deep into his neck cutting the General's head off. He dropped the hold on the right wrist and stepped backward. He turned and glanced at Zenith. Neither said a word but looked at the body of the dead man.

They heard Hulk running up the stairs, "We got company." Hulk ran into the room and looked at the seven dead men and all the blood. He saw his two friends standing, looking at each other with Dak holding his sword over the now decapitated dead General.

Dak placed his sword in the sleeve and picked up his other sword. He then picked up General's Cuez's head by the hair and followed Zenith to the stairway. Hulk said, "We've got to retreat." They ran down the stairs. Hulk ran over to the window and was

227

watching. Dak ran toward the doors. "Open the doors," Dak commanded.

Hulk pulled up on the metal stop inserted in the floor keeping the doors from opening. Hulk looked at Dak and then noticed he was carrying the head of the General. He pulled the doors open. Dak stepped on the porch facing the squad as one of the captains and several guards approached. They slowed when they saw Dak and Zenith walk out on the front porch. Hulk stepped out from behind Zenith with his bow up and ready.

The Captain held his hand for his men to halt. He noticed the two dead guards on the front porch. Dak tossed the General's head down the stairs with the head stopping at the captain's feet. "It is over. Your General Cuez was a Blueblood and now he is dead. You need to lay down your swords, or we will kill you."

"What? You have lost the battle. Your men retreated."

"We did not lose the battle. That was a decoy, so we could kill this bastard general of yours. You men now are free of his control. You need to drop your weapons."

"Bullshit. Now, we will kill you three."

Dak pulled his knife from the holder over his left shoulder and threw the knife, burying the blade all the way to the hilt in the man's neck. The captain fell backward dead. Dak asked, "Who is next in command?"

The man on the far side of the yard had kept inching forward. He fired his arrow toward Dak. Zenith stepped forward and blocked the arrow with her sword. Hulk quickly changed his aim and released his arrow. The shot hit the man in the center chest.

"Rush them."

The three ran back into the building with Hulk locking the double doors by ramming the metal stop attached to the bottom of the doors into the holes in the floor. The men started beating on the doors. "This will hold for a couple of minutes tops," proclaimed Hulk.

Dak asked, "Anybody got a better idea? They called my bluff."

Zenith smiled at the thought of the bluff. She said, "I will find the back door." Dak picked up a cross bow from the dead guard he had killed earlier and loaded it. He looked at the other dead guard Zenith had killed and jumped over him lying in the floor as he followed Hulk to the rear hallway.

Zenith glanced through the window next to the door, "I found the back door, but there are soldiers waiting on the other side. We are surrounded."

Hulk yelled, "The front door is being breached. We have no choice."

Dak motioned for Zenith to open the rear door. She moved to the side behind the wall as she released the handle of the one door. The door swung open. Dak and Hulk fired their arrows through the open door. Both hitting soldiers stationed outside. Hulk stepped behind the wall and loaded another arrow. Dak and Zenith both pushed out the door with swords pulled. Dak immediately dove to the ground, dodging several arrows. Zenith blocked two arrows.

Hulk stepped from behind the wall into the doorway and shot his second arrow. The Normand archer standing in the middle between several other archers was hit by the arrow in his center chest. Hulk then rolled behind the wall and out from behind the door opening. Dak yelled! "We must retreat. We cannot get through this way. There are too many of them." He and Zenith jumped back through the door as three arrows stuck into the exterior door.

They heard the front door being breached. Dak ordered, "Go up the stairs. We will make our stand upstairs." The three ran up the stairs. Dak picked up a shield and handed it to Hulk and then slid one over to Zenith. He held the third shield up, "We fight to the death." They stood at the top of the stairs and waited. They heard a horn blow in the distance. They heard men from the rear of the building running around the side elevation toward the front. Hulk peered over the rail and did not see any Normand soldiers charging through the doorway or up the stairs. He looked at Dak and Zenith and shook his head no.

Zenith looked at Dak with a puzzled look and ran toward the balcony. She and Dak looked out the window peering over the battlefield. "Billy Ray has ordered an all-out assault on the front lines," yelled Dak. Dak noticed movement and glanced to the south and saw coming up the beach was several hundred men on horseback. He noticed Vulture was leading the crusade. The men from New Foundland had ridden the horses to the ocean on The Ocean Front Trail west of their location and then followed the shoreline south. There were no Normand soldiers in their path at the shoreline. The fighters entered the battle and immediately attacked the battle lines from the rear. The Normand soldiers had been out flanked and were driven inward toward the middle of the battlefield. With Vulture's men attacking from the rear on horseback, the New York men were able to breach the gate and force the Normand soldiers to retreat toward the middle of the battlefield.

Hulk walked over next to Dak. "I will be damned. The New Foundland fighters must have rested and recovered from their siege and decide to volunteer to come south and fight."

Veronica surprised them when she walked next to them as the three stood in a row watching the battlefield. She had her bow out and arrow loaded. "You know you really should watch your backs. I killed those four remaining guards right after you closed the door. The rest of the guards heard the horn and headed for the battlefield. Those four remaining guards did not watch their backs either."

Hulk then said, "I guess you shot them in the back?"

"They should have turned to fight. The fourth one finally realized someone was killing his comrades, and he ran. He also took my arrow in the back."

Hulk smiled, "Let's jump off the balcony and go kill a few Normand soldiers."

Dak said, "Why don't we walk down the stairs and out the front door and kill them all?"

***

The battle raged for more than another hour. The Normand army commanders had not considered they could have been out flanked from the shoreline and attacked from the west. Their scouts had not reported any other warriors in the area. They also had not considered the four warriors attacking from the rear and killing General Cuez.

Zenith jumped on the back of a horse that was tied off and immediately rode into the battle killing Normand archers standing in the rear firing their arrows over the infantry men into the battlelines of her men.

Veronica ran in behind the rear line of archers and started shooting the archers from the rear. They were all focused on the battle in front of them. She settled on one knee and shot the archer at about ten feet in the back. Her quickness to reload an arrow was the part of shooting she excelled. Her ability to load arrow after arrow was quicker than Robin Hood. She shot another archer at twenty feet in the side as he was about to release his arrow. As she reloaded another arrow, the Normand archer noticed the man next to him fell over in pain. He looked at Veronica and jumped for the ground. Veronica adjusted her aim and released the arrow hitting the fourth man located forty feet away in the side of the head. The third man pulled his arrow and was trying to load his bow. He was nervous and the arrow slid off the string in his right hand. Veronica shot him through the chest as he was bringing his bow up for a shot. She quickly fired at the fifth man in the row hitting him in the right shoulder. She watched as Zenith was over two-hundred-yards approached the archers on horseback and cut three of the archers down as she rode behind them heading away from her.

Dak and Hulk ran toward the back lines of the east battle lines in support of Eric of Newport and his men advancing on the bridge. Hulk walked up behind the captain of the Normand army and cut his head off as he was yelling commands to his soldiers. Dak had likewise killed the archer commander and then used his shield to block arrows as he would charge and kill the archers. Once the archers were distracted, the fighting on the bridge was no longer a stalemate. The Cliff Tops archers would fire arrow after arrow. The Normand soldiers would use the shields to block the arrows. The infantry soldiers would spear the cowering soldiers hidden by the shields on the bridge. The battle on the bridge was brutal. Once Dak was able to kill enough of the archers to create a path to the bridge, he ran into the fighting soldiers with both swords, killing Normand soldier after Normand soldier. Hulk followed him and was trying to protect his rear flank. Dak made it to the middle of the bridge and yelled through clinched teeth with his two swords above his head for the men from Cliff Tops to rally behind him and follow him into battle.

Trey and Tommy Boy were the first two to cross the bridge. They saw Dak and followed Dak into the flanks of the battle. Now, with one gate and one bridge fallen, Billy Ray led his ten soldiers into the war. He had been watching from the knoll. He knew it was now or never. They had to win. They could not afford to lose and retreat was not an option. Billy Ray waited until one of the bridges was opened. He knew, with Vulture and his men pushing the west flank toward the middle, he and his men would attack the now open bridge on the east and help surround the Normand army.

Dak would catch the sword blade of the Normand soldier in between the small blade of his left Sai sword and the longer blade and twist just enough to hold the Normand soldier's sword in place and in some instances pull the soldier forward or at least make the soldier lean forward. He would then finish the soldier with his blade of his right hand. He either would cut an arm or a foot. Gutting the Normand soldier took an extra second, and he had no time to spare before the next soldier was attacking him. Either way, with a severely injured appendage, the soldier would fight no more. Dak knew he needed to protect his back from an attack, but he kept pushing to the next man and then the next. He in one instance caught two swords at the same time with his blades in both hands from two soldiers attacking from each side. He turned and kicked the Normand soldier in the head with a Karate kick and then returned to the other soldier, killing him by blocking his swing and then ramming his sword through the soldier's neck. He then turned back to the soldier he had kicked and immediately sliced him down his face as he hit him with his fist and then the short blade of his sword from his left hand. There was never time to consider any other option other than swinging the two swords, blocking swords, and killing the next soldier.

Trey, Tommy Boy, and Hulk worked as a team with shields up and killing the opposition as they moved toward the middle of the battlefield. There were still archers in the area shooting into the ranks of Cliff Tops men. Hulk yelled at Tommy Boy, "Dak has left our group. He has no one backing him up. I am going to try to help him." Hulk ran thirty feet across the battlefield, fighting soldiers as he went. He could not quite reach Dak for the soldiers blocking his path.

Little Jimmy hit several Normand soldiers with the hammer end of the spear. He also stabbed his spear through several of the Normand soldiers on the bridge. He would move forward two yards and then be forced backwards two yards. The bridge battle had turned brutal with blood on the decking on the bridge from men from both sides. Little Jimmy had been hit by an arrow in the upper right shoulder fired from an archer over eighty-five feet away located on the back row. Little Jimmy had gotten so mad he bull-rushed the middle of the bridge guards pushing them backwards, knocking them down. He stepped forward with the arrow in his shoulder and blocked another arrow from an archer at ten-feet away. The archers kept firing arrow after arrow at his men. He hit two infantry men with his hammer and then his spear. His men followed him across the bridge taking on the Normand soldiers with swords. The New York tribe archers had been trained to provide cover fire as the infantry men advanced across the bridge. They fired arrow after arrow into the fighting men.

Veronica turned to face the archers in the far east area of the battlefield. They were over two-hundred feet away. She knew they were close to the limit of her range with her small bow. She aimed high. She figured if she missed the front archer maybe the second or third archer would be hit as the men stood in a row. Her first arrow missed the first archer and hit the second one in the ankle. She immediately adjusted her second arrow and hit the first archer in the back. She fired her final arrow higher hitting the third archer at close to two-hundred-twenty feet.

She ran to one of the first archers she had killed and pulled his pouch of arrows from his dead body. She moved to the middle of the battlefield. She saw her father, Little Jimmy, take the arrow in his shoulder. She tracked the archer and took a deep breath releasing the arrow hitting him in the face. She looked back at her father. He had rushed over the middle of the bridge. She looked east and saw Dak fighting from the east pushing toward the middle bridge and Hulk trying to reach him. She knew they should be fighting as a team. She noticed Tommy Boy and her brother, Trey, with their backs to one another using their shields to block arrows and then fight the infantry men. She turned to see Zenith had turned her horse and was blocking arrows and then killing the archers as she was heading back toward her. Vulture, Hershel, and their men had been stalled and were fighting on the west front. The Normand soldiers had collapsed inward and created a natural wall with the shields.

Veronica looked around her to make certain she was not being stalked. She aimed at another archer and hit him in the back at thirty feet away. She fired three more arrows in the general area where Dak was outnumbered hitting three infantry men. The Normand soldiers had realized the trenches were a death trap, and they had to fight the men from behind them. She knew Dak and Hulk were going to be overrun. She fired arrow after arrow into the infantry men rising out of the trenches.

The battle seemed to turn once Billy Ray and his horse riders crossed the bridge and killed the archers on the east ridge. All the Cliff Tops men advanced across the bridge and circled behind the Normand soldiers in the middle of the battlefield. Once the Normand archers had all been eliminated, the beginning of the end started for the Normand infantry soldiers. The Normand soldiers from the east flank had no support and were being attacked from the front and two sides. Zenith had ridden next to Veronica and jumped off her horse. She picked up a bow from the dead Normand soldier, and she and Veronica both fired arrow after arrow into the infantry men.

The east flank of Normand soldiers had all been killed. The soldiers in the middle had been overrun and killed. The Normand soldiers on the west flank had fought hard and then realized all their comrades had been killed. The horn sounded after seventy-two minutes of fighting. The warriors stepped backward and looked at the Normand soldiers.

Little Jimmy had been shot by a second arrow in his back. The silk shirt and extra padded vest had protected him. He stood with two arrows, one in his back and one in his shoulder, and looked at the Normand soldiers and demanded they drop their weapons. "You will be killed if you do not drop your weapons. You need to surrender." The Normand soldiers looked over the battlefield and saw all the dead men. The one front soldier facing Little Jimmy threw his sword down and then the rest did one after another.

Chapter 25

Aquarius bowed as he stood before the Merlin Senate. Senator Dale announced, "Let the interview begin." Aquarius raised his head and stared straight in front of him. Senator Dale turned to his left and motioned for Senator Blackmon to begin.

"Let the record reflect this man before us, Aquarius was on a special assignment at the request of this Merlin Senate for one-hundred-twenty-three days. What do you have to report?"

Aquarius looked at his boss sitting at the end of the panel, "On the forty-third day of the journey, Samuel and I were attacked by a large contingent of Midlanders. As we were fleeing, Samuel's horse stumbled, and both he and his horse fell to their deaths into a dry-creek bed. I was able to flee north and elude the Midlanders. I regret to report General Samuel is dead.

"I kept traveling east in my attempt to accomplish the mission. On the fifty-first day of the journey, I met a fellow traveler. His name was Thomas. He indicated my daughter and the young sword fighter had perished into a nuclear waste pit several weeks prior and never returned.

"Thomas was certain there was no way to travel to the east coast from where I was located unless I would be willing to brave the frozen tundra in the far north. He indicated to travel further east, I would first have to travel north through the jet stream into the harsh cold desert. I was unprepared for the below zero daytime temperatures and the nighttime temperatures would be as low as negative seventy degrees."

Aquarius turned his head and looked at Senator Dale in the middle, "Based on my situation, I turned and headed for Merlin. I regret I was unable to travel all the way across the continent to the east coast and the city of Cliff Tops."

Senator Blackmon asked, "Do you have proof Samuel is dead?"

"I do not have proof. I could not check on him for fear of being captured. I can tell you; he fell down the embankment over fifty-feet from the top of the cliff before he landed headfirst in the rock covered bottom of the gorge. There was no way a man could have survived the fall."

Senator Blackmon said, "I have one follow up question. Do you have proof of your daughter and the young man named Dak being killed or dying in the waste pit?"

"I do not have proof of their deaths for fear of traveling into a nuclear waste pit. However, I do have a written statement signed by the man I encountered. Thomas states they traveled into the nuclear waste pit and would have died inside the danger zone. Here's the statement." He handed the statement to the clerk.

Senator Dale stared at Aquarius, and it was obvious to the others he was trying to discern how to cross exam him. Could his story be proven otherwise. He then spoke, "Let the record show, Aquarius has failed to be successful on the mission entrusted to him by this same Senate. He has also failed to provide proof of his traveling companion, General Samuel, being alive. However, we in the

240

senate will move forward with the following, General Samuel, Zenith, and the man named Dak will be recorded in our records as being deceased as noted in this interview."

Chapter 26

As Billy Ray walked by the front yard, he saw General Cuez's head on a picket attached to the white fence. He walked into the building, "We killed over one-thousand-one hundred Normand soldiers today, and we lost approximately one-hundred-twenty-five men. We have over two-hundred wounded. Some of the wounded men kept fighting after they had been hit by an arrow or cut by a sword. I would say all-in-all we had a successful battle."

Dak sat on the floor with Zenith next to him. They both looked tired. Trey and Tommy Boy were sitting across from them, drinking water and resting. Hulk and Veronica were both lying on benches trying to sleep.

Dak looked at Billy Ray, "Vulture and his men made a huge difference. They out flanked the Normand lines. Did you know they were going to be here fighting with us?" Everyone got quiet.

Billy Ray looked around at the young warriors. They were covered in blood, sweat, and dirt. They all looked tired and hungry. "Yes, I knew they were approaching from the shoreline. They were our ace in the hole. We only had the one shot of winning this battle. We had no way to reinforce our position and no supply lines. Either we were going to win today, or we were going to retreat and run to our home. They had us out-numbered and could have chased us all the way to Midnight Hole."

Dak asked, "Why did you not inform us Vulture, Hershel and their men would be fighting with us?"

"Dak, your mission, and your unit's mission was to kill General Cuez. You four then were going to leave on the raft. I was not certain when Vulture and his men would arrive. I did not want you four sitting behind the enemy line waiting for a battle that might not take place. I was not certain they would not encounter a Normand patrol on the way and not make it. I knew we needed them, but I also knew they might decide not to fight with us."

Zenith looked up and asked, "Now what?"

"You guys need to eat, drink, and rest. Some of us will head home tomorrow with the wounded. Some will need to stay and set up a network and a functional resistance group. King Solman now will know he is in a war with a formidable adversary. This will make him unpredictable and more cautious. Vulture and Hershel are out recruiting men to fight and try to hold this harbor. We sent some men out to commandeer the anchored boats. War is coming. This was a great battle, but this was a small part of the war to come. We lost too many men. We cannot afford to lose one-hundred-twenty-five men in our next battle."

Dak looked at Billy Ray, "He did not send the assassins from Asia."

Billy Ray looked at Dak, understanding the significance of what he said.

Hulk sat up on the bench, "What you did out there on the battlefield was not how we had been trained. We were trained to fight as a team. You moved off so fast toward the middle of the battlefield, I could not reach you." He looked at Dak with a stern look, "I almost got killed trying to reach you and provide you support and protect your flank."

Billy Ray looked at the faces of his two sons and then at Dak.

Dak glanced up, "But you did not get killed. Did you?"

Hulk looked at Dak, "Man, you are my best friend. What is going on?"

Dak announced, "We all about got killed today in the Battle of Harpers Ferry Harbor, but we did not. We will live to fight another day. This war, I am afraid, it is in the infancy stage. King Solman will not stop until we are all dead."

Chapter 27

Vicky announced, "I am a little lightheaded. I do not feel good this morning. I believe instead of horseback riding with you today, I must go lay down."

Samuel watched as Vicky walked up the stairs. He did not say anything. He knew she was not feeling good and wanted to be by herself. He walked outside to the snow-covered ground. He walked over to the blacksmith shop and picked up an ax and a bow saw. He knew they all needed additional firewood and coal. No one had been cutting firewood or mining the coal. Some of the men were away hunting seals, and Billy Ray had led his army south.

Vicky laid down in the fetal position and finally fell asleep. When Mia opened her door to check on her, Vicky was surprised it was afternoon. She was very hungry. She and Mia walked down the stairs talking. Vicky ate four pieces of chicken while Delores and Mia watched. She wiped her mouth, "I have never been so hungry. I do not know what has gotten into me. One minute I feel great and then another, I am nauseated. I felt very nauseated this morning, and I slept past lunch." She glanced up as Delores was watching her eat.

Mia smiled and looked at Delores and then back at Vicky. "I believe you are pregnant. Vicky had a mouth full of food and stopped chewing. "There is no way," she mumbled. She finished chewing her food with a look of desperation and wiped her mouth with her napkin. She stood up and walked out the door without saying another word. Vicky looked around as she descended the stairs. She waved at a couple of towns people. She saw Samuel driving a horse pulling a wagon full of firewood. He pulled up next to her. "I cut all this wood by myself." He seemed to be proud of his work.

"Hi Samuel. We need to talk. Can you park that wagon and let me tell you something?"

He applied the brake and the horse stood still. He hopped down. He looked into Vicky's eyes. "Let us walk up toward the cliff top and the view." She looked around to make certain no one could overhear her as they started walking.

"Did you not want me to cut the firewood? With a great number of the men out hunting or fighting down south, I thought I could help."

"No. The firewood was a great idea." She then raised her thumb upward in reference to the firewood. "I just need to talk to you about something else."

Samuel looked at the ocean once they crossed the crest of the hill. Vicky looked at the view and then turned toward Samuel. "Well, Samuel there is no easy way to tell you this, but just tell you." She hesitated and took a deep breath, "I am pregnant."

Chapter 28

Dak stood next to Zenith and watched as Billy Ray addressed the warriors. The one-hundred-seventy-two prisoners stood in the wire pen that had been erected for the enslaved towns people. "We had a great victory here. I am sorry for the loss of our soldiers, but we showed the world we are willing to fight and protect one another. The armies to the south will know we will be a force to be dealt with." He paused and let the shouting die down. "The story of this battle will travel, and others will join our cause. We will stand together as brothers and as one." He paused again for the shouting to die down. "I thank the men from the New York tribe for believing and fighting with us in two battles we have now won." He paused for the shouting again to die down. "I thank the men from the villages lead by Vulture and Hershel. We could not have beat this large army without your help." He hesitated for thirty seconds until the shouting dissipated. "I also want to thank the men and women of my tribe from Cliff Tops who did not back down in the face of overwhelming odds."

After the shouting and celebrating, Vulture yelled for Billy Ray, "General Claiborne, what about these Normand prisoners?"

Several men in the audience yelled, "Kill them!" The Normand soldiers looked at Billy Ray from behind the fence.

Once it got quiet, an elderly man from Harpers Ferry Harbor yelled, "They killed my boys and starved my neighbors as they kept us in the pin. We need to kill them." The audience yelled to kill them. Another man yelled, "They killed hundreds of the people from this village. Kill them."

Another man yelled, "They killed my brother and raped his wife and hauled his kids off to be slaves." The audience all started chanting, "Kill them."

Billy Ray held up his hands for everyone to calm down, "I will meet with advisors, and we will decide on the fate of the prisoners."

***

On the fourth morning after breakfast, Eric of Newport and Little Jimmy stood and watched. Dak walked over and said, "Zenith is a little sick. She has not been feeling good the last two days. She says her stomach is upset, but then it passes." Little Jimmy deadpanned with a look at Dak. "I know what she has." Eric smiled.

Eric of Newport then added, "I believe I also know what is making her sick. The symptoms are very noticeable."

Dak looked at both men very worried.

Little Jimmy reached his shoulder area where the arrow had hit him and rubbed the area and said, "Don't worry. She does not have the B12 Virus. She does not have those types of symptoms."

Billy Ray walked over. Dak said, "Good morning, General Claiborne."

248

Billy Ray looked pissed, "You can cut that shit out about me being a general. I am a soldier and that is the way I would like to be remembered."

Little Jimmy and Eric of Newport both laughed.

"What is wrong with Zenith? Is she sick? You two left a day and half earlier than we did. I thought you two would be further ahead of us on the road home," declared Billy Ray.

Little Jimmy smiled and blew out some wind as he kicked the dirt on the ground. Dak looked perplexed. "These two were about to tell me what is making her ill. They both said it was very common. I am just glad to hear she does not have the B12 virus. Her blood system should fight off all viruses. She should be immune from viruses." He looked nervous.

Eric of Newport looked at Billy Ray, "The illness she has her blood will not fight it off. She gets fatigued easily." He raised one finger. "She has an upset stomach of the morning which causes her to vomit." He held up a second finger. "She has cramping." He held up the third finger.

Billy Ray laughed and said, "Lord have mercy. No wonder we caught up to you on the trail home."

Dak looked worried. Zenith stood up from where she had sat next to the creek and upchucked. She approached the four men. Three of the four were smiling. Zenith asked, "Have you not seen someone have an upset stomach? I would have liked to have some privacy."

Billy Ray smiled and exclaimed, "All three of us have witnessed this at least once." He pointed at Eric of Newport and Little Jimmy. "With our wives and then about eight months later the problem is over until the next pregnancy."

Chapter 29

"You know, Dak, you don't have to help me on and off the horse." She pushed her body tight into his body under the large fur cape. "I can wash myself in the river without you holding my hand. I will be okay."

"Zenith, I am trying to watch out for you. I do not want you to slip and fall on those wet rocks. You're pregnant."

She rolled over and kissed him on the check. "I can do these things myself. I know why you are rushing home, so you can make certain I stay indoors until the baby comes."

"Are you not scared?"

"Yes, Dak, I am scared. I am seventeen-years-old and have a baby growing inside me. My mother died during childbirth."

"I am scared to death."

"I am the one with the baby inside my gut. What are you scared about?"

"I am afraid I will be a failure at being a father. I know nothing about being a dad. I never had a dad."

"You will be a great father. I remember when I first rode into Cliff Tops and all the kids ran up to you for you to pick them up. You will be a great father."

"I remember Eric of Newport and Little Jimmy talking when we all were hunting for seals years ago. Eric told Little Jimmy, the best time to teach a child the golden rule, work ethic, how to love, and about God is during the hobbies with the child. The child will be more apt to listen during the interacting of the hobbies and will want to learn."

Zenith looked at him, "See there you will be a great father."

Dak stared at the ceiling on the tent, "The greatest fear I ever had was six days ago. Did you know I was scared to death when we both were facing General Cuez? I could tell he was trying to draw you in closer. He was going to kill you."

"He was going to kill both of us. I knew you could not beat him with one sword and with him having a sword and a hatchet."

"Zenith, you left your entire side open. If he had swung his hatchet a fraction lower, he would have killed you."

"I figured he would swing the hatchet. The hatchet was not the kill shot. He knew you would hesitate after throwing your sword. I also knew we only had the one chance. He missed, and I countered with my sword on a hard jab that sliced through his arm all the way into his humerus bone. I also knew his second swing coming for my head was his kill shot." She kissed Dak on the cheek. "I love you. I had to take the chance, or he was going to kill you after he killed me."

They kissed and held each other. They both confessed their love for one another. "I just do not know about all this killing. When is it going to stop?"

Zenith pushed his hair away from his forehead, "I believe this is just the beginning. The killing will never stop. In my basic training to be a Blueblood warrior, the instructor taught us how to emotionally accept we have taken another's life, and how to live with the death of the opponent. We were taught killing is the natural order with humans."

Dak said, "Cane killed Abel. The Holy Bible is full of violence."

Dak then mentioned they would need to build a home. He asked Zenith if she wanted to be in close to Cliff Tops or out further in the mountains or along the coastline. She indicated she had not thought about a home. "I wish we could live in peace. The land near the Midnight Hole is good land for cattle and sheep. It is a warmer climate than Cliff Tops."

She looked at him wondering why he mentioned the land. "How far behind us is the army?" asked Zenith.

"Billy Ray, Little Jimmy and Eric of Newport and our friends were going to go hunting for deer. They were taking their time. Billy Ray was held up a couple of days talking to Vulture and Hershel and other leaders about the need for them to oversee the land and the people. He was hoping they could set up some form of government for the people. We need all the people to commit to preparing for the wars to come against the armies in the south. We really need their help. When Billy Ray caught up with those others, they decided to go hunting." He looked away. He then said, "Billy Ray did as he said. He met with his advisors. I was not asked to attend the meeting since you and I had headed home. Vulture, Little Jimmy, Eric of Newport, Hulk, Tommy Boy and the other captains and generals. They voted to turn the prisoners over to the villagers, and Vulture ordered all of them to be executed." He stared at the ceiling. "I could not image decapitating that many men. There is some much hatred in this world, and this war is exposing the dark side of our race. When will we ever learn?"

Zenith looked at her husband, "The Normand army and King Solman has started the war. After people see what we have seen, hatred hidden deep inside of us is being exposed. You know Dak, that is why I fell in love with you is because you were not full of hatred. You have passion for what you believe and empathy for those in need. You try to do the right thing. Please do not change." She kissed him on the cheek.

Dak then added, "Little Jimmy indicated he was not certain why my mother was not happy with my actions being the acting King of Cliff Tops. She obviously did not like me killing Sie."

Zenith was surprised, "Why would he say that? He jumped off his horse and was watching for the men of Meadow Bottoms to fight you. Little Jimmy was with you."

"Evidently, Mia had mentioned to her husband, Little Jimmy, that Queen Vicky was aware of the situation in Meadow Bottoms and was preparing to meet with them to address all the issues in a peaceful manner. Then, she was shot by the two assassins."

***

Dak looked ahead as they rode out of the pine forest. "We made it to the Midnight Hole." He could see farmers and ranchers hauling hay in a wagon. He could see soldiers watching and standing guard. The two rode at a slow pace. When they crossed through the burned down village, they could see the graveyard with the markers of the villagers above the graves. When they made it to the turned-over wagon, two guards rode out to meet them. At first, the New York guards were careful and blocked the road. Zenith pulled back her hood and showed them her blond hair. "I would suggest you two get out of our way. You do not want to piss off a pregnant woman."

The two guards smiled and allowed them to pass. Dak was relieved when they finally made it to Cliff Tops. He saw Robin Hood walk out of the four plex wearing a sling for his shoulder. There were several kids following them, and people were watching them ride toward the fourplex. Dak jumped down and then helped Zenith down. He gave the horse reins to a boy who took the two horses toward the stable. The stable boy announced, "I will take your personal items to The Dive." Dak nodded his head okay at the young man.

Dak walked over and hugged Robin Hood and then Zenith walked over and hugged Robin Hood. Both men smiled at each other. Dak said, "Do I have a story to tell you. We sure did miss you in the battle of Harpers Ferry Harbor." He smiled, "The guys will be here soon. They went hunting. How is the shoulder?"

Robin Hood showed his arm in a sling, "The shoulder is improving every day. It will be okay. It was great news to hear about the battle. I wish I could have been there with you. I missed out on all the glory. It has been a bit boring sitting around talking to the women."

"Yeah. We have not been bored."

Robin Hood smiled, "It is great news to hear about the pregnancy."

Dak looked a little surprised. He pointed to the fourplex as to tell Robin Hood they needed to go inside, "Yes, it is. Zenith and I will see you later." He reached over for Zenith's hand, and they walked into the fourplex and then the kitchen.

Delores looked over as they walked through the doorway, "Lord have mercy. Look what the cat drug in." She smiled. "We figured you guys would be back tomorrow."

Mia and Casey both smiled. Mia said, "It certainly is good to see you returning. Where are my three?"

Little Jimmy and Trey are hunting deer with some of the other guys. Veronica is riding back with the main army. They are a couple days behind us. She is the acting nurse for the wounded. During the battle, Little Jimmy was shot twice by arrows." Dak smiled, "The arrows pissed him off, which helped us win the battle."

She smiled. Mia then said, "He must feel okay if he went hunting."

"It is great news about the pregnancy," said Casey.

Zenith smiled, "The morning sickness comes and goes. But overall, it has not been too bad." She patted Dak on the arm. "He takes good care of me."

Delores, Mia, and Casey all three tried to hide the surprise. They all paused with no one saying a word. Finally, Dak said, "Yeah, Zenith is ready to see Doc Johnson. We would like to make certain she and the baby are okay. We are interested in knowing how far along she is."

Delores came over and hugged Zenith and then Mia and Casey hugged her and assured her they would help her through the pregnancy. Vicky walked into the kitchen and hugged Dak. She then hugged Zenith. "It is so good to see you." Dak looked at his mother, knowing the last time they had talked both had been upset.

Delores, Mia, and Casey all started laughing but were trying to hold it in. They all three excused themselves and walked out of the kitchen, and Dak heard them open the front door to the fourplex. Dak asked, "Are you not excited about the pregnancy? Everyone else seems to be excited about it."

Vicky looked a little off guard. "Yes, I am very excited about the pregnancy. I was not certain how you would feel." She looked out the kitchen window and could see Delores, Casey, and Mia standing in the road laughing so hard they could hardly stand. She saw Delores pointing at the kitchen and telling one of the other women in the town something very funny.

Zenith said, "At first, I was a little scared, but I am excited." Vicky looked at Zenith and smiled as Zenith smiled back at her.

Vicky's expression turned to a look of confusion and a little surprised and said, "I am glad you are happy for me."

"Of course, I am happy for you. You will be a fantastic grandmother. Zenith and I are both happy for you." Vicky felt shocked and looked confused. She turned when Wayne walked into the kitchen.

Wayne smiled and announced, "It is so good to see you two. We were all so worried about the battle. I am sorry our combined army with the New York tribe lost those men, but you killed nearly two-thousand Normand soldiers. The messages were running about two weeks behind. Damn, it is good to see you."

Dak looked at Wayne "The battle was a great victory." Dak did not want to talk about the killing. He was having nightmares when he slept. He wanted to change the topic "We were just talking about the pregnancy when you walked in."

Wayne replied, "Yes, everyone in town has been talking about the pregnancy. We all are so excited. Do you think the people in Harpers Ferry Harbor will stay united and fight King Solman's troops in the years to come?"

Dak replied, "This battle was nothing like the Battle of New York. We hope they understand the threat from the south." He looked stern. Then he said, "Zenith and I need to go see Doc Johnson."

Vicky glanced over Zenith's shoulder out the kitchen window and saw four more people laughing along with Mia, Casey, and Delores in the town street.

Wayne asked, "Are you alright? The reports did not mention you were injured. Why do you need to see the doctor?"

Zenith smiled, "Because we want to make certain the baby is doing okay."

Wayne looked very surprised, "So you are pregnant also?"

Dak looked at his mother and then Wayne, "Zenith is pregnant. Who else is pregnant?"

Wayne looked at everyone and then smiled, "I will be damn. I forgot to send a pigeon to Old Thomas. I better get right on that." He immediately turned and walked out of the kitchen and onto the dirt road. Vicky glanced again over Zenith's shoulder and saw Wayne bending over laughing as the others walked toward him. All were laughing.

Vicky rubbed her forehead and then looked at the two. She walked over to Zenith and hugged her. Dak asked, "Mother, who else is pregnant?"

Vicky turned and smiled, holding her arm around Zenith, "Dak, your mother is pregnant."

Zenith hugged Vicky, "That is great news. That is not what we expected, but what wonderful news. Dak, you will be a father and a big brother in a few months."

Dak was still confused, and his eyes narrowed as he glanced at his mother's stomach, "You are pregnant? Did you and Wayne get married?" He knew his mother and Wayne had always been close friends, but he never thought of them dating. They had never shown interest in being romantically involved with each other.

Vicky looked at Dak. She felt a little nervous. She reached up and rubbed her cross attached to her necklace. She then walked over next to the counter and placed her hand on the countertop and slowly turned to face Dak. "No. Wayne and I did not get married. I have never dated Wayne. Wayne is not the father. Do you need to sit down?"

Dak was perplexed his face reflected worrisome expression. His mind was trying to figure out how, when, where, and most of all who. He blurted out, "Who is the father?"

Samuel walked into the kitchen over to the counter and placed his arm around Vicky.

Vicky smiled and said honey, "Zenith is also pregnant."

Dak looked at Samuel. His nose flared, "You Blueblood bastard. I am going to kill you."

Chapter 30

Wrinkles appeared in her forehead as Vicky glared at Dak and then at Wayne. "That was quite a show you put on two days ago. What do you have to say for yourself?"

Dak looked at Little Jimmy and then Billy Ray. "Mom, I am sorry. I am truly sorry, but do you have any idea who that man is?" He looked at his mother with scorn. "You do not understand he has killed thousands. He would have either killed me in Merlin, or I would have killed him in the trial by combat. The only reason we did not fight was he was out doing his job and killing some defenseless families."

Vicky cut Dak off. "How dare you come into my kitchen, pick a fight, and then bust through our window. You two fell out the window in front of the town people. Do you know how bad this looks on me?" She paused as she stared at Dak. She added, "You took charge and became the King of Cliff Tops and decapitated a citizen. A king is not reckless and immature and does not act in this manner."

"I did. The bastard you speak of committed treason. He talked all the men in Meadow Bottoms into not fighting in the Battle of New York. All your male advisors were present, endorsed the sentence of death, and I cut his head off."

She clenched her jaws, "Do you not think I would have handled the situation? I would have made certain they understood without the capital punishment being enforced. What is the difference between us and the Normand soldiers if we kill our own people?"

Dak could not control his temper, "It was your fault."

Vicky narrowed her eyes. "How was it my fault?"

"You need to announce your heir to the throne. This is a Monarchy government. You did not provide direction for the leadership while you were lying in bed about to die."

"You killed a man."

"I did. I would do it again. We need everyone fighting with us. We cannot win this war if half our tribe has decided not to fight. We need better leadership."

"Wayne will be the king in my absence. How is that for clarity?"

"That is a great choice. Wayne is a good man. I do not want to be the king of this village. I thought the village needed leadership in your absence, and I thought I could help." He looked down at the floor.

"Zenith and I have decided to move to the cliffs out from the Midnight Hole. We talked to ranchers in the area, and the land is for the taking."

Vicky was stunned. "Samuel is not a bad man. He loves me. You need to give him time."

"It is not Samuel. I want to start something on my own. We talked to a couple of ranchers on the way back through from the battle of Harpers Ferry Harbor. The herds are scattered. There is enough stray cattle and sheep to start a ranch. Several of the ranchers were killed."

Billy Ray folded his arms as he stood with a puzzled look on his face, "What about the war?"

"The war might not come after the battle of Harpers Ferry Harbor. But if it does, I will fight and protect my family and friends. Zenith and I did more than our share in the battle of Harpers Ferry Harbor."

"Samuel indicated King Solman will march north in the spring," announced Wayne.

Dak interrupted Wayne. He was frustrated. "He does not know what King Solman will do. You need to be worried about the Blueblood army in Merlin marching west. I have met the Merlin Senators. They are all corrupt. They will do what is best for their wallets. Samuel is one of them. Our world will get smaller from all sides until there is no tomorrow."

Vicky narrowed her eyes with a look of concern. "Wayne, Little Jimmy, Billy Ray, and Eric of Newport all pledged their support for you. They have reported you did excellent, and you need to be rewarded."

"I am very grateful for their support. I will always remember them standing with me." He looked at each of them. "But not everyone supported me." He looked at Delores and then back at his mother, the Queen. "None of the females supported me. Delores would not give me her support. I know behind the scenes Casey and Mia did not support me. Veronica supported me, but she won't take orders. Zenith loves me, and she will not be ordered around by me either. A king must have total obedience and support of all in the realm."

Little Jimmy smiled. "You better hope Zenith is carrying a boy, because if she has a girl, I got news for you, Dak, your daughter won't listen to you either."

Wayne tried to show some humor, "Dak, that is the way females are. Do you think Delores listened to her father? Do you think your mother, our queen, listened to her father while she was growing up?"

"I have decided. I will go south and build a ranch. Zenith and I will move in late spring or early summer." Dak stood and walked out.

Vicky ducked her head in frustration. The men looked at each other. Billy Ray finally announced, "I have work to do. Come on Little Jimmy. Let us see if we can make some better hatchets." Eric also followed them out the door.

Wayne looked grim. "No one mentioned to me that Dak was not happy living here. I will go and talk with him."

Vicky was upset, "Please leave me alone."

***

Little Jimmy observed the hot metal rod he was holding in his gloved hand with the large channel lock pliers. He then looked over at Eric of Newport who was attaching a wooden handle to a hatchet. Little Jimmy said, "I believe Dak is going to leave. I do not believe he is bluffing. Billy Ray thought he had his feelings hurt when his mother made him the leader of the army." Little Jimmy shook his head no. "He was in the middle of the worst fighting I have ever seen in Harpers Ferry Harbor. They were dead men everywhere. The dead were stacked up like firewood. Hell, I know I was shot twice by arrows. If not for the padded vest and silk shirt, I might be laying down south in a grave."

Eric looked stern at Little Jimmy, "So you think the fighting and killing has got young Dak wanting to move?"

"I am just saying all that killing and the danger of being killed can get to a man. He has already killed more men than all of us combined. Plus, he worries about Zenith. He loves that girl."

Eric looked sincere. "I know one thing for certain. He saved our lives by volunteering to go on that mission. I listened to Hulk talk when we were hunting. Dak and Zenith killed the six guards and then killed General Cuez." He hesitated and looked at Little Jimmy eye-to-eye. "He cut General Cuez's head off. The entire floor was covered in blood. We would not have come out of there alive if we had gone."

Little Jimmy looked at Eric as he picked up the hammer and placed the hot metal on the anvil to flatten the end. "Wayne and Vicky also mentioned he is mad about Samuel dating his mother. You know the two will be married soon. I don't see Dak moving based on his mother getting married."

Eric replied, "I was in the middle of the front lines just like you were. We both know about the killing and all the bodies. There is no way one could visualize that battle unless they were there."

Both men looked up as Samuel walked into the blacksmith's shop. His two hatchets were strapped to his back with the handles sticking upward for him to reach over his shoulders and pulled them for combat. He had a four-foot-long sword in his belt along with his knife in his boot. He had another knife strapped to his left side, so he could reach it with either hand. Little Jimmy turned and started beating on the metal trying to knock off the surplus metal debris attached to his spear and flatten the end. He was trying to make himself a second weapon. He wanted a very sharp blade on one end made of metal and a wood rod to lighten the weapon. He wanted the rod to be perfectly balanced. Eric of Newport glanced at Samuel and asked, "What can we do for you?"

Samuel noticed some resentment from some of the people in the tribe. He and Dak had not talked since the fight with them crashing out the window. "Our Queen would like a couple of hatchets like mine. She has been practicing with mine and believes they are better than swords in combat." Little Jimmy kept hitting the metal and did not answer.

Eric wrapped the leather band around the handle and finally asked, "So you want one of us to make her some hatchets?"

Samuel hesitated. He first thought about hitting Eric of Newport. No one in Merlin would have ever ask that of him. They would have started work immediately. "Yes, our Queen desires it immediately."

Little Jimmy kept hitting the metal. Eric said, "We both are busy. We are making us additional weapons, and the shop is backed up with other orders."

Samuel looked at Eric. "I said our Queen is ordering you to make the two hatchets."

Little Jimmy turned, holding the red-hot metal in one hand and the hammer in the other. "Did you not hear him? He said we do not have time. I do not see the Queen in the blacksmith shop making the request. If you want to make her a couple of hatchets, then by all means, go harvest some buried metal buried and have fun. We are busy."

Samuel approached and placed his hand on his sword handle as Wayne walked into the blacksmith shop. He saw the men looking angrily at each other. Wayne yelled, "Hold it right there." He jumped between the men. "Samuel, you need to leave. These men are working for me. We have several pressing items that need to be crafted."

Samuel fastened his sword with the strap back over the sword grip and walked out.

"What was that all about?"

Eric of Newport looked at Wayne, "He came in here and demanded we make Vicky two hatchets. Hell, if it is that important, he can give her his two hatchets."

Little Jimmy started beating on the metal. "I told him to make them himself. We are busy."

"Guys, you don't want to pick a fight with him."

Eric said, "We do not work for him. We are free men; our families are free. The people in this tribe are free. He needs to understand that."

Wayne looked frustrated. "The last man that spoke like that had his head removed over in Meadow Bottoms. You might want to watch what you say. Where is Billy Ray? I need to have a word with him."

Eric replied, "He said he was going to talk to Hulk, Tommy Boy, Trey, and Veronica. He wanted to know why Dak is so upset."

Wayne looked perplexed, "We know why. His mother is pregnant with a man Dak does not respect. Plus, Vicky named me the heir to her throne."

Little Jimmy turned to Wayne, "That is not why he is upset. He was acting a little strange before the Battle of Harpers Ferry Harbor and then after the battle, he was not the same. He and Zenith kept to themselves. They traveled back by themselves." He rammed the hot metal into the bucket of water. The men watched the steam rise. "Wayne, that battle was the worst fighting I have ever seen. You and I have been in some tough situations in the old world with Mrs. Vicky, Eric, and Billy Ray, but nothing like that type of killing. The ground on the front lines were covered with blood. You could hear men crying in pain and begging for help as they were going into shock."

Eric said, "I still remember the first time I killed a man. I killed two men within seconds of each other saving Mrs. Vicky. I felt righteous killing them. They were going to do some bad things to Mrs. Vicky. I used a gun and was standing fifteen feet away. I still remember it every single day. This is a lot different. This is all up close and personal with a sword, hatchet or sometimes an arrow. With the sword and hatchet, you are looking the other man in the eyes or killing him from behind standing so close to him you can smell him. You hardly ever kill a man with the first swing of a sword or the first arrow. You normally must finish him up close. All those butchered men and women can mess with your mind."

Wayne was stern. "So, you think the reason he is wanting to leave our tribe has to do with what he has been through?"

Little Jimmy looked over, "Something was bothering him before he found out about his mother and Samuel and before she announced you as the heir to the throne." Wayne turned and walked out.

Chapter 31

Vicky walked to The Dive, where Zenith and Dak were staying with their friends, and she knocked on the door. Zenith opened the door and asked her to come in. "Dak and the others have gone fishing."

Vicky smiled, "I know. I was wanting to talk to you." She smiled. "How are you doing?"

"I am tired and constantly needing sleep. Dak will not allow me to do much. He waits on me hand-and-foot. He is so protective. I had to beg him to go fishing. I told him I was craving fish just so he would leave." She laughed.

Vicky smiled, "I was wanting to discuss your plans. Hulk told Billy Ray that Dak was going to travel to the Midnight Hole and start on your ranch and future home." She hesitated hoping Zenith would fill her in on the plan, and why they should move.

Zenith looked at Vicky, "He has made up his mind. He wants to start something of his own." She smiled. "I go where he goes."

"So, you would like to stay here? We can build you a home here."

Zenith suspected Vicky was going to try to manipulate her to change Dak's mind. She was curt, "I would like to stay here until after the birth of my child. I feel more comfortable with Doc Johnson assisting with the birth. We will move in early summer."

"You know war is coming."

Zenith looked out the window. "War is coming. In my opinion, the people here in Cliff Tops are not safe. I agreed to go south and fight because I thought we needed to push General Cuez and his army further south. I believe we should have kept moving south setting up resistance fighters. Dak is right, the Senate in Merlin will send troops west. May I ask you a personal question?"

Vicky smiled at Zenith, "Yes of course you may ask me a personal question."

"What is Samuel going to do? Is he going to protect your child?"

Vicky was surprised with the question. "Certainly, he will protect our child. Why ask?"

"Did he tell you that the Senate in Merlin has outlawed any births between a Blueblood and a normal person? The babies are killed immediately after the birth if they are not aborted in the first trimester. The Blueblood controlled senate has ruled, and they do not want the genetic code to be altered. The only way to keep the blood line pure is to control the breeding."

Vicky immediately reached for her tummy and felt horrified. "No, he has not mentioned that to me. He seems to look forward to being a first-time father. I assumed the Merlin Senate passed that legislation years ago and now have accepted half breeds."

"The official line as the law is clearly stated, no half breeds, but yes a few have been permitted to live in Merlin."

She stared at Zenith wondering about her unborn child's safety. "Is Dak, okay? I mean since the Battle of Harpers Ferry Harbor? He seems to have changed."

271

Zenith looked at Vicky, "We were lucky to have killed General Cuez. The general was overconfident. If only one of us had attacked General Cuez, he would have certainly killed either one of us. After we killed General Cuez, Dak changed. He ran into the battle without support from Hulk or me. He went into an uncontrollable rage, killing the Normand soldiers. Hulk tried to talk to him after the battle, and Dak walked off. I believe the killing bothered him. He has nightmares. Us moving away may help him. His passion I believe is he would aspire to be a rancher." Zenith looked Vicky in the eyes, "When going through my training to be a Blueblood warrior, we were trained by two Blueblood commanders. They were not allowed to compete in the warrior tournaments. They were thought to be the best sword fighters in the world. I now know, Dak is better than anyone alive I have seen with a sword, and that will always follow him." She turned away and looked out the window. "Living by the sword, protecting the innocent, and doing the right thing always follows men like Dak. He will never be allowed to be a rancher."

Chapter 32

Dak had risen earlier in the morning and kissed Zenith on the forehead as she slept. He placed a few pieces of coal in the fire. He walked out the rear porch of The Dive and looked at the view over the ocean. He was thankful his nightmare of the war had spared him, and he slept all night with his wife curled up with him under the warm blankets. He knew she was tired and needed to rest more with her pregnancy. He felt refreshed and loved the view watching as the sun was about to appear over the eastern horizon. It was a cold, clear morning, and the village was still asleep. The newly fallen snow helped make the view picturesque. He looked at Little Jimmy and Mia's small cottage and saw the smoke from the chimney. He turned and noticed smoke coming from the four chimneys at his mother's fourplex. He glanced at the rest of the homes and thought of the pretty, peaceful village. He saw smoke coming from the black smith's shop and heard the start of someone using a hammer hitting metal. He wondered who would be up at this time in the morning. He walked at a fast pace to the doors. Normally the doors were left open to allow the excessive heat from the forge to escape the room. He observed Samuel facing the rear while beating on a hot piece of metal. He eased the door open and entered. He leaned against the wall and observed Samuel as he was trying to make something.

"You are doing that all wrong. Once you have melted the metal into a liquid form, you need to reheat the metal to six-hundred degrees Fahrenheit. Then, you need to coat the metal in the oil and saltwater solution at sixty degrees. Otherwise, the metal will be too soft. We use a high-carbon steel forging method to perfect the hardness in a weapon."

Samuel looked over from the anvil and saw Dak leaning against the door casing. "Are you here to finish our fight?" Samuel turned and stared at Dak.

He yawned, "Not right now. Maybe later." He stared back at Samuel. "My mother told me if I hit you again or pushed you out another window, she was going to have me arrested. She seems to be very protective of you." Dak hesitated, "Maybe if she leaves, we can have round two."

Dak walked toward Samuel. "You need to start over. The form used needs to be better defined. The hammer and anvil are not meant to shape the metal into a perfect form. The hammer and anvil are used to chip away the excessive overage. You need to start with a perfect form. Billy Ray keeps his forms in the rack over by the wall." He pointed at the back wall. "If you do not like one of the established forms, you need to construct your form the way you desire. Then, pour the liquid metal into your form. Cool it quickly before it has pockets of carbon set up in it. The carbon is what weakens the metal." He reached toward Samuel. "Let me see that."

Samuel watched as Dak walked toward him. He lifted the hot metal with the channel lock pliers. Dak asked, "What are you making?" He stared at the glob of metal with a perplexed expression.

"I am making our Queen two combat hatchets."

"So that is what this glob of metal is. It takes time. You are rushing the process. You need to start over and forge the metal and pour the liquid metal into the perfect form. Then, if needed, forge it a second time to make certain the shape is to your liking. You need a more precise pattern for the liquid metal to form the instrument you are making. The process takes three days, not a half a day if you would like the hatchets to turn out correctly."

Samuel looked at Dak, "You know how to do this?"

"Yes, I know how to make hatchets. I will show you, but first I need some information from you."

"What do you want to know?"

"When Zenith and I met the six guards in the room with General Cuez, we were lucky to have survived. The only reason we are not dead is that General Cuez was too ignorant. He was not dressed in body armor. He felt safe. He allowed us to kill his six guards as he watched. If he had attacked us in conjunction with his six guards, he would have killed us. Even with his six guards lying dead, he still felt he was superior. I fought Apollo in the trial by combat. He was the youth winner and the man that came in second to you in the Blueblood tournament in Merlin. I won in eleven seconds. I could not have beaten General Cuez without Zenith. He said he had killed eight Bluebloods prior to our battle. Like I said, we were lucky to have won. What do you know about the Blueblood genetic line that originated from the old German Country?"

Samuel peered with surprise at Dak, "They are very deadly. They are psychopaths engineered for one purpose, to kill. They are better than us Bluebloods from Merlin in fighting. We realized for us to survive we would need to hunt them down in large numbers and kill them. There were a few of them that survived the Transition Period. The ones we have killed were loners. We tried to capture one of them for information eleven years ago, and we ended up killing him after he had killed several soldiers in a border town south of Merlin. He killed nine of my best soldiers and one Blueblood before I rammed my spear through his heart. We tracked his kind down and killed a few of them and then they disappeared. We have not run into them since." He looked directly at Dak. "Did General Cuez show signs of pain once he was wounded?"

"He was wounded and could not lift his left arm, but now that you mention it, he showed no signs of being in pain. I believe Zenith fractured his humerus and cut through his upper arm muscle when she drove her sword into his upper arm. Now that I think about his expression, he never showed signs of being in pain. The expression was one of anger for allowing us to injure him."

"They feel no pain. They are engineered with a condition called Congenital Insensitivity to Pain which is a form of Peripheral Neuropathy. You can burn them, you can hit them with a bat, and they show no signs of pain. We killed three females. They seem to have learned to fit in better than the males. They were harder to locate. See this scar on my side." He lifted his two shirts. "The bitch got me. I walked right by her. She was in disguise. I mistook her for a very elderly lady. I saw her move out of my peripheral vision, and I grabbed her sword and held the blade with my left glove hand as it was sticking in my side. She thought I would go for my sword with my right hand, but instead I pulled this knife from my back and rammed the blade through her face." He pulled his knife he had attached to his upper back behind his neck.

"I believe I killed one of the genetic mutant warriors from Germany when I killed General Cuez."

He looked at Dak in shock, "If General Cuez was in fact a Blueblood from Germany, then King Solman is also. General Cuez would not have taken orders from King Solman unless he feared him. They only obey someone out of fear, otherwise they are loners that kill for joy."

Dak looked at Samuel, "I believe King Solman is a Blueblood, and I know Senator Dale is a Blueblood. Both might be from Germany. What do you know about Senator Dale?"

"Senator Dale was not with the first-generation Bluebloods that lived through the Transition Period. We lived in pods in the Artic and survived the Transition Period at great cost to my people. Several Bluebloods starved to death. They were in isolated pods during the long winter with no way to obtain food.

"Senator Dale claimed he was in a pod, and he was the only one to have survived from that pod. He showed up in Merlin during the construction sixteen-years ago, and no one ever questioned him. He has been on the senate ever since."

Dak said, "I believe the three were working together. There might be more." Dak looked back at Samuel. "Now, since General Cuez is dead, there are at least two more psychopath engineer killers. The question is which one is alpha, King Solman or Senator Dale?"

Samuel looked at Dak, "I do not know which one is in charge. They will both send their armies to attack us. They will show no mercy, and they will kill every one of us. In addition, you should not have sent Aquarius back to Merlin. Senator Dale will figure out he is a spy and have Aquarius put to death."

"Aquarius was made aware of the risk. We need someone in Merlin to introduce us to the resistance fighters. We will need their help at some point. I am more concern with the army in Merlin than I am the one headquartered in Southern City. I need Aquarius to be our eyes and ears. Aquarius knows he will need to disappear before Senator Dale and his soldiers find out what he knows. None of us are safe, and you are correct, there is a good chance we all are going to be killed." He looked at Samuel in the eyes. "You mentioned us. Where do you stand?"

Samuel turned and looked at Dak with a stare. "I stand with my Queen and unborn baby. I will fight for them with my last breath."

He stared at Dak, "I love your mother. There is no greater enjoyment in life than to be in love and bed a beautiful woman."

"I will make my mother these two hatchets. We will need to start over. I need you to listen to my plan while we work on these hatchets. We cannot sit back and do nothing."

Chapter 33

Aquarius walked in the hall and approached the door with the inscription above the header, 'Department of Finance'. He knew these men and women would not be receptive to his unscheduled visit. He worked as a clerk for Senator Blackmon who was one of nine Merlin Senators. At least one of the nine Merlin Senators, was always presenting legislation to lower the tax which would be conflicted with the department of Finance. Aquarius knew the Senators must take this position to make the pretense they were trying to help the people of their prospective districts. He also knew the Senators passed laws allowing for tax breaks for the wealthy. One of the largest tax breaks was for the farmers and called the Farm Tax Rate Discount (FTRD). The Senators in turn purchased farms or were provided opportunities to become partners with farmers. Consequently, the senators were able to not only not show revenue from the income from the farms but also, they could write off all other income. The Senators were excused from paying taxes. The Senators also passed a law which forced farmers to have to purchase a farming permit and without the permit, they could not conduct the business of farming. One of the ways to obtain a permit was to be a partner with a Merlin Senator. Otherwise, the process could drag on through the planting season and then the farmer would not be able to plant his crop. The Finance Department oversaw acquiring tax income and every time a Senator purchased a business or became a partner in a business, that business no longer paid taxes and the income stream to run the government was decreased.

Aquarius opened the door and walked to the front desk. He noticed the name plate for the receptions, Rosa Cruze. "Mrs. Cruze, my name is Aquarius, and I work for Senator Blackmon."

Mrs. Cruze looked to be a young lady in her early twenties with dark skin and dark hair. Her attire accentuated her beautiful body, and he had remembered meeting her in meetings with the Senators and her boss the prior year, Mica Sprous. Aquarius knew she would not be able to help him with his request, but he also knew if he was able to intimidate the young lady, he might have an opportunity to meet with the Director, Mica Sprous. He elected to speak in English. He figured English was not her preferred language. People from all over the continent traveled to Merlin to live. The people were trying to leave the areas where the warlords were dictators and in constant conflict with each other. The young lady looked at Aquarius, "How may I help you?" She smiled.

"I need copies of the national tax records for the past two years with the reports broken down by industry." He smiled and waited for the response.

"You may complete the form Mr. Aquarius, but we cannot release the records to you unless the director, Mr. Sprous or the Merlin Senate authorizes the request. The tax records and reports are confidential." She reached for a form and a piece of paper.

Aquarius replied with a sharp tone, "I said I worked for Senator Blackmon, and you need to retrieve this information for me now." He noticed her head jerked around as she looked at him, and he could see the fear in her eyes.

"I will be right back." The young lady bolted for the door behind her.

A few seconds later Mr. Sprous appeared in the doorway. He looked at Aquarius with his eyes narrowed and wrinkles appeared on his forehead. "What gives you the right to come into my office and raise your voice to one of my employees?"

Aquarius looked at the director with a stern expression, "I can assure you this is of the utmost importance. I work for a senator, and I am making the request in conjunction with my right as a senate employee." He glanced at the other five employees who were sitting in the open office. "Maybe you and I can discuss this in private in your office?"

Mica stared at Aquarius, and Aquarius could tell he was considering his request. Mica was a second-generation Blueblood. Only the first-generation Bluebloods had one name. The second and third generation Bluebloods had two names. Out of respect and customs, the younger Bluebloods were required to extend certain courtesies to the first-generation Bluebloods. Mica's wrinkles on his forehead disappeared, and he smiled at Aquarius, "Certainly, come on back to my office."

Aquarius walked forward and followed Mica into the corner office located on the third floor of the Senate Building. Mica closed the door behind Aquarius and motioned for him to have a seat. He then walked behind his desk and as he sat he stared at Aquarius. "My receptionist has indicated you have requested the prior two years tax collection reports for all industries. Is this so?"

Aquarius walked to the corner side window and peered out over the city and the view looking over the interior city wall which surrounded the Blueblood safe sanctuary. Further out Aquarius could see the fields of cotton, corn, and farther to his right he could see a large horse ranch. "I am jealous of your view." He reached down with his left hand and secretly unlatched the lock on the window casing. He then turned and walked back to the center of the room. "That is correct. I was wanting to review the data and then see if I can formulate a new legislation for Senator Blackmon to introduce in the form of tax relief for the poor and also to clarify if there is a method to raise taxes for the wealthy who do not appear to be paying their share. Our government as you must know is funded by the poor working class."

As soon as Mica heard the words raise taxes for the wealthy, he knew Senator Blackmon was not in the loop. He relaxed in his chair and leaned back, "Does Senator Blackmon know you are making this request of the Office of Finance?"

"No. He does not. The clerk's job is to assist the Senators in making needed reform, and I need the information to see if I can first come up with a more amicable solution to the high tax rate for the poor. His constituents would benefit."

Mica leaned forward in his chair and announced, "You can complete the form and then I will deny your request."

Aquarius's eyes narrowed and his jaw was stern, "You will stand up and look me in the eyes and provide me the respect I deserve. I am a first-generation Blueblood."

Mica abruptly stood and his eyes narrowed, "Your request is denied. Now get out of my office, and Aquarius I understand you may be looking for a job in the near future. Senator Blackmon is done with you, and the other rumor is you abandoned General Samuel and left him for dead in the Midlander Territory. You will not receive respect much longer. You know what happens to unwanted people like you. Now get out."

Aquarius turned and walked out of the office and then by the pretty secretary and out of the main office by the clerks as all watched him exit.

***

Aquarius ate his food without looking across the table at his wife. She sat down and looked at him. "I understand you went to the Office of Finance today and acted like a clown." She glared at him.

He took another bite of food and glanced at his wife. She then said, "I went and talked to Senator Dale. I explained our situation with you sleeping in another room. I also explained that my status was to be a wife of a Merlin Senator. I understand you will be getting fired tomorrow from your clerk's job." She hesitated, and he took another bite of food. "He will grant us a divorce, and I will be united with another."

"Who."

She looked confused, "What are you asking?"

Aquarius looked her in the eyes, "Who will you be paired with? I would like to congratulate that poor bastard for having to live with you." He took another bite of food.

She slammed down her fork and knife. "You could have been a general in the army. You were then scheduled to be the next senator appointed, yet you settled to be a glamours secretary. You are a failure. What happened to you?" She stood and walked into her room as he developed a slight smile and took another bite of food.

***

Aquarius looked at his watch and noted it reflected two A.M. He quietly got out from under the cover and placed on his dark clothing and then his running shoes. He then picked up his small pack and fastened the latch around his waist and placed a dark colored backpack on his back. He slowly walked to the door and listened. He then proceeded to open the door to his room and then his apartment door. Once on the city street, he started jogging toward the Senate building. He ran for a less than a minute to the west side and stood in the shadows watching for the guards. He noticed the streets were clear. He proceeded to jog across the street. He used his key and unlocked the door and entered the lower back entrance and immediately started running up the interior rear stairs. He went to the door leading to the roof. He jimmied open the door with his knife and walked to the brick chimney vent and picked up his hidden rope. He did not hesitate and tied off the rope to the chimney. He looked over the side of the building and noticed the street was clear. He used the rope and lowered himself ten feet down the side of the building and stood on the window ledge. He opened the window and entered.

Aquarius went to the large file cabinet and pulled the reports for the tax listed by industry. He also pulled the file listed Farm Tax Rate Discount and Farm Tax Applications pending. He looked at Mica's desk and considered if he had time. His distaste for Mica urged him to the desk, and he opened the side drawer. He noticed the first file labeled NIV. The rest of the files were in alphabetical order. He knew the longer he was in the office, the greater his chance of being caught. He took a deep breath and knew he needed to leave. Time was not on his side. There were too many guards stationed around the Senate building and several walking the city streets. He considered the letters abbreviated, NIV. He said to himself, "NIV." He took the file and placed the file in the backpack next to the other files and traced his steps back to the roof.

He opened the first story rear door and noticed the area was clear. He jogged to his friend, Doc Vandergriff. The doctor and his wife were waiting. "Did anyone see you?" Aquarius looked at Doc Vandergriff and replied with a shake of his head no.

"We need to hurry. I also brought an additional file abbreviated NIV. It was the first file in the second desk drawer. All the other files were in alphabetical order."

Doc Vandergriff handed the prior tax year report to his wife, and she immediately started copying the long ledger. Doc Vandergriff sat down and started copying the other ledger. "We need to hurry, so you can return the reports. He will notice the file from his desk is missing." He glanced at Aquarius as he copied the reports.

Aquarius started reading the notes and the reports in the file. The room was quiet until Aquarius clenched his jaws and declared, "Those bastards. NIV stands for Normand Investments."

Chapter 34

It was a beautiful spring day four months later. Vicky hugged Dak and told him she loved him. Vicky hugged Zenith. They hugged Wayne, Billy Ray, Eric of Newport, and Little Jimmy. Dak and Zenith said goodbye to the women and other towns people. Dak walked over to Samuel. He stuck out his hand and the two men shook hands. "You need to take care of her and your baby. I am counting on that."

Samuel looked at Dak knowing he was concerned about the Merlin Senate sending an assassin to kill the child. "I will die for both my Queen and our baby."

Dak replied, "I am counting on you to do the right thing. If someone kills my sibling, my mother would never be the same." Dak released his handshake and went and helped Zenith into the wagon and then Dak headed the wagon for the New York tribe territory and then further on to his new ranch in the territory of the Midnight Hole.

Hulk, Trey, Tommy Boy, Robin Hood, and Veronica waved goodbye to the towns people as they rode the horses leading the wagon.

Several hours later, the group cleared the tunnel and entered the village of the Midnight Hole. Zenith noticed the village had been somewhat rebuilt. She could see a feed store, a church, a tavern, and hardware store with people moving between the stores. She had not been in the area since she and Dak traveled through the Midnight Hole after the battle of Harpers Ferry Harbor four months prior.

Dak looked over at Zenith. "I promise. You will love your new home. Robin Hood and Hulk captured over fifty stray cows. We already have a large herd. Everyone pitched in. We still have a lot of work to do."

"I can hardly wait. I know your friends worked hard. I wished you had allowed me to participate in the work. Women who are pregnant can still work."

Dak acted as if he did not hear her. "We will camp here for the night and finish the trip tomorrow." Zenith looked at Dak. She knew he was traveling slow for her sake. Her midsection had started growing. Doc Johnson figured she was starting her third trimester.

Hulk rode over to the village and talked with the newly elected mayor in Midnight Hole as the others set up camp. The mayor talked several times over the past few months with Dak and his friends about the future. The group spent weeks at a time building the ranch and worked out deals with the local ranchers to assist. The towns people elected a sheriff, and the community was starting to grow. The ranchers built the large barn in one day while Dak talked with a stone mason about the construction of the home. The community helped. The Mayor asked the people in the Midnight Hole community and the forest regions to assist. He knew war was coming and having Dak and his wife Zenith, a full blood Blueblood, living in the community was going to provide an extra level of protection. Dak and his friends had a reputation after the Battle of New York and then the Battle of Harpers Ferry Harbor to be famous warriors. The mayor and the community were aware of gangs of bandits that traveled from town to town killing and stealing. The bandits would be reluctant to attack the Midnight Hole knowing the community was protected by Dak and Zenith.

The group sat around the fire watching the blaze and enjoying feeling of the warmth as the fire burned hot while cooking the four chickens. Robin Hood announced, "Do not worry about dessert." He looked at Zenith. "Well maybe you will not have dessert since this dessert is the type you smoke and with you being pregnant, you can watch us have a smoke."

Trey said, "I knew when we came down here, Dak, to help with your plantation, Robin Hood would locate the man by the name of the Weed Eater and obtain us some pot."

The group laughed. Robin Hood then said, "I not only found him, but he and I are friends."

Hulk laughed, "Damn, Robin Hood, I knew you would come through for us."

Zenith looked at Trey and then at Dak, "So, we have a plantation?"

Dak smiled, "Wayne and Billy Ray delivered the portable sawmill for us to use right before the cold weather last winter. The local men had several logs cut from the prior year. They cut all the planks and let them dry in the weather for the past four months.

The people in the community helped us. Once the stonework was completed, the rest of the home was completed in three weeks. You will see your new home in the morning."

The group continued to talk and laugh. They enjoyed each other's company. The winter in Cliff Tops had been cold with temperatures below zero every day and most nights were double digit degrees below zero for a month and a half. Spring had arrived without war. Everyone was on edge waiting for the battle that never came.

Zenith smiled as they rode under a sign that proclaimed the name of the home as Zenith Point. The home was huge, laid out to house several people. The home had six stone chimneys and walls of stone and logs. The roof system was made of cedar shakes with eleven different slopes. The barn was huge, and the entire campus was surrounded by a stone wall. A large number of cows, goats, and sheep roamed the fields to the south and west of the home. The home foundation was built of stone and set at the edge of the three-hundred-foot cliff overlooking the Atlantic Ocean. Zenith was at a loss for words with the beautiful home. She then noticed the large number of armed men. At first, she had not noticed the army camped out to the south of her new home in the woods and the fields.

She beamed at Dak. "I truly love my new home. I love the view overlooking the ocean. Where did all the stones come from to make the walls?"

"We harvested the stone from the cliffs. There is plenty of stone in this region. The army is improving. Hulk is a natural teacher, and the others are very good at teaching combat. Some of these men had never shot a bow and some had never fought with a sword. Robin Hood and Veronica forces each man to fire at least one hundred arrows a day. They will not allow them to advance to the more difficult shots until they master the easier shots." He smiled at Zenith. "No one has advanced to shooting at moving targets. A person cannot master the bow in three months. We need time and this training lasts for four weeks and then the men and women must return to their villages."

"Do they all have swords?"

Dak said, "Yes, Billy Ray showed several of the men how to forge swords and arrow tips last winter. He provided them the forms. They have plenty of metal. There is an old train track they discovered in the north mountain region. They have harvested the iron rails from under the ground. They are not ready to fight a large Normand army out in the open, but we will fight with what we've got."

Dak looked at Zenith beside him in the wagon. "I love you. War is coming, and we need to attack them when they are not expecting it. I just hope our army is strong enough."

"Do you not think you should have told your mother that you were considering attacking King Solman?"

Dak looked forward at the home as the wagon slowly traveled over the dirt road. "I do not agree with my mother and her passive ways. Most of the older people in our tribe opinions and thoughts have been shaped by the old-world governments. We now know the earth has been reshaped and the natural resources are in high demand. The armies around the world will try to conquer us. We will have to learn to live and die by the sword."

Chapter 35

Aquarius walked into the infirmary with his hand on his chest and complained to the receptions he needed to see a doctor. "Doctor Vandergriff told me to come and see him if I had additional chest pains. He told me to tell you to alert him I was in the lobby."

The female receptionist looked at Aquarius, and she noticed the flushed look on his face and worried look in his eyes. She immediately stood and motion for Aquarius to step through the door. She asked him how long as his chest been hurting and asked several other questions. She took his blood pressure and then indicated she would return in a minute.

Aquarius had a seat in the hall and tried to look at nothing but the floor, knowing all the eyes in the waiting room were focused on him as the patients could see him when the door opened. The nurse came to the door a few seconds later and requested Aquarius to follow her. She led him to a room. "The doctor will be in to see you shortly. Is your chest still hurting?" After he answered her questions, she closed the door.

Doctor Vandergriff walked into the room, "What are you doing coming in here like this. Did anyone follow you?"

"No one followed me here. I was able to place the files back into the cabinets as planned last night. Then, today I was fired.

"I have the proof. Senator Dale is paying for the Normand army to attack the southern part of the continent. He lied about not knowing about the war. He is taking income that should be paid in taxes, exchanging it for gold and sending the gold by ship to King Solman. The plan is brilliant."

"Hell man. How did you get this proof?"

"I borrowed the proof from his office. He might be on to me."

Doctor Vandergriff rubbed his hands together, "You broke into Senator Dale's office in the daytime? They will kill you and anyone that is associated with you."

"I know. I need to get this information to your contact in the underground. I also need to send a message by ship to a place called Cliff Tops. We need to hurry. I have the proof here in my satchel. These conniving bastards are investing in the land which will be conquered by King Solman."

Doctor Vandergriff seemed to consider the information, "Why Cliff Tops? That place is all the way on the other side of the continent." He realized the answer before he finished his question. "You mean to tell me; Zenith and the sword fighter are alive? What happened to Samuel?"

"Listen Doc, I need your help. I know you have contacts, and you can get a message to Zenith. She may be the only one that can help. You owe me."

"What about Samuel? Did you kill him?"

"When I left Cliff Tops, Samuel was in jail."

"In jail? How did he get arrested? No way that man would allow those common town's people to arrest him. What is the charge?

"I was surprised he got arrested. The charge was murder. The son of the queen claimed Samuel was the third Asian assassin, but he knew Samuel was not the killer. It is complicated. Samuel did not protect the queen, and she was shot by two assassin's poison tipped arrows."

"Protect the queen? How long did it take the queen before she died."

"The Queen of Cliff Tops did not die. What I discovered was they wear silk undergarments. The silk does not tear and creates a barrier between the organs, and arrowheads. Once hit by an arrow, they pulled the arrow and silk out of the damaged area. The process limits the injury."

"Let me see what you have and be quick about it."

Aquarius opened his satchel and pulled the gold exchange information. He pointed out to Doc Vandergriff how the total amount of income from taxes had been decreasing for the past three years while the tax rates have doubled. "The Senators and their partners do not pay taxes, and here is the real kicker. Their extra income which they should be paying in the form of taxes is used to purchase gold." He then pulled the folder with the titled NIV. "They are dividing up the land to be owned by themselves. It is like a large investment, and they are using the Normand army to acquire the land. They wish to own the entire continent."

He showed him the information on the ship called the Meridian. "The Meridian will be hauling the gold to Southern City to pay for the army. It will be escorted by two warships. Here are the dates. We need to make certain Zenith can stop the Meridian at sea. We need to hold the tax information until which time the Meridian has been destroyed and the gold is lost. Otherwise, they will be on to us. Then, we leak this other information about this government's involvement in the war and expose Senator Dale and his groupies."

Doc Vandergriff looked up from glancing over the data, "This information could start a civil war. They will kill anyone of us who they think knows about this."

He turned to face Aquarius, "We must make your visit appear like a doctor's visit. I will have the nurse take some of your blood to the lab in the university. She will check your vitals again. I will give you a work excuse, and my records will reflect you have gas which caused the chest pain. You will need to stay out of sight. Can they track these documents back to you?"

"I was in his office earlier today signing divorce papers and took the documents. I need help to hide. I have risked my life for this information."

"How did you take the documents with him present?"

Aquarius smiled, "The chaos I created provided me an opportunity." He winked at Doc Vandergriff, "I accused my wife and Senator Dale of having an affair. The yelling got so loud Senator Dale had to escort my ex-wife out of his office. You know if she is found to be unfaithful, she will not be allowed to marry a senator. I took the folder before he returned."

"Is it true?"

Aquarius smiled, "I believe you and Senator Dale are the only two that have not bedded my ex-wife. What can I say? I married a slut."

Chapter 36

The screaming stopped, and Dak heard the crying of a baby. He felt so relieved. He rushed into the room. Doc Johnson arrived the prior day and helped with the delivery. He looked at Dak. "Congratulations. This one is a boy. There is a second baby." Dak felt in shock and was paralyzed as he stood motionless. He saw the nurse holding the baby boy under the arms while another nurse gently cleaned the child with a damp cloth. He noticed Doc Johnson jumped over to the other side of the bed. He said, "I can see the crest of the head. Zenith you will need to push." Dak's vision rotated to his wife lying in the bed. He noticed the soiled sheets and the strain and the pain in her face. He noticed the one maid was wiping the sweat off her red face as the doctor had positioned himself to receive another child. He could not re-act and stood still. He thought he heard someone say, "I believe he is going to pass out."

***

Dak had never been happier holding the two baby boys. "Time has passed so fast the last six months. I can hardly remember their births."

Zenith smiled, "Time has passed. You seemed to be truly happy, and you seemed to feel blessed by the Lord. The guys are already six months old. They are sitting up and are ready to eat real food, but I will never forget the births." She smiled and looked at Dak, "Why did you faint?" She turned her face to the door with a large smile, "I am so thankful for the women working for us helping me raise the kids."

Dak Knew he did not faint, and he handed the letter to Zenith. "We received this from a courier from Cliff Tops. The letter originated in Merlin."

Zenith looked concerned and reached for the letter. She opened the note handed from Dak. She read the letter twice and looked at the third page with a map of the west coast. She looked up from the note. She felt relieved knowing her father was still alive.

Zenith turned to Dak while holding the letter, "My father has risked his life to send us this message. My father has indicated the boat full of gold will be leaving from Merlin to King Solman in Southern City in four weeks. The boat is called the Meridian. There will be a convoy with two other ships. We need to sink the ship named the Meridian. Dak, I want to be part of this journey. We need to leave immediately." She handed the letter to Dak. He read the message and the part about the importance of sinking the gold. He then noticed the end of the letter where Aquarius declared his love for Zenith. "I love you daughter."

Dak looked at the map on page three and noticed the path of the three ships and how they would travel near the tip of the peninsula near the city of Tanger.

Dak looked at Zenith, "This is all starting to come together. Now we know how King Solman is financing his war. The Merlin Senate is sending him gold. They are using the Normand army to conquer our land and the land south of us. He is waiting on the gold to pay his army. Then, they will attack. They have promised the land they obtain to the men in Merlin. They have promised our land to two of the senators. We will fight."

Zenith looked at Dak, "The nursemaid's can keep our two boys. We will need to sink the ship off the coast of Tanger. If we can stop King Solman from receiving the gold, we will set his army and war campaign back months and maybe years."

"I will prepare the others for the mission. My mother can keep our sons. They will be safer in Cliff Tops. I will send a message back with the two riders. Captain J.J. is waiting for the messenger from Merlin before he leaves the port. We will also be on that vessel." Dak wrote a quick letter and walked to the front porch and handed the letter to the messenger from Cliff Tops, "This message is my response. For Queen Vicky's eyes only. Make certain the Queen understands Captain J.J. does not leave the port without us." The two men acknowledged the order and mounted the horses and rode toward Cliff Tops.

Dak walked back into the large room where Zenith was waiting. "We will need to cross the southern hemisphere. We will need a guide to assist us across the continent and sailors to attack that ship at sea. Those newly formed mountains might be full of nuclear waste pits and are going to be challenging for us to cross. I do not

301

know if anyone has ever charted that region. All we know is what we heard when we were at war in the south. The journey will not be easy. I understand the low gap in the mountain range is over seven-thousand feet and will be a challenge to cross. We will leave tomorrow."

Chapter 37

Wayne walked into the bedroom. "My Queen. Dak has sent a note from a personal carrier."

Vicky looked surprised and smiled thinking everyone started calling her the queen after the two battles. She felt cautious looking at the envelope he was holding. She handed her two twin daughters each a toy. "What is the message?" She glanced at Wayne and noticed the wax seal on the letter was not broken. She motioned her head for him to open the letter.

Wayne announced, "The messenger said for your eyes only." He cut the seal and unrolled the letter. He read the message to himself. He looked perplexed and rubbed his forehead, "I can only assume Aquarius has reported to Zenith and Dak a secret. There is a large gold shipment which will be transported by a convoy of three ships in three and half weeks heading down the west coast from Merlin." He paused and looked surprised. "The gold is headed to King Solman in the port located at the Southern City." He grimaced as he repeated, "The ship will set sail from Merlin. Dak has indicated the mission is to sink the ship carrying the gold."

Wayne looked at Vicky playing with her two twin daughters. "He is sending his two sons to stay with you until this mission is complete. They will sail south with Captain J.J. They know Captain J.J. cannot take them to Tanger. He does not have a Right of Passage granted by the Normand high command."

Vicky smiled. She had not seen her grandkids. Her hands were full with her two six-month-old daughters which were born three days after Zenith had given birth to the twin boys. "Now we know for certain, we will have to go to war at some point with Merlin and all those Bluebloods. I need to tell Samuel."

Wayne looked at Vicky, "I am not certain I would tell Samuel. This mission needs to be kept top secret. If the word gets out about all this gold, the secret will not be a secret."

Chapter 38

Hulk walked up to Dak's porch. "We had a rider close to one hour ago from down south with our three-month updated report from Hershel. The army is prepared. However, most of the men have returned to their villages to farm and ranch. The entire region is on notice, and the men have sworn to return to arms when the Normand army heads north. More and more of the farmers and ranchers are starting to contribute to the war effort in the region."

Dak looked at Hulk, "That is a blessing. Any other news?"

Hulk looked at the back page of the report, "There is always problems dealing with the bandits and warlords. The ranchers west of Harpers Ferry Harbor have reported that a group of six men rode into their sanctioned property and killed two men working for one of the ranchers and took twenty head of cattle and five horses."

Dak cut Hulk off, "Why are you reporting this particular issue? There are bandits killing people every day in the south."

Hulk made eye contact, "The killings and theft of the livestock is not carried out by the normal run of the mill bandits. The report reflects this could be Midlanders coming across the mountains from the west coast." He looked at Zenith who walked out on the porch dressed in her war paraphernalia. He studied her for second, "The other ranchers in the area have reported someone has been stealing their livestock for months. There must be a pass across the mountains to the west coast. The animals could be taken and sold, they believe, on the west coast at a port called Tanger." Hulk looked at Dak, "There was also a report based on the navy register on the ships in the harbor after the battle of Harpers Ferry Harbor, not all the Normand sailors were located. Vulture believes these bandits are sailors who deserted the Normand navy. The ranchers are asking for our help. Vulture is refusing to send the army. These ranchers did not support us in the battle of Harpers Ferry Harbor."

Dak looked at Hulk, "Round everyone up. We have an urgent mission which we must leave on now. Zenith and I are sending our kids to Cliff Tops. This is going to be dangerous. Did you say there were some Normand sailors not located?"

"Yes, best we can gather, there were close to seven-to-ten sailors that were not on the ships anchored to the left of the channel." He did not want to bring up the fact the Normand prisoners had all been executed by Vulture and his men. He knew Dak and Zenith did not agree with Billy Ray's decision to turn the prisoners over to the villagers.

***

Zenith looked over at Dak as they rode side-by-side, "Do you not want to tell your guys why we are going to sink the ship?"

Dak looked at Zenith, "I am afraid once gold is mentioned, the story will spread. I do not care about the gold. I just want to sink that ship. Losing that much gold will set King Solman back months, which will buy us additional time to prepare our army. We

306

must slow him down until we can be better prepared. Our small army needs time to train. If anyone finds out what is on that ship, everyone will want to steal the gold. The word will spread like an out-of-control wildfire. We need to keep this mission focused on one thing and that is to make certain the ship sinks with the gold to the bottom of the sea. We will travel by boat to Harpers Ferry Harbor and recruit Hershel to assist us with our additional travels."

***

The group stepped off the vessel and was happy to see Hershel. They sat in a pub and drank drinks and ate steaks. Vulture walked into the pub with four other men and updated Dak on the training of the soldiers and the plans to defend the area. He further explained they are in constant need of supplies and money. The pub was loud with laughter and drinking. Dak was sitting across from Hershel. He leaned over the table and whispered, "Do you know anyone we can trust who can sail a ship?"

Hershel looked into the eyes of Dak knowing the question was a serious issue; otherwise, Dak would not be asking. Hershel glanced around the room and noticed Zenith, Trey, Robin Hood, Tommy Boy, Hulk, and Veronica all talking to the other people in the pub. They all seemed to be having a good time. Dak on the other hand was serious. The mood was joyous with everyone celebrating the win of the battle from last year of Harpers Ferry Harbor.

"How fast do you need sailors?"

Dak looked stern and whispered, "I need them tonight. Hershel, this is urgent, and you need to keep this to yourself. Can you help me?"

"There are some trading ships that are able to slip past the Normand blockade and come to the docks. They are smaller vessels. The larger ships are located on the west coast. The Normand navy has control of the ocean and the traders in the large vessels are not allowed through their blockade. The only ships with the Certificate of Safe Passage are the warships."

Dak interrupted him, "No. I need sailors who can fight a battle at sea. I also need a fast ship."

Hershel looked at Dak, "Fight a battle at sea? Where at sea?"

"Tanger"

Hershel now looked around and saw Vulture glancing from the other table at him and Dak. He leaned toward Dak, "Tanger is located on the furthest west point of our continent located on the peninsula of the other coast. The Normand Navy has the southern routes all blocked."

"Yes, it is. Can you help me or not? I really need your help."

"I do not have contacts on the other side of our continent. Of course, I will help you. I have been told there is a harbor south of Tanger with several sailing vessels which routinely dock in that area while the sailor's rest. What is the mission?"

"I understand there were a few Normand sailors not accounted for after the battle last year and some livestock being stolen west of here in the mountain region. Are they related?"

Hershel studied Dak trying to discern his thoughts. "Yes. They were supposed to be on the troop-carrying ship. The crew was never located. We suspected they hid somewhere in town and sailed out of the harbor in a small sailboat under the cover of darkness. The small sailing boat was reported missing the next morning. We found the rowboat in shallow water south about twenty-five miles on a remote beach on the coast. The rowboat was missing from the sailing vessel." He glanced around toward Vulture and his table. "Vulture ordered the Normand prisoners all killed. There were no captured sailors left alive. So, you believe these cattle thieves are the missing Normand sailors and not Midlanders?"

Dak whispered, "I believe I know where the missing sailors are hiding. I need them alive, and I need their help. For the most part Midlanders stay in their territory. The Normand sailors would not return south, and they know what Vulture will do to them if they are caught. These men must be them. We leave at first light."

***

The next morning at sunrise, the group headed west across the plains and into the mountain region. They camped four nights before arriving at the ranch on the journey. The rancher and his two sons watched as Dak and the rest of the riders approached. The eight riders rode quickly into the large ranch. The elderly rancher stepped off his front porch accompanied by a younger lady. Dak explained they were going to track the cattle and horse thieves. The rancher explained, "The ransom is two gold pieces per bandit."

Dak studied the rancher. He talked with an accent from one of the old Asian countries. "Where are you from?"

"It does not matter where I am from. Do you want the job?"

Dak immediately did not like the rancher and his lack of hospitality. Before Dak could respond, Hulk commanded, "I tell you what. You can take your gold and shove it up your ass with a red-hot poker, and the next time the Normand army attacks you better have all your cowhands, your gold, and yourself along with your sons fighting in the army of Harbers Ferry Harbor. Now, have one of your sons show us the trail."

The ranchers did not show any surprise and told Hulk his oldest son would show them the north pasture, and where the two workers were killed. They would not dare cross into the mountains because the bandits would kill them. There were also nuclear pits in the mountain region. Dak ordered the son to lead the way.

The son looked to be fourteen and repeated himself as he spoke. Dak figured he was uneducated. He mispronounced the words as he explained the theft as they all rode to the field location in the western area of the ranch. The son pointed to the tracks leading into the wooded area heading into the mountains. "These tracks were left the last time they took from us. The tracks are sixteen-days old. They hit the range to the south of us thirty days ago and killed one of the rancher's employees." The son did not know the distance to the west coast. He had been told the nuclear contaminated area was west and located across the first mountain range. He indicated he would go no further west.

Hulk got off his horse and inspected the horse tracks. He motioned for the group to head toward the mountains in hopes of crossing in the lower gap of the large mountain range. "We will follow the tracks. I bet they lead us to the gap in the mountains."

***

As Dak and the others rode to Hulk's position, Hulk announced, "We have followed the tracks for four hours. They must have found a trail through the mountains."

Dak looked ahead of him at the large mountains, and he knew they were going to be a struggle to cross. "Yes, the men must have found a pass in the mountains. Why else steal the livestock and take them west."

***

Hulk rode down the creek bank to the waiting group and declared, "These are the horse thieves. The one horseshoe on the left rear of one horse is cracked. This is the same print back at the ranch. They are camped at the bottom of the valley. We are not picking up radiation since we went south and crossed the other mountain range."

Dak asked, "How many men are there?"

"Six. They must have sold the livestock. They appear to be headed back this way."

Dak looked at his group and then back at Hulk, "Let's surprise them, but do not kill them. I need to talk to them."

***

Zenith looked at Dak, "Are you certain your guys are in position?"

"I hope they are. You and I will need to tie off our horses and walk into the camp. We need to find out if these men are in fact the missing Normand sailors. We need their help to sink the Meridian. We have no one else who can sail a ship."

Dak and Zenith walked in close and stayed hidden behind the trees and small bushes. The camp was set up near the creek in the open woods. Dak counted six men from his spot behind the thick group of small trees. Dak signaled to Hulk. Hulk signaled back they were all ready. "Here we go."

"Hold it right there," Dak commanded. The six men jumped toward their swords and bows. Robin Hood crawled down the hill and was hidden in the thick rhododendron trees. He fired an arrow and hit the pine tree next to the head of one of the men, "The next arrow won't miss."

Hulk and Tommy Boy came in from the west up the creek bank with their arrows loaded on their bows.

Trey and Verónica ran into the camp with their arrows loaded moving from side-to-side as they pointed their arrows at the six different men.

Dak commanded, "All of you need to raise your hands, or you will die."

One man looked at his sword leaning against the tree. Dak followed his line of sight, "I would not do that if I were you. I know what you are thinking. 'Can I reach my sword before I take an arrow in the back?'" Dak stared at the man with a scar on his face. "Everyone hands up."

Hulk walked into the camp and picked up the weapons and threw them in the creek. He then ordered, "Everyone line up and get on your knees."

The middle-aged man with the scar on his face asked, "What is the meaning of this? We have not done anything wrong."

"You stole five horses and several cows from the other side of the mountain. Not to mention you have killed at least three cowboys. We tracked you."

"That was not us," said the man with the scar.

The men all got on their knees in a line.

The man with the scar snarled, "We have not stolen any livestock. You have no proof."

Hulk hit the man while standing behind him in the side of his head and ear with the broad side of his sword. The man fell face first into the leaf covered ground.

Dak and Zenith walked further into the camp. Dak ordered, "Pull your shirts up in the back." The men seemed surprised by the request. They all wavered.

Dak ordered, "Do not make me tell you a second time." The five men still on their knees pulled their shirts up exposing a brand burned into the middle of the lower back. Dak motioned for Hulk to pull the shirt up of the man lying on the ground. Hulk pulled the shirt up and motioned no brand.

Dak said, "Shoot them if they move." Robin Hood and Veronica covered the front of the men with the bows leveled at them and the arrows pulled tight, and Tommy Boy and Trey covered them from the rear. Hulk stood next to the man on the ground with his sword pulled. Dak motioned for the man on the end to move forward. Dak noticed he looked to be the youngest and seemed to be the most frightened. He was shaking while on his knees. Dak ordered, "Tie their hands behind him. I want to talk to these one." He pointed at the young man on the end.

Hulk tied their hands. The young man looked scared. Dak walked him out of hearing range near the running creek. "You have been branded by the Normand army. I understand this means you are a slave. Now is the time to tell the truth. We know you and your friends stole those horses and cows. Were you one of the sailors who escaped in the battle of Harpers Ferry Harbor a few months back?"

The man looked baffled. "Please don't. I know you are going to kill us."

"Well, I could kill you. Horse thieves do need to be hung, but I might grant you amnesty if you answer my questions honestly."

The man looked at Dak, "Amnesty?"

Dak looked into the scared man's eyes. "Do you know I was the man who cut General Cuez's head off? You need to start talking before I get impatient. Now answer my questions."

The man was frightened, which caused his body to shake involuntarily and stuttering when he talked. He also acted confused. He knew this posse was aware he and the others were in the Normand army. "Yes. I watched as our army was being crushed. I saw you in the middle fighting. I saw her fighting. For heaven sakes, she is a Blueblood warrior."

The man with the scar could see Darnel talking to Dak. He raised up on his hands and knees and yelled, "Darnel, you better keep your mouth shut." Hulk hit the man with the handle of his sword in the head. The man fell face first on the ground with blood oozing out his scalp.

"Yes, she is a Blueblood warrior. Darnel, you need to answer my questions."

"Yes, five of us were captured in the Southern City and the surrounding provinces and forced to be sailors in the Normand navy. We watched as they killed some of the civilians and burned their bodies. We were given a choice to fight with them or be burned alive. During the battle of Harpers Ferry Harbor, we were hidden in the corner building. That is the office of the captains. We were being instructed on our next mission when the battle began,

315

and we watched the battle unfold. At first, we thought the Normand foot soldiers were going to win. The man with the scar was a captain and ran from the battlefield when your horse soldiers entered the battlefield from the beach and out flanked his men. He hid with us in the basement of the office. We stayed hidden and in the dark of night, we rowed a small rowboat out to sea."

"Who killed the three cowboys?"

"I swear I never killed anyone. The captain with the scar is a killer. He killed the cowboys."

"Can you and your five comrades sail a ship?" Dak asked.

The man looked at Dak with a confused expression, "Yes, Ronny, the third man in line, is an excellent sailor. He worked in that capacity before the wars down south. The Normand captain of the boat would allow Ronny to order the rest of us sailors to adjust the sails while he worked the rudder. He knows ships better than anyone I know. He understands how to travel in the wind of the ocean with the sails and a rudder."

"What about the man on the ground bleeding?"

"Like I said, he was a captain in the infantry division for General Cuez. He is no sailor. He killed two of the sailors in my unit who were trying to escape from his command after we saved his life that day of the battle. There were originally seven of us." Darnel glanced at Dak, "He is a true Normand soldier. He is a cruel man."

"Where do you take the stolen livestock?"

"The valley meets with a second valley leading northeast. We circle back around north and sale them to a rancher in the mountain region."

"So, you do not cross the great mountains?"

"No. they are nuclear contamination in those mountains. We stay clear of the areas west.

Dak turned Darnel around and walked him back to the others. "Keep quiet and get on your knees next to the others." The men on their knees glanced at Darnel trying to understand what was going to happen next. Darnel kept shaking and stared at the ground.

Dak walked behind the row of men. He acted like he randomly picked Ronny. He walked him next to the creek to drown out the conversation and asked him the same questions. Ronny indicated he loved the sea. "I can sail a ship in any weather. I mastered the sailing of small sailing vessels before the Transition Period. After the Transition Period, I was stationed on a large sailing vessel that transported all types of trade items." He looked at Dak. "Me and those other men have been to the Asian ports. I hated when my crew was captured in the inlet of Southern City, and my wife and kids were hauled away. I hate the Normand army. They tell us they have our families in a safe location. The captain went back into the office that night before we escaped. We had no way to know what was so important. He crawled up the stairs and entered the office and came back with the list with our family names and their location. The report was encrypted. We understand the threat against our families. They will be killed if we do not serve, and he

317

mentions that fact to us daily. The list is in his saddle bag lying on the ground next to the black saddle. They are holding our families as hostages down south, and we are forced to serve them. We really have no idea if the captain is telling the truth, and our families are alive. He forced us to paddle north up the coast, and we circled back down the beach on foot. We stayed hidden out of your daily patrols. We watched as all those prisoners were killed two days after the battle." He looked at Dak.

"Killing all those men was not my doing."

Dak walked Ronny back to the line and forced him to his knees. He looked at Hulk and then walked over to the saddle bag and removed the folder and papers of the names of the families. The encrypted paper was not readable without the codebreaker. Dak demanded, "Hulk, place the captain, the man with scar on his face, on one of the horses with a noose around his neck. I have confirmed he is a murderer and horse thief."

The man tried to fight Hulk as he was being picked up from the ground. He looked at Dak as Trey walked a horse toward the man. "You have no right to judge me. We are at war with the rebel scum. I am a soldier in the Normand Army. I demand to be returned to the south in a prisoner trade."

Dak looked at Hulk and Trey, "Please place this murderer and horse thief on the horse."

The men looked at the Normand soldier sitting on the horse with the rope around his neck. Dak announced, "This is what we do to someone who commits murder and is a horse thief." He slapped

318

the horse on the rear, and the man with the scar on his face was left dangling by the rope with his hands tied behind his back. He choked for a few seconds and then died. "Now the rest of you can join him, or you can work for me. If you do what I ask, and we are successful in our mission, I will grant you full amnesty."

"What are you going to ask us to do" asked Ronny?

Another man who had not spoken asked, "How can we trust you to provide us full amnesty? Your army killed all our comrades."

Dak looked at the men on their knees and snapped, "Your army has done far worse. The Normand army has committed war crimes against the innocent people in the south. They have butchered the innocent, and you men know this." He looked at each man as they ducked their heads. "We will travel by horse to the City of Tanger and steal a ship. The mission is to sink another ship headed for King Solman in Southern City. I will provide you additional information as we get closer to the deadline. As far as trusting me, you will need to weigh your decision and tell me now. I would appreciate you being honest."

"The third man looked at Dak from his knees, "We are going to cross the mountains through the nuclear waste areas? We will all be walking dead men."

Dak looked at the man. "We have not one but two monitors which can detect radiation. We have no intention of walking into a nuclear contaminated area."

Ronny glanced at the man on his knees next to him to the right and then the left. He then looked at the dead caption swinging back and forth hanging by the rope. "So, all we need to do is sink a ship at sea, and you will not kill us or force us to walk into a nuclear waste pit?"

The other man on the end that had not spoken announced, "Full amnesty means you will release us?"

Dak looked at the men. "I will not kill you unless you keep committing murder and stealing livestock from people inside the realm where I reside. In addition, we do not want you to rejoin the Normand army. I do not desire to have to fight you twice. You need to let me know right now. You need to give me your word and pledge your allegiance to me. You also need to understand if you break your word and your allegiance, I will hunt you down and hang you along with your families." He held the folder in his hand for all to see and pointed at the man hanging dead by his neck.

Ronny said, "I am with you." The other four men motioned their heads they agreed.

Dak announced, "Then repeat after me, 'I will pledge my life to General Dak Donahue and die to protect him until which time he releases me of my pledge. If I break my pledge, the sentence is death by hanging." The men repeated the pledge.

Dak announced, "We need to ride west to the coast. We have very little time to spare."

Chapter 39

Hulk was tired from the three days of crossing the mountains. He said to himself, "There is nothing flat. We are either going up or down in this damn terrain." He had been the scout on the mission and had to forge the path west cross the mountains. He had been on alert for a possible ambush and nuclear radiation for the past ten hours. He monitored the area for radiation every half-hour. He had elected to ride on the ridges of the mountains to try to avoid the possible ambushes from bandits. The mountains near the top of the ridges had very little foliage but were steep, rough, windy, and cold. He looked north across the valley and mountains east of their location. He could see a large void in the land where there must have been a nuclear waste pit. He considered if Ronny and his men knew they had possible traveled into a contaminated area with the stolen livestock. With the mission pending, he elected not to mention it. He slowed his horse and took a drink of water.

He knew Trey and Tommy Boy were also tired. They had been assigned to watch Ronny, Darnel and the other three men as they rode horseback to the coast. Hulk could sense his friend Dak was not telling him the entire story. He had approached Dak and asked about the mission on the long ride. Dak changed the subject, and the final time Dak ordered Hulk not to ask questions about the mission. He would let him know when the time was right, and they must cross the mountains faster. Dak kept pushing.

Hulk checked the air for radiation, and the monitor was clear. From the ridge he could see the ocean located maybe fifty miles west of his location. He admired the view from the ridge as he waited for the rest of the group to approach him at his vantage point on the ridge and announced, "Once we descend this mountain and cross the flatlands west of us, the coast is a few miles west of the river. You can see the river leading to the Pacific Ocean. He pointed west. The City of Tanger should be north of us a day's ride. I suggest we camp at the flat land at the bottom of the mountain."

Robin Hood walked his horse next to Dak, "Hell yea. We need to camp, eat and rest. I am tuckered out. I also have some good weed to take the edge off. Dak, what I have noticed is everything you and Hulk look at while we are on a journey like this is you are a hammer, and you pretend everything else or everyone else is a nail. You two have beat the shit out of me."

Zenith and Trey both smiled with Tommy Boy saying, "Hell yea. I agree. You two are hammers. This has been horrible crossing these mountains."

***

Hulk walked by Dak, "Why do I feel you are not telling us the entire story? Why do I get the feeling this ship called the Meridian is not just any ship? We are here at the coast. I and the rest of our team want to know the parameters of the mission, the risk, and the instructions."

Zenith walked over and heard Hulk's statement. "He needs to know. He needs to understand the importance of the mission. Dak your friends are loyal to you. They have a right to know what we are facing."

Dak considered Zenith's statement. He glanced at Hulk and thought about how Hulk had changed over the past few years. He was sterner with his emotions and did not smile near as much as he had when they were boys growing up together. He now allowed his hair to grow long in the back and tightly cut around his ears. Dak glanced at the fire and the food in the frying pan sizzling as the meat warms. He then glanced at Robin Hood preparing an additional ground hog along with the four other rabbits they had shot on the journey as they crossed the flat lands. Robin Hood had also changed. He was more reserve with his opinions but still demonstrated his sense of humor which help make them all laugh. He now had allowed his hair cut short and had a short beard. Dak was tired and he knew his fellow travelers were spent. He saw Veronica walking toward the spring to bathe. Her hair was now hanging to her waist. Dak thought she had changed the most out of his childhood friends. She was more outspoken and more confident in herself. Dak turned and noticed the sailors were all watching her disrobe and wash herself in the open for all to see. She was sitting in the water next to a large granite rock with her back to the men acting like she did not know they were watching. He noticed Trey was feeding the horses and extending the lead rope, so the horses could reach the creek leading away from the spring. Trey had now allowed his hair to grow long and had the hair pulled into a ponytail. Hershel and Tommy Boy were sitting and talking with the five sailors next to the second fire all facing the view of Veronica. Tommy Boy had also allowed his hair to grow long and had the hair pulled into a long ponytail hanging down his back. Everyone was tired and hungry. Dak turned to face Hulk and Zenith. He knew Hulk was still angry with Veronica, and he did not wish for Zenith to suspect he was enjoying watching Veronica while she bathes. He also knew none of the sailors and Hershel would dare approach Veronica with her three hundred twenty-pound brother nearby. Dak said, "Aquarius has reported a game changer in the form of a secret. Hulk, the ship called the Meridian is carrying three treasure chests with at least one-hundred-fifty-thousand gold coins in the cargo bin. We were correct with our assumption the Senate in Merlin is financing the war for King Solman. The mission is simple." Dak hesitates and shrugs his shoulders, "We need to sink the ship before that ship arrives in Southern City and reaches King Solman. We need the help of these sailors to sink the ship." Dak stared at Hulk.

Hulk hesitated and glanced at Zenith, "Why don't we steal the gold?"

Zenith responded, "If Senator Dale is suspicious the leak came from inside the city of Merlin, he will locate the leak. He will have my father executed. We need to make this look like the boat accidentally sunk at sea or was randomly attacked and sunk."

"How much is the one-hundred-fifty-thousand gold coins worth on this ship?"

"Hulk, this is Merlin gold. One hundred percent solid gold. There is enough gold on the ship to buy several trained armies. That is why we have not mentioned the cargo. The story of gold would travel fast throughout the region. The fewer in the know the better," replied Zenith.

Hulk looked surprised. He set still and contemplated the mission. "I think we need to tell our squad. They deserve to know. The ship might be guarded by Blueblood warriors and certainly other highly trained guards."

Dak looked at Hulk, "The Meridian is escorted by two heavily armed battleships. Our intel does not suggest there are Bluebloods traveling to Southern City on this mission."

Hulk shook his head no. "You think these five prisoners can sink this ship called The Meridian?"

Dak looked at the sailors and commanded. "Ronny, come here. I need to have a word with you." Ronny stood and walked over to the three. Dak noticed Ronny faced him and Zenith and positioned himself so he could still see Veronica while bathing in the background. Dak announced, "In forty-eight hours, a merchant ship by the name of the Meridian is going to be sailing south along this coast. If you want to be free, your job is to sink the ship. The

325

ship will be escorted by two heavily armed battleships carrying several hundred troops. How do we sink this ship?"

"Sinking one merchant style ship might not be as difficult as you think if we have the right equipment. We would need a fast agile ship, a Ketch style sailing vessel, and be waiting out at sea. The wind is always blowing from the west, and we could drive the smaller ship right through the side of the target ship. The best time is in the darkness of night or during the rainstorm with fog. The merchant vessel would be traveling slow in those conditions. The men on the ship would not be expecting an attack, and we would ram our stolen ship into the mid-section of the merchant ship. The cargo ships are not designed to stay afloat once the midsection has been breached. The problem will be escaping the two battleships after the collision."

He glanced at Zenith, "We will need to steal a sailing ship which is designed for speed, and one we can maneuver on a dime. We must have a Ketch sail type ship which has two masts, three sails, a mono-hull, and a deep keel. All three sails will have to be dropped just prior to the impact, so they are not damaged. The Ketch sail, the main sail, and the front sail will have to be reset after the impact. We will need to weld a protected shield to the front of our ship and with a sharp point to cut through the side of the merchant ship and also reinforce the bow of our vessel."

Hulk was impressed with Ronny's wish list and the exact needs to sink the boat. "Have you done this before? You seem to be very exact with your needs."

Ronny looked at Hulk, "I have been forced to consider this exact type of mission while working for the Normand navy."

Hulk smiled at Ronny, "The second alternative. What if we aspired to steal the ship or the cargo? Have you considered this alternative?"

Zenith and Dak both looked at Hulk. Hulk then said, "We need to examine all possibilities." Dak had known the sin of greed. No man could resist the temptation of never having to want for something ever again. Wayne often would say, 'Money could not buy happiness, but rich people were happier than the poor.'

He also remembered the stories from the older people in his tribe talking about how ruthless and greedy men could be. A large American oil company had sold oil to the enemy, the German Army in WWll. The large pharmaceutical companies had raised the price of a lifesaving medicine to where only the rich could afford the drugs, and the poor were allowed to die a slow death. He remembered the preacher had listed greed as being one of the seven cardinal sins when he taught him and the friends about the Bible and the decision to accept God.

Ronny looked at Hulk. "You are asking two different questions. The large warships might not be able to catch us if we sail clear after the initial assault, but they could follow us, and they would have greater speed capabilities. The fast-sailing ship I am envisioning we use is not made to survive a high-speed impact and then out run a larger warship. The warships would need to be sabotaged. The Normand Navy uses the Schooner type sailing vessels with square sails with top speeds fifty miles per hour under perfect weather conditions. During inclement weather they travel close to ten miles per hour. They are faster with all those sails, but they cannot turn directions very quickly. They however are very deadly with those harpoons position on the bow and stern decks. The Ketch sailing vessel is quicker and easier to maneuver with speeds close to forty miles per hour. At slower speeds, the Ketch sail vessel can easily outmaneuver the warships because with an experience crew it can be turn on a dime. I have the crew."

Zenith spoke before Dak had a chance to stop the conversation about stealing the cargo. She could tell Dak did not want to consider stealing the cargo. He wanted the ship sunk. "How would we sabotage a warship while the ship is at sea moving south along the coastline?"

Ronny looked at Zenith, "Sabotage the sails and one of the three masts. It would take an experienced crew at least three hours to take down the damaged sails and reinstall the backup sails. If you could damage one of the masts, the ship will not perform correctly at sea even if the other sails are reinstalled. It is designed for the three masts to have multiple sails tied off. That would provide us enough time to escape." He looked at the others.

Zenith asked, "How would we hijack a ship at sea and deal with the crew?" Dak looked at Zenith knowing what she was considering.

Ronny smiled, "In the seventeen and eighteen hundreds, pirating was at an all-time high in the world. I studied this before the

Transition Period. There are three ways to be a successful pirate. First, the pirates would sneak up to the ship at sea under the cover of darkness and use grappling hooks and ropes to board. The second method is they would outmaneuver the other ship at sea and use the threat of cannon balls to blast it out of the water. The third way, the merchant ship would give up and surrender without a fight at the sight of a pirate ship. The merchant ship would drop its sails and provide the walking blank to be boarded.

"I would suggest number one. The Normand navy is not going to surrender, and they have way too much fire power with their harpoons and fighting men to attempt a sea battle." He smiled looking at Dak and then Zenith. "The assault would have to be conducted under the cover of darkness with stealth and agility utilized as the primary asset. The pirates would have a minute maybe two before the crew responded from below deck. Otherwise, the crew would have to be killed. There is no way that many crew members could be trusted to be in on a mutiny. May I ask, what is the cargo we are trying to steal?"

Dak took a deep breath, "Let us eat." He wanted to consider the possibilities. He knew that much gold would help their war effort, but he also knew he did not want to take any chances. The gold must not reach King Solman.

***

The squad rode back into the camp. Trey announced, "Ronny located the perfect vessel tied off at the lower dock inside the small inner coastal water way. We borrowed some additional ropes from the pier." He dropped the two large ropes on the ground. "Stealing the unguarded boat will not be an issue. We will tie off a large metal plate on the front of the vessel to reinforce the bow during the impact. The plan is coming together." Dak remembered how sick Tommy Boy, Robin Hood and Trey had been on the prior trip at sea before they sank the ships in the harbor. He knew he, Zenith, and Hulk would have to be on the ship with the sailors. He did not know if he could trust the Normand men or not. He looked around at the riders, "Where is Hulk?"

Trey replied, "Hulk announced I was in charge. He then rode off by himself heading south."

Dak thought, "Damn him."

***

Dak watched as Hulk came riding the horse on a dead run back into camp with Hulk pulling back on the bridle as the dust flew from under the hoofs. Dak commanded, "You violated a direct order of mine." Tommy Boy and the two Normand sailors all stared at Dak who was angry. "The mission must start any minute. We do not have enough time for you to go off and do whatever you were doing. What were you doing? Looking for the middle-aged whore Becky?"

Hulk dismounted and smiled at the name of Becky, the woman he had met in New Foundland. He knew he would never live her down. He looked around the camp and noticed Ronny, two other Normand sailors, Zenith, Trey, and Robin Hood were not in camp. "I have a plan."

"We do not have time for your plan. I needed you to lead the mission to steal the sailing vessel and prepare it for the assault. Yet you placed Trey in charge."

"Listen to me. I have a plan where we can keep the cargo, and no one will find it." Dak was upset. He wished he had never told Hulk about the gold. Hulk tied off his horse and walked over to Dak. Dak turned and tried to walk away.

Hulk grabbed Dak by the arm and turned him. Dak snapped, "You have been poisoned by the gold and your greed." Hulk glanced at the two Normand sailors and knew they had heard Dak. "Will you listen to me?"

Dak was mad. He realized the Normand sailors had heard his remark. "I should have never told you. I knew you would make this mission worse. You do not understand. We need to sink the ship with cargo on it. That is all we need to do."

"Listen to me. I have a plan. It will work. You must trust me and the rest of our team. Do you remember my plan of starting the stampede in the Midnight Hole. That plan worked. This plan is easier. Just hear me out. When the other guys return, let me present the plan and let us vote on it." He then whispered, "We could use that gold."

Dak was about to hit Hulk. They had not fought since they were eleven. Before that time, they fought at least once a year and then the next day they were best friends. They would often laugh and talk about the fights when they were young.

The Normand soldier yelled and pointed out to sea. They have the stolen ship. Dak looked west and saw the ship moving fast across the open sea. The crew was heading toward the pier where they were now camped.

Hulk said, "Dak. Trust me on this. This is a good plan, and we keep the gold. It is a win win scenario. Kings make this type of decisions, and you are destain to be a king."

***

Veronica was the first to speak. "I like the plan. We need to verify if our sailors are as good as they say they are."

Robin Hood looked at Dak, "I like the plan. I would suggest we sweeten the deal with our newfound friends, so they will be at the top of their game. They already know gold is involved."

Zenith looked at Dak. "The plan could work. We need that gold for the upcoming war as much as King Solman. I vote we sink the ship and take the gold."

Dak looked frustrated at his friends, "My plan of sinking the ship is a one phase plan and is simple. There are too many moving parts to this plan. We do not know how good these Normand men are at sailing a ship. We do not know if we can trust them. I do not like the plan with four phases. Plus, once the story is out of the theft, every gang, tribe of people, cut throats, and army will be trying to steal the gold from us. We will have painted a large bullseye on our backs."

Trey interrupted Dak and looked at Dak, "If the Normand sailors lie to us and steal all the gold, we still win. Dak, your objective is keeping King Solman and the Normand army from using the gold to buy an army. If they steal the gold, we win. They are not going to give the gold to the Normand army. The best I can tell, they hate King Solman." He held his arms out and palms up to his side providing body language saying what difference does it make.

Dak blew out his breath and looked at his friends. He shook his head no and smiled, "I cannot believe you guys. If the gold ends up in the coffers with King Solman we lose. All for nothing. What the hell. I am in. This better work. We can now add pirating to our resumes."

Chapter 40

Delores walked into the upstairs nursery and announced, "Our queen's entire upstairs apartment is a twenty-four-hour nursery." The women laughed.

Mia was rocking one baby boy. Casey was playing blocks with the other baby boy. Casey's daughter was feeding the baby girl while her sister slept. Mia said, "Our Queen needed a break. She and Samuel are riding along The Ridge Trail. She likes the view on top overlooking the ocean."

Delores smiled as she picked up some items on the floor. "The ladies will be sleeping and preparing for the midnight shift. Raising the four kids takes the entire community."

Mia asked, "Have you heard from Dak or any of his friends?"

Delores knew Mia was worried about her son and daughter, Trey and Veronica. All the parents were worried. During the Transition Period and afterward, everyone knew of death, but none of these parents knew the emotional challenge of losing a child. "No, I asked Wayne about them during the last council meeting. He said he had not heard any word. It has been twenty-one days since they left south on the boat. Wayne would not elaborate on the mission. Matter of fact he acted like he wanted to avoid the conversation. He walked out as soon as I asked about where they went.

"I asked Billy Ray about the mission, and he indicated he did not know the scope of the operation. Vicky and Wayne have not revealed to Billy Ray or anyone on the council the mission guidelines. We do not know what they are doing." Delores thought about her husband not telling her. Certainly, Vicky would have shared the scope of the mission with Billy Ray. He must know. She looked over at Mia, "Wayne and Billy Ray are going to ride out west and take Old Thomas some supplies. I believe they wanted to get out of baby duty." She smiled and thought about her husband and Wayne holding the babies. Then she thought of him not telling her about the mission. "Wayne should divulge the mission to Billy Ray while they are camping. They are going to be gone for four or five days. When they come back, I will find out."

Mia said, "All I know is a message was hand delivered by a man riding from Midnight Hole. The message was wax sealed and given to Wayne by the courier. The courier told Wayne the message was to be opened by Queen Vicky and no one else, and Wayne went straight to Vicky with the message. They never discussed what was in the message."

Mia looked over at Delores, "Casey told me two days prior a courier had been on Captain J.J.'s ship when he entered our jetty. The courier had an urgent message for Zenith, and he was adamant he had to hand deliver the message to her. When he was told she was living in the Midnight Hole community, he immediately demanded a horse and a guide to lead him to her. He had an

335

unusual accent. Eric of Newport thought the messenger was from Merlin."

Delores looked perplexed. "No one has mentioned the courier to me. We had our biweekly meeting with the council two days ago and nothing was said about the mission or the message. We added a chair on the council, to accommodate the people of Meadow Bottoms. They now are represented by Barney Simpson, who was elected to the council by the people of Meadow Bottoms. He came with several demands, and Vicky finally raised her voice to him. She said having a chair on my council does not mean you have the same say in the affairs of Cliff Tops as I do. At the end of the day, I will rule, and what I say is the law." Delores remembered looking at Wayne. She knew when Vicky was pushed, she was a fighter and a leader. "Barney apologized and said no more during the meeting."

Delores announced, "You could have heard a pin drop for a few seconds in the meeting. I believe Barney suddenly recalled what happened to Sie."

Chapter 41

Dak looked at Zenith, "Hold on. This is going to be dangerous."
Dak could tell Zenith was determined. He knew if this part of the
mission failed there was no back up plan. The conditions were
cold, windy, dark, and the waves were continually rolling the
sailing vessel up and down as they cut through the ocean. He could
not allow the mission to fail. He could not fathom the thought of
the Meridian sailing into the Southern City Harbor for King
Solman to have his gold to pay for his armies.

Dak looked over at Hulk and noticed Hulk used leather straps to
wrap around his waist and the rail on the opposite side of the deck.
He seemed to be staring at the deck while holding on with both
hands. He noticed Ronny used leather straps also to tie himself to
the supports next to the wheel controlling the rudder. He was
squinting trying to see through the darkness of night in the rain.
When the lightning struck in the sky, the crew could see the
battleship moving south along the coast. The course was set. One
of the crew was near the top of the mast in the bird's nest seat
watching and yelling course changes to Ronny. Two other sailors
were ready to receive the order from Ronny to adjust the sails. The
other sailor was in the cabin waiting to come on deck and support
the crew members. They knew they had to adjust the two sails and
then drop them before impact. The sun was a couple of hours from
rising in the eastern horizon and the rain had slowed to a drizzle in

the wind with close to twenty-five miles per hour and gusts close to thirty-miles per hour. The swells in the ocean were ten-to-fifteen feet high. Dak thought, "I have never been so miserable," as he held onto his side of the boat railing. He and Zenith had tied themselves to the railing and prayed the ship did not turn over. Drowning while being tied to a flipped ship was no way to die. He knew Ronny had said they needed inclement weather to surprise the other boats, and he seemed relieved when they set sail in the night with rain and wind. He said to himself, "How could anyone have the fortitude to sail a vessel in this weather? I hate this shit." He then glanced at Ronny working the wheel turning the rudder with the constant rain and cold wind blowing against him. He thought, "The man looks fearless."

Dak was surprised when he noticed the huge warship was ten feet away. He could just about reach the hull hanging over the rail. The vessel had literally appeared from nowhere. He noticed Zenith had the same reaction as he did with the surprised look on her face, and her body reacted with a jerk backward. Caption Ronny, yelled, "Now."

Hulk released his leather straps and came running across the boat and jumped for the railing on the warship. The two ships rubbed, and the smaller ship lunged outward. Ronny had explained the key was not to allow the small sailing vessel to get caught underneath the large warship as it rose in the swells.

Hulk tied off the rope he had around his shoulder and then proceed to the cockpit of the warship.

Dak and Zenith followed Hulk as they also jumped to the other vessel. Ronny ordered his additional sailor to the deck to be prepared to adjust the sails. Hulk made his way to the cockpit. The lieutenant saw Hulk approaching and at the last second realized he was not one of the Normand sailors. He tried to yell, and Hulk cut him with his sword across his neck. The man fell over being held up by the straps and harness attached to the wheel casing as he bled to death. Dak immediately ran toward the bigger sail and climbed the mast. He cut the sail ropes as he ascended. Once at the top he slid down the top rail cutting the ropes holding the sails in place. Zenith had done the same with the smaller mast and sails. Once on the deck, both worked quickly to cut the ropes on the bottom framing causing the sails to blow into the ocean. Dak used his hatchet to cut the goose neck attached to the boom on his mast. Hulk released the dead sailor from the harness and dropped his body overboard. He tried to hold the wheel straight and keep the rudder straight so as not to alert the crew below. The large ship started to change course and speed once the sails were cut.

Ronny had been yelling for his two sailors to adjust the sails. He was trying to stay even with the large battleship. The men turned the cranks trying to slow the sailing vessel while trying to make certain the ship did not get pushed under the large warship and crushed as the waves tilted the ships up and down.

Dak took Zenith's hand. He pulled her across the deck which was constantly moving upward and downward. They made it to the rail. "We've got to jump now." Zenith did not hesitate. She cleared the rail of her vessel which was sitting lower in the water. Dak turned to Hulk and motioned for him to follow. Hulk started toward the rail as Dak climbed the rail and jumped. Dak landed and rolled as the ship sloped downward at twenty degrees in the large wave. Dak slid across the slick deck trying to grab anything to stop his momentum. He finally reached the railing with his left hand of the opposite side of the deck. He then gripped the railing with his right hand holding himself with the one hand from falling into the sea. His midsection had slid under the bottom of the rail and his entire body went under the wave as the vessel dipped lower into the wave. One of the sailors slid to the rail and reached Dak's arms. He positioned his feet against the rail post and used the leverage to pull Dak onto the ship's deck as the ship rotated back upper in the wave. Dak had thought he was going overboard as he held to the rail as the boat shifted upward in the wave.

As Hulk started to move to the rail, he was grabbed by someone from behind. He turned and dodged the swing of a fist. The large ship was rocking up and down. The guard lost his balance and slid into Hulk with both men falling to the ship's deck and sliding to the far rail. Hulk knew he needed to jump now or never. Ronny had explained they could not match the speed of the larger ship and the larger ship would crush their smaller vessel as it rocked out of the water.

Dak stood on the deck with the help of the sailor and watched for Hulk. Zenith had made her way to the cockpit and yelled at Ronny, "We will wait on Hulk. He has not jumped."

Ronny yelled, "We will be crushed. We must pull away." He was very adamant. Zenith could see the fear in his eyes. She looked back at the large ship as it rocked upward. Their smaller vessel was pulled closer. It appeared her ship was being pulled underneath the larger ship as they both rocked in the waves. Ronny yelled, "We must cut the line and pull away."

Zenith looked up at the side of the large warship as the wave rolled the side high in the air. She did not see Hulk, and she felt the smaller vessel was being pulled under the large ship. "We are going to be crushed. I cannot hold us away any longer. We go now or we don't go."

Zenith thought about the mission and the importance, "Cut the rope and pull away."

Ronny yelled frantically at the sailor to cut the rope connected to the warship. Ronny yelled at the other sailors to adjust the sails. The sailors immediately started cranking the sails which pulled the sails into position. Once fully up, the sails caught the wind. The ship had a sudden jerk as it changed direction and cut a path away from the warship.

Hulk unfortunately was on the bottom with the large guard trying to hold him down. Hulk knew he had to jump from the ship. Either he was going to clear the rail of the deck of the sailing vessel, or he would drown. He pushed the man upward. The guard resisted and head-butted Hulk. The head butt had not been expected. Hulk felt the sudden feeling of blacking out as he struggled with the obese man as the back of his head hit the deck caused by the head butt to his forehead. He gritted his teeth, and one big surge pushed the big man upward and to the side as the deck shifted in the wave. With one quick motion of his right hand, he found the handle of his knife strapped to his thigh. As the man started falling back down, he braced him up with is left forearm as he positioned the knife in his right hand and pierced the man's ribs. Hulk saw his eyes register the wound. He then slid out from under the man and tried to stand with the ship rocking and tilting upward. He ran up the slope of the slick deck. He reached the rail and pulled himself over the side and jumped. He realized his vessel had pulled away, and his leap was going to be short. He saw the sailor cutting the rope and pulling the end back aboard the ship. The sailor looked up and saw Hulk in midair. He could tell Hulk was not going to clear the rail of the deck. The sailing vessels are not designed for someone to climb onto from the water. They are designed for speed with slick well sanded hulls and narrow smooth rolled bow to cut through the water. Unless the sailing vessel is stopped and a ladder is dropped down from the rear deck, the chances of climbing aboard a sailboat is practically zero. The sailor threw the rope upward toward Hulk. Hulk reached the rope and then hit the side of the ship, falling into the ocean. Hulk heard the sailor pleading for him to hang on as he glanced off the side of the vessel and entered the water.

Dak had made his way to the cockpit located in the rear of the wheel. He felt the sudden jerk of the sail catching in the wind as the motion caused him to fall and slide across the deck. He heard

Ronny yelling for the two sailors to adjust the sails. Zenith pulled herself over to the rail to the stern of the boat. She at first did not see Hulk. Then he tried to raise his head from the ocean while being pulled by the ship. She hollered for Ronny to stop the ship. She ran next to him, "He is hanging on to a rope."

Ronny looked confused. "I said stop the ship. He is being pulled."

Ronny registered what Zenith was telling him. He yelled for both sailors to drop the sails. "We must cut the speed. Drop the sails."

Dak crossed to the deck and reached the rope tied off to the front cleat and started pulling Hulk inward. He could see Hulk lying on his back holding the rope above his head. Zenith reached the rope and started helping Dak pull the rope. Ronny tied the wheel in place holding the rudder straight. He ran to the stern of the boat and dropped the rope ladder. He started yelling, "Pull. He is still holding on."

Once Hulk was about five feet away, Ronny jumped over the rail and climbed down the rope ladder onto the small rear platform. He reached for the rope and started pulling, "Hold on."

Hulk could feel the strain in his forearms and the pain from his shoulders as he was close to letting go. He rolled his body over and reached for the rope ladder. Ronny grabbed him by his shirt and pulled him on to the platform. Ronny knew he must hurry to the deck, "You will need to climb the ladder. Follow me up. We must hurry." Hulk shook his head in understanding as he laid on his back breathing hard on the platform.

Once he climbed the ladder, Hulk laid on the deck. He could feel his forearms and shoulders were both hurting from the strain. His hands were blistered under his gloves. The cold ocean and the wind were freezing him. Ronny yelled, "Get him below deck. He needs to get warm." He then turned to the three sailors, "Raise the sails." He knew they had lost time and now were going to be behind schedule. Ronny ran to the wheel and unfastened the straps. He looked upward at the sailor in the bird's nest. "Sneedy. Report."

"We are clear of the battleship. There is no visibility south of us. I have lost visual contact. I do not see the Meridian."

Chapter 42

The wind was steady at close to twenty-five miles per hour and the medium size sailing vessel had been able to gain ground on the Meridian. Now, the day light was approaching with the lighter sky in the far eastern horizon, but the cloud cover was still present with a constant rain preventing the sun light from spreading across the surface of the ocean. The cloud cover in the far eastern sky was however thinning and the morning sun light was trying to break through the dark clouds as they shifted from the west to the east. Sneedy could see the silhouette of the other large warship sailing further ahead of the Meridian. He yelled the position of both ships to Ronny. The plan was to hope no one on the Meridian noticed the other large warship was nowhere to be seen. Ronny explained the plan and directed the vessel further out to sea and then he would angle the vessel at maximum speed to cut off the Meridian before anyone noticed them approaching from the seaward side. He knew the lookouts on the ship would be stationed to watch the landward side of the ship. He also knew the ships would communicate by lantern every ten hours. The rain and cloud cover had been a blessing to shield their fast approach and to also postpone the signals between the three traveling ships.

Ronny had been nervous about the planned collision. He stared at his magnetic compass and tried to adjust the speed of his ship. He just did not like ramming a smaller vessel into the side of a large ship. In theory the plan would work with the contact from his ship being above the water line with the sharp reenforced bow cutting into the broad side of the wood merchant ship. He also understood, in realty both ships could sink together in a mess of wood.

He then smiled to himself and thought, "If they were successful, he would buy his own ship and maybe a shipping company. He dreamed about how they would be sailing the small vessel away with the gold. Enough gold that he could own his own company, hire his own crew, and live anywhere in the world." He then refocused on the task and knew he would need to hit the ship hard enough to cause a gouge big enough to cause the Meridian to slowly sink. Dak, Hulk, and Zenith needed time to locate the gold and transport the gold to their ship. Once he and his fellow Normand navy men had been told about the gold on board, they were all in with stealing it. None of them liked the Normand army, and they felt they had nothing to lose. He now was more scared of failure and being forced to living poor. He liked Dak and his mannerism and his personality. He did not want to let his new friends down.

Dak and Zenith walked out of the cabin. They both walked to the cockpit and stood next to the wheel. Ronny glanced their way and asked, "How is Hulk doing?"

Dak smiled. "He is grateful for your crew throwing him the life rope. He is warming up. He has changed clothes. He is a tough man. He said the last four feet was the scariest point during all that mayhem. He was afraid he would lose his grip being so close and then not make it."

Ronnie grinned, "We were dragging him like bait when we used to shark fish. I am surprised a huge Tiger shark did not take the bait." He smiled. "Good. The second stage is going to be more difficult and dangerous. We need all the strong-tough men we can gather. The chests are going to weigh close to five-hundred pounds each. I pray they are stored on wheels, so we can lock them in place and move them around on our deck."

He looked at Zenith and Dak, "You better be ready and have Hulk on deck in about five minutes. We are running out of time. So far, they have not spotted us. The Normand sailors on guard will be preparing for the routine dawn signal between the ships. They will not like having to come out on the deck in this rain and signal the other ship. The weather I suspect has caused the delay We are running out of time." Dak and Zenith both looked at the one-hundred-and-sixty-foot ship flying a Normand flag with the ten large sails pulled tight in the wind. Dak glanced at the other three sailors. He considered his options. He knew he had to trust these men. Two men were perched holding onto the ratchets waiting for Ronny to yell another command and the other two were lookouts. He noticed they all had safety harnesses strapped to their bodies holding them secure to the deck.

Zenith looked at Dak and could read his mind. She knew he was considering if Ronny and these men could be trusted. She said,

"You need to tell Hulk to get his sword and bow and come on deck. We go live in less than two minutes."

Ronny hollered his commands and at the last second as he turned the wheel hard to the right. The two sailors turned the ratchets causing the sails to shift. The sailing vessel leaned sideways as it turned perpendicular to the Meridian. The ship picked up speed. At fifty feet away, Ronny yelled for everyone to brace for impact and motioned for the sailor in the bird's nest to come to the deck. At ten feet away, he yelled, "Drop the sails and brace for impact."

The entire crew did as they were ordered and then braced for certain impact as the side of the Meridian got closer. The two sailors tied themselves to the rail and were prepared to pull the quick release on the ropes. Ronny had done the same and tied himself to the wheel framing. He locked the wheel in place, so the rudder was not moving. Hulk, Dak, and Zenith were holding on tight. Dak looked at Zenith, "I am surprised I allowed you and Hulk to talk me into this."

Zenith regripped her hold on the rail, "You love me because I am not boring." She smiled at Dak.

"No sweetheart, you are not boring, and I do love you."

Ronny had instructed them where he thought the gold would be stored. It would be below deck in either the front or rear storage compartments. They had to retrieve the gold boxes and carry the gold to the rail and transfer the gold to their sailing vessel with close to fifty guards on board.

Dak glanced at Hulk across the deck. Hulk shook his head and provided a thumbs up sign. Dak shook his head at his friend and smiled.

Dak could see the Meridian pull in front as he peered forward over the bow of his boat. The rain had picked up, the ocean was choppy, and there was no sign the sun might break through the cloud cover. The clouds moved west across the sky and brought even more rain. Dak thought it looked like waves of rain falling. He said to himself, "Here we go. Damn, I hate this."

The front of the sailing vessel collided with the seaward side of the larger ship about one third the way from the bow. The initial jar had been absorbed by the eight people on the sailing vessel. The front of the sailing vessel had busted a deep rut in the side of the Meridian with the sailing vessel angled upward.

Dak did not hesitate. He ran up the deck and jumped over both ships rails and landed. He immediately killed a guard that approached him. He picked up the guard's sword and ran to the door to the cabin and stuck the sword cross ways through the door handles trapping the men below deck.

Hulk and Zenith both jumped across to the Meridian and fired their arrows hitting two different men. Zenith and Hulk ran toward the rear of the Meridian and up the ladder. She pulled open the rear storage department. There were some grates, and nothing that resembled a treasure. They were labeled with food, oil, or some other commodities.

Hulk turned and headed for the cockpit. He fought his way through three men and reached the cockpit where he killed the first mate with his sword as he was strapped in a harness to the wheel.

Dak looked at Zenith, and she shook her head no. He turned and ran toward the bow of the lower deck. He blocked one guards swing and then bull rushed the man pushing the man over the rail. He turned just in the nick of time and blocked another soldier's sword swing. He did not hesitate. He then countered with two fast swings and drove the man backward. The man hit the rail walking backward, and Dak rammed his sword through the man's gut. Dak reached the hatch and saw the large lock. He bent down and tried to remember his mother's directions on how to pick a lock as he reached in his vest pocket for his tools. He rammed the tension wrench into the lock hole and held it stern at the bottom and then slid the City Rake tool into the top of the lock and pushed it gently. The lock opened. He threw the lock to the side and flipped the latch. He looked up and flipped backwards dodging the sword swings from one of the two guards.

Zenith ran and ascended the ladder and blocked the arrows fired from the Normand soldiers on the bow of the boat. She ran to the hatch looked at the only item, that being the three treasure chests. She dropped into the forward hatch and opened the first box. She was surprised at how pretty gold clittered in the morning cloud cover sky. The shiny gold coins were all stacked in perfect rows held together in small wooden dividers. She jumped upward and pulled herself from the storage compartment and exited the forward hatch. She turned to fight. The Normand soldiers were emerging from the bow cabin exit door one after another. The bow exit door had not been sealed closed. The Normand sailors were running out the front hatch ready for battle. Dak killed the two men he was fighting and turned to fight two more. He felt the pain of the arrow striking him in the shoulder. He turned and felt the pain of the arrow hitting him in the leg. He bent down to one knee. Hulk jumped down the ladder as Zenith pointed to the gold boxes located in the front hatch. "I will cover you." Hulk did not waver. He strained as he pulled the first box full of gold onto the deck and aligned the box toward the railing. He pushed the box as the boat deck was slanted to the rail where he then strained to pick the chess up over the rails. He dropped the chest to the deck of the sailing vessel and the waiting sailor.

Darnel struggled to drag the large chest and tied the rope around the handles to the cabin wall. Hulk turned and ran back to the forward hatch and pulled both boxes to the deck and drug both to the rail and dropped them to the deck to Darnel.

Zenith ran to Dak and help him descend the ladder. "We have the gold. We need to leave now."

The passage was blocked below deck where the sailing vessel's bow had pushed through the bulkhead and blocked the passage under deck for the guards in the forward cabin of the ship. The only exit door was locked with the sword Dak had positioned in the two handles. The Normand guards could be heard with the frantic screaming for help below deck. They had tried to bust

351

through the door at the top of the steps where Dak had placed the sword holding the door shut.

The two sailors working with Ronny were in position to protect the retreat as they fired arrows upward at the Normand soldiers.

Ronny was excited with fear and yelled, "We need to disengage and pull backward, or we are going down with that ship."

Hulk turned toward him with his sword in his hand, "We are not leaving them behind. You better not pull back until everyone is on board. If you do, I will kill you." Hulk ran back up the bow of the ship. He looked over the rail and saw Dak standing fighting three men. Zenith was blocking arrows and charging the archer's position. Hulk jumped back over the ships rails and killed two of the men fighting Dak by slicing one in the back and ramming the other with his knife in his left hand through his side. Dak pulled his knife from his leg strap and threw his knife killing the third sailor. Hulk grabbed Dak's arm and pulled him to the rail. Dak slid down the bow of ship on to the deck. Hulk turned and saw Zenith kill two men and then turned and ran toward his position. She knew they had to pull away fast. She had to choose to turn and fight or jump. The arrow hit her in the upper back, and she fell into Hulk's arms. He picked her up and held her as they both slid down the bow of the ship.

Ronny hollered, "Now release the sails. The Bartholomew and Sneedy winched the ratchets, and the sails started to lift. As the man on the stern was turning the winch an arrow pierced his back. One of the solders looking down from the deck of the Normand vessel fired the arrow. The sailor fell into the rail, flipped over the rail as the vessel dipped into a swell. The man lost his grip and then fell into the dark ocean waves. Hulk ran to his position and finished turning the crank forcing the sail to rise to open. Hulk then ran dodging multiple arrows behind the cabin. The wind started to pull the ship backward. The sailing vessel started moving backward slowly at first away from the deck of the Meridian. The Meridian sunk to the deck railing and appeared to be sinking faster now the ocean water had filled the front compartments.

The sailing vessel was slowly drifted away from the Meridian. Dak and Zenith both laid behind the cockpit and hid from the large number of arrows being fired by the guards on the Meridian. Finally, Ronny announced, "We are clear."

Hulk ran over to Dak and Zenith. Dak pulled the arrow out of his shoulder and cussed in pain. He then pulled the one from his lower leg. He crawled next to Zenith and broke her arrow leaving the steam sticking out of her back. He held her. He then looked at Hulk, "Get her below deck." Hulk picked her up and carried her below deck. Dak followed Hulk.

Ronny looked at the three-treasure chests and yelled for the other sailor to secure them to the cockpit. He then tied the wheel straight and locked it into place. He ran over to the main sail and adjusted the sail. He yelled at the Bartholomew to adjust the other sail. He ran back to the wheel. He looked toward the horizon and could see the third ship had turned and now was headed directly for their position at full speed. He yelled, "We've got company. Be prepared to lift the Ketch sail." He knew they needed top speed and the Ketch sail needed to be lifted at the correct time once they had turned.

Dak pulled Zenith's overcoat off and then her protected padded vest. He pulled her shirt off. He reached the silk shirt and the arrow. He pulled the stem outward and at the same time as he pulled the silk shirt out of the puncture wound. He pulled her shirt up and placed a bandage on the wound and held it firm. "I believe you will be okay. The arrow hit a little left of your spine. The padded vest and the silk shirt worked. We need to stop the bleeding. The puncture wound is maybe an inch deep. I do not believe you have internal organ damage. The arrow did not pierce through the silk liner."

Hulk looked at both Dak and Zenith, "Thank God mom knew the history of the Mongol Army in the end of the eleventh century and the great Genghis Khan, and how they used silk to protect their warriors from arrows mitigating the damaged to the soldiers."

Dak announced, "The sailors use small bows with short arrows. The arrows do not have the velocity of our bows."

Zenith turned and looked at both Dak and Hulk, "The arrow still hurt like hell. I knew I was going to get hit, but I also knew I had to jump to our boat."

The three heard Ronny yelling, "We have company. We must turn, and we must get moving."

Dak looked at Hulk and grabbed his arm. "If we are about to be overtaken, you need to promise me you will throw the gold overboard." He stared into Hulk's eyes, "Tell me you will."

Hulk looked at his friend, "All the gold is not worth your two lives. I will do the right thing. I am sorry." He turned and ran out the hatch.

Ronny yelled, "Come here and hold the wheel straight. I must turn the head sail, so it is working with the main sail. Otherwise, you need to prepare to be boarded." Ronny ran to the sail and pulled the cords. He dropped the smaller sail and turned the boom. Hulk ducked as the boom support flew across his head space missing him by inches. Ronny ran back to the sail and pulled the cord tight lifting the main sail. Sneedy ran to his position and helped him. Ronny told Sneedy, the top support is broken from the lurch. You need to climb the mast and tie the sail off. Otherwise, they are going to shoot their harpoon through our sails and stop us dead in the water." The young sailor showed no fear and did not hesitate.

Hulk could see the large battleship gaining ground and getting closer by the minute. He could see the men on the front of the ship with spears, swords, and bows. He could see the large harpoon aimed at their ship. The sailor climbed and tied off the sail. He dropped down the upper shroud. "We've got to get the sail aligned," yelled Ronny.

Hulk yelled back at Ronnie, "What is the range of their harpoon?"

Ronnie yelled back at him as he ran to the sail, "You will know when they fire the damn thing."

The sailing vessel was moving with the small sail, but the large ship was bearing down on them and still gaining. Ronny pulled the cords for the mainsail while the other man cranked the sail upward. The sail caught at the top and hooked in the toping lift. Ronny yelled to the Bartholomew lift the Ketch sail. Ronny looked tired and exhausted. He watched the sail rise and felt the boat pickup speed. He and the other sailors walked back to the cockpit. "They will not be able to catch us. I believe I can keep us out of range of their harpoon. Now part three of the mission."

Hulk looked at the four men who were exhausted. "I am sorry we lost your friend. He died a brave man."

Ronny looked at Hulk and shook his head as he acknowledged the death. "His name was Bryan. He was a good man. He is not the only brave man on this ship. You three are crazy."

***

Hulk heard Sneedy hollered from his located in the bird nest, "There is the marker at two o'clock."

Ronny looked where he was pointing and saw the flag waving at the entrance to the inlet. He turned and looked at the large battleship heading directly for them close to a quarter of a mile behind them. He told Hulk to turn the wheel left once, as Ronny and the two other sailors adjusted the two sails. They headed for

356

the inlet. The rain had slowed but the wind and cloud cover had not changed. Dak and Zenith walked out of the cabin holding hands. They had changed clothes, and both glanced at the three boxes of gold. Hulk said, "I hope phase three of my plan works as smooth as phase one and two."

Dak looked at Hulk, "Yes, I agree. So far only one is dead, I have been shot twice, Zenith had been shot once, and we pulled you for one-hundred meters while you dangled by a rope fighting for your life behind the ship. So far, everything has worked perfectly." All three laughed.

Ronny smiled as he turned the wheel, "What do you do for a living? This is nuts." They all laughed again.

Dak looked at Hulk as he walked holding Zenith's hand. Both were in pain from the arrows. They both grimaced in pain each time they took a step. "Speaking of phase three. What is your get away plan?"

Hulk smiled, "This really is the easiest and simplest phase. I checked the inlet out yesterday. There are two ways to proceed on the river heading in from the ocean. The wind is always blowing from the west and should carry the boat to a rendezvous point to meet Veronica and the others further inland. We will off load the gold and head home on fresh horses. Veronica should have commandeered a wagon to assist with hauling the three-treasure chests to the base of the mountains. The boys will set a trap for the warship and then move our horses to meet Veronica. The fast way is through a narrow river passage to the left of the inlet. This way is shorter with less head current and a direct shot. The second way is through the wider part of the river going right which is longer and more time consuming."

Dak limped over toward Hulk, "Why would the Normand warship not be able to catch us? It sounds like we are traveling into a dead end. You know we cannot outrun them."

Hulk smiled and held his hands up to say I am not finished.

Zenith said, "All they must do it get close with those harpoons, and they can sink our ship."

Hulk looked to the side as they were entering the inlet. He then smiled, "This is where my plan really is next level. Matter of fact, you two are going to accuse me of being a genius."

Dak smiled with a grimaced expression, "A genius?"

Hulk said, "We want the Normand warship to follow us through the narrow passage. Once they commit to the short route, we can stop them. I have an ace up my sleeve."

Zenith tried to smile as she looked at the smile on Ronny's face, "An ace up your sleeve. I bet this is really good."

Hulk beamed with confidence, "Once the Normand ship follows us, they will not be able to turn around in the small inlet. They cannot back up with the wind blowing in from the west. The inlet is plenty deep enough, but one problem they will face that we will not is my ace in the sleeve." He smiled, "Robin Hood is going to finish cutting a huge Sycamore tree once we pass his spot in the narrow river part and once the Normand vessel commits down the narrow passage. The large tree will block them from proceeding after us. It is that simple. I am a genius."

Zenith looked at Hulk with a questionable expression, "Robin Hood is your ace up your sleeve?"

Dak said, "Mary, sweet mother of Jesus. Hulk, please tell me you are not counting on Robin Hood to save our asses?"

***

As they were approaching the inlet, Ronny ordered for the front sailor to drop the Ketch sail. They entered the smaller inlet and glided across the smooth water. They adjusted the two sails to decrease the speed, so they could maneuver the vessel in the narrow inlet. Ronny announced, "The Warship is closing fast. We need to stay in ten feet of water, so the keel does not drag. Drop a rope and give me a measurement." Bartholomew ran to the cleat and lowered the rope. "We are in fourteen feet of water."

***

Tommy Boy looked at the ax edge and proclaimed, "This damn ax is too dull to cut this large Sycamore tree. I cut the lead in the tree deep enough, but we need a sharp ax."

Trey announced, "We stole the dullest ax within one-hundred miles. Someone should have taken time to sharpen the damn thing."

Robin Hood climbed the tree with the use of a rope leaning backward against the tree as he ascended to the top. He tied off the pull rope. He then slid down the pull rope. Trey pulled the rope tight and then tied the rope off to another large tree. Robin Hood announced, "One more time, and the two ropes should hold our leaning tree." Tommy Boy started cutting into the back side of the tree while Robin Hood scaled the tree the second time.

Robin Hood slid back down the second rope, and Trey tied the second rope off to another tree. Robin Hood announced, "You are about a quarter through the tree. You need to cut at least sixty to seventy percent through. We do not want the tree to fall prematurely. We want tension on the two ropes holding the tree." Tommy Boy hit the tree about fifteen quick times and then waited as he wiped the sweat from his forehead. The three agreed they were good. The tree could only fall in one direction that being the way it was leaning toward the inlet water way. The wind provided additional reassurance as it was blowing the same direction the tree was leaning.

***

Robin Hood sat down on a log and proclaimed, "I believe now is a good time for a smoke." He pulled his pouch from his interior pocket.

Trey smiled, "You only have this one job. Robin Hood, you better not mess this up."

"That is correct. We have the tree tied off. We have the tree cut about seventy five percent through including a perfect lead cut. All we need to do is cut the tree the rest of the way once Dak, and the ship move on by. I can cut the ropes and watch the tree fall. I am certain I will not get so high; I cannot finish this by myself. You two may take the horses and go check on Veronica. She should be at opening in the field where the river turns to the north."

Trey glanced at Tommy Boy, "Maybe you should go check on Veronica and take all those horses with Tommy Boy. This is one of the most important steps in the plan for us to block the channel, so we can escape."

Robin Hood lit his marijuana cigarette. He took a puff. "Dak did not want to leave with the five Normand sailors. He does not trust them. We pulled this easy assignment because we all puked so much on our prior voyage." He looked at his two friends and blew out smoke. "I wonder how the first two phases went of this operation." He smiled and took a drag. "I know I would not have smoked any weed if I had been invited to that party. The only way I could have survived another boat trip like we had prior is being stone cold high." He pointed to the ocean. "Dak may have thrown the treasure over the side of the ship. I could tell he was against the plan to try to steal the gold. He figured the entire job would be safer if the gold was at the bottom of the ocean."

Tommy Boy smiled, "If Zenith had not spoken in favor of stealing the gold, that gold would have been dropped over the side or sunk with the Meridian."

361

"I am glad to be on land. I hope I never get seasick again. Damn, I was miserable," said Trey.

Robin Hood smiled as he smoked the joint, "It might not have been so bad if you two had hit the drain in the floor. I would not have gotten sick, but I laid down on the floor near the interior wall. Your puke ran over on me as the boat tilted in the waves. I had no idea what all that was on me until the smell hit me. I was covered in your puke. That is when I got sick." He pointed his index finger at his friends.

The three friends laughed, and Tommy Boy said, "Now, let me have a smoke. I do not want you to get so high you do not drop this tree. Maybe Trey you need to smoke some of Robin Hood's pot before he gets too high."

"I have plenty of pot."

Chapter 43

Veronica directed the wagon with the team of horses to the inlet where Hulk told her to meet them. She looked into the sky trying to locate the sun to judge the time of day. The cloud cover and rain had been constant all morning, and the sun was still behind the clouds. She was a little apprehensive as she waited knowing the owner of the wagon and team of horses would be looking for them. The wagon tracks would not be difficult to follow across the wet ground. She hoped Dak, Zenith, and Hulk had been okay. As she sat under the tree for close to one hour, she saw five riders descending the small hill on the trail toward her. She walked from the tree to the wagon and climbed into the seat and waited. She lifted her bow and unleashed the strap on her sword. As the riders got closer, she noticed the five riders were armed as they each were holding bows with swords hanging on their sides. She noticed the rain had stopped, and the sun was breaking through the cloud cover sky as she sat still and tried to act normal. The first rider pulled his horse to a stop and the other did the same. She pulled back her hood on her cape. She wanted them to notice she was a lone female. The older gentleman looked at Veronica with her smile. He glanced around to verify if there was anyone else in the area. The low-lying area was apt to flood during the rainy season, and the tree line was back several yards from the inlet water way as she peered east. The area around the large tree was open and covered in weeds and high grass with a few trees lining the riverbank with this one large Live Oak tree that spread out across the open field. To the west along the river the woods were thick with underbrush and large trees.

"You stole my horses and my wagon."

Veronica smiled again and looked each man in the eyes and studied them. "I did no such thing. How dare you accuse me a being a horse thief." She smiled. "I actually borrowed your horses and wagon. I will not allow you to accuse me of being a horse thief."

"Borrowed? You took them without asking."

The man to the left was younger and asked, "What are you doing with our horses and wagon way out here all alone? Are you waiting on someone?"

Veronica looked at the handsome young man. He appeared to be in his late teens or early twenties. She could tell he was the son of the first man who had spoken. They had the same body type with dark skin and dark hair. Both positioned themselves in the saddle the same and possessed the same mannerisms. They both wore expensive looking leather boots, vest, and hats. The other three were hired help.

Veronica smiled at the young man and made eye contact. "I am waiting on someone. After we use your wagon and horses, I will make certain they are returned to you. Like I said, they are being borrowed."

The older man said, "Why don't you get off my wagon, and we will take our rig back with us. We are going to arrest you and turn you over to the sheriff in Tanger."

Veronica smiled at the older man, "These horses are fine stock. This wagon is good equipment. How much would you charge me to rent this equipment and animals for a few hours and maybe a day?" She smiled again at the two men.

The older man looked confused, "You stole my horses and my wagon and now you want to know how much I charge to rent them?"

She held her hands out with palms up in a compromise suggestion, "I will pay double." She smiled at the older man then the younger man.

The younger man smiled as he rode closer to the wagon, "You do understand. It is the trust thing. Can we trust someone who stole our horses to begin with?" He smiled at Veronica. "How old are you?"

"I am eighteen. Do I really look like a horse thief to you? I am sitting still in the open. I am not running away. How much?" She smiled at the young man and pulled her cape back to her back and allowed the men to see her figure in her snuggly fit silk top.

He rode closer and stopped next to the wagon and was studying her. He liked her appearance and her confidence. "How much money do you have on you?"

"I have no money right now. I will pay you soon."

All five men laughed. The young man looked at her bow and her sword. The sword handle was worn black leather, and the bow was curved and smooth. Both appeared to have been used often and appeared to be high quality with a synthetic looking string on her bow and not the leather strings like he and his men used. He noticed her pretty smile and nice appearance, "Where are you from? I cannot place your accent."

"We are from a place furthest north along the east coast. Some of our army is from a place located north where the Continental Trail ends called The Midnight Hole. The city I am from is called Cliff Tops, which is portrayed as the furthest city north on the eastern part of our continent."

"Miss. You are a long way from home. Why would we trust someone who lives that far from us?"

"Because it is the right thing to do." Veronica smiled again.

The older gentleman asked, "Who is we?"

"Me, my king, and his soldiers are at war with the Normand empire. They have attacked my city of Cliff Tops and another tribe just south of us called the New York Tribe, and we have fought them. We pushed the Normand empire south of Harpers Ferry Harbor. Now, we need to commandeer this wagon and horses for a few hours and then I will personally return them. I swear I am no horse thief."

The older man cautiously approached. He stated, "You are a rebel. We have stayed out of the wars east and south of us. We are neutral."

Veronica knew she needed to buy time. "You are neutral until which time King Solman wants these horses, your land, your rights, and these men to fight in his army. You will not be able to stay neutral very much longer. You will be forced to choose sides. I hope you do not wait too long and lose your opportunity to defend yourselves. I am sorry, but war is here and now. If you do not stand and fight, you will lose everything that is dear to you. I have seen the innocent men, women, and children all rounded up and killed. There is no mercy only death."

The older man seemed a little nervous when Veronica mentioned the war and King Solman. "Look we do not want any trouble. You need to get off my wagon. We will be taking those horses back with us."

Veronica smiled at both men, "I cannot do that. I need this wagon and these horses. We have borrowed them from you. We do not want to keep them. We will make certain they are returned when we are finished." She smiled.

The man to the right pulled his sword. Veronica hollered, "No. Do not kill these people. They are innocent." At first the five men looked puzzled, as they did not see anyone else in the area.

Tommy Boy and Trey rode out of the brush with the bows cocked. The men were surprised to see two large men approaching from the west along the riverbank. She looked at the older man, "We will be happy to pay you double the cost of rent for your wagon and horses. Otherwise, my men will kill all of you."

The older man looked at Trey and Tommy Boy with their arrows leveled in their bows pulled tight riding at a slow pace toward the group, "There are three of you and five of us."

"Like I said, my men will kill all five of you. They have each killed over one-hundred Normand soldiers in two different battles and several different skirmishes. Killing you, your son, and these three farmhands is not necessary. Please allow us to pay you rent for your wagon and horses."

The older rancher looked perplexed. Veronica seemed to think he must have another agenda. She thought, "Why not take the deal? Why risk his son's life?"

He looked at the two large men approaching, each with multiple weapons and the appearance of being warriors and then looked at Veronica, "Okay. We will return here to meet you this afternoon. You will need to pay me a gold coin for the rental of the wagon and horses." The five men turned and rode away.

Chapter 44

The rider kept spurring the large horse in the side forcing the animal along the beach. His horse was blowing out air from the nostrils fighting for the next breath with sweat running down both sides. The rider was relentless and kept pushing forward without concern of over taxing the horse. The man would reach behind him and slap the horse multiple times with the whip pushing the horse harder and harder. The horse strained to move faster in the sand covered beach. The man pulled the horse hard to the left as they approached the rock embankments located at the shoreline and rode away from the beach up the three-hundred-foot incline and across the ridge. He could see the sails of the large ship about to enter the harbor. He whipped the animal again and again, pushing the horse to the limits.

The horse ran down the steep embankment and across the flat lands to the river edge. The man jumped off the horse with the long whip in his hand. He ran to the riverbank as the ship was entering the river and exiting the ocean. He waded out from the sandy riverbank in the river waist deep and slung the whip three times with the whip spinning in the air above his head. He let loose the whip and the whip end rapped at the top of the railing. He wasted no time and scaled the large warship. He pulled himself across the ship's railing and looked at the waiting soldiers. The commander stepped forward as Damen pulled his hood back revealing his entire head and face covered in tattoos. The commander hesitated when he noticed Damen's deformed but pointed ears. He then noticed the powerfully built repulsive looking man with a long knife on one hip and a sword on the other hip. The captain noticed the man appeared to be very unafraid and a very able warrior. There was no fear in the mysterious man who had just climbed aboard.

"What is the meaning of this?" The captain sternly commanded.

Damen looked at the soldiers facing him. He then stared at the captain while placing his right hand on his sword. In his harsh accented voice, Damen commanded, "Do not allow that vessel to escape. You need to increase your speed. If they escape, I will hold you responsible. You must stop that ship." Damen turned and walked into the captain's chambers.

The captain watched as Damen closed the doors to the cabin understanding his life may depend on his crew and their ability to overtake the fleeing vessel. He commanded, "Two guards are stationed here." He turned and walked to the front of the vessel. He peered over the bow and saw the other vessel turning the curve in the river and then disappear behind the mountain with the river flowing outward to sea and the wind blowing close to twenty-miles per hour inland, the opposite direction from the current. He commanded, "Check the depth."

The sailor dropped the rope overboard, "We are at fourteen feet deep."

The captain walked to the aft of the ship and commanded, "Take the shorter route to the left and maximum speed ahead."

Lieutenant Springer's expression turned skeptical, "But Captain."

Captain Wallace turned to his Lieutenant and interrupted his sentence and clenched his jaws. "I said full speed ahead. We will take the same path as them."

Lieutenant Springer turned to the helmsman and relayed the order for the helmsman to turn the rudder directing the ship left into the small canal. The helmsman then relayed the order for the sailors to adjust the forward sails. The lieutenant was aware of the risk of sending the large ship into a small section in the river between the island and the bank of the river. He also had seen the warrior that had just boarded their ship and knew the captain had no choice. They were going to follow the other vessel.

Chapter 45

Robin Hood smoked his second joint and relaxed. He started looking at the cut in the tree. He thought Tommy Boy could have cut another inch or two. The huge tree had grown with the trunk leaning toward the river and the large limbs were reaching over one hundred-fifty feet toward the early morning sunrises. There was no question which way the huge tree would fall either by cutting it or by natural causes. He looked at the tree and considered his high slumber and the task of finishing cutting the large tree. He stumbled, standing up right and then bending over to retrieve the ax. He swung the ax ten times and said to himself, "Hell fire, this is one dull ax." He sat down and leaned back and stared into the cloudy sky. The rain felt good hitting his body. He thought the clouds were turning in circles. He smiled to himself, "It is good to be high." He smoked another joint.

Robin Hood woke to the sound of someone yelling at him. He had trouble focusing. He had lost track of time. He tried to remember where he was located. He saw the river and asked himself, "Why am I sitting in the rain in the woods near a river? What am I doing, and why Hulk is standing on a sailing vessel yelling at him?" The view was foggy as he noticed a vessel had already past his location. He heard Hulk yelling, "Cut the damn tree."

He stood and walked next to the tree on the inlet side to the river embankment and looked down to the river edge. He then saw the sailing vessel with Hulk, Zenith and Dak standing to the rear watching him. The vessel had already floated past, and he then looked seaward and saw the large Normand warship gaining ground and was closer than he thought possible. He jumped toward the ax and felt the adrenaline spike in his body. He swung twenty times trying to hit the tree in the perfect spot. He kept seeing chunks fly out with each swing. He hit low and then high missing his target. He looked seaward and saw the large warship approaching with archers lined up along the railing. He looked up at the tree and noticed the ropes they had tied off were both tight. He looked east and saw the stern of the sailing vessel turning around the farthest corner with Hulk, Dak, and Zenith watching him. He felt panicked being high and trying to swing the ax as needed. He stumbled as he ran to the trunk of the other large tree fifty feet away and swung at the first rope tied to the large tree. He swung a second time while cussing the dull ax and his aim. He ran to the tree and the second rope, and it took two swings to cut the rope. He ran back to the tree and frantically started hitting the tree. The chunks kept flying out. He knew the tree was meant to block the passage in the narrow inlet. He started sweating and the fear and panic started to set in emotionally. He switched sides and hit the tree from the other side. The ax was not making enough headway. Some of his swings were missing the mark but most were hitting with very little results. He felt he was hitting too high or too low. The large pole for the sails running out from the ship's bow was about even with him. He knew the archers would shoot him once the large ship advanced another twenty feet if he stood in front of the tree to swing the ax.

Dak looked at Hulk, "It would appear your ace up your sleeve has gotten himself messed-up on his pot. You should have taken the pot from him before sending him out there to cut the tree and stop the warship."

Zenith added, "Hulk, your friends never take things seriously. This kind of stuff keeps Dak up at night worrying about what you and the others will do or not do. You guys need to be reliable."

Hulk looked hurt and frustrated at Zenith. Zenith then added, "Now you know what if feels like to come up with a plan and others do not listen. You guys need to be more mature. This is war and not some child's game. I am tired of hearing your stories as you five grew up acting as children. I wish to hear the stories of you acting as adults doing what adults would do not what a child would do."

***

Robin Hood knew he had to make these last swings count. He swung down and then swung even and watched the chunk fly through the air as he shifted the ax for another swing. He did not hesitate and swung down and then even and watched another chunk fly as he recoiled and prepared for the next group of swings.

He repeated the swings eight more times. The archers now had a clear shot at him from the bow of the ship twenty yards away. The inlet was twenty feet deep out from the tree and narrow with the flow of the current unnoticeable to the eye and the wind blowing constantly close to twenty-miles per hour west into the inlet. The tree was situated close to ten feet higher than the river with it leaning toward the river. He dove to the ground and then rolled behind the large Sycamore tree which was close to five feet in diameter. The arrows were hitting all around him and hitting the tree. He could hear a man yell to kill the man behind the tree. He pushed the tree and felt it sway. He pushed the tree again and again timing the pushes with the tree swaying back and forth. As the tree swayed more and more with each push, the arrows kept hitting the tree and the ground all around him. He pushed the tree one last time as he strained with every muscle as hard as he could push with his hands above the cut mark, and his boots dug into the muddy ground. He heard the pop inside the tree and felt the instant relief with the sound of the tree giving way. He stepped back and watched the tree at first slowly fall. The huge tree picked up momentum and with nothing to break the fall, the tree crushed the midsection of the large wooden ship. The initial sound of the tree colliding with the middle mask, both rails, and then the deck of the ship was deafening. The large sails collapsed under the weight of the tree limbs. He heard men yelling and noticed the ship was stuck in the water way. The weight of the large tree tilted the ship sideway, and the large tree trunk cut through the deck and both sides of the ship rails and the hull.

Robin Hood was tired but relieved and said to himself, "That was damn close." He picked up his bow and pack and ran for the woods and headed for his horse tied off hidden in the brush. Once he cleared the tree line with the thick vines, he stopped and turned. He noticed the sailors attempting to release the lifeboats while others were trying to assist men trapped under the large tree. As he started to turn and run, he then noticed a man in a black cape exit the lower cabin. The man did not move like other men. He stood out on the deck with his cape and movements. He was not in a panic and seemed to move with a purpose. Robin Hood could not help himself and lowered himself to one knee hidden in the thick veins and wooded area. He was intrigued watching the man. He watched in a frozen state from his hidden spot. Robin Hood knew he needed to run to his horse and hurry to the rendezvous spot and meet his friends, but his interest in watching the man had peaked. He had never seen a man dressed like this man or move like this man. The man was confronted with two guards as he took a few steps from the cabin. Robin Hood was surprised as he watched the man kill the two guards on board with very little effort. He then stepped over their dead bodies and proceeded to the large fallen tree and the captain located in the mid-section of the vessel.

Chapter 46

Dak announced, "We need to load the gold in our saddle bags and tie off other bags across our horses. The team of horses cannot pull the wagon any further. The mountains are too rough, and the trail is too steep."

Each of the riders filled their bags and laid the bags across the front of the saddle with a sack of gold hanging off each side. The two extra pack horses were also weighed down with coins of gold. Veronica announced, "I will take the wagon and team of horses back to the rancher. I will catch up with you in a day or maybe two days." She smiled as she thought of the young rancher and the crush, she had developed for him.

While he was filling his saddle bags with the gold coins, Hulk glanced at Veronica, "Why would you do that? We need to head east and then north across these forsaken mountains before someone tracks us. We cannot outrun a posse carrying this gold."

"Because it is the right thing to do. I told the rancher and his son we were renting the wagon and his team of horses, and we were not stealing them. We might need their help in the future against the Normand army. We need all the friends we can find."

Dak looked at Veronica and could tell her mind was made up. He like Hulk did not agree with her, but he felt maybe they did need additional friends in this part of the world. Dak also felt relief with the mission and now they had the gold. The first three phases had worked and were complete with Hulk's plan but not without difficulty. The fourth phase was for them to cross the mountains an escape with the gold. He smiled, "Okay, Veronica, you need to stay on The No She Trail, and you will avoid the nuclear pits. The trail as Robin Hood has named it will take you through the low gap in the mountain, and you should be able to catch us in two days and no more than three days. We will be pushing hard through the ninety miles of rough mountains. We will resupply ourselves with not only rested horses but other supplies at one of the ranches on the other side of the mountains. We are not going to wait on you. There is too much risk of us being caught in the open with all this gold."

She turned the wagon around and headed back toward the coast with her horse tied off to the rear of the wagon. Robin Hood led the rest of the men upward toward the first ridge of the mountains. He had marked the trail on the prior trip, and they all were content carrying the gold. They were all dreaming of what they could buy with their share.

Chapter 47

Damon heard the large tree crash into the deck, and he felt the sudden jar of the entire ship. He stepped out on the aft cabin and saw the tree lying across the midsection and men trapped under the tree yelling in pain. He noticed the sailors abandoning ship and others trying to drop the lifeboats. He stepped forward and was thirsty for blood. His master had instructed him to monitor the three ships as they passed Tanger Port heading south along the coastline close to a quarter of a mile from shore. He realized when he could only see the one battleship and it was in pursuit of an unknown vessel not flying a flag, something had happened at sea.

He saw the two guards approaching as they stepped in his path with their hands resting on their swords. Damon could tell they were more concerned with making it to land and were not really wanting to block his path. Damon however quickly pulled his sword and stabbed the one on the left through the unprotected neck. He then rotated his sword and cut the second guard across his arm and then stabbed him through the chest plate and into his heart. He stepped over the two dead guards and walked forward. At first, the lieutenant could not see his face or outfit with his cape over his body and his hood tight over his head. When Damon walked toward the lieutenant, Damen pulled off his hood and his robe opened showing his well-defined muscled chest and his intent to kill anyone that tried to stop him.

The lieutenant stared at the figure approaching him. He observed the appearance of one who was deranged covered in red tattoos on his head and face. He had additional red tear drop tattoos down the side of each cheek and neck. His four front upper teeth were yellow and all four were sharp incisor teeth. Damon looked at the captain standing next to the lieutenant as the sailors were abandoning the ship and also stepping back to allow Damon passage. Damon lifted his sword and announced, "My master does not accept failure like this. This is not acceptable." He cut the captain's head off with one quick swing. He then walked to the tree debris and killed a wounded man who had been pinned under a tree limb screaming for help. The large tree branch had pushed the man face down on the deck with his head pinned between his feet. One quick swing of the sword cut the top half of the man's head off. The second sailor could not pull his hands from under another tree limb and was begging for help. His hands were crushed by the weight of the tree.

Damen quickly turned to the next sailor trapped and rammed his sword through the man's heart. The two sailors trying to remove the tree limb stared at the monster who had just killed the helpless men and their captain. Damon walked by the stunned lieutenant and then bent low and walked under the large tree trunk and quickly to the front of the ship killing the three guards in his path who pulled their swords and tried to stop him. The first guard had commanded for Damon to stop, and he pulled his sword. Damon pushed the guard's sword to the side with his sword and rammed his knife from his left hand through the breast plate. The guard fell backward and died as he hit the deck. The second and the third guards both spread out pulling their swords in a threatening manner, but there was not enough room as Damon walked by the cabin and the rail of the boat. Damon quickly pushed the second guard's sword to the side and then rammed his knife through the man's face mask. The third guard tripped over the second guard as he fell dead. Damon rammed his sword through the man's mid-section and walked to the bow. He glared at three additional sailors cowering against the rail. They looked confused at Damon as he was a thick, strong looking man with no hair and dressed as a satanic warrior.

Damon placed his sword in the sleeve tied to his left side. He stared at something in the tree line and then he jumped over the rail of the ship and lowered himself by the rope to the water where he swam to the land. He got out of the water and ran into the woods following the inlet water way while the horrified sailors watched him.

The large ship partially sunk with the stern of the vessel resting on the bottom of the river. The sailors and guards on the bow of the ship jumped into the water and swam to the shore. The tree had fallen and cut through the wooden ship with the large trunk resting on the main middle support framing under the collapsed deck. The river water was pouring into the bottom of the ship causing the ship to tilt toward the land side and the riverbank.

The one sailor sitting against the rail looked at his dead captain and three other dead guards on the deck, the two guards near the cabin and the two dead men pinned under the tree. He looked over at Lieutenant Springer, "Who is that monster? He killed his own men. We are on his side."

The lieutenant walked toward the sailor, "That man must have been a Blueblood Warrior. We need to jump. The front of the boat is going down. You best forget you ever saw him. He could have killed every one of us."

Chapter 48

Veronica smiled as she pulled the wagon into the open area near the inlet. She had tried to ride fast but the old muddy roadway was bumpy with gullies caused by rain over the years. She decided to slow her pace and remove her robe and her top shirt. She smiled to herself as she knew the tight-fitting silk undershirt best showed her figure. On the long ride, she had considered her relationship with her friends. Dak had met Zenith, someone not from their tribe. She knew at one time, she had a crush on Dak, but he wasn't in love with her. She could tell Dak and Zenith loved each other. Hulk and Robin Hood were like brothers to her. Tommy Boy was still a little shy and immature. He was the youngest of the five friends. She loved Trey, her younger brother. There were no other males for her to consider to be romantically involved. She wanted to flirt with someone. She wanted someone to flirt with her. She knew how she felt late at night when she was alone in her bed. She was starved for a man to old her romantically. She knew her body had matured quicker than her male friends, and she ached for the touch of a grown man. She could tell how men from her tribe and the men from the New York tribe looked at her, and they appeared to be interested. She also knew most men were married or scared of her father, brother, and her friends. She smiled as she drove the wagon thinking about the young rancher. She liked his looks and his smile. He seemed to be nice, confident and wealthy. She hoped to see him again at the inlet. She considered what she would say, and how she would stand trying to figure out how best to be noticed by him. As she approached the inlet, she saw the rancher leaning against the tree. The sun was bright, and the temperature was nice. She recognized him as being the man on the black horse who had first talked to her. She looked around in hopes of seeing his son, the young rancher. She stopped the wagon as she placed the brake on and jumped down. She talked as she turned to walk to her horse. "I am sorry, I am running late. I guess you thought I was a liar, and I was not going to return the wagon and horses. Tell your son we appreciate the use of these fine animals." She glanced at the rancher and smiled.

She lifted open her flap on her saddlebag on her horse and realized the man had not replied or moved. She pulled a gold coin from her saddleback and turned toward him. She thought maybe he was upset that it took her so long to return or maybe he could not hear. Something did not feel kosher with the situation as she approached the man. She glanced around the area, and he had not moved. She walked within ten feet of him under the large Live Oak tree and looked at the rancher. His hat was pulled down covering his forehead and some of his face. She noticed his eyes were frozen open. She felt something wet drip on her arm. She became distracted and looked at her arm at the blood drops and then she looked up in the tree close to twenty feet and saw what appeared to be multiple skinless bodies hanging from ropes. Her mind was confused, and she was trying to process what she was seeing hanging in the tree. She looked at the ground next to her feet and saw the remains of a person's entrails and blood. She then looked at the man with a questionable expression and noticed his fingers were missing. The part of his face she could see under his brim hate was pale white. His head and hat suddenly fell forward, and the head rolled toward her on the ground.

With his head falling to the ground in front of her, Veronica first was scared, and then she froze when she realized he was a standing dead man. She could not process what she had seen and now the man's head rolling toward her shocked her. She was slow to respond. Her brain tried to register what happened, "Why had this man been killed. What caused his head to fall to the ground. The bodies were skinned hanging in the tree. Is this real?"

She saw the scary figure step from behind the man and the tree as the rancher was headless and the body fell forward. Veronica realized the rancher was being held up by a large knife which had been stuck in his back and the knife was being held by an ugly evil looking demon. He was covered in red tattoos, black leather vest, and black pants with a robe hanging loosely around his upper body. His arms were muscular and covered in tattoos. His body was a powerful looking strong man. She realized his arms were moving forward toward her with a brass knuckle grip on his large knife. The handle was shiny brass knuckles which covered his left fist. The knife had a curved twelve-inch blade covered in blood. He looked demonic with his dingy colored sharp front teeth when he smiled. Her mind finally registered the threat, and she knew she did not have time to pull her sword. She dropped the gold coin, and she went low with a frontal kick to his left knee as he quickly approached.

She hit the fast-approaching Damon in the front left leg pushing his leg inward at the knee. She was surprised. The kick had not at first seemed to have affected the monster, and his abilities to rush her. He slowed down a little as he pivoted to the side and provide her an opportunity to rotate to her side and roll backward. She quickly stood. Damon pressed the attack as he reached for her. She quickly moved to the side and used her left arm to push both his reaching right hand and the left hand holding the knife to the side. His motion continued forward as he passed to her left side and as he became even with her, she timed her punched perfectly as she delivered the perfect hard right fist to the ribs. As she tried to drive her knuckles through the ribcage using her body weight as leverage to punish him. As she viewed the side of his head during and after the punch, she noticed his pointed ear which had been trimmed and only a small portion of the fatty material and ear cartilage was attached to his head. Her adrenalin spiked as her mind immediately registered the threat, "This man is a rogue Blueblood."

The strike landed perfectly and should have forced the man to his knees. She had been taught the ribs are easy to fracture in combat, and the person will always retreat with the acute throbbing. She had not moved and had anticipated him falling or at least bending over caused by her forcible punch to his ribs. She elected to use this opportunity to pull her sword as she realized the

386

punch did not distract the man as he turned and grabbed her left arm with his right hand and pulled her toward him. He had not hesitated and swung his left fist and hit her in the side of the head driving the brass knuckle part of the knife into her temple. She looked up toward the tree with her vision spinning and saw the hanging bodies as she desperately tried to force her body to pull away. Instead, she fell backward as her vision became blurred, and she blacked out as she landed on the ground.

Chapter 49

The man gritted his teeth as he flew backward in the air. He tried to prepare for the hard landing. He hit with a thud as breath escaped from his lungs. He knew the adversary would show no mercy. More excruciating pain racked his body from the savage kick to the face. He would fight no more today.

His partner did not fare as well. He had swung at the man with a right hook. His swing was blocked, and the large man stepped forward with a vicious chop to the front of his neck. Desperate to breathe, the man grabbed his neck. King Solman punched the man in the ribs. The man fell against the wall gasping for breath while enduring the agony of the two broken ribs. He also would fight no more today.

King Solman was not concerned. He walked to the rear of the gym and continued working out on the punching bag hanging from the ceiling.

The assistant walked toward the sparring arena. He trembled with concern as he knew King Solman would not hesitate to execute him for delivering the bad news. He had witnessed the psychotic actions of the King when he became angry. He trembled as the two guards allowed him to pass as he walked into the workout room.

King Solman watched the assistant approach. The assistant bowed his head as he stopped and stood still waiting for King

Solman to motion for him to speak. The assistant knew the two King's Guards would not help. There was no one else in the arena, and he was at the mercy of a brutal psychotic man. King Solman motioned for him to speak.

"My Lord. I have news from your three-ship convoy sailing south along the west coast. Captain Roosevelt commandeered a small cruiser from a trading company to bring you this news."

King Solman placed his hand on the punching bag and eyed the assistant. Hearing that Captain Roosevelt had seized a cruiser meant something bad had happened to his ships. He nodded for him to proceed. "Two days ago, the Meridian was hijacked and sunk with no survivors. Both warships which were escorting the Meridian were attacked. One was sunk in the inlet about thousand miles north. The other warship is undergoing repairs."

He growled through clenched jaws, "What did you say?"

The man quivered, "My Lord. We are still trying to gather information from the survivors. This sounds unlikely, but the report has indicated Captain Roosevelt's ship was at sea following the other two ships in the convoy. Three unknown persons boarded his ship in the darkness of night during a rainstorm. The sails were sabotaged, and the gooseneck was cut in half. The crew will have the needed repairs completed in three days and the ship will be seaworthy.

"The report indicates once the combatant's ship pulled next to Captain Roosevelt's ship, the three pirates spent less than two minutes sabotaging the ship and sailed away. Your sailors had no time to defend the ship, and the harpoons could not be loaded in time to fire at the pirate ship."

His face was red and distorted with anger as he yelled, "I demand Captain Roosevelt and all the sailing crew members be brought to my court. What was Captain Wallace and his battleship doing in an inlet?" He wondered how and why this happened? No one knew what the Meridian was carrying, and no one would attack his navy at sea. The other world rulers had no navy. He considered killing the messenger but spared his life. He thought, "This is war. I need to learn who did this and crush them. Someone had orchestrated this well-designed attack at sea. Who could have accomplished such a feat?" His thoughts turned to finding who must have betrayed him.

The assistant interrupted his thoughts. "There is one more item mentioned in Caption Roosevelt's report as reported by Lieutenant Springer who was assigned to Captain Wallace." King Solman's steel eyes glared at the man. The messenger fumbled his notes as he read the message, "An unidentified man boarded the warship as the ship entered in the inlet and talked with Captain Wallace. Captain Wallace was in pursuit of the pirates inland when a large tree was cut and destroyed his ship." The assistant looked at King Solman and stopped reading his notes, "The report from Lieutenant Springer indicates, once a large tree fell on your ship, the unidentified man killed Captain Wallace, five guards, and two sailors."

King Solman's eyes narrowed, and wrinkles appeared in his forehead, "Who is this man?"

The messenger stuttered, "Sir, the lieutenant claims in his report the man is a Blueblood warrior, and he disappeared on foot going inland after the pirates. He killed seven men and decapitated Captain Wallace in front of the crew for allowing the pirates to escape."

To Be Continued.

ACKNOWLEDGMENTS

***

To my editor Carolyn Pegram for all the hard work.

To Chesnie Nichols for the book cover and formatting.

To big sister, Sherrie Rutherford, for all the loving help in writing book six.

www.ingramcontent.com/pod-product-compliance
Lightning Source LLC
Chambersburg PA
CBHW070837260626
47170CB00007B/2402